THE CURSED QUEEN'S DAUGHTER

Elly Blake

LITTLE, BROWN AND COMPANY

LARGE PRINT EDITION

This book is a work of fiction. Names, characters, places, and incidents are the product of the author's imagination or are used fictitiously. Any resemblance to actual events, locales, or persons, living or dead, is coincidental.

Copyright © 2026 by Elly Blake

Map copyright © 2026 by Virginia Allyn

Cover art copyright © 2026 by Micaela Alcaino. Cover design by Sasha Illingworth and Tuesday Hadden. Cover copyright © 2026 by Hachette Book Group, Inc. Interior design by Carla Weise.

Hachette Book Group supports the right to free expression and the value of copyright. The purpose of copyright is to encourage writers and artists to produce the creative works that enrich our culture.

The scanning, uploading, and distribution of this book without permission is a theft of the author's intellectual property. If you would like permission to use material from the book (other than for review purposes), please contact permissions@hbgusa.com. Thank you for your support of the author's rights.

Little, Brown and Company
Hachette Book Group
1290 Avenue of the Americas, New York, NY 10104
LBYR.com

First Edition: February 2026

Little, Brown and Company is a division of Hachette Book Group, Inc. The Little, Brown name and logo are registered trademarks of Hachette Book Group, Inc.

The publisher is not responsible for websites (or their content) that are not owned by the publisher.

Little, Brown and Company books may be purchased in bulk for business, educational, or promotional use. For information, please contact your local bookseller or the Hachette Book Group Special Markets Department at special.markets@hbgusa.com.

Library of Congress Cataloging-in-Publication Data
Names: Blake, Elly author
Title: The cursed queen's daughter / Elly Blake.
Description: First edition. | New York : Little, Brown and Company, 2026. | Series: Thirstwood ; book 2 | Audience: Ages 14 and up | Summary: "A warrior daughter of the forest king strives to protect her family and bring her long-lost mother home, even as she begins a romance with the son of the king of shadows." —Provided by publisher.
Identifiers: LCCN 2025029937 | ISBN 9780316396028 hardcover |
ISBN 9780316396226 ebook
Subjects: CYAC: Fantasy | Forests and forestry—Fiction | Magic—Fiction |
Romance stories |
LCGFT: Fantasy fiction | Romance fiction | Novels
Classification: LCC PZ7.1.B586 Cu 2026
LC record available at https://lccn.loc.gov/2025029937

ISBNs: 978-0-316-39602-8 (hardcover), 978-0-316-39622-6 (ebook),
978-0-316-61043-8 (large print)

For my niece, Zoe,
the fiercest warrior I know

THE AMBROSE MOUNTAINS

The Scar River

Pixie Village

WELKINCASTER

Sylvan Village

THE SINKING SEA

THIRST

North

HUMANS

Sylvan Village

Entrance to the Cryptlands

HEXDUN VALLEY

SCARHAMM

The Grotto

Erebus's Tree

WOOD

Prologue

> The Old Ones came into
> existence before death.
> Hence, they have no true fear.
> —Excharias, Sylvan poet

Damon stood before his father, the King of Iluna. Shadows swirled around his throne, a writhing mass of spirits that served as both weapon and shield. No knife could cut them, no arrow pierce them. No one could defy the ruler of this slice of eternal night.

Especially not his son.

King Erebus beckoned with one gem-clad hand. "Step closer."

Damon obeyed. If he hesitated, the shadows would sense weakness and converge on him.

"I give you freedom, do I not?" the king asked.

Damon gave the only acceptable answer. "Yes, Father."

The king leaned forward. "I give you leave to wander all the places my roots can take you?"

Damon nodded. He sensed he was being led toward an accusation, but he didn't know his crime.

"All I ask in return," the king said softly, "is that you bring me anyone who dares violate my sacred shrines."

Damon bit his tongue. *Sacred shrines.* A few scraggly trees and rocks where people used to worship—remnants from when his father held sway in the world above. They were no more than magical detritus now. King Erebus used them as traps, claiming the spirits of folk unfortunate enough to stumble upon them.

"We need fresh spirits to feed our realm," the king reminded him, lifting a hand to caress one of the ribbons of darkness, his rings a bright, sparkling contrast. "These shadows are yours as well as mine. Have you forgotten?"

An explosion of hatred heated Damon's chest. If they were his shadows, why did they do nothing he wanted? If they were his, why did he despise them?

"No, I haven't forgotten." *Where is this going?*

"Yet," his father said, his tongue sharp on the word, "you haven't brought me a new spirit in weeks."

Damon bowed his head. Merely one of the regular lectures, then. "I have met no one in the woods." A lie. In reality, he'd seen many creatures, some of whom had come perilously close to his father's traps. But Damon had no urge to damn any of them.

"Prospect says different," the king added. "His crows have spied you neglecting your duties."

Damon's head snapped up. Quick rage pumped through his veins as he searched the dark corners of the room. The Court Seer was always lurking somewhere nearby. Damon could feel it—Prospect's malevolent glare an itch on the back of his neck.

Many of the throne room's inhabitants drowsed or slept on black velvet divans or on the cold, hard floor, their snores audible. They were mostly forest folk, a few Azpians, and one or two humans who'd been invited to this realm to make merry before succumbing to the king's enchantment. Soon they would be given a choice to leave. But none would go. Damon tried not to look at them. Their fate turned his stomach.

"Few folk stroll the forest at night. Even Sylvans avoid the woods under a full moon."

"Then what do you say to this?" The king flicked his fingers, and shadows parted to reveal a tall woman with greenish-gold hair, skin with a hint of bronze, and hazel eyes. Though her posture was proud and determined, her clasped hands trembled.

Damon was at the age when his voice cracked and hoped it would not betray his dismay. "A Sylvan."

"Not just any Sylvan." The king smiled with more genuine mirth than usual. "You can't even bring me a common spirit, and Prospect has brought me Coventina, the Sylvan queen."

Damon's stomach clenched, helpless against a twist of sympathy. His father had caught a prize he would not give up easily.

The woman took a breath and turned toward the king. "Your Seer claims my daughter violated a sacred boundary. I came here to refute his claim. Everything in Thirstwood belongs to the Sylvans."

Damon noticed that she didn't seem affected by his father's charm. Most folk who came succumbed to it almost immediately.

"Not," said King Erebus, his lips curving up, "everything." He stroked his chin in a way that put his gems on display. "Some things in the mortal world still belong to me. Places where humans worshipped me retain vestiges of my power."

The queen was silent for a moment. "What do you claim my daughter did?"

"She climbed a tree," Prospect interjected, his nasal voice grating on Damon's nerves. "A tree that belongs to the King of Iluna."

"All children climb trees," the queen said, her voice rising. "It does not give you any right to my daughter!"

"And I thought Sylvans never lied," the king said with deceptive gentleness. "Children who climb *my* trees belong to *me*."

The queen sucked in a breath, perhaps realizing she didn't know for certain. "If what you say is true, why does no one know of this?"

"Your husband knows," Erebus insisted, his eyes bright with conviction. "The Sylvan king is well aware that someone must remain here to pay penance for violating my boundary. Perhaps he thought the brambles he placed around my tree would be enough of a deterrent." Erebus smiled. "But my magic is a strong lure, especially to those of a certain curious nature. Now one of you must pay the price. You or your daughter."

The queen's jaw worked before she spoke. "I will not agree to this until I've spoken with my husband. Until I've verified your claims."

The king paused for a moment, then inclined his head. "Go home for the answers you need. But if, my willow, you think you can escape your fate, know that you are cursed from this moment to wither in illness while you are away from here. You may fight it, but eventually, you will succumb. You will die if you do not return."

"I'd rather die than condemn my daughter to this place," the queen spat.

"Your death will not protect her," the Court Seer interjected. "When you die, I will come to claim her spirit and yours on behalf of my king."

The queen let out a shocked breath, stepping toward the king. Her expression was so furious, it made Damon want to take a step back. "You filth—"

Fast as a winter's sudden gale, shadows snaked up her arms and held them. She snarled, baring her teeth, her fists clenching.

But Damon knew well these shadows could not be battled with strength. "Father." He didn't mean to protest but couldn't hold his tongue. "Her daughter didn't know it was your tree."

He wasn't surprised by his father's mocking laugh or the sneer that accompanied it. There was a human belief that if milk soured, it was a result of the King of Iluna laughing. Damon sometimes wondered if a bowl of milk was curdling somewhere in human lands above.

Turning his attention back to the Sylvan, the king spoke calmly. "I await your choice, Queen Coventina."

Damon let out a relieved breath when the shadows let the queen go.

Three years to the day, the Sylvan queen returned. She was thinner, paler, her face drawn with exhaustion. But her hands no longer shook, and she wore the most determined expression Damon had ever seen.

Prospect slid from the shadows like a bad smell, his angular form floating more than walking, a silver chalice gleaming in his stained hands.

Damon's eyes burned from the taint of magic, and he blinked to clear them. He hated the cup. Despised it.

"I offer my spirit," Queen Coventina said, her voice strong despite her frail appearance. "I offer myself in Theodora's place."

The king grinned, his body relaxing. He made a motion toward Damon. "My son will administer the cup."

Prospect chuckled at the shudder Damon couldn't control as the frigid chalice was placed in his hands.

"The touch of its metal brings a powerful burn." The Court Seer's smile was cruel.

"Not as powerful as your stench," Damon hissed.

Prospect's furious expression made him smile. If he ever became king, the first thing he would do would be to rid himself of the Seer, one way or another.

Damon looked up at Queen Coventina, and his smile faded. He saw someone brave and strong who'd been trapped by his unscrupulous father. She didn't deserve this.

"Drink," he said, his disgust at this task making his voice harsh.

The queen gasped at the cold burn of the metal, her hands unsteady as she tilted the cup. Silver limned her once-pink lips, the shine spreading down to her chin and neck, and up over her nose, continuing to her lashes and brows until her hair was silver, too.

The cup dropped with a clatter as her arms grew into branches, her legs becoming roots that dug through the black stone floor and into the ground below. Her trunk stretched taller, taller, until it was twice the height of the throne, its branches bending away from the king as if trying to escape. In moments, she was nothing more than a hauntingly elegant tree.

"Another spirit for our kingdom," the king said with obvious satisfaction. "A queen's life force will be far more powerful than most in protecting us. We are favored by fate."

Favored. Damon wanted to spit that it had nothing to do with destiny and everything to do with his father's lack of conscience. But instead, he bowed, then turned toward the path that wove between rows and rows of silver trees. The shadows followed, hounding him with mocking echoes of the king's laughter.

Someday, I will be free of this place, Damon promised himself. *I will never be like him.*

The shadows howled as if they'd heard his thoughts.

1

> Autumn is a harbinger. Leaves turn red. The moon bleeds. The wind bites, carrying a warning that to some, the coming season will be their last.
>
> —Excharias, Sylvan poet

Thea sat in her copper tub and stared at her knees as they poked out of the soapy water, wondering at the sense of dread that hung over her like a dark cloud. Where was the satisfaction she used to feel after a fight? When her patrol had encountered Skratti raiders earlier this evening, she and her fellow Sylvan Huntsmen had attacked. She'd slain a handful of enemies, sending their spirits to the Netherwhere, from which they would never return to trouble the living. The remaining raiders had fled.

So why did she have this cold sense of danger creeping up the back of her neck? She was at home in her bedchamber in Scarhamm, a fortress protected by archers and guards and mystic wards. There was nowhere safer for a Sylvan to be.

Add to that, it was her name day. Even now, guests were arriving for a revel in her honor.

Thea sank deeper into the water, trying to shake her strange mood. Maybe it was the fact that she didn't trust the newly formed truce with their greatest enemy.

For a decade, the forest-dwelling Sylvans had been at war with the Dracu of the Cryptlands over what their queen had considered a theft: A Dracu boy had unwittingly given an artifact of great power to a Sylvan girl, and she'd kept it. The girl was Thea's younger sister, Cassia, the artifact an amber ring called the Solis Gemma, whose gemstone emitted a glowing blast that harmed any creature who couldn't live in sunlight, like the Dracu. Six months ago, a Dracu named Zeru, the one who'd gifted the ring, had abducted Cassia to get it back.

But retrieving the Solis Gemma hadn't been so easy, and Zeru had been forced to work with Cassia to discover the ring's history: that it was created by the Ancients as a tool for growth and restoration. Its gemstone had been misused during the Ancient Wars as a weapon to murder thousands of forest creatures called moss folk—by the Sylvan king, no less. A shameful history that he'd hidden from everyone, including his daughters.

It was too much to absorb, and Thea had not yet accepted all of it. She wondered how Cassia managed to seem...well, happier than she ever had before.

Cassia was one year younger than Thea but leagues apart in personality. A gentle soul who hated fighting, Cassia had finally refused to use the Solis Gemma against the Dracu after years of trying to meet her father's demands. Thea had understood that, and when it became clear her sister had deep feelings for Zeru—a Dracu, of all creatures—she had tried to understand that, too.

Or bit her tongue when she didn't.

But when Cassia invited her sisters to visit a mysterious cloud region called Welkincaster, Thea had declined. She belonged here in Thirstwood. She had blood trees to protect her and Skratti blood to polish her blade. That was enough to keep her content. Or had been until recently.

The Dracu were keeping to their terms of the truce, but the Skrattis—goblins who dwelled underground in the Cryptlands and were often allied with the Dracu—had started coming above and raiding Sylvan villages. Hence the increased patrols that had kept Thea and the other Huntsmen busy over the summer.

But battle was part of life. Thea had grown up during a war. A few Skratti raids could not explain her growing unease.

She pulled herself from the water, dabbing the moisture from her long limbs with linen cloths left on the stool next to the tub, and stood in front of the crackling fire to dry. Gooseflesh broke out over her arms as a cold draft of air came from the chimney.

And suddenly, resting on the hearth at her feet, was a neatly folded pile of cloth.

Tension whipped up her back as her pulse slammed. *Had that been there a moment ago?* Was she so distracted lately that she would miss something right in front of her?

She snatched up the top garment and shook it out: a short-sleeved blue gown with seed pearls on the bodice and a belt of bright green silk cinching the waist. Underneath lay a pair of thin stockings and green slippers embroidered with white thread.

A name day present from one of her sisters? It would be the type of thoughtful gift Enora might choose. But it was so unlike anything Thea had ever worn. Most of her gowns were simple and dark, and this was bright and fanciful. Thea frowned at the idea of what Enora could be trying to convey. That she should try new things? That her dresses were too plain?

As Thea held the gown closer for inspection, she inhaled. A shock ran through her as she detected the unmistakable stink of magic, and the scent brought back a memory she'd tried unsuccessfully to bury.

One night, when Thea was eleven years old, a sound from the hallway had woken her from sleep. She'd opened her bedchamber door to see her mother descending the stairs. Worried, she'd followed, surprised at how quickly her mother was moving. After all, her mother had been ill for the past three years, from the start of the war with the Dracu. Some said the war had been too hard on her gentle nature. Others guessed that a Dracu witch had put a curse on Queen Coventina. Mages and Seers had been brought in from surrounding villages, but no one had been able to cure her, and the queen had grown listless.

But her mother showed no sign of weakness now. Thea could hardly keep pace as a back door that led outside closed behind her mother.

Half-curious, half-scared, Thea traversed the courtyard and left the safety of the gates, keeping her mother in sight. Where was she going? Sylvans could go to their birth tree to recover if they were ill or injured badly enough. But the Sylvan queen shouldn't go out at night, much less alone, not when they were at war with the Dracu. And did she really mean to leave without saying goodbye?

Thea almost called out, but the king was so secretive about the location of their family's birth trees, Thea thought perhaps her mother would turn around and go home if she knew she was being followed. Then Thea might never know where the tree was. She decided to be a silent guard until her mother reached her tree, then she would step out and confront her.

The paths of Thirstwood brought them to an area of elms and willows and walnuts. Her mother put her hand to the trunk of a gnarled walnut, a surprisingly large and old tree, not what Thea would have imagined as the birth tree for her elegant mother. Thea remembered when she was younger, a tree that looked just like this one that had been covered in brambles. Drawn to it for some inexplicable reason, she'd cleared away the thorns and climbed the tree, something about its menacing branches challenging her.

Thea was about to call out when her mother's voice broke the silence. "Come, then," said the queen, "and claim me!"

Thea's gasp was muffled by a gust of wind. A man stepped from the shadows at the roots of the tree. She saw that he was handsome and wore bright gold rings on his fingers. He'd smiled at her mother and took her hand, drawing her forward.

Then he'd kissed her.

Thea froze in shock until a sudden, blinding light forced her to shield her eyes. The next moment, her mother and the man were gone.

After frantically calling her mother's name, she'd recovered her senses. She was alone in the forest at night during a war. There was a stink in the air that reminded her of the Seer's workroom. Magic. She could not battle magic. She'd rushed home to find help.

In the end, she'd found no help at all.

Thea came back to the present to find she'd crumpled a slipper in one hand.

"Show yourself!" she commanded. Her voice echoed more than it should in her modest bedchamber. In answer, another frigid breeze caressed her bare skin.

Unsettled by the scent of magic and the horrible memories it stirred up, Thea threw the gown into the flames, followed by the stockings and slippers. A huge gust of air came from the fireplace, forcing her to step back to escape the cloud of ashes. As the wind died, she dusted her hands to rid her skin of the feel of that fabric.

With determination, she donned an old gown, taking refuge in the practical. As she turned back once more to glance at her fireplace, she could almost believe she'd imagined the strange dress.

But for two blackened seed pearls nestled among the ashes like staring eyes.

2

> There are three things a Sylvan needs: sun, water, and revelry. Without these, our spirits wither.
>
> —Excharias, Sylvan poet

The great hall of Scarhamm was a large, paneled room with columns stretching up to a beamed ceiling. Windows faced the garden, inviting pink bands of sunset to warm the wooden floors. Normally, the hall was filled with trestle tables numerous enough for most of the Huntsmen, but for revels, the tables were cleared away. Tonight, the beams and columns were wrapped with red leaves from blood trees interspersed with gold leaves of autumn. Lamps hung at intervals, burning with a warm light as the sun's rays faded outside. A trio of pixie musicians played lute, drum, and pipe to a festive rhythm.

Thea made her way through the crowd, stopping to speak to several Huntsmen before reaching her father. Atop a raised dais, the king's throne was carved from a massive oak, its sides raw bark, its back sprouting branches that reached toward the ceiling. Thea bowed her head respectfully. Her father did not attend many revels, and she understood he was only present now for her sake.

To everyone else, the Sylvan king was a majestically imposing figure. Born in a time when folk had been wilder, his far larger stature and the broad, white antlers springing from his head were signs of his great age and power. Though enemies shook at his approach, and even allies had trouble meeting his darkly assessing gaze, Thea was accustomed to her father's intimidating presence.

The Sylvan king's eyes warmed as she straightened from her bow. "You killed four Skrattis last night," he said in a deep, approving rumble.

She gave her father a modest smile. "Five. They fled before I could take more down."

"They shouldn't trouble us again for a good while."

"Not if they have a grain of intelligence left rattling around in their heads," she agreed, "which is questionable after we knocked so many of their skulls about."

The Sylvan king never laughed, but his lips twitched, which was comparable to hilarity in anyone else.

Thea felt a slight pang, noticing the respect her father showed her in this moment, something her sister Cassia had never received. But everyone agreed Thea was the child who was most like her father—fearless, relentless on the battlefield, a natural defender of the forest folk. Thea planned to dedicate her life to that defense, which for a Sylvan could be hundreds, even a thousand years. If you didn't die on the battlefield.

The Sylvan king motioned to one of the servants. "Bring my daughter some of our best ale."

Thea nodded her thanks as a tankard was placed in her hands. "Thank you, Father."

His nod was one of approbation. "Good name day, Theodora."

As Thea bowed and turned away, she caught sight of the Court Seer's wooden seat, carved in the shape of an owl to represent Noctua, the Ancient patroness of spirits and divination. The seat was empty, as usual. Veleda rarely came to the great hall, as she didn't seem to enjoy attention. Or revels. Or people.

For a moment, Thea thought of asking Veleda about the mysterious dress. But Thea despised magic. She hated the chants, the rituals, and the ephemeral entities Seers called upon to divine the future. Sometimes Veleda prayed to the Ancients themselves to send her a vision, which seemed like a fruitless exercise. The Ancients had never once helped Thea when she'd asked.

Anyway, the Seer was absent, and it was Thea's name day revel. She took a cleansing breath and examined the assembly. Since the signing of the truce with the Dracu, more forest folk had started coming to Scarhamm. The hall was half filled with winged pixies, small household folk called lutins, lake-dwelling naiads and their cousins the river nixies, as well as other allies who lived under the protection of the Sylvan king. While the Sylvans were about the same size as humans, most forest folk were diminutive in stature and lived in small groups. They didn't have the strength, training, or numbers to defend themselves, which meant the Sylvan Huntsmen were their last and best protection against enemies who would kill them and steal their land if they could. Enemies included humans and Azpians, the folk like Dracu and Skrattis who dwelled underground beneath the forest.

One of the naiads looked Thea over as she passed. "Good name day, Thea! Is that the same dress you wore last year? Sylvan, you need new gowns!"

Thea straightened her shoulders. It *was* an old dress. She preferred to let people think she didn't care how she looked. After all, she was a warrior. There was no place in her life for fine or delicate things.

Saving Thea from having to reply, Tibald, the weapons master, entered the hall, his thick arm raised in greeting, drawing shouts and raised tankards. The jovial, bearded elder had trained every Sylvan Huntsman in Scarhamm, except for Tordon who was older still—the oldest Sylvan alive, except perhaps for the king himself. Their exact ages were a mystery.

"Thea! A toast to your name day!" Tibald said, waving Thea over to a tray of drinks. Thea's older sister turned from where she'd been talking with a group of nixies. Enora's silvery blond locks were braided in a crown on her head, a stark contrast to the nixies, who left their hair loose or braided with water lilies. A handsome nixie winked at Thea, and she nodded to him with a smile.

"Ready, name-day girl?" Enora asked, picking up a tankard before moving to Thea's side. She was dressed in a dark green gown that contrasted with her pale hair. "You know you're expected to outdance us all."

"Consider it done," Thea assured her with a confident grin.

As they toasted and drank, the Second Huntsman, Burke, entered with a group of friends, each with varying levels of swagger. Burke stopped for a moment, straightening to his full, considerable height to show the perfect fit of his jacket, then bowed to Thea with a murmured name day greeting. Thea gave him a nod and watched as he approached the throne, bowing deeply to the king before speaking. She saw the gleam of respect in her father's eye. No doubt Burke was detailing his success in the skirmish with the Skrattis, as she had done. It was obvious to everyone that Burke hoped to be the next First Huntsman.

Too bad for him that Thea would be taking that role. She didn't feel the need to announce her plans, opting instead to show that she was better suited. And with the Skratti raids, she was gaining more opportunities. Burke boasted precision and skill, but so did she. And there was one crucial difference between them. He played by the rules, whereas there was nothing she wouldn't do to protect the people she loved.

Noticing Burke's head stray toward the door, Thea turned to see Cassia entering the great hall, her pale, feathered wings and gold freckles warmed by firelight. Her flaxen hair was left in loose waves. Enora embraced her and complimented the daisies sewn onto her white dress, drawing a shy smile.

"Where's your Dracu?" Thea asked with a mischievous grin. "We won't kill him, you know. Probably."

Cassia's eyes narrowed on her sister. "Can I vow to Zeru he won't end up in a cell if he comes here?"

Thea and Enora exchanged looks. Neither of them knew what their father would do if a Dracu showed up in Scarhamm, even one Cassia trusted with her life.

"Your silence," Cassia said wryly, "tells me all I need to know."

Enora looked uncomfortable, but Thea shrugged. "Find any scuccas on patrol?"

Though Cassia no longer used her ring as a weapon against the Dracu, it had proved vital in the fight against scuccas—creatures made from sticks and moss and animated with trapped spirits. Though most of them had been destroyed when Cassia had battled the Seer who'd created them, Selkolla, some lingered. Some of the scuccas were peaceful, apt to hide if a Huntsman caught even a glimpse of them, but others had been skulking through Thirstwood and attacking forest folk.

Cassia's hazel eyes were distressed. "Not today. I think they hide from me. Maybe they can sense the ring and its ability to release their trapped spirits."

"At least you slayed the mad witch so she can't create any more of them." Thea tried to sound reassuring.

"Thea," said Enora with disapproval.

Oh, right. Cassia had a weak stomach for violence. "I mean since you caused the witch's death by vengeful Ancient."

Cassia's eyes warmed with humor. "It's all right, Enora. I'm not that squeamish. Anyway, I think the scuccas are aimless without her guiding them."

"Nothing we can do about all that for now," Enora said, grabbing another horn of ale. "Tonight, we celebrate our sister's name day. To Thea!"

Thea grinned, raising her own mug in reply, then hesitating before drinking. "Where's the Sproutling?"

"Behind you!" a voice piped.

Thea turned to see her youngest sister, Rozie, coming toward them, ginger curls wild, though someone had made a valiant attempt to tame them with pins. A losing battle if ever there was one.

"Like my dress?" Rozie spun in a circle, her arms out. Her yellow dress was sewn with orange leaves so when she twirled, she looked like a leaf mound in motion.

Thea grinned. "I don't know whether to embrace you or rake you into a pile."

Rozie giggled, shaking the skirt out with her hands. "The seamstress said she was inspired by my hair. The season of autumn come to life! Or something."

Thea reached out with her free hand and tucked a curl behind Rozie's ear. "No one livelier than our Sproutling."

Enora handed Rozie a cup of nectar, chuckling when she tried to switch it for ale. For the next few hours as they danced and laughed, Thea was able to push the truce, the Skrattis, and the mysterious dress to the back of her mind.

Nothing could touch them here. Selkolla was dead. The Court Seer had reinforced the wards, keeping magic attacks and enemies at bay. Scarhamm was still the safest place a Sylvan could be.

3

> Beware when the forest folk gather. Pixie wine is the doom of many a Dracu.
> —Gaxix, Dracu philosopher

As Thea exited the gates the next evening, Enora and Burke were waiting at the tree line, their breath visible as clouds of fog. Patrols were gathering, some Huntsmen already dispersing, their green-and-brown uniforms swallowed by shadows as they moved into the trees. The sunset stained Scarhamm's stone walls with a splash of red, as if a giant had been slain at the gates and slapped a bloody hand against the wood. The spikes that had once displayed the severed heads of Dracu were now empty, but Thea had no trouble remembering each one. It felt to her as if the war had ended yesterday rather than months before.

"Have you recovered?" Burke asked, his smile taunting.

Thea's mind went to the mysterious dress at her hearth, and she stared hard at him. "From what?"

Enora's eyebrows went up. "From your name day revel?"

"Oh, that." Thea rolled her shoulders. "I had two hours' sleep. I've survived on less."

Burke chuckled, a knowing look in his hazel eyes. "If you were suffering, you'd never admit it."

"Then why ask?" Aware she was being more irritable than usual, she strived for a neutral tone. "Where are we assigned tonight?"

"Same as two nights ago," Enora said, tilting her head to the right. "The area around the Grotto."

Burke's grin widened. "I could use a drink."

Enora gave him a warning look. "We'll be going in for information, not pixie wine."

"Why not both?" Burke quipped.

Thea grinned as they started down the path. She never minded this assignment. You could learn a great deal by asking questions or sitting and listening at the bar. Though forest folk could be shy and reticent to share information outside their own people, most of the customers were willing to talk to the Huntsmen. They knew Sylvan patrols were vital to protecting them.

The threats were many, and not only from the Skrattis and other Azpians. Humans who lived on lands adjacent to Thirstwood were an ever-present danger as well.

Once, humans had respected the land folk who'd inhabited wild spaces, considering their woods, fountains, and rocks as sacred, even giving offerings to appease them. But as humans cleared and cultivated the continent, the folk's connection with the land and its power weakened. Their numbers diminished as humans multiplied. Finally, humans had called the land folk monsters and demons, using that as justification for hunting and killing them. When the danger of extinction became too great, the Sylvan king had led the tree-dwellers into Thirstwood for their own protection. For a long time, stories of the blood trees trapping and suffocating intruders had been enough to keep people away.

But humans were becoming bolder. It had been too long, some said, for them to remember the old stories. They'd begun clearing trees at the forest's edges, using the timber to build towns and villages. There were not enough Sylvan Huntsmen to fight off more than a small army of humans. Only the Sylvan king's blood trees stood against the encroachment that would cause the death of all forest folk.

Thea tried not to dwell on things that she could do nothing about. She focused on her duty, which for now was patrol. She kept vigil with Enora and Burke along the woodland paths, ducking to avoid low branches and inhaling deep lungfuls of crisp air scented with peat moss and the coppery tang of blood leaves. A thin silver mist hung like garlands from the boughs, as if some misguided spirit had tried to decorate for a revel. But the only music was the rustling of birds and nesting squirrels. The moon rose, shivering under a quilt of clouds, and Thea felt no warmer herself. But after all her injuries, she had practice ignoring discomfort.

The night wore on with no sign of a disturbance. Finally, the lantern lights of the Grotto came into view, its frost-rimmed windows glowing with welcome.

Burke chuckled. "Is Wick ever going to fix that foundation? And the roof? The place is falling apart."

Enora shrugged. "Part of the charm."

The Grotto's roofline *was* rather sad, but the rectangular stone-and-timber structure had sat empty for ten years during the Sylvan-Dracu war, bearing the weight of snow winter after winter without repair. Missing windowpanes had merely been covered by boards, and the steps sagged drunkenly to one side, while masonry crumbled at the building's base. Wick, the proprietor, was a gregarious lutin and more concerned with persuading her customers that it was safe to return to the Grotto than replacing mortar and glass.

Still, lutins were household spirits, folk who lived indoors rather than in wild spaces. A building like this would be connected to Wick's spirit, which probably meant she had not fully recovered from the war herself.

As far as Thea was concerned, the sagging roof was as much a Sylvan responsibility as Wick's. One more reason to keep Thirstwood safe.

Enora entered first, waving to a group of five naiads seated at a round table near the bar. They were dressed in their usual flowing greens and blues, with water lilies tucked into their hair. They wore jewelry made from shells and fish scales, polished or painted so that it sparkled in the warm firelight. Thea scanned the rest of the space, taking inventory. A dozen patrons chatted over ales. A swamp dweller was seated by the window, staring down into his tankard between swigs. Two pixies sat atop a single barstool. And someone was seated by the fireplace. Only broad shoulders and a dark head of hair were visible above the back of their chair.

Wick was talking to the naiads, throwing her head back as she laughed. Her curvy figure seemed to fit her generous personality, though she could be fearsome if someone misbehaved in her establishment.

"Thea, you talk to the pixies," Enora said, unbuttoning her cloak. "Burke, you take the swamp dweller." And tossing her cloak onto a hook, she moved toward the naiads. Enora was friends with some of them, so they were most likely to share information with her.

Burke grumbled something under his breath, but he strode off to perch his large frame awkwardly on a rickety chair next to the figure by the window. The swamp dweller was a rare creature. He had fins coming out of his face, and his skin was bright green. In the summer, he was scarce, spending every moment in the marsh. But the colder nights of autumn and winter drove him to places like the Grotto that offered a warm fire. His name was unpronounceable to a Sylvan tongue, so most called him Fen.

Thea made her way to the pixies, ducking under cobwebs that hung down from the ceiling. "Well met, Winter. Mind if I sit here?"

Winter was one of the pixies who frequented the Grotto along with his cousins Spring, Summer, and Autumn. Spring and Summer must have stayed home, perhaps not willing to venture into the cold night.

"If you wish," said Winter, his tone cool but polite. "Better than sitting on *us*, Giantess."

Thea forced a smile at their nickname for her as she took her seat, wondering why the pixies always seemed intent on testing her patience. Still, she couldn't help staring for a moment at their delicate wings. Their pastel shades had an opalescent quality, changing colors depending on the light, and they were so thin they were almost transparent, much like butterfly wings. When she was a child, Thea had loved butterflies, spending hours playing in her mother's garden, mesmerized by the tiny creatures' beauty and grace. Winter's wings were a pale, icy blue, and his long hair so blond it was almost white, contrasting with his dark brown eyes. Autumn's wavy hair was more auburn than copper, her eyes golden brown, and her wings a pale orange.

"What are you drinking?" Thea asked. "Pixie wine?"

"We merely call it *wine*," Autumn replied sourly, raising the thimble that served as a tankard. Thea took a breath, wondering how to fix her mistake.

Before she could speak, Wick returned to the bar, her gap-toothed smile breaking the tension. "Welcome, Thea. You're on duty?"

Thea nodded. "Tea, please."

While Wick bustled with a kettle over a brazier, Thea turned to Winter and Autumn, rehearsing how to ask them if they'd seen anything suspicious in the area. Thea hated dancing around things, but pixies did not like a direct approach. And despite their beauty and delicacy, the two of them together were rather disconcerting. Their rapid gestures and darting eyes made Thea feel more alert, and she had to tell herself not to be affected. It was vital she didn't upset them. Pixies were the Huntsmen's eyes and ears, flying to nearby villages and reporting enemy activity to Sylvan patrols.

If they felt like it. And if their goals aligned with yours. And if they didn't harbor any grudges against you.

Thea searched for a soft opening and noticed Autumn's pristine white gown. It was simpler than her usual clothing. "I like your dress."

Autumn's brows came together. "You mean my sacred robes? I'm in training to become a Seer. I'm apprenticed to Veleda, you know."

Thea did not know. She avoided the Court Seer of Scarhamm as much as possible. Which left her at a loss as what to say next. Finally, she came up with, "Are you finding it interesting?"

"Her tutoring is adequate." Autumn lifted her tiny shoulders in a delicate shrug. "A touch pedantic for me. But you know, she is a Sylvan."

Thea cleared her throat to buy herself a second to think of a polite reply. "Yes, we must seem rather plodding to you. Pixies are nimble." She hoped the compliment would massage any ruffled feathers.

"They can't help it," Winter said, taking a sip from his thimble. "Trees grow slowly. As do Sylvans. But they can be taught."

Thea bit the inside of her cheek. She hated not being able to speak her mind. For the past several years, the only diplomacy she'd employed was granting enemies a quick death. She did not have the patience for this.

"If you'll pardon me," she said, standing, "my sister needs me." It was true in a general sense.

"She seems perfectly content to me," Autumn observed, her eyes shifting from Enora to Thea. "You're not looking for an excuse to leave us, are you?"

Thea's tongue stuck to the roof of her mouth. She could not lie. If a tactician knows anything, it's when to retreat. "Excuse me." Turning on her heel, she made her way across the room, cursing under her breath. She'd bungled that. Why had Enora assigned her the pixies? She'd rather have talked to Fen, even if his conversation was dangerously boring.

As she neared the table of naiads, Enora shook her head subtly as if to say, "*Not now*." She must be learning something the naiads were reluctant to share. Thea gave a slight nod and headed to the fireplace. Wick had returned to the bar and was talking with the pixies, probably saying all the right things to smooth over Thea's abrupt departure.

"Difficult things, aren't they?" a deep voice said from behind her.

Thea spun to face the chair, which she'd somehow forgotten was occupied. It wasn't like her to be unaware of anyone in her vicinity. A tall, lean young man with a face hidden by shadows lounged in a relaxed way, one leg stretched toward the fire, the other bent. She examined him. Velvet and silk clothing. Rings glittering on his fingers. Too refined for the Grotto.

"You look surprised," he said, the firelight illuminating well-shaped lips. "Did I startle you?"

Her shoulders tightened at the blunt reminder that she hadn't been alert to her surroundings. "I was distracted."

He turned to look at the bar, then back at her. "The pixies were rather rude."

"*Eavesdropping* is rude."

He smiled, showing even, white teeth. "It's almost as if they know you have a temper and were trying to ignite it. Is your anger a thing worth seeing?"

"Maybe." Thea took a step closer. The shadows were strangely thick so near the fireplace.

"You'd like a better look at me, I suppose," the stranger said, his tone neutral, almost bored. He murmured something and the firelight fell on his face, illuminating him. Thea's breath caught in her chest, an instinctive reaction as her mind tried to understand what she was seeing. He couldn't have been Sylvan because his ears did not come to a distinctive point at the top. He was too tall to be any of the other forest folk. And he couldn't be a human because she had never heard them described as ethereally, devastatingly handsome. Which he was. Also, a human would have been devoured by the trees long before it could find its way this deep into Thirstwood.

The longer she looked at him, the less she could think. His eyes were dark, his hair darker, and shadows clung in defined arcs under his pale cheekbones and jaw. She could look at him all day.

Go closer, some instinct said.

"Breathe," said the stranger.

Thea blew out an angry breath. She never forgot to breathe.

But she had.

Someone opened and closed the door, admitting a gust of wind that rattled cups behind the bar, carrying with it the scent of blood. Though Thea wasn't as connected to the trees of Thirstwood as Cassia, she sensed the forest's anticipation, a muted but distinct awareness, the blood trees readying for violence.

This stranger was a threat, and the forest sensed it.

"Who are you?" she demanded, her hand resting on her sword hilt.

His eyes glittered as he looked her over. "Straight and tall as a pine, lovely as a willow, fearsome as a winter storm."

Her upper lip curled. "That's from 'The Ballad of the Sylvan King's Daughters.' Don't listen to lutin bards. They don't hold truth in as high regard as Sylvans do."

His smile didn't reach his eyes. "I don't see the lie. Well met."

A frisson of awareness slid over her arms at the way he looked at her. "Who are you?" she demanded again. "I've never seen you here before."

He made a gesture as if tipping a hat, shadows swirling over his fingers. "I'm a traveler. You may think of me as a friendly stranger."

"Only forest folk are welcome here." She made a quick decision, knowing her sister and Burke would agree. "As you've trespassed, I'm taking you back to Scarhamm for questioning."

His melodious chuckle made her want to close her eyes as if she were listening to beautiful music.

"You trespassed first," he replied.

Thea had to take her eyes off him, if only to prove to herself that she could. *So beautiful.*

He tilted his head. "You don't even know what you did. Do you?" The shadows swirled around him, touching his forehead and cheeks as if to reassure themselves he was there. *She wanted to touch him, too.* "If I had any feelings," he murmured, "I might think that was sad."

His vagueness and the pity in his tone set her off. She grabbed for his arm, prepared to haul him back to Scarhamm.

Her hand passed through him as if he weren't there.

A chill ran from her neck to the small of her back. *Impossible!* "What foul magic is this?"

"I'll tell you." He leaned in, his grin returning as he watched her shiver. "*If* you wear the dress."

4

> What we call magic is the power of the Old Ones harvested by the Ancients, left behind by their footsteps when they retreated from our lands. It lingers in the air we breathe, the water we drink, and the fire that warms us. If we sit quietly and listen, sometimes we can hear the whisper of their words.
> —The Little Book of Spells

Thea inhaled sharply, turning to call Enora, but when she looked back at the chair in front of the fire, it was empty.

Her eyes darted from the chair to the bar to every shadowy corner. Could he have slid out of the tavern without her noticing?

Suddenly, a strange image appeared all around her. Several thin, metallic trunks and delicate branches floated into view. For a moment, the room was filled with silver trees.

Her feet rooted in place, Thea watched the vision fade, the jerk of her heart slamming as wildly as if she were in a fight. She blinked as her mind suddenly went fuzzy. Why was her pulse racing? Had the interaction with the pixies upset her that badly? She looked at the chair in front of the fire. Hadn't someone been sitting there a moment before? Confusion coursed through her as Enora approached. "What's wrong?"

"I…" Thea cleared her throat, searching for a reason for her turbulent emotions. "I offended the pixies."

"Oh, is that all?" Enora's posture relaxed. "I knew you would."

"Excuse me?" Thea asked, irritation providing a welcome change in focus.

Enora smirked, but her eyes asked forgiveness. "Don't be mad. I only wanted you to keep them busy so I could talk to my friends without them overhearing. I could tell something was wrong from the look on Kaiya's face."

"Did you learn anything?" Thea asked, still unsettled at the feeling that she'd lost track of what was going on around her.

Enora nodded, her expression worried. "Let's rescue Burke and get going. I'd rather tell you closer to home."

Burke wasted no time in saying goodbye to Fen. Thea nodded to Wick, who grinned and waved before setting two more thimbles in front of the pixies. The pale-haired pixie, Winter, raised a brow at Thea, but Autumn didn't spare them a glance. Burke opened the door, and the three Huntsmen left the warmth of the tavern.

The brisk air sharpened Thea's senses, making her aware of her surroundings. Patrol always required vigilance, but she had a lingering sense of unease that seemed out of proportion to the night's encounters. Enora had something to share, but that wasn't unusual. They often heard warnings from the forest folk, and whatever the threat, they would deal with it. She ran over the conversation with the pixies in her mind but could find no cause for concern, aside from her own mistakes, which in retrospect were minor. The pixies had been ready to find fault, as they always were.

Lost in her thoughts, Thea hardly noticed the silence of her companions until an hour had passed. Enora didn't speak until the sky started to lighten as they neared Scarhamm. "The naiads are on edge," she said, her voice pitched low. "I know this will sound odd, but Kaiya said they've caught glimpses of silver trees in the woods, like nothing they've ever seen before."

Thea's head jerked up, a vague memory flitting through her mind, there and gone. "Nearby?" If she, Enora, and Burke were the closest patrol, they should head there immediately.

"No, you don't understand," Enora replied. "They're not real. They appear in the forest, but when the naiads go near, the trees are not actually there. It's like they're figments."

Burke's voice lacked its usual lightness as he added his own report. "Fen has seen them, too. He thinks they're somehow coming into our world from the land of spirits."

Thea considered that. "Trees from the land of the dead?"

Enora made a doubtful sound. "It doesn't seem likely. Noctua keeps ephemeral beings bound in the Netherwhere. And Father's protections on the forest keep out anything that shouldn't be here. Veleda even adds her own wards around Scarhamm."

"But how strong can those wards be?" Burke asked. "The Skrattis have been entering Thirstwood." He lowered his voice as if he were afraid someone might overhear. "Even when it's not a full moon."

Thea had wondered about this, too. All the Huntsmen probably had. She assumed the elders were aware of the threats and were doing something to handle it. Because if strange things were appearing in the woods, that was a direct threat to the safety of the Sylvans.

Thea would not take any threat lightly.

After a few hours of much needed sleep, Thea dressed in her practice gear. Though she'd spent the night on patrol, she would still be expected to put in time on the training grounds. Not that she minded. Sparring was always a good way to work out her frustrations.

But first, she wanted to speak to Tordon about the sightings of silver trees. Given his age, he knew all the old history. She checked the war room, the kitchen, and great hall before trying the library, a modest room crammed with dusty codices and scrolls. Orange rays of sunrise streamed in from leaded windows high on the paneled walls, drawing rectangles of light on a long, scarred pine table where Tordon was leaning over a map, his hand absently running over his short dark curls. He looked up as she entered, his eyes brightening as he saw her.

"Ah, Thea. I'm planning the patrols for tonight. Your father and I have been trying to discern a pattern to the Skratti attacks. Maybe you can help me." He motioned to the map, which he'd covered with small wooden carvings of soldiers. "I've marked all the previous skirmishes. I'm hoping your young eyes will pick up something I'm missing."

Thea stared at the map for a few minutes, lingering on each location, trying to see any connection. Some areas were boggy, some dry, some populated with forest creatures, some relatively empty.

"I'm at a loss," she finally admitted. "It used to be they'd find burial mounds or other places where the ground was disturbed. Now they seem to be able to come up anywhere."

Tordon rubbed the bridge of his nose. "None of these areas have openings to the Cryptlands. I thought at first it could be the work of the Dracu, but Cassia's friend Zeru verified that his queen is holding to her side. The Skrattis are ignoring her edicts, and she isn't happy about it."

"Maybe the Dracu is wrong," Thea suggested, not willing to trust the word of a longtime enemy.

Tordon's eyes met hers. "You don't like him."

She couldn't rightly say that, so she shrugged. "Don't know him."

Tordon leaned against the table. "I remember a time when the Dracu and Sylvans were not at war, nor even at odds. Yes, I am that old, child. And yes, you are a child to me, so stop scowling. I get a sense that Zeru—he does have a name, you know—truly cares about Cassia. And he helped us greatly with negotiating the truce."

Thea felt chastised. She hated admitting she was wrong. "I suppose."

He chuckled. "You'd do well to listen to me. Take your allies where you can find them."

"Speaking of allies," Thea said, seizing the opportunity for a change of subject, "some of the forest folk are worried. They've seen something strange." Briefly, she told him about the reports of silver trees in the forest.

Tordon listened attentively until she'd finished, his brow furrowed over serious eyes. "But the trees weren't truly there?"

She nodded. "When the folk moved toward

them, they disappeared." The groove that appeared between Tordon's brows did not look promising. Perhaps he was as confused as she and Enora and Burke had been. "You don't know what they could be?" she prompted finally.

Tordon sighed, his eyes settling on the map. "For all we know, it could have been a trick of the moonlight."

Thea lifted her brows in surprise. "But the naiads have seen the trees, as well as Fen, the swamp dweller."

Tordon pinched the bridge of his nose. "I'm sorry, Thea. I don't have the answers." As if realizing he sounded abrupt, he looked up and gave her a genuine, if tired, smile. "But let me think on it some more."

Thea nodded. "Thank you." But as she left the library, her mind whirred with questions.

Tordon's phrasing was too careful. *I don't have the answers* was different from saying he didn't know. She found her chest tightening with an unusual restlessness. If something dangerous was coming, didn't they all need to know what was going on?

As Thea arrived at the training yard, both Burke and Enora were already there with a group of Huntsmen. Enora was facing off with young Cedric, going easy on him from the looks of it. Cassia was there, too, practicing knife-throwing at a target on the far end of the yard, her golden wings catching the sun with every movement. Rozie was sitting on the sidelines as a spectator, her coppery hair making the training yard brighter. Tibald sat on a rock, his hands crossed loosely over his belly, watching it all.

"Face off with me?" Thea asked Burke.

He gave a quick nod. "Gladly."

Soon, they were sparring, and the wooden swords made a satisfying sound with every contact, which relieved some of her tension. Burke seemed to appreciate her frenzied pace, matching her vigor.

"Can't stop thinking about what Fen said." His eyes looked haunted, though his movements were as sharp and clean as always. "What are those silver trees? I don't like an enemy I can't see."

Thea nodded. Her stomach was tied in knots, the sweat cold on her skin. Not only were silver trees appearing in the forest, a dress that stank of magic had appeared in her bedchamber. Inside the walls of Scarhamm, where Veleda's wards shouldn't let anything in. She'd tried to put it out of her mind as some kind of joke, but the coincidence was too telling.

Distracted by her thoughts, Thea mistimed her parry and took a blow on her shoulder. It caught her off balance and sent her down on one knee. Rozie shouted in surprise as some of the Huntsmen gasped. Thea saw a glint of gold as Cassia rushed closer.

Tibald stood up, his expression concerned. "It's been years since you let your guard down like that." When she gave him an angry look, he put his palms up. "It's only the truth. Maybe your night patrols are catching up to you. Rest and try again tomorrow."

Tibald's kind tone only made it worse. She stood and brushed herself off, hoping her braids hid the worst of her blush. When she looked up, Burke was staring at her with a mixture of triumph and disbelief. Her hand twitched, ready to hit the smug smile off his face, but that would only make her look like a sore loser. Maybe Tibald was right that she needed rest. She had no stomach to continue sparring now.

She felt the weight of her sisters' and fellow Huntsmen's stares as she turned to leave. She wasn't used to being seen as weak. She wanted to snarl at them all that she was fine. But it would be a lie.

Rozie trotted along beside her as she headed toward the fortress with long strides. "I've never seen you get hit, Thea! Is something wrong?"

Thea slowed her steps to match Rozie's pace. "It'll never happen again."

Cassia caught up, concern in her hazel eyes. "You're not hurt?"

Enora joined a moment later, her chin jutting at a determined angle, her eyes narrowed on Thea. "Care to explain that unprecedented show of inattention?"

Thea shrugged. She didn't want to mention the silver trees in front of Rozie, and though Enora was clearly worried, no one was more disturbed by the lapse than Thea. "Something is off," she said finally.

"I know what you mean," Cassia said, lifting her head and sniffing the air, reminding Thea that her sister's senses were keener now. "I feel it lately, too. I wish I knew what was causing it."

The four sisters walked in silence for a few moments.

Rozie broke the hush.

"If you're not on patrol tonight, I'll give you Mr. Himmy to sleep in your bedchamber," she offered, naming a black-and-gray cat who was one of her favorites. "He hogs my pillow, but he's so mean he'd rip anyone to shreds if they tried to hurt you. He always helps me sleep."

"Thanks for the offer," Thea replied, "but I don't want to take him from you." More importantly, she didn't want Rozie's notoriously grumpy cat anywhere near her.

"Rozie, who are you expecting him to rip to shreds while you sleep in your own bedchamber in Scarhamm?" Enora asked, alarmed.

Rozie shrugged her slight shoulders. "Who knows? We didn't expect shrubs to try to kill us until a few months ago."

Though Enora laughed, a coil of tension wound tighter in Thea's chest.

"Well, murderous plants aside," Cassia said, "we all need sleep. We should get some rest before the revel tonight."

"Another one?" Thea asked.

Enora turned to her in surprise. "There was a time we longed for revels again. What's wrong with you?"

"Maybe I don't trust this truce." And the fact that there were new threats: silver trees in the forest that weren't really there and a dress that had mysteriously appeared on her hearth. How could she make merry when she didn't know what was going on? When she was starting to feel like she couldn't protect her sisters?

"Veleda says Sylvans need bright, happy things to flourish," Rozie pointed out.

Thea scoffed. "Veleda spends her days in a dark workroom in the cellars. What does she know about bright, happy things?"

"Well," Cassia said, "if it's brightness you need, I keep inviting you to sunny Welkincaster and you keep refusing me." She raised a pale brow. "Unless you've changed your mind...?"

Thea hated to disappoint her gentle sister, so she smiled as she said, "Someday, maybe."

But not right now. Her gut told her some dark threat was growing, unseen. And her instincts were rarely wrong.

5

> Elders claim that other realms exist side by side with our world, though the pathways there have been lost.
> —Excharias, Sylvan poet

Needing sleep after her patrol, her conversation with Tordon, and her humiliating loss of control while training, Thea decided to go back to bed, only waking when Rozie burst through her bedchamber door a few hours later. "It's time for the revel!"

Thea sat up and pushed the tangle of hair from her face. Rozie was dressed in green trousers and a flowing tunic, both too large for her. "Where in the nine realms did you get that outfit?"

Rozie straightened proudly. "I found a trunk full of clothes left behind by one of the old Seers."

Thea didn't know how to tell her sister that the flamboyant costume did not look right on a twelve-year-old girl. "It's too big."

"I'll grow into it," Rozie said, hand on one hip. "Anyway, get dressed! We don't want to miss the beginning."

"I'm not going," Thea said, hoping a steely-eyed stare would have some effect. "I don't feel like dancing."

Rozie bolted to the side of her bed. "You don't understand! There are drudes! *Drudes!*"

Thea wrinkled her nose, trying to remember. "Those folk from the mountains?"

"Yes!" Rozie put her hands together. "They juggle glass and fire, and they do all kinds of tricks! I've been begging to see them for three years and Father asked them to perform for us tonight!"

Thea noticed the excited flush on her sister's cheeks. "This is clearly a momentous occasion."

As Rozie passed near the fireplace, she reached down and scooped up something. "Is this your dress for tonight?" She shook out the garment, her expression impressed. "I like it!"

Thea's lips parted in shock as Rozie held up a gown she'd never seen before, the fabric dyed the hue of faded lilacs. On the hearth were a pair of stockings and slippers—black with purple flowers embroidered on the tops.

Seeing Rozie's hands on the dress made something inside Thea go wild. The idea of her youngest sister being tainted with some unknown magic, of it having any effect on her—

Thea leaped from bed and ripped the garment from her sister's hands.

Rozie stared at her with wide eyes. She blinked a couple of times before her lip trembled. "I wasn't going to do anything to it."

Thea's heart contracted as she registered the hurt in her sister's expression. "It's not that." How could she explain without scaring Rozie? "It's a surprise." Though her throat tightened at the misleading statement, it was vague enough, and partly true enough, that she was able to speak it. The dress had, in fact, been a surprise to her.

"All right," Rozie said, eyeing her cautiously. She moved with careful steps, as if Thea might do something unexpected and dangerous. Which she supposed she just had.

Thea's heart stuck in her throat as the door closed. She shut her eyes, fury building in her chest. The garments were no longer an annoyance but starting to feel sinister.

Now that Rozie had seen the dress, she would expect to see it on Thea, but there was no way—not without knowing more about the risks. Tossing the garment back to the floor, Thea threw open the doors to her armoire and chose a simple brown dress.

By the time Thea reached the great hall, the revel was in full swing. The Sylvan king was not in attendance, but the drudes, diminutive mountain folk wearing colorful garb, were warming up in an open area off to the side. A few dozen Huntsmen, some in green-and-brown dress uniforms, others in colorful garb, danced with lutins, naiads, and river nixies. Thea admired the clothing of the water folk—dresses woven from delicate green muskgrass and swamp milkweed, belts made from cattails—and their hair braided with marsh marigolds and water hyacinths.

Thea scanned the room for newcomers but decided she had no wish to introduce herself to anyone tonight. Instead, she danced with Gawen, a stable boy her own age who she'd found a quiet corner with now and again. As their hands joined in the dance, he asked her with his eyes if she might be interested in stealing off now for such a thing.

Normally, she would. But something was making her neck prickle. And suddenly, she was not looking at Gawen at all.

A stranger stood in his place. But no, she'd seen him once before. She had a memory of meeting him in the Grotto! Somehow, the incident had fled her mind as soon as he'd disappeared, but now it came rushing back to her.

He is here! In the great hall of Scarhamm! The thought of an intruder getting past the wards made Thea's heart stop for a moment before crashing in horror.

The stranger was dressed in finery once again, a fitted, dark jacket and trousers made of some soft material. His snowy white shirt was pristine. Silver cuff links glinted at his wrists, and rings shone on his fingers. He was even more handsome than Thea remembered. She felt the same pull toward him, but it was mitigated by the wrongness of his presence.

"Keep dancing," he said, smiling urbanely as if he'd been her partner the whole time. "It will seem odd if you stop."

Her pulse slammed, but her head felt light. Her hand went to her dagger, but she didn't bring weapons to revels. Maybe she should.

His eyes went to her hand. "There's no need for whatever weapon you seem to be searching for. You can't hurt me with it, anyway."

"How did you get in here?" she hissed, her voice breathless when she'd meant to sound threatening.

He ignored the question. "What is this you're wearing?" He waved a hand up and down, a slight frown marring his features. "It doesn't do you justice, Theodora. The dress I sent is much nicer, and it will fit you better, too. Why don't you go back up to your bedchamber and change?"

"I will do no such thing."

His eyebrows lifted, and she could not help noticing how thick they were and how nicely they framed his dark eyes. "If you prefer to wear a grain sack to a revel, who am I to argue?"

Thea's hands curled into fists, longing to teach him some manners. But before she could do anything, she found herself staring at Gawen, who was regarding her with huge, wide eyes. "Thea? Are...are you well?"

She looked around for the stranger but saw only Huntsmen and guests. It took her a moment to find her voice. "Why wouldn't I be?"

"Well," he said slowly, his eyes wary, "you said

some things that didn't make sense, and... you looked like you were going to hit me."

She cringed, noticing several revelers looking her way. She could remember a stranger standing there in Gawen's place. Had she imagined it? The details were already fuzzy in her mind. They must all think her mad. Oh, and now Enora was coming over. Thea had no urge to answer questions when she didn't even know what had happened. She needed to be alone.

Without another word, she turned and strode from the great hall.

Thea took the stairs leading to the bedchambers two at a time, hoping to outrun her shorter sister.

But Enora's voice came from too close behind her. "I couldn't hear what you were saying, but Gawen looked horrified. What happened?"

I don't know. But if she admitted that, Enora would pester her with a thousand questions she couldn't answer. "I'm tired," Thea said, speaking a truth to avoid lying. "I'm going to bed."

"Thea." Enora leaped three stairs and spun to block her way. "Tell me what's going on!"

In a cheap move, Thea reached out and tickled

Enora's side, then slipped past her and into the bedchamber. But her sister was quick to recover, pushing her way in before Thea could slam the door. She'd seldom seen her sister so agitated. Braids had come loose and were coiling over her shoulders. How very un-Enora-like.

She understood her sister's confusion. Usually, Thea shared every detail of every fight, every jest, every encounter with a soft-voiced groomsman or stable hand. But now she could barely remember what had happened.

At Thea's silence, Enora's tone hardened. "We've always trusted each other with everything. Why don't you trust me now?"

Thea took a breath, trying to calm. "It's not about trusting you, Enora. I do. More than anyone."

Enora folded her arms, her gaze probing. "You're keeping secrets." She glanced around the room as if searching for clues to her sister's strange behavior. Her brows furrowed as she glanced at the floor near the hearth. "What's that?"

Thea's pulse quickened as she saw the gown on the hearth. Furious that she'd forgotten about that, too, she wanted to pick the dress up and hurl it into the flames. But that would only make her sister more curious, and she needed to be alone.

Enora's eyes narrowed at Thea's silence. "It's been years since you had a new one made."

Thea shrugged, searching for a reply that wouldn't lead to more questions. "I'm full of surprises."

After a final, searching look, Enora finally turned to leave. "I hope you get some rest." The door shut with a bang.

Thea sat on the edge of her bed and stared at the hearth, tempted to drive her fist into the stonework just to ease her frustration. She hated magic, but it was time for her to visit the one person in Scarhamm who might be able to explain everything.

6

A Seer's workshop is a dangerous place.
—Excharias, Sylvan poet

AFTER TRAINING THE NEXT MORNING, Thea headed to the workroom of the Court Seer, which was located on the chilliest, wettest, lowest level of the fortress. As Thea reached the bottom of the staircase, her foot splashed into a puddle and she shivered, the autumn temperature of the Scar River already anticipating winter. Frigid water flowed into crevices, making it impossible to keep the floor dry. The entire thing seemed to be in a state of decay.

The damp, empty cells that had held Dracu captives during the war seemed to echo with agonized voices, though Thea knew it was merely the wind howling through cracks. She couldn't remember the last time she'd been here. It smelled of mold and neglect. She had no idea why Veleda chose to have her workroom here when she could have had any empty one in the upper floors of Scarhamm.

Thea found the warped wooden door half open and let herself into the room. Veleda's back was turned as she hunched over her worktable, her curly brown hair held loosely in a scarf, half of it escaping and trailing over her shoulders as she ground something with a mortar and pestle.

Thea glanced around the overcrowded chamber, which was lit with a single candle jammed into an animal skull, the flame lighting its empty eye sockets. The shelves were crammed with too many vials, bottles, and bones, and a menagerie of odd things no one in their right mind would collect. Her nose wrinkled at the smells of divination—crushed herbs and earthy things she couldn't identify.

Veleda finally turned to face her. "Thea?" She set down the mortar and pestle, staring at the bundle in Thea's hands. "What is that?"

Hello to you, too. Thea held the garment toward the Seer. "I need to ask you about this. It appeared on my hearth."

Veleda gave her a doubtful look. "What do you mean it 'appeared'?"

"I mean that one second my hearth was empty

and the next it had a dress and stockings and a pair of slippers on it. This is the second one."

The Court Seer looked unsettled. "But that can't be. It would have to get past my wards."

Thea took a step closer. "Do you want to examine it?"

Veleda reared back, pointing instead to a corner. "Put it there for now."

Her reaction was odd, but Thea tossed the gown into the corner, watching as a thick bunch of cobwebs caught it, cradling it like a prize. "Don't you ever let anyone clean in here?"

Veleda took a shuddering breath. "I can't believe you don't feel it."

"Feel what?"

"The power coming from that dress." Veleda leaned against her worktable, a hand to her head. "Old. Strong." She rubbed her eyes, then blew out a breath.

"I could smell magic on it," Thea said, realizing a Seer must be able to sense things she could not.

Veleda's eyes shifted in thought. "Tordon told me what you heard on patrol the other night. Silver trees, or figments of them, appearing in the forest."

Thea nodded, wondering at this sudden topic change. "Do you think that relates to the dress?"

The Seer frowned. "It concerns me that we have two strange things of unknown origin. Where are they coming from? How are they getting into Thirstwood and even into Scarhamm itself? Your father's command over the roots creates one layer of protection, and my warding spells create another. So my first worry is about those wards."

Thea nodded, waiting in silence for a moment. "It sounds like you have another concern."

Veleda sighed, her frown deepening. "Silver trees...that is...strange. I worry..." She stopped, shook her head, and met Thea's eyes. "There are also mystic buffers between realms, between our world and other, much more dangerous ones, and those buffers are the first and most important barriers that protect us."

"Other *worlds*?" Thea asked, tension tightening her spine. "You mean like the Netherwhere?"

"Yes, that's one," Veleda said, speaking slowly as if thinking. "Another example is the welkins, which Cassia found with the help of her ring."

Thea shook her head, wondering why the Seer was jumping to wild conclusions. Surely there was a simpler explanation for all this. Another witch working for the Azpians, perhaps?

Veleda spread her hands. "We know very little about the pathways to these other places. There's a rare old book called *Old Ones, Ancients, and the Folk*, which used to be in your father's library."

"Used to be?"

Veleda glanced around as if she might find the volume somewhere underfoot. "I can't find it of late. But it talks about places where the barriers are thin between worlds. The figments of silver trees could be a sign that something is trying to get through. The appearance of this dress in your bedchamber is even worse. It means something can get inside our walls."

An icy finger traced Thea's spine. "I know my father's power in the forest prevents Azpians from coming aboveground." It was hitting her that she knew very little about the magical component of what kept Sylvans safe. "And you reinforce the wards on Scarhamm's walls and inside. You're saying there's more than that protecting us?"

Veleda nodded. "What I'm describing are more like divisions between places, perhaps more like curtains or veils that can be drawn aside if their magic is depleted... They could break down."

"And whoever or whatever is in those realms could come into ours?" Thea couldn't believe what she was hearing, but she couldn't deny a threat just because it sounded fanciful. As a Huntsman, it was her job to protect the Sylvans from all threats.

Veleda worried her lower lip with her teeth. "If my theory is correct, we could think of the silver trees like a drip that shows a crack in a dam, a warning of what could come if the veil's magic is not restored, and if your father's power and my wards are unable to stem the tide. Our priority must be to find where the cracks are. We are not as safe in Scarhamm as we once thought."

"Do you think the dress comes from the same place as the silver trees?" Thea asked, following that thought to another. "What would happen if I put it on?" After all, it might be a way to find out more about all this.

"Thea," Veleda said, her tone sharpening. "Promise me you won't wear it. In fact, I want you to burn it. There's no way to know what could happen."

Somehow, that warning only made Thea more curious. "I promise I won't wear the dress," she said. *This particular dress.* She would promise no more until she knew what was going on. "And I'll burn it back in my room."

Veleda seemed satisfied by that and went back to worrying her lip. "I wish there were more Seers to help me."

"Autumn said she's apprenticed to you," Thea reminded her.

Veleda frowned. "Yes, but she's early in her training." Annoyance crept into her tone. "She's rather obstinate, too. Like most pixies."

Thea couldn't argue that. But obstinacy was necessary sometimes.

"She claims to keep Seeing an elm tree and a fountain," Veleda went on absently. "She's convinced it's some kind of warning. But I recognized those as symbols associated with your mother." She shook her head as if dismissing the vision. "I told her no warning could come from your mother, who is in a deep slumber in her tree."

Thea stiffened, knowing that last part wasn't true, but in agreement that her mother could have nothing to do with the current mystery. The queen had run off with some man years ago and no longer seemed to care about her family or the Sylvans at all.

"After what you've told me, I have even more work to do," Veleda said in a firm tone, "but if you see anything unusual, promise you won't keep it from me."

Thea stiffened at this implication that she might be secretive. She'd always had the sense that Veleda didn't trust her, though she didn't know why. "Of course I won't."

Veleda pointed to the corner. "Don't forget the dress."

Dutifully, Thea went to the corner and picked up the purple pile of cloth, annoyed that the Seer didn't even seem to want to examine it. Thea had promised to burn it, so she would.

But she didn't think that would be the end of this.

7

> Our world is the land of Nerthus, where folk and humans live, but other places exist behind a thin curtain that separate them. Solis has realms of eternal sunlight, and Noctua rules the nine realms of the Netherwhere.
> —*Old Ones, Ancients, and the Folk*

Patrol that night was quiet but for the continual hooting of an owl. Owls were thought to be Noctua's mortal representations, carriers of omens, warnings, and even good luck to those who treated them well. Or something like that. Thea had never paid much attention to superstition. Now she was starting to wonder if many of the things she'd thought of as fanciful stories had some connection with truth.

"That owl won't shut up," Burke said, his tone unusually bitter.

"What's wrong with you?" she asked, scanning the dark woods for signs of movement. "You never minded before."

"I don't know," he admitted, holding the lantern higher. "I keep thinking I see flashes of silver among the trees."

The path did seem darker tonight, the moonlight not finding its way past the canopy. There was no wind, which meant it didn't feel as cold, but the stillness was eerie.

"Don't let the swamp dweller's stories rattle you," Enora said, but her voice held a hesitation she couldn't hide. "I'm starting to wonder if the naiads were imagining things. We've seen nothing strange."

"I don't like the feel of the trees," Burke said, which might sound like nonsense to some, but to Sylvans, it was a comment worth noting. The trees could sense threats, and if you listened, you could pick up some of their tension.

Thea halted, taking a moment to attune to the forest. Something was amiss. Her voice was pitched low as she said, "No sign of anything strange, but I wonder if we should check back in with your naiad friends."

"We'll stop at the tavern again," Enora said

with a nod, "see if anyone has anything new to report."

They found the Grotto nearly uninhabited despite the mild weather. Thea's eyes went to the chair by the fireplace, relaxing slightly when she found it empty, though she wasn't sure why. The swamp dweller sat at his usual table. The only other occupant was the pixie Autumn. She was curled up asleep on a barstool, her red hair a bright little spot against the dark wood. Her quiet snores were barely audible. She looked rather sweet when she was asleep, Thea thought.

"What's keeping everyone away?" Enora wondered aloud, though of course no one answered. Wick was polishing tankards as if her life depended on it, her brows drawn together in worry. She didn't even seem to notice them.

Thea and Enora exchanged a confused look. Wick usually greeted every customer warmly as they came through the door.

"I'm going to find out if Fen has seen anything new," Enora said, leaving Thea by the door and moving to the table where the swamp dweller sat. Burke was already heading over to the same table.

Thea sighed. That left her with Wick and the

pixie. She headed over to Autumn, hoping to redeem herself after their last conversation. She sat quietly, not wanting to wake her. When Wick looked up and saw Thea, she put her hand to her chest. "I didn't even see you come in."

"You seem distracted," Thea observed softly. "What's going on?"

Wick chewed her bottom lip. "I don't know. It's been so quiet. I've sold next to nothing the past two nights. Fewer and fewer folk are going out."

Thea looked around. "Autumn is here."

"She comes every night," Wick said, a fond smile curving her lips. "She said she needs a drink after her lessons with Veleda." Wick winced. "Sorry, but that's what she said."

Thea waved that away. "I'm not close with the Court Seer. I recently went to see her, in fact, and she wasn't much help."

"Mark my words, Autumn will be a great Seer one day," Wick said. "She has a gift. One of the things that makes me a good tavern owner is that I can size people up."

"As it happens, I need someone to help me with a magic problem." Thea's eyes shifted to the empty chair by the fireplace, though she wasn't sure why.

"What's wrong?" Autumn asked, wiping drool from her mouth with her wrist. Her eyes were bloodshot, her words slurred.

"You've had too many thimbles," Wick chastised. "You need to drink water." She went over to a tin pitcher and poured water into an extra-large thimble, setting it on the bar. Thea picked it up carefully and offered it to the pixie.

Autumn sat up, swaying to one side so that Thea had to put a finger out to stop her descent off the edge of the seat. "I only drank what I needed to stop the visions."

"Visions of what?" Thea asked.

Autumn gestured, swaying dangerously once again. "Trees, trees, trees. So many. Unhappy trees."

Thea moved her hand to stop the pixie from tumbling the other way. "The forest does seem unhappy tonight."

"Not thissh forest," Autumn slurred. "Silver one. Coming through. Jingle, jingle. Sounds like chimes when the silver leaves blow in the wind."

Thea sucked in a breath. "You've seen the silver trees?"

Autumn nodded. "They're coming and going. Soon, they'll come to stay. And then our trees will be silver, too. The spirits warned me. But no one believes me. Not even Veleda."

Thea's anger surged. "Why doesn't she believe you?"

Autumn frowned darkly, her pouting pink lips like a miniature rosebud about to lose its petals. "She says I'm too index... inex... innersperienced."

"Inexperienced?" Thea suggested.

"What I said!" Autumn put her head down, closing her eyes. "But I know what I saw. And the only way to stop them is..." She closed her eyes, trailing off.

Wick leaned in, and Thea urged her on. "What?"

"It's not that she doesn't believe me," the pixie said, apparently forgetting what she was saying. "It's that she doesn't want to."

"I'm sure you're right," Thea agreed. "But what's the way to stop them?"

"Stop who?"

Thea sighed and offered the small tankard of water. "Drink this. You need it."

Autumn drank, choking on the last mouthful. "Water. Ew. Do you have any blueberry juice?"

"Right away," Wick said, moving off.

Suddenly Autumn's eyes seemed clearer, meeting Thea's urgently. "I only said that to get her to go," she whispered, leaning toward Thea. "I'm not supposed to tell anyone but you."

"What is it?" Thea asked. Wick was already pouring the juice, and it didn't take long to fill a thimble.

"You're the only one," Autumn said. "A silly Sylvan. But that's what the spirit said."

It took a moment for Thea's mind to make sense of that. "A spirit told you I can stop the silver trees?"

Autumn nodded. "I've been Seeing an elm tree and a fountain. Veleda says those are symbols of your mother."

The world shifted under Thea's feet. What did it mean? She'd dismissed the idea before, but was it possible her mother was trying to communicate with this pixie Seer?

"What else did you See?" Thea asked.

The pixie took a lock of her hair and twisted it between her fingers. "She spoke to me. She said, '*He knows the truth.*' But I don't know who she meant."

At that moment, Wick returned, handing the thimble of juice to her patron. "Try this, dear." Autumn thanked her, sipping delicately.

Thea's mind raced. There was only one person who knew what really happened to her mother.

8

It is easier to cut out a tongue
than a lie that has spread.
—The Sylvan king

Thea stood before her father in the war room, her hands behind her back, her posture straight, chin up. She had requested this audience, but now she wished she were here for any other reason. She would rather speak of attacks and stratagems, even poor chances on the battlefield. Anything but the thing she had come to ask him.

She let her eyes roam, calmed by the familiarity of the space. The war room was large with scuffed wooden plank floors and stone walls covered in weaponry, each stained and showing signs of wear. A long oaken table ran down the center of the room, its surface dented from decades, perhaps centuries, of use. The Sylvan king stood at the head of the table with the great maw of a fireplace at his back. It gave a rather impressive effect when paired with the fire that lit his eyes when he was angry.

Normally, Thea loved this room. She soaked up its energy when she and the senior Huntsmen pored over maps, planned attacks or counterattacks, or reviewed defenses. With its scents of battle, its old wood furnishings and broken weapons, its rugged surfaces, this room was symbolic of the history of the Sylvans themselves. It spoke of the grit of her people surviving against impossible odds, fleeing from humans and then finding themselves threatened by Azpians who outnumbered them by many times. Worn and weary, but still here.

The Sylvan king shifted, bringing her attention back to him. "What is it, Thea?" her father asked. He sounded more tired than usual, and there were lines under his eyes that Thea had never noticed before. She wondered why he looked weary now, when the war with the Dracu was over. Perhaps he didn't trust this truce, either.

She realized she was scared of his reaction, but instead of fighting it, she allowed it to sharpen her mind the way she did before a battle. Fear was there, but she didn't have to be ruled by it. "I have reason to believe our wards are being tampered with. Veleda has Seen signs of this but hasn't yet found the source."

He gestured sharply as she paused. "Go on."

Thea assumed from his lack of reaction that he was already aware of the problem. Still, she wasn't sure if the Court Seer would have shared this next part if she was uncertain of her visions. "Veleda has Seen symbols associated with my mother. I can't help but wonder if there's a reason."

A profound silence followed. For a second, Thea felt as if she were being crushed by it. Her breaths came shorter, her chest aching with dread. The harsh look in her father's eyes took her straight back to that awful night.

After her mother had disappeared with the handsome stranger, Thea had run home as fast as she could. Her father had been waiting at the gates, almost as if he'd expected her. His antlers were stretched wide and pale against the darkness. His eyes were red with anger in an otherwise expressionless face.

"Call the Hunt!" she'd gasped, out of breath. "Mother disappeared in the woods. A stranger took her—"

Her father looked down at her and said, "Hush!"

At his tone, Thea had gone abruptly silent.

"Your mother has gone into her tree to rest," he said in a harsh tone. "You saw nothing but that."

Thea stared at him, shocked that he was so adamant. "No! She didn't go into her tree—"

"She did." The Sylvan king's voice deepened to a bass note of warning. "She is ill. She is in her tree. She has gone there to rest until she is well again. Do you understand?"

Thea had stared up at him, uncomprehending.

"*Do you understand?*" he'd repeated, more threat than question.

When his meaning became clear, Thea's mouth had dropped open. The Sylvan king was asking her to lie? Most Sylvans couldn't. What Thea's father was asking was unthinkable.

"I can't *lie*," she'd said, her voice barely a breath.

His lip had curled with contempt, one of the few times she'd ever seen it directed at her. Her stomach had contracted with shame. "I said nothing about lying," he said in a harsh rasp. "Your mother is in her tree. You will say nothing to contradict that."

Thea nodded, chilled by his implacability. An order from him could not be disobeyed.

The next morning, King Silvanus had told the court that his queen had gone into her tree to rest. It was clear he would brook no questions. Still, Cassia had timidly asked when their mother was coming home. The king had stared at his daughter with a dreadful coldness. Tibald filled the gap with reassurances that the queen would come home once she was well.

From then on, Enora had taken over the role of caregiver to her younger sisters. Soon, it became clear their mother was not going to return any time soon. If ever. Rozie cried at night, her sobs tearing at Thea's heart.

But Thea couldn't cry. Everything had stayed locked up inside. Her grief was different from her sisters' because she knew what they didn't. Her mother was not in her tree. She had gone off with a man. Willingly. The knowledge made her feel separate and alone.

Over time, it was easier to feel anger than sadness. And why shouldn't she be angry? Her mother hadn't cared about the pain and destruction she'd wrought by abandoning them for...a Seer, perhaps? A mage? Thea would never forget the stink of magic in the air that night.

She'd hated magic ever since.

As Thea stood in the war room waiting for her father to reply, she found the heat of impatience growing inside her. But showing it would do no good. She swallowed her frustration and searched for the best way to ask him. "Please, Father. Can you finally tell me what happened to Mother?"

The Sylvan king's eyes lit with fire. Thea should have stopped there. She knew well when she was in danger of going too far. But this was too important. "I don't ask for myself," she said sincerely. "This is a threat that I don't understand. I'm trying to protect our people."

The flames in his eyes grew brighter. "You dare imply I don't have our people's best interests at heart?"

"No," Thea said, realizing her mistake. "I only meant—"

"My Huntsmen receive information when I deem it necessary. Are you still one of my loyal Huntsmen?"

"Of course, Father, but—"

"Push me further and you will find yourself removed from patrol. Do you understand, Theodora?"

Thea gasped. He had never spoken to her like this.

"Dismissed," he said, the flames in his eyes telling her he meant it.

Thea could not feel her fingers as she turned and walked to the war room door. As she opened it, she felt a chill on the back of her neck, and the shadows seemed to dance on the walls.

It almost looked as if they were laughing.

9

> The Sylvan elders tell us there were once many realms connected by doorways, and that folk passed freely between them.
>
> —Excharias, Sylvan poet

Thea returned to her bedchamber, her hands shaking with anger. The sun had set while she'd been in the war room, and only a faint purple twilight glowed through her window. But it was enough to see a new folded pile of clothing on her hearth. She snatched it up to throw it into the fire, but her arm froze, trembling. She couldn't let her temper rule her. Not when this dress could be the key to information no one else would give her.

She paced the floor, fuming. Her father had never treated her with such blatant disrespect. He could be harsh, even cruel at times, but she'd always made allowances, knowing the protection of the Sylvans was his priority.

Though she tried not to dwell on things she couldn't control, she found herself thinking more and more of the shameful secrets Cassia had uncovered. Not only had the Sylvan king killed the moss folk, he'd bound restless spirits to some of the forest's trees, making them bloodthirsty. In doing so, he might have murdered the original Sylvan spirits. Thea had been as horrified as her sisters by the revelation. But she told herself that, in the end, their father *had* realized what he was doing was wrong and had dismissed the Summoner he'd hired to do that awful work. He'd made those mistakes while trying to protect his people from the humans hunting them and the Dracu raiding their villages. Thea also had a strong protective side, and sometimes it led her to rash actions. How could anyone else know what it felt like to carry the fate of an entire people on your shoulders?

Thea hadn't expected him to welcome the subject of her mother, but neither had she anticipated his fury. She only wanted to help. To find a way to face the danger together. Instead, her father's reaction had shown her she had to handle this alone.

But who was the threat? Selkolla was dead. Without the Dracu fighting at their side, the Skrattis were easier to subdue.

Indecision and inaction were things she despised. She stopped pacing and forced herself to think, lining up everything she'd learned, the way she'd catalog an enemy's movements.

There were other worlds besides this one, and the veils between worlds could break down. In addition, the Sylvan king's powers had to be weakening. Silver trees were appearing and disappearing in the forest. Figments of things that weren't really there. A Seer—albeit a pixie apprentice—had visions of the silver trees taking over Thirstwood and claimed to have spoken with her mother.

Thea looked down at the fabric still clutched in her fist. There was one thing she hadn't yet tried. Maybe she was a fool for doing this, but she'd rather be a brave fool than a cowardly one. She couldn't let a threat to Thirstwood go unanswered.

Not wanting to act rashly, and needing time to calm herself after the clash with her father, Thea had a bath in her copper tub, scrubbing until her skin shone. When she was done, she combed out her hair until the brown waves crackled in the firelight. By the time she was done, she felt ready. She put her hair in a loose braid, tying the end with a scarf, then began to dress.

When she unfolded the pile of clothing, she saw that it wasn't a dress but three garments: a striped skirt, a white blouse, and a black corset vest. The stockings were so fine they were near transparent, the texture silky under her fingertips. A shiver went through her as the smooth fabric slid over her toes, then calves, then thighs. She attached the first stocking to a garter, then donned the second. Next, she strapped her own leather holsters to her thighs, each containing three daggers. Whatever happened, she would not be without weapons.

The blouse fit her comfortably, the fabric soft. The sleeves were puffy, creating a rounded effect, ending mid-forearm with laces. The heavy skirt was striped black and white, its length sufficient for her long legs, as if it had been measured for her by a careful seamstress. Finally, the black fitted corset went over the shirt. When laced up, it molded to her lean curves like a second skin. As she put the black satin slippers on, a warm feeling poured through her. The moment she secured the second slipper on her foot, she felt a change in the air. A breath of something that was not from Scarhamm, not of the forest at all.

Her foot took a step toward the door. Another. It was as if her feet had minds of their own and had decided where they were taking her.

The clothing is enchanted. Perhaps the slippers were the final piece that completed the spell.

On impulse, she grabbed her short sword and strapped the leather belt around her waist, fighting to slow her steps as she adjusted the scabbard. As she finished securing the buckle, her attention strayed from her steps and her feet sped up, taking her out her door, along the hallway, and down the stairs at a breakneck pace. With concentration, she slowed again as she passed through empty corridors leading to the fortress's entrance. When she arrived at the main gate, it swung open as she neared, and three Huntsmen passed inside—a patrol returning. They ignored her as she moved past. It was almost as if they couldn't see her. *More enchantment?* Not stopping to question it, Thea swept outside.

The forest opened up around her, the dark

paths familiar even by scant moonlight. Thea didn't know where to go, but her feet did. The enchanted slippers didn't hesitate even as the path forked, continuing forward as if they knew the way. Only the sounds of small animals and nesting birds accompanied her on the walk.

After a time, she came to a familiar glade. Suddenly, she recognized the walnut tree. This was where her mother had disappeared. Memories of shock and fear twisted her stomach as they flashed through her mind. The slippers brought Thea to a halt near a thick root. Before she could decide what to do, the root moved toward her.

Instinctively, she leaped back, startled. Even if it were a blood tree, which it did not appear to be, it should never harm a Sylvan. But as she tried to move farther away, the slippers nudged her toward the root. When she resisted, the soles of her feet grew so hot she feared a burn. She reached down to pull one slipper off, but the fabric slid from her fingers.

The root came toward her, weaving to follow her no matter how she tried to move away. Sweat broke out over her upper lip. She pulled her sword from her scabbard and did the unthinkable: She hacked at the tree root. Sylvans did not harm trees unless absolutely necessary. But this was not a normal situation, and she'd had enough of this magic, whatever it was. The root shivered and retracted, a sound like pain reaching her ears. A moment later, it stabbed out toward her, wrapping around her ankles like a thick, wooden rope. Thea grabbed the trunk of the tree, her fingernails digging into the bark.

A white dot appeared in the air a few inches away. It grew and grew until it became an oval of light surrounded by translucent tree roots, their tips moving like tentacles.

A doorway.

Thea swallowed, her mouth as dry as a late summer drought, her heart beating heavily in her chest. She had faced huge Skrattis and quicksilver Dracu in battle with less fear. But she'd made her decision, and there was no second-guessing it now. It was her responsibility to protect Sylvans from all threats, even ones drenched in sinister magic. She closed her eyes against the brightness and pulled her fingers from the bark, allowing herself to be drawn forward.

From one breath to the next, light turned to darkness. There was a disorienting moment when time lost meaning. The single breath she took could have lasted a second or a hundred years.

As Thea inhaled again, she found herself standing on flat ground. There was no scent of moss or pine, only something metallic that lingered in the air. She turned in a circle. Twinkling lights blipped in and out, more like lightning bugs or moon sprites than lanterns, judging by the way they wheeled and floated in the air. They appeared to be far away. She moved in that direction step by slow step, her hand on the hilt of her sword.

Pale shapes appeared some distance ahead. As she drew closer, she saw that it was a swath of delicate silver trees, probably the same figments both Kaiya and Fen had reported. A sudden memory struck her. She'd seen them once before, in the Grotto. How had she forgotten?

There was an eeriness to the silver wood that set her nerves on edge. No birds sang. No small animals rustled. There was no undergrowth. No green. Nothing but the trees with leaves as delicate as ice.

She walked slowly toward one, her hand coming to rest on its thin trunk, half expecting to pass right through it. It was solid and icy cold.

Metallic. With her middle finger and thumb, she flicked the trunk of the tree, shivering when a clang reverberated from it. She let her hand fall. There was a clear path of black stone winding between the trees. She followed it, a gentle crunching sound accompanying each step. At least the slippers had stopped forcing her feet forward. Perhaps their job was done now that she was here.

As she walked, she looked around in wonder at the silver wood. Speaking softly, she greeted the nearest trees.

"Fellow Sylvans, well met," she murmured in a friendly tone. "Will you wake from your slumber and speak to me?" It was the polite greeting in case any of the trees had Sylvan spirits in them, if those spirits were still sentient enough to answer.

When no answer came, she continued on.

She halted when her foot sank into water, so black it blended with the onyx stone underfoot. A lake or river? The lights she had seen earlier floated in the distance, their reflections rippling on the water's calm surface. She wondered what she was supposed to do next.

A pinpoint of light moved closer, and a shape

floated into view. Thea tensed, not trusting anything in this place. But it turned out to be a small boat, low in the water, a lantern on its prow, its black hull blending with the darkness. The boat appeared to be empty, and yet oars turned as if pulled by invisible hands, rotating soundlessly in their oarlocks.

The vessel halted next to her, sliding against the shore. Thea shuddered at this evidence of enchantment. She wasn't afraid of water or boats, but this was different. Once she set foot in this magical craft, she had no idea where it might take her. But as this was her only option to go forward, she reluctantly stepped inside. It rocked until she sat on a wooden seat, guiding her sword to lean against her leg.

"Hello?" she called. No reply. The boat slipped soundlessly across the water, the oars cutting the surface with a gentle plash. The bow turned toward the floating lights. Thea made out another shape as they drew closer, a tall structure as dark as the onyx path. When the boat bumped up against an unseen shore, she stood carefully and stepped out.

Fine gravel crunched underfoot. As she approached the lights, the structure shimmered into view—a castle of dark stone with windows aglow. The gravel path led her to a pair of arched double doors that stood open. With their shape, they looked almost like two beckoning hands.

Thea stood there for a moment, torn between curiosity and caution. You didn't saunter into an unknown place that could be full of enemies. Instead, she walked around the side and peered in a window.

It looked like a ballroom. It was decorated in black with touches of silver and white. Polished black floor tiles reflected silver candelabra and sconces with flames that did not look real. Some sort of mage light, perhaps.

Thea counted twelve couples dancing in orderly formations, their clothing varied and colorful. All manner of folk were included, from pixie to lutin to Sylvan, though no one that Thea recognized. Even a Skratti was dancing, her polished tusks reflecting the warm light. Thea blinked, never having seen a Skratti in formal clothing, having always encountered them in battle gear. Still, the sight made her hand move to her sword.

"Scouting your enemies?" said a low-pitched voice.

Thea turned with the speed of her training. From a few feet away, a shadowy stranger grinned at her, his pale face catching scant light from the castle windows. The same man she'd seen before—twice! But the planes of his face had more dimension now, even as shadows swirled around him.

"Are you the one responsible for bringing me here?" she asked as the memories came crashing back. As she examined the texture of his pale skin, his dark lashes, the glint of light in his pupils, she recalled meeting him in the Grotto and seeing him again in the great hall. She didn't understand how she could have forgotten him.

He lifted a dark brow. "Do you like the dress?"

10

> Little remains of the writings of ancient Seers, as most of their art was spoken, passed on from master to apprentice. But there are indications that some things act as conduits between realms quite naturally. For example, the roots of trees are essentially bridges that carry life, so they can be spelled to lead to other places.
>
> —Old Ones, Ancients, and the Folk

As mirth reached his eyes, Thea found herself in a sort of stupor. The shadow stranger was even more knee-weakeningly handsome than she'd thought. She wanted to step closer. To touch his cheek to make sure he was real.

He made a movement with his hand—drawing a weapon?—that woke her out of her daze. It was a split second, but she had no time to think, whipping out her blade.

Before she could do more than draw it, shadows swirled over her sword, yanking it to the side with such force that she nearly lost her grip. Gasping, she moved back a step, putting space between them. The shadows came at her, twisting like scarves tossed in the air. She sliced toward them only to find they were not solid at all. The blade went through as if they were nothing more than breath... then caught as if stuck in a rock. The contradiction of that blanked her mind as the impact jarred through her hand so painfully, her fingers convulsed. Her loosened grip was enough for the shadows to disarm her. The sword floated in the air. She was about to grab for it when it wobbled and fell toward the ground. She caught it nimbly by the hilt, slashing out again.

The shadows swept at her from different directions, too many to fight. She deployed her finest sword work to keep them off. It lasted until one wrapped around her wrist at the same moment another went for her neck, tightening like a noose. She gasped and choked, one hand reaching up to grab it.

"Enough," the stranger commanded. "Return to me."

The shadows loosened from Thea's neck slowly, almost as if they were sulking. But they moved back to him as ordered, swirling in an agitated orbit.

"I would apologize," he said, tilting his hand so the darkness wove between his fingers, "but you drew your weapon on me. I'm afraid my shadows don't like that."

Thea returned her sword to her scabbard, watching him carefully. Those things were not just shadows, but he'd made his point. She couldn't harm him. "I thought *you* were reaching for a weapon."

His eyes were warmly appreciative. "You *are* fast for a Sylvan."

His comment on her speed reminded her of the pixies' remarks. So what was he, then? "Which makes it sound as if you are not a Sylvan."

He merely tilted his head to the side, showing his rounded ear.

"Not human, either," she said. "Humans don't appear as figments, nor do they have shadows that are both spirit and solid."

He lifted an eyebrow as if enjoying her reasoning. "Definitely not human."

"Not a lutin, kobold, or drude," she said firmly. "You're so tall, I have to look up at you, which is rare for me."

"You are quite tall," he agreed, his tone neutral enough that it was neither compliment nor insult.

"Naiads have hair like seaweed," she went on. "Dracu have horns. Skrattis have tusks." She waved a hand at him, indicating his lack thereof.

He grinned. "Regrettably tuskless." At that lopsided flash of teeth, something fluttered in her stomach.

"I have it," she said, snapping her fingers. "A pixie."

He chuckled, and the sound traveled up and down Thea's arms like a light touch. "Perhaps I am not one of the land folk at all."

Her suspicions deepened. "Who are you, then?"

Hand to chest, he made a slight bow. "Damon, at your service."

"And what does Damon's service involve?"

His smile became wicked.

Thea felt her cheeks heat at her unintentional innuendo. "I didn't mean…"

He laughed softly again, as if enjoying her discomfiture, his smile so warm it made something ache in her chest, which triggered an alarm in her mind. She did not react that way to strangers, especially ones who were clear threats. Some magic had to be at work here.

He might have noticed a change in her demeanor because his own became more formal. "There are only a few more hours until morning when you need to be back home." He gestured toward the ballroom. "Will you dance?"

Thea stepped back, though she was reassured by his claim that she was to go home. "I didn't come here to dance."

"Didn't you?" His smile twitched. "The slippers. The dress. What did you think they were for?"

"I had no idea, though now I assume for your personal amusement." She noted the way his mouth twitched at that. "Where am I?"

"Ah, Sylvan," he said with a shake of his head. "That is not how things work here. I don't answer questions for nothing. You have much to learn about my realm."

"Since it's your realm, you can tell me." She lifted the hem of her skirt, watching as his eyes followed the movement. A wash of heat flooded her bloodstream, making her dizzy.

His effect on her was unnerving. Twitching one of the daggers from its sheath, she let the skirt fall. "Or should I try to get past those shadows again?" Longing to redeem herself from the last attempt, she threw her blade at his thigh.

The shadows caught it, twisted it, and handed him the dagger. As she'd thought.

Her lips twisted. "Worth a try."

"If you've had your fun," he said, offering her the hilt.

Thea sheathed the knife, frowning as he offered his hand. He was affecting her badly enough already. Instead, she retraced her steps to the front of the castle, striding ahead of him.

"We can dance without touching," she said firmly, stopping as she reached the doorway. "I don't trust this place or anyone in it." She eyed the Skratti with suspicion.

"Fine," Damon agreed, moving to stand beside her. "However, you can't dance with a sword." He pointed at a statue of a woman supporting a round disc over her head—clearly the Ancient Solis, holding the sun. "Put it there. It's no use to you anyway. We've established you can't hurt me."

Thea leaned her sword against the statue, turning to find that Damon had followed her. He wasn't standing close, but she still felt the power of his presence as if he were. "It's not only you I'm worried about."

"Ah." His brow furrowed. "I thought there was some sort of truce between the Sylvans and Azpians."

So, he was at least somewhat informed. "The Skrattis have been breaking it."

"You folk and your squabbles." He looked thoughtful for a moment. "Well, there's only one way to find out if this Skratti has a thirst for Sylvan blood." He gestured toward the dance.

Not much of an invitation, but Thea would not shy from a confrontation. She needed answers, and if he wanted blood on his dance floor, so be it.

11

> The most dangerous things are
> often the most beautiful.
> —Gaxix, Dracu philosopher

Damon kept his word. As Thea joined him in several country dances, he did not touch her. When he was within arm's reach, however, she could feel his shadows, fleeting caresses like the brush of cold butterfly wings. She tried not to let it bother her, focusing on her surroundings and what she could learn from observing this strange place.

The black and silver decor of the ballroom faded into the background, making the dancers stand out even more. Some wore fine clothing and jewels that sparkled under the flickering light from the sconces and chandeliers. Others wore plain clothing, ripped and specked with dirt, as if they'd stopped work in the fields to join the dance. Everyone moved in strange harmony, their eyes never meeting hers. Thea paid special attention to the Skratti, waiting to be noticed and perhaps threatened. But like all the others, she seemed focused on the dance.

As the steps in a promenade brought Thea close to a Sylvan, she smiled politely. He was unfamiliar, which meant he was probably from one of the outlying villages. "Well met, friend."

A glassy-eyed stare was his only reply.

Thea's skin went clammy. None of them were speaking to each other, and their eyes held a sort of dazed joy.

Finally, the music, which was coming from some unseen source, rang out with a few final notes and went silent. Damon smiled and bowed. The dancers bowed to him. Thea grabbed a handful of skirt and inclined her head. Damon motioned her toward a corner of the room.

From there, she cast an eye over the folk once more. They weren't speaking, nor had they clustered in groups the way everyone naturally did at a revel. They acted like puppets with their strings cut. "They're enchanted, aren't they?" she demanded in a low voice.

Damon smiled, but the mirth didn't reach his eyes. "I prefer to think of it as a pleasant descent into slumber. They dream while they dance."

Her gut told her this was a more dangerous place than she'd realized. "They're trapped here, and they don't seem know it." It was obvious he knew what was going on, being the only one who didn't share the others' stupefaction. "And you're responsible."

His eyes met hers more directly than they had before, though he didn't exactly look angry. His eye color, she noticed, was not as dark as she'd thought—more the indigo of evening than full night. The flames from the sconces reflected in his pupils like early stars.

"You are very blunt," he said, the only possible sign of annoyance in the precise way he enunciated. "To a fault, I would say."

She crossed her arms. "There's no fault in telling the truth, Shadow Stranger. You'd rather I pretend everything is fine here?"

"Shadow Stranger," he repeated. His smile was almost wistful. "Is that what you call me?"

She shrugged, disliking that he seemed to enjoy the nickname.

"No longer, I would think." He tilted his head down toward hers. "We've exchanged names like two civilized creatures. We enjoyed several dances together. Surely you can call me by my name."

His voice was like a soft brush in her mind, a gentle bid that she relax. She stiffened against the impulse to lean toward him. "If you say so, Shadow Stranger."

His eyes were sharp as they looked her over. She had the sense she'd confused him somehow. "There are some who would take offense at your brazen straightforwardness. I recall the pixies were not so enamored with your bluntness."

"Your speech is very formal," she said. "I'm guessing whatever your brand of folk happens to be, they are long-lived. Are you very old, then?"

His posture went rigid. "I am twenty." He paused. "Or thereabouts."

She lifted a brow. "*Thereabouts* means you're not twenty yet, I'd wager." She glanced around the ballroom, noting its pageantry was as dated as the oldest parts of Scarhamm. "And yet you speak like Tordon, one of the oldest Sylvans alive."

"No one has ever complained about my speech before," he said, rather stiffly. "And I'll be twenty in nine days." He paused, his eyes searching hers for something before he added, "And yes. We are long-lived."

She noted he still hadn't told her what kind

of folk he was. "I'm guessing you don't leave here often."

He regarded the ballroom coldly. "Not as much as I'd like."

"You've been to the Grotto," she mused aloud. "If you go there more often, you can hear how people speak..." *Wait.* She did not want him in the Grotto, the place where forest folk shared secrets. He didn't belong there. Him or his silver trees. She frowned, an unpleasant thought occurring. "Your magic is making me want to share things with you, isn't it?"

"You are very clever." His appreciative glance sent prickles of heat creeping up her neck. "Cleverness should be rewarded. I suppose it will do no harm if I admit that the more time you spend with me, the more you'll want to tell me things. And the more you tell me, the more you'll want to spend time with me." He watched her for a moment, smiling at her glare. "Your frown is quite severe. You did ask."

Thea put a hand to her stomach. Fighting his effect on her was taking a physical toll. She measured the distance to her sword. "I see now why you told me not to worry about the Skratti. I think you are more dangerous than any Azpian."

He laughed. "There is no doubt about that."

They regarded each other in silence, Thea using her best blank stare that gave nothing away. Damon's expression was openly curious. She couldn't help noticing the jut of his cheekbones. The way the cut of his jacket emphasized his shoulders. The night sky of his irises beckoned to her, promising something that made her dizzy. It felt like the time she had climbed the tallest hill near Scarhamm and looked up at the star-studded expanse with no trees in the way. The vastness had made her head spin. She pressed her hands together to focus her attention. "You said you'd tell me about your magic."

His smile returned, as warm as a blaze that has been fed fresh, dry logs. "I don't recall making such a promise."

"In the tavern," she clarified. "I asked, 'What foul magic is this?' and you said you'd tell me if I wear the dress. Have you used your own forgetting spell on yourself?" She motioned down at herself. "I'm wearing what you sent. Now it's your turn to keep your side of the bargain."

"Information isn't given away here," he said, his eyes a little cooler. "It must be earned. I'm not sure that putting on the dress was enough to answer a question so personal."

She gasped, unused to liars and oath-breakers. "When you make a deal with a Sylvan, you have to keep it. Not sure whether you worship the Ancients here, but breaking a Sylvan vow will incite Noctua's wrath. You'll pay a price, shadows or no."

"It wasn't a vow, but even if it were, what sort of dire consequences should I fear?" His skepticism was obvious.

Thea searched her mind for the stories. "Once," she said, "a man promised to marry a woman and reneged on his vow, marrying someone else instead. He died of a fever on his wedding night."

"Coincidence," Damon said, looking unimpressed.

Thea held up a finger. "A kobold once promised Noctua to give away all his possessions if she would heal his wife, who was ailing. She was healed but he kept a stash of gold tucked away, thinking the Ancient would never know. His wife died that night."

He shrugged. "Her fever returned. It happens."

The cold way he said it gave Thea a chill. She chose a recent story she knew was accurate, related directly by her sister Cassia. "The Seer, Selkolla, promised not to harm a Dracu she held captive, but she did. In moments, her own undead creatures consumed her."

"That one I like," he said, his head tilting. "Though I still can't tell you what you want to know, I did promise information for a dance." He reached out to take her hand, stopped—perhaps remembering his promise—and dropped his arm. Thea's hand tingled in anticipation of the touch that never came. "When you were a child," he said softly, "you climbed a tree in the forest. But it was not your tree to climb."

She waited for him to continue, but he merely stared at her with a look of anticipation. Could he be referring to the giant walnut whose roots had brought her here? What did that have to do with anything?

"That's it?" she asked, disappointed. "That's all you'll tell me?"

He dipped his chin, looking equally disappointed. "For tonight."

She exhaled sharply. "It might not have been

my tree, but it is a Sylvan tree. All the trees in Thirstwood belong to the Sylvan king."

Damon shook his head. "What I said is true. If you want more, you'll have to come back tomorrow night."

Her hands curled into fists. "But you said the more I see you, the more I'll want to return here. If I come back, I'll be in greater danger."

"I suppose you're right," he said, his smile warm again. "If you are afeared of the danger, perhaps you should burn the clothing once more." He took a few steps to retrieve her sword before handing it to her with a courtly flourish.

She took her sword, roughly pulling the leather around her waist, furious at his vague threats. "No one says *afeared* anymore," she told him snidely.

He made a motion in the air and spoke. "Return them home."

There was a rustling sound that grew louder and louder. Suddenly, a tree root snaked through the castle doors, coming to a halt amid the dancers. One by one the dancers stepped onto the root as if this was something they did all the time. The oval of light appeared, bordered by roots—the same portal that had brought Thea to this place of darkness.

He nodded toward the root. "If you don't try to hack it to pieces, it'll go much better this time."

So he'd seen her use her sword on the tree earlier that night? It hollowed her stomach out knowing he could see what was going on in the forest even when she hadn't known he was there.

With no other choice, she stepped on the root. It twitched to life with her feet attached, taking her to the portal. As she went through, she had the same sense of time shifting. When she came to a halt, she was back in Thirstwood in the very place the slippers had taken her hours before, next to the walnut tree. She didn't know where the other dancers had gone. Perhaps they'd been taken to their homes as well.

She looked up, surprised to see that it was close to morning. The sky was a shade lighter than Damon's eyes.

"Are you here somewhere, spying?" she asked aloud, turning in a circle. "Damon?"

Nothing. But a cool breeze brushed the back of her neck, reminding her of Damon's shadows.

As she made her was back to Scarhamm, her

mind reeling with even more questions now than when she'd put the dress on, she told herself to stop thinking about him, that she would never go back to his realm now that she'd satisfied her curiosity.

But as a Sylvan, she knew a lie when she heard it.

12

A wise Sylvan leader never loses control.
—Excharias, Sylvan poet

Thea longed to go straight to bed, but it was already time for training. With sluggish movements, she removed the skirt, shirt, bodice, and stockings and began dressing in her practice gear. The clothes still stank of magic, so she threw them into the fire, then the slippers, watching them fold in on themselves like flowers blooming in reverse.

A part of her ached a little as she watched them burn, as if she'd thrown away something important. But that made no sense, so she turned away and got dressed.

When she arrived at the training yard, most of the Huntsmen were already sparring in pairs, the familiar clash of practice swords like an uneven drumbeat. The air was damp, the sky heavy with the promise of rain. The cold brought her back to herself. Something about that shadowy realm had blurred the line between truth and fancy. She'd felt as if she could hold up a lantern and the whole place would have turned out to be made of parchment.

At least she could remember it. Perhaps Damon's spell to make her forget him only lasted until she visited his realm. She despised that he'd affected her memory, even temporarily.

Burke twirled his wooden sword as he approached, his long strides eating up the yards as if eager for her arrival. No doubt he was jubilant after knocking her down the last time they'd sparred. His grin was somewhere between teasing and insulting. With no sleep and a full day ahead of her, Thea chose to be insulted.

"Morning, Thea. Ready for another go?" His tone ignited a fire in her belly.

"Any time."

"Are you sure you're up to it?" His tone dripped concern. "I could give you another week or two to recover."

She had to force her jaw to unclench. "Dead certain."

At his nod, she attacked. Her pride still stung that he'd gotten the better of her, that moment of inattention so unlike her that it would be fixed in everyone's minds today. She needed to redeem herself.

She swung her sword in a predictable strike, hoping he'd let down his guard if she held back. Instead of falling for it, he met her move for move, his footwork as impeccable as always. On the surface, he was the better swordsman, his precision and economy of movement unmatched among the Huntsmen. But she had something he didn't—an inner fire that would not allow her to give up. And she meant to remind him of that.

Within seconds, it became apparent they were not merely sparring. They were both trying to prove something. *He wants to be First Huntsman*, she thought. *But I want it more.* This wasn't a contest for First, but it felt like it. Some of the Huntsmen ceased their own practice, and in a few minutes, half the Sylvan army was encircled around them. Thea saw the glimmer of excitement in Burke's eyes and suspected he was enjoying the audience.

Sweat covered her forehead and arms as she parried his every strike, trying to get inside his guard. She watched the sweat bead and slide down his face, satisfied that she was putting him through his paces, too.

As she told herself to be patient, she saw that something serious had entered his eyes, something behind the joyful glint of an eager performer. He wanted to win.

Part of her understood. She knew she would enjoy the renown of being the best Sylvan warrior, the most feared Huntsman of the Sylvan army. There had always been a murky lack of definition in her title, as if being the king's daughter was enough, and she shouldn't want to also be ranked among the Huntsmen.

The title of First was changed by the king every few years, claiming it was healthy for the younger Huntsmen to compete for a chance at leadership. The current First, Alof, had been in the role nine years, so it was soon time for a change. Enora was also a natural leader, but she wasn't ambitious. She fought because it must be done. She didn't crave fame or glory. She was content as long as everyone she loved was secure.

Thea wanted that, too. But she felt safest when she had control. She wanted the power to protect those she loved.

She *would* be First.

When Burke made a tiny mistake, Thea took the opening. For a second, she thought she had him. But he'd set her up. She was unable to block as he hit her wooden sword so hard it flew from her hand.

"Sure you won't take another day to rest?" he mocked.

Without thinking, she kicked him. Hard.

He snarled, "Desperate, Theodora?"

The kick had been cheap, and she knew it. But his taunt made her lose all sense. Her body took over. She drew her knife. She'd moved the blade an inch toward Burke's throat before she stopped herself, her hand shaking violently.

All around them Huntsmen gaped. Thea froze, horrified. She hadn't meant to do that. This wasn't like her at all. Had her brush with magic already affected her somehow?

Enora strode forward and took the knife from Thea's hand, which had gone numb. It was clear her sister was furious. There weren't many people Thea feared, but she cared what Enora thought of her, and that gave her sister the power to hurt her as few people had.

"Inside. Now," Enora commanded.

Thea followed without a word, her stomach sick with guilt. As they reached the edge of the crowd, Rozie stepped forward, but Tibald put a hand to her shoulder. "Let them go, Sproutling. There'll be time enough for you to find out what's going on." His eyes met Thea's. "For all of us to find out."

As soon as they reached the upper level of Scarhamm, Enora turned on her, her cheeks flushed. "What in the nine realms was that?" Her eyes were as stormy as the rain-laden sky.

Thea took a breath, stalling. "What do you mean?"

"What do I *mean*?" Enora looked like she wanted to wallop her. "You drew your knife on a fellow Huntsman!" Enora's eyes were wide with a blazing concern that made Thea's stomach churn with guilt. "Something is wrong!"

"Don't push me, Enna," Thea said, using the childhood nickname, feeling cornered and needing a breath. "I know I've been acting strange—"

"Strange!" Her sister threw her hands up. "Just now, you looked like a wild thing. The violence in your eyes when you went for Burke!"

Thea felt her breath becoming shallower, her sister's fury not helping her to calm down. "We always fight. We're both vying for First."

Enora's mouth fell open. "Well, in that case, what an excellent way to show Father you're ready to lead. Do you even hear yourself?"

Thea closed her eyes. "I went too far. He pushed me, though."

"He pushes everyone! He's a braggart and a show-off. You've never let him provoke you like that. What made you draw your knife?"

Thea bit her lip, trying to find some self-control. "I don't know. He used my full name."

Enora's eyes sharpened with understanding. "Theodora. Like Mother called you."

Feeling her jaw clench tight, Thea nodded.

"Mother will come home one day," Enora reassured her, some of the anger leaving her voice.

"I'm not so sure about that." Thea felt the truth crowding her tongue. "There is something I haven't told you," she said. Abruptly, her lips pressed together, and not by her own doing. It felt as if her tongue was glued to the roof of her mouth. As terror threatened to consume her, the tightness eased, and she took a shuddering breath.

"What?" Enora asked impatiently.

Thea was furious. She'd already told Veleda

about the dresses. Why couldn't she tell Enora? It had to be some enchantment keeping her from saying anything about Damon's magic. Finally, she managed to choke out, "Maybe you'd better talk to Veleda."

Enora looked more outraged. "Either tell me or don't, but don't tease me, Thea. You can be thoughtless, but I've never known you to be deliberately cruel."

"I don't mean to be—" Thea started.

Too late. Enora slammed the door so hard, the walls shook. A picture fell from its nail, the wooden frame cracking in two. Thea bent and picked it up, the space behind her eyes tight with regret. It was a small painting of her and her sisters that Rozie had done when she was seven. A cherished piece of art.

Her chest tightened with anger. First, she'd lost control, and now something was preventing her from talking about Damon.

She would go back to the shadow realm tonight and demand answers.

13

In times past, there was a great harmony between the folk. All was abundant, and everything was shared. When the Ancient Wars forced the folk to take sides, harmony became strife, and enmity was brewed like a rich, dark wine, aging into hatred.

—Excharias, Sylvan poet

If she was to be up all night, she needed sleep. Thea threw her clothes off and fell into bed, fading into slumber as soon as she was under her covers. The next thing she knew, her door was crashing open.

"Get dressed," Enora said as she rushed in, grabbing a shirt off the chair and tossing it onto the bed.

Thea rubbed her eyes. By the darkness outside

her window, she judged that she'd slept later than she'd intended. "What's going on?"

Enora's voice shook with anger. "Skrattis. Near the Grotto. They came out of nowhere. Our pixie scouts say this could be the worst attack yet."

Thea was on her feet in a second. "Why aren't the blood trees dealing with them?"

"We'd all like to know," Enora replied.

Thea grabbed the shirt and put it on. She rushed to her wardrobe for the rest of her clothes.

Cassia appeared in the doorway, her golden wings tucked to her back, her cheeks flushed as if she'd hurried to get ready. "I'll fly ahead. Scout things out."

As Thea turned, she glanced at her hearth. A dark pile of clothing sat there—deep plum with gold stitching. Tingles of shock went down her spine. She looked away, not wanting to draw her sisters' attention there. Another dress must have appeared while she'd slept. A chill breeze curled through her bedchamber, reminding her that danger was seeking her out in the safest of places. Scarhamm was the best-warded place in Thirstwood. She still didn't know why Damon was targeting her or why he wanted her to wear the dresses and attend his awful dance. But she couldn't assume he was acting alone. What if the Skratti attack was a ruse to get them to leave the fortress unguarded?

"Stay here to guard the walls," she told Cassia, knowing her younger sister would do what she asked. "If anything... strange approaches, use your ring and blast them with enough light to send them fleeing."

A tense silence followed.

"You think there's a threat to Scarhamm?" Enora demanded, stepping closer. "There aren't enough scuccas left to be a real problem. As for the reports of silver trees, they are just figments of things that have no substance. Do you know something we don't?"

Thea bit her lip. She wasn't sure what threats they could be facing, and even thinking about telling Enora about the shadow realm made her throat tighten.

"I don't like all these unknowns," she said, frustration coming out as anger.

"I hate the idea of not being with you, but you have a point," Cassia said, glancing at Enora for agreement. "We've underestimated threats before and nearly paid a steep price."

Enora let out a long breath. "True. You should stay."

Cassia lifted her hand to show the deceptively plain yellow gemstone. "If I see any scuccas, I'll use my ring. I'll head to the watchtower until you return."

With a final worried look, Cassia swept out. But Enora remained, clearly intent on getting answers.

Thea grabbed her boots and sat on the edge of her bed to put them on, refusing to meet her sister's eyes. "I'll be down in a minute."

"You can't avoid my questions forever," Enora muttered before stalking out.

Thea hated when Enora was angry with her, but she had no time to ruminate on it. She strapped on weapons as fast as she could and rushed downstairs. In a few minutes, she was heading out the gates along with a large group of Huntsmen. The night sky was clear, but a north wind stung her cheeks. The sound of many footsteps blending together was normally a comfort, but tonight, it somehow made her feel more alone. Her secrets weighed down on her, dragging her toward the roots that she now knew could carry her to places she'd never imagined.

The clash of swords was audible before she saw the Skrattis through the trees. Huntsmen patrols in the area had already engaged with the enemy. The moon wasn't full, but near enough to illuminate the sparsely forested area. Thea rushed into the clearing along with the others.

A Skratti stepped from behind a tree to greet her with a swing of his cudgel. She ducked and came at him with her sword. He turned to take the cut on his bare shoulder. These particular Azpians seemed to take pride in not wearing armor, their scaly hides protective. But she cut him deeply enough that blood shot out. He merely laughed, dipping his head to block her next jab with a tusk. He managed to push her toward the edge of the clearing. She saw Enora's pale head out of the corner of her eye, knowing her sister could hold her own but always feeling more comfortable when they were close. There were so many enemies.

Too many.

Backed against a tree, she dodged and felt the brush of a weapon against her hair. Senses heightened, she worked on avoiding the Skratti's swipes. Suddenly, he screamed, his arms wheeling as he leaped back. A bird swooped down from above, its beak aimed at the Skratti's neck. A crow?

More birds swept in, diving at the combatants. Shrieks and startled cries came from all over the clearing. The birds came fast, attacking and retreating.

With her attacker occupied, Thea moved in to deal a killing blow. But an arm snaked around her waist, pulling her toward the trees. She slammed her elbow into whoever had grabbed her, breaking free and spinning to face another enemy.

A familiar pair of dark eyes glared into hers. "Was that necessary?"

Damon!

Recovering from her moment of distraction, she shot a look at the clearing. The Skrattis were retreating, the crows chasing them as they fled. Relief tore through her to see Enora safe and very few injured Huntsmen on the field. She hoped none were dead. They'd been badly outnumbered this time.

But her blood still hummed with the need to fight. "I had that Skratti!" she said bitterly, turning back to Damon.

He stepped closer, his expression darkly

skeptical. He looked out of place in a light gray velvet jacket that was clearly meant for the ballroom. Thea was startled to realize he was actually here, not just a spirit haunting her as he had at the Grotto. "He had you cornered."

"I was waiting for a chance, which I would have found if you hadn't hauled me away."

He lifted his chin. "Your absence from the dance necessitated a trip. Imagine my shock watching you nearly bludgeoned by a goblin-made cudgel." His frown was severe. "Is that really how you want to die?"

His assumption that she couldn't defend herself was insulting. "What do you care, Shadow Stranger?"

He crossed his arms. "Still avoiding my name. I thought we'd made progress."

Thea gave him a skeptical look. "Progress toward what?"

"Civility?"

"Politeness is overrated." She looked up, noticing the shadowy shapes had gone. "Were those your birds?"

"No," he said, deadpan. "By coincidence, a murder of crows swept in and targeted your enemies at the precise moment you needed help."

"It must be nice to lie so blithely," she observed, not hiding her annoyance.

He adjusted his cuffs. "You're welcome."

"Thank you, I suppose. Though I don't trust your motives."

His eyes cooled. "I thought you wanted answers. One of my father's trees is near enough that we can travel by root. It won't take a moment." He offered his arm, the implication clear. If she wanted any more of his knowledge, she had to accompany him to the dance.

She took a step back. "I can't leave without telling someone. They'll worry."

"What would you tell them?" he asked dryly.

She opened her mouth and closed it. He had a point. She couldn't exactly tell them the truth. And she couldn't lie.

He lifted one hand and made a gesture toward the trees. There was a rustling sound, and a root appeared at their feet. *How can this stranger command anything in Thirstwood? Only the Sylvan king should be able to do that.*

Thea looked over to where Enora's hair reflected moonlight. Her head was turning side to side, as if she were searching, wondering where Thea had gone, maybe starting to worry.

A flash of light forced Thea to shield her eyes. She blinked to see a portal opening in front of her. Damon stepped toward it, holding out his hand.

"I will answer a question," he promised. "More than one."

Thea couldn't refuse this offer. She *needed* answers to protect her family and home.

With one last guilty look at Enora, she went.

14

> Over time, the folk staked out territories, created boundaries, and protected our ownership over lands. Some call this the "human way," claiming that we have been corrupted by our contact with these fragile, short-lived beings who grasp at whatever permanence they can find in the rocky tides of their days.
> —*Old Ones, Ancients, and the Folk*

THEA STUMBLED AS SHE STEPPED OUT, disoriented by her passage through the portal. Damon grasped her elbow to steady her. At his touch, a bolt of awareness sent warmth into her veins. A heady calm made her feel softer, lighter. Damon's expression was unreadable. The way his head was tilted down toward her and the look in his eyes made her think he was aware of her, too. Or watching for her reaction.

She blinked. These feelings were clearly his magic at work. "What about our no-touching rule?"

"I apologize." He dropped her arm and stepped back. "It was instinct to keep you from falling."

Her reaction to his touch was instinctive, too, but that didn't mean she wouldn't fight it. Taking a deep breath, she looked around. They were in an area with silver trees at the edge of a large expanse of water. The floating lights could be seen in the distance, so that was probably the isle with the castle on it.

"Is this a lake or a river?" she asked, more to break the tension than anything.

"A river," he said. "Our version of the Scar, I suppose."

"What is this place called?"

"It's called Iluna." Damon paused. "Some call it the Forgotten Realm."

"Why was it forgotten?"

He merely shrugged. "That story is too long to tell."

She sighed. Asking him questions was like begging for crumbs.

He set off along the shore. Thea's boots crunched over the fine black gravel, her eyes struggling to adjust to the darkness. In seconds, the empty boat from her first trip came gliding closer, a lantern on its stern casting light on the black water.

Damon made a polite gesture for her to embark. Thea climbed aboard, bracing her hands on the sides. Once she was seated, Damon stepped in, dropping to another seat behind her. The oars turned in a steady rhythm that propelled the boat across the water. Thea faced forward, so she could see the lights flickering over the outline of the castle. Its black stone seemed to absorb illumination, almost as if it didn't want to be seen. The windows, however, were uncannily bright. *Come inside*, they invited. Music floated on the windless air, tinny and muffled, as if it were being piped from far away.

Thea turned so they were facing each other in the boat, and Damon's shadows came closer to her face, as if they were examining her.

She pulled her head back. "You need to teach them manners."

Damon made a grasping gesture, and the shadows returned to him, hovering around his shoulders like a fur collar. "It's taken me years to have this much control over them. I doubt they will ever be—how should I put it—*civilized*."

She turned her head to the side, unnerved at the way he sounded so affectionate about the cold darkness that swirled around him. "That's no excuse to stop trying."

A low chuckle made heat rise to her cheeks. She was not immune to the rich sound of his laugh. Thea decided to take a chance that he'd answer one of her big questions. "I read that one of the Old Ones was banished long ago along with his shadows. Is this Erebus's realm?"

Damon hesitated. "Do you know that most humans won't speak his name?"

She didn't like the sense that he was stringing her along, offering answers but giving nothing of value. "Did you know you answered a question with a question?"

He blinked, but his lips curved up. "We have a rule here that questions can only be answered after a dance. You're asking so many."

She widened her eyes at him. "You said you would answer more than one."

"Most of the people who come here are not so curious," he said, turning his head to look at the castle. "At least... not after one or two nights."

Thea wondered if that's when the enchantment took hold of them. She reminded herself she could be vulnerable. It was her second night, too.

Soon, the boat scraped gravel on the opposite shore. Damon disembarked nimbly, offering his hand to her. She ignored it until he dropped his arm, and preceded him into the castle. She counted twelve couples stepping in time to the music, mostly the same folk from the previous night, but also a lutin she hadn't seen before, as well as another Skratti.

Thea almost felt sorry for the creature—strange after she'd been battling Skratti raiders not an hour before.

"Join me?" Damon asked.

They stood at the end of two columns of dancers. The songs were much as before, but wearing her leathern breastplate made the experience altogether different. Also, it chilled her to see the blankness in their eyes, the way they smiled at nothing. She was ready to be done with this.

"Did you even see the dress I sent you?" Damon asked.

"Not more than a glimpse," she replied coolly.

His expression filled with mock accusation.

"My finest yet. You should see the attention to detail."

She gave him a doubting look. "You say that as if you stitched it yourself."

"I did have a hand in it. I gave the tailor instructions and paced until she closed the final stitch."

Thea gave him a wry look. "I'm sure she loved you looming over her while she worked."

His dark eyes gleamed. "I so badly wanted to see you in the gown. But you look just as enticing in your leathers."

Thea told herself not to listen to his practiced flattery. But her skin heated at the compliment and the way he looked at her.

After several dances, Damon gestured toward the same corner where they had spoken the night before.

As soon as they reached the spot, she leaned against the wall, remembering one thing she definitely wanted to confront him about. "I was trying to tell my sister about the problems with our wards and suddenly, I couldn't speak. Was that your doing?"

"Not directly," he said, lifting his chin. "Anyone

who has been touched by shadows can't speak of this realm to outsiders."

Thea crossed her arms, staring at him. "I hate everything about this realm, your shadows, your rules. What you're doing to those people."

He turned his head to watch the dancers. Did he feel any regret at all? "Do you know how strange it is that you have been here for two nights and are not like them?" he asked.

A chill ran through her at the thought of becoming like the others. Would that happen to her if she kept coming back? "You didn't answer earlier about whether this is Erebus's realm."

His eyebrows lifted, and he shook his head. "He would be horrified to learn his infamy has faded in the lands above. For you to even need to ask."

That statement basically confirmed that it was. She decided to hit him with one of her most important questions. "Do you know what happened to my mother?"

The shadows that moved continuously about his face stopped. Damon's eyes bored into hers.

She refused to be put off. "Did my mother run off with him? With Erebus?"

He shook his head. "No."

Her hands curled into fists. "You said if I danced here, you'd answer more than one question."

He took a step closer. "There are some things I simply can't tell you, at least not directly." His eyes shifted in thought, as if he were weighing his words. "I'll say this much: A lost Sylvan can be freed, but only if another is offered in her place."

Thea's stomach plummeted, her pulse stuttering. "Are you talking about my mother? You're saying she's not free?"

One of the shadows moved to his ear, and he tilted his head as if listening, which was unnerving to see. "They're searching for you. Your sister with wings is flying over the forest. Your elder sister is ready to hie herself off with a search party into the Cryptlands. If you don't want that to happen"—he nodded toward a root snaking in through the opening portal—"hurry."

"Wait!" She still didn't have any more information than when she'd come here.

"Take her home!" he commanded.

And the damnable root did just that.

Thea found herself under the walnut tree. She'd assumed she'd be deposited at the same spot she'd come from, near the Grotto. Hopping to her feet, she kicked the root for good measure. It lay there like a root.

"Now that is a sight you don't see every day." The small voice came from somewhere to her left. "A Sylvan kicking a tree."

"Show yourself," Thea demanded, instantly on guard.

"Just me, Giantess." A tiny figure flew into view: Winter, the pixie.

"Were you spying on me?" Thea asked, relieved it was not a foe. Or not exactly. Winter's sharp tongue might sting, but it wouldn't kill her.

"I was here first," Winter said haughtily. He wove through the air, forcing Thea to look left and right to follow his quick movements. "But what if I were? Spying is what we do, remember?"

"Not on Sylvans." Tension crawled up her back at the darkness all around her, concealing who knew what. It had to be near dawn, but it was still too dark to see.

"Scarhamm is that way," Winter said, pointing. "In case you didn't know."

"I'm aware." Annoyed with the pixie's condescension, she set off, her long legs eating up the yards. She had to get home before Enora actually took a search party into the Cryptlands. Who knew how that would affect the peace pact with the Dracu, and someone could easily be killed.

"You're very noisy," Winter observed, flying alongside her.

"I'm not trying to be quiet," Thea replied. "I'm in a hurry."

"You also look angry," he said. "Care to share?"

Probably hoping for some gossip to take to the Grotto, Thea thought. "I can't tell you." *Literally.* "I wish I could."

Winter sighed. "Autumn says that all the time lately. *I can't tell you.* It's irritating, but I know she's been bothered by visions of the silver trees, and this is where most folk have seen them. I thought maybe if I came to the shadow king's tree, I'd see one myself."

Thea stopped and spun to face him. "Are you referring to that walnut tree?"

Winter floated up and down, almost like a nod. "Of course."

Thea gasped. "You know about…him?" The magic wouldn't let her say his name.

He looked perplexed. "Don't you?"

"Not until recently. None of my tutors ever mentioned him."

The pixie gave her a sour look. "Your father likes to keep control of what is known in his stronghold. But the rest of the forest folk have ways of passing on history that are not tied to parchment or vellum. We speak of these stories to protect one another. You see, there are places here that do not belong to the Sylvan king."

"Everything in Thirstwood belongs to him," she said, voicing a truth she'd been told her whole life and wondering why her mouth felt tight when she spoke it. "We all have our own tree that gives us strength and life force." Even if she didn't know where hers was.

Winter flapped a hand. "Yes, yes, we all know the pride you Sylvans take in your connection with the forest. But other folk live here, too, outside the safety of Scarhamm's walls. We have to know the truth of things to survive."

Thea tried not to chafe at the pixie's implication that Sylvans did not. "Then tell me this truth: Who does this tree belong to?" she asked. "What does he look like?"

Winter shook his head, as if she were being

obtuse. "They say the shadow king is more beautiful than the stars and as cruel as the void that holds them."

Thea's heart raced. Damon fit that description—the beautiful part, anyway. And he had to be cruel to invite those folk to his dance where they became enchanted. The question was, what did he do to them, ultimately?

"Your patrol is near," Winter said, his head cocked to one side. "I have to get home to check on Autumn." He flew off, his light hair visible for a minute before he was concealed by trees.

The baying of her father's hounds interrupted Thea's thoughts. They must have caught her scent. The howls changed to excited yips as they spied her, bursting through the underbrush to jump on her. Bracing her legs so she wouldn't be bowled over, she laughed as she patted their heads and scratched behind their ears. She loved the hounds, always had.

Enora appeared on the path, running full out. "Where in the nine realms of the Netherwhere have you been?" she asked breathlessly. "After the battle, we couldn't find you." She came to a halt, grabbing her sister in a tight embrace and letting her go to look her over. "I feared the worst."

"I'm sorry," Thea said, hating that she'd worried anyone.

"Were you injured?" Enora demanded, looking her over.

"Not unless you count some cuts and bruises."

Enora's eyes snapped to hers. "Where did you go?" When Thea said nothing, her voice hardened. "We were worried half into our graves. Cassia has been flying for hours. Curse it, where is she?" She looked up at the canopy. "Someone needs to flag her down."

Thea's guilt intensified. "She wouldn't have found me no matter where she searched."

Enora rounded on her. "Thea, what is going on?"

"I can't tell you." She winced, remembering Winter saying how annoying that line was. To escape Enora's clear anger, Thea started walking, mindful of the hounds as they wove a haphazard trajectory, crossing back and forth to sniff in the grasses at the edge of the path. Burke and Cedric appeared around a bend, jogging toward them. At the same time, a whooshing overhead told her of Cassia's arrival just before she gracefully landed in front of them, sweeping her wings to her back.

"Thea." Cassia rushed forward, her eyes wide with worry. "Are you hurt?"

"She's fine," Enora said sourly, still clearly furious.

Thea smiled at Cassia and embraced her. "Were you going to heal me if I was?"

Cassia bit her lip, holding up the hand that wore the yellow gemstone. "The ring works best with plants, but of course I'd do my best."

"The way you make things grow, I'd worry you'd make me taller," Thea said, managing a smile. "The Ancients know I don't need any more height."

"Glad we found you," Burke interrupted. "Strange things are happening to you lately. What's going on with you, Thea?"

She pressed her lips together, annoyed at his blunt question. But then she remembered how she'd drawn her knife on him, completely overreacting to his getting the better of her.

"Didn't mean to threaten you in the training yard," she said, her eyes falling for a second before she forced herself to look up at him. "I'm sorry."

"I accept your apology," he said, inclining his head graciously. A little dramatically, in her opinion.

But she was grateful. She didn't need to make enemies right now.

As Thea returned to Scarhamm with the search party, the Sylvan king stood in the open gates, Tibald and Tordon on either side of him. Tordon nodded politely in her direction, but Tibald wore an expression she couldn't read.

Thea halted, feeling as though she'd been caught out.

"You disappeared during a battle," the king said without preamble. "Were you injured?"

Thea swallowed, her mouth dust dry. She couldn't tell them a shadow stranger had taken her to dance in another realm. Even if she'd been able to, it would sound so ludicrous they might think she was lying, which would be more shocking than her disappearance.

"No." That was all she could say that was truthful.

Tibald's voice was confused. "If you weren't injured, what happened to you? Was it something to do with those birds that appeared? Still can't figure out where they came from." When she merely grimaced, he added, "We searched the whole area. For hours. You have no explanation?"

Thea shook her head.

The king took a step forward, his chin tilting down so that his antlers looked like curved swords about to fall. "Where did you go, Theodora?"

His harsh tone made her wince. But she had said as much as she could. Even at the thought of telling her father the truth, her mouth tightened. "I didn't run off," she managed, realizing a defensive answer only made her sound worse. "I..."

Thea met her father's eyes. "I have no excuse," she admitted, unable to think of any explanation that wouldn't make her throat close up, whether from a lie or from speaking of Damon.

She hated this. She couldn't even truthfully promise it wouldn't happen again. Everyone must think she had run off or hidden during a battle. A sick churn started deep in her stomach, bringing the taste of bile.

"Unacceptable," her father said, his deep voice rumbling with disapproval.

Thea tried to keep her face impassive. She didn't know how to make this right. "I wish I could explain it." She met her father's eyes again, waiting, hoping he would remember that she had always been ready to put herself at risk to defend her fellow Sylvans, and that she had never before shied from a fight.

But she could see the distrust in his eyes and knew she had lost something important.

Tordon stepped forward, his calm voice breaking the tension. "We were all worried, but it sounds as if you are not sure what happened, either. Perhaps some enemy magic was at fault here. There are strange things afoot. Scuccas still roam the forest, though they have no master. The Skrattis no longer wait for a full moon. We must stand together against this threat."

Thea nodded, grateful that he'd stuck his neck out for her.

Her father directed his next words at the rest of the assembled Huntsmen. "These attacks are escalating. It all points to a potential strike at Scarhamm. I need everyone on duty tonight." His eyes met Thea's, his voice lowering to a near whisper. "Consider this your last chance to redeem yourself."

Tibald's tone was pragmatic. "We will need everyone to be out in the forest tonight."

Cassia stepped forward, her wings catching sunlight. "I can scout by air."

"Cass," Enora said, pausing a moment before adding, "you should invite Zeru to patrol with us."

"What?" Thea blurted, turning to her sister in shock. "Why?"

"Isn't it obvious?" Enora said, her expression making it clear she was still angry at Thea. "He has wings! And the Dracu have a talent for stealth."

"I don't think we need him," Thea replied, her back stiffening. Though Zeru had given her no reason to dislike him, she didn't trust him. Everyone else seemed willing to overlook how he'd abducted Cassia to steal her ring, and when he couldn't take it from her, he had found a way into her heart.

"You can take your hand off your sword, Thea," Cassia said, her expression annoyed.

Thea relaxed a fraction. "We have many talented Huntsmen who can move with great stealth," she said.

"Burke will be with you," the king added, as if Thea was worried about being protected rather than the whole patrol being betrayed by an Azpian. She couldn't believe their father agreed this was a good idea. Her eyes went to Burke, who gave her a shiny grin.

Tibald frowned. "Get some sleep. We meet here after the evening meal. And for Noctua's sake, wear your darkest gear and quietest footwear. Burke, I can hear the squeak of your new leather boots a mile away. You're going to alert the Skrattis the moment you step outside the gates."

"Not that bad," Burke muttered, but he dipped his head and stalked off, presumably to spend a few hours softening the leather.

Enora turned to Thea, her expression unreadable. "I'll see you tonight. Don't run off this time, hmm?" Before Thea could reply, she had turned and was striding toward the fortress. A mixture of regret and anger stabbed Thea in the chest, her sister's disdain unfair but understandable since Thea could explain nothing about her disappearance during the fight.

Cassia stayed behind, waiting until Thea finally sighed and looked at her. "You know you can tell us anything, don't you, Thea?"

Thea tried to smile. "Thank you, Cass."

But her stomach twisted at the knowledge that she couldn't. And that even Cassia would likely be angry when Thea abandoned her patrol again tonight to go to Damon's dance.

15

Someone with a knowledge of Summoning may be able to open a closed door between realms. In some cases, an item or pair of items has been spelled to open doorways, acting as lock and key. If used correctly, these items can transport a living creature through a spirit path that leads from one realm to another.

Of course, these are lost arts, and perhaps that is best.

—A SEER'S GUIDE

CLOUDS COVERED THE MOON AS THE patrols spread out from Scarhamm's gates. Thea and her group, which included Enora, Cassia, and Burke, headed north along the banks of the Scar River. Burke and Enora carried lanterns, the glow illuminating the expanse of water to their right and nearby trees to the left, while Thea carried a satchel with some dried fruit in case they needed food over the long night. A path along the riverbank allowed them to move quickly and quietly.

They'd walked for a few minutes when Cassia shot a grin back at the rest of them. "Zeru is up ahead."

"How do you—?" Thea hadn't heard, seen, or scented anything. Then she remembered that her sister's ring was connected to an amulet Zeru wore around his neck, the mystical bond made stronger by the emotional bond they shared.

Thea shivered at the idea. She wouldn't like someone knowing where she was at all times. She enjoyed her freedom too much.

The lantern light picked up movement as Zeru emerged from the trees, his bat-like wings tucked to his back. Average height with a lean, wiry build, his sharp features had always seemed rather shifty to Thea. But when he smiled at Cassia, something blossomed in his face, something that made him... intriguing. He embraced Cassia without a single regard for three sets of watching eyes, though Cassia used her own wings to screen them from view. Their kiss was longer than it needed to be, in Thea's opinion. But then her mind went to the way she'd felt around Damon, reliving the sweep of heat she felt when she looked at him or when he touched her.

"If you're done slobbering on her," Burke said, his voice twanging with impatience, "can we finally be on the move?"

After several more tauntingly long seconds, Zeru pulled away from Cassia, his green eyes glowing with mirth as he looked toward Burke. "We haven't seen each other in a few days. Some catching up was in order."

"Catch up on your cloud," Burke all but snarled.

Enora ignored this byplay, regarding the Dracu with an assessing look. "Can you move as quietly as you claim?"

Zeru nodded once, then disappeared. There had been a blur of wings but no sound, only a slight breeze and shift of leaves. He was almost invisible but for the glowing green eyes.

"You're going to watch my sister's back?" Thea asked, staring hard at him.

"Always," Zeru said. It sounded like a vow.

Cassia grinned, her happiness so clear it made

Thea's chest ache. She had to admit, it was possible the Dracu was good for her sister.

"You two scout by air and meet us north of the gorge—the dry riverbed that branches off the Scar," Enora said. "If we don't see anything by then, we should head east. Azpians have been known to come up in that area."

Though Zeru lifted a brow at Enora's reference to his people, he and Cassia made use of their wings, lifting to the treetops and out of sight. For the first hour's walk, Thea's senses were on full alert. But she was aware she was distracted, her mind in two places. She couldn't help but wonder what kind of dress was sitting in front of her fireplace.

After a while, the river curved east and they kept to a former tributary that had been dammed up and left to dry. Enora and Burke were moving faster while Thea let herself fall behind, hoping her ears would pick up any signs of scuccas or Skrattis.

A scream sounded ahead. *Enora!* Thea dropped her satchel and sprinted in the direction of her sister. Her first thought was that Enora had lost her footing and fallen into the riverbed. The cliff was a good twenty feet high in that spot.

What she didn't expect was to see her sister floating in midair, being held in the talons of some massive creature. Its dark silhouette stood at least twelve feet tall. The thing had arms and legs and a head, but no facial features. At first glance, it reminded her of a scucca. Sticks formed a sort of skeleton, but instead of moss and vines holding it together, this creature's body writhed with snakelike shadowy forms. *They look like Damon's shadows*, Thea realized, but so many more, all moving as one being, connected and coordinated into this monstrous thing.

Drawing her sword, Thea sliced at the creature's legs. As the steel made contact, it sank in and stuck, as it had when she'd tried to hurt Damon. She heaved back but could not pull it free. With wrenching force, the blade was yanked from her hands. Cold air brushed against her skin, raising hairs on the back of her neck.

Enora twisted madly, but her arms were held, her blades out of reach. Her legs were no longer visible. It looked like the creature was devouring her.

Thea searched for Burke. He was on the opposite side of the gorge, scrambling down to get back to them. He must have crossed to scout the other side and not seen the creature until it had Enora. Cassia and Zeru were nowhere in sight. Thea thrust her arm at the shadow creature, her hand feeling wet leaves and twigs. She gripped whatever she could and pulled, trying to yank the thing apart. A stick broke free and she stumbled back with it in her hand. The creature gave a wordless roar, swiping an appendage at her. Thea dodged, trying to draw it toward the trees. It took a lumbering step in her direction.

"There's water at the bottom of the gorge!" Enora cried. "Maybe—" Her speech was cut off as she grunted in pain, her arm disappearing up to her shoulder.

Thea understood. If the thing was made of sticks and rocks, maybe it would come apart in water despite its shadows. As the creature leaned toward her, she kicked the rock under its foot. The problem was, if the thing went down, it would take Enora with it.

"Grab on to me," Thea shouted, wishing for wings. Enora was at least three feet out of reach.

Burke's long-legged stride slowed as he caught sight of the thing. "What—"

"Help us!" Thea ordered, dislodging another rock from under the creature's shadowy feet.

Burke flung the lantern aside, rushing to help. As much as it looked insubstantial, the scucca or monster or whatever it was seemed to be standing on the ground. As the rocks shifted, its body started to sway.

"Don't stop!" Enora cried.

But she was at least twelve feet off the ground, and the gorge would add another twenty feet to her fall. As the stick legs lost their footing, Enora struggled to free herself, but vines and twigs still held her. Her eyes widened as the creature careened toward the edge.

"Enna!" Thea shrieked, her stomach dropping to her boots. All she could do was watch as the creature went over the cliff, taking her older sister with it.

16

> Azpians know there are lower realms that house creatures wild and elemental. We avoid those beings as much as possible, but there may be others unknown to us. What creatures lurk in forgotten realms? Perhaps they are best left alone.
>
> —Gaxix, Dracu philosopher

The rhythmic beat of wings came a moment before Zeru appeared, diving like a hunting hawk. Arms outstretched, he yanked Enora out of the shadowy creature's grip a moment before it descended into the gorge below.

Thea's eyes were half-blinded by dirt, her fingers bloody from pulling at rocks, but she shouted with relief when she saw that Zeru held her sister securely. As he carried Enora from harm's way, Thea peered down into the gorge.

Burke's dropped lantern illuminated the riverbed, which held a few feet of stagnant water. All that was left of the thing was a jumble of sticks gleaming under the water's surface.

Hauling herself up, Thea breathed a sigh as she spotted Enora's silver hair where it should be—attached to her head, which was attached to her body, which was firmly on solid ground.

"Are you all right?" she asked, her stomach still churning.

Enora brushed off leaves and ran her hands over her head twice before tucking loose strands of hair behind her ears. "Dizzy as if I drank five too many glasses of fruit wine." Her laugh was shaky, her lopsided grin bright with the heady relief that comes from a near escape.

"Was that a scucca?" Burke asked, staring down at the remnants of the creature.

"A cursèd large one, if so," Enora replied, plucking twigs from her sleeves.

"Not like any I've seen," Zeru agreed, tucking his wings to his back. "The others were held together with moss and vines. This one contained something dark that moved."

Thea's chest ached with the need to share information about the shadow realm, to warn her sisters and the rest of the Huntsmen. But even thinking about it made her mouth close up. Would she fare any better trying to write down the truth? Her fingers twinged with a cramp at the notion.

"Even if it was a scucca," Enora said, "who would have made it? Selkolla is dead. At least... that's what Cassia thought. Is there any possibility she was wrong?"

"No," Zeru said firmly, but his green, glowing eyes showed a hint of panic. "Where is Cassia?"

"Wasn't she with you?" Thea demanded.

"She insisted we split up to cover more ground." He spat what sounded like an Old Azpian word, then spread his wings, their claws shining in the lantern light, and lifted like an arrow shot into the sky. A moment later, he was out of view.

Burke ran his fingers through his hair and brushed at bits of plant matter lodged there. "He seems more concerned with finding Cassia than with making sure the threat is neutralized."

"First of all," Enora said, stepping to Burke and tilting her chin to look up at him, "finding my sister *is* the priority right now. Also, that Dracu just saved my life. And he's part of our patrol, so get over whatever your problem is with him. You may be Second, but I was put in charge of this mission. Right?"

Burke looked annoyed but chastised. "Understood."

Thea admired Enora's ability to be both calm and firm. She really could be First if she wanted.

A few seconds later, two pairs of wings caught the lantern light, one of them golden and moving quickly toward the ground.

Cassia met the ground hard, scudding to a stop on loose stones, her hands hitting the dirt to break her fall. She pushed up, rushing to her sisters. "Are you hurt?"

"I could ask you the same," Enora said, smiling to reassure her sister.

Zeru alighted gracefully a second later, shaking his head as he went to stand next to Cassia. "You have to slow down as you land," he muttered, but Cassia didn't seem to hear him. She grabbed Enora's hands, looking her over.

"Couple bruises but I'm fine," Enora assured her.

Burke chimed in dryly, "I'm fine, too, in case you were worried."

"She wasn't," Zeru said without sparing a look at the Huntsman.

As Enora told Cassia and Zeru the details

of what had happened, Thea looked around, a prickle of awareness on the back of her neck alerting her that they weren't alone. Taking her time, she scanned the surrounding trees. A hint of movement caught her eye. She drew her knife in readiness, but her instincts weren't saying "*threat.*" More that someone was trying to get her attention.

And she had a feeling who it might be.

Seeing that Cassia and Zeru were taking all of Enora's and Burke's attention, she moved toward the trees.

As she reached the edge of the tree line, a silky voice spoke from the darkness, making her shiver with recognition. "I thought I made it clear you were to come to the dance every night."

Thea drew up short, her eyes searching but not finding him.

"Where are you?"

Damon stepped into view. As always, his handsome face stole Thea's breath. If she could have dreamed someone like him, she would have. The urge to touch him did not seem to be fading, no matter how she fought it. He must have traveled by root once again to bring her to the dance. *Or is he here for another reason?* Last time, he'd made his shadows into birds to scare off the Skrattis. Could he have created the shadowy scucca monster?

"Was that thing yours?" she demanded in a harsh whisper.

Damon took a step closer, his brows knitting. "What thing?"

She gestured in the direction of the riverbed. "A huge creature made of sticks held together by shadows. It grabbed my sister and nearly tumbled her over the gorge." Thea's skin chilled remembering how she'd been helpless to save Enora.

"I don't know what you're talking about," Damon said, his expression confused.

She watched him closely for a moment, trying to decide if she believed him. "Do you know about the scuccas that Selkolla created?"

Damon nodded. "Moss creatures animated with trapped spirits. I heard the Seer who created them was killed."

"Some of them linger in the forest. But this thing was much larger. And it was held together with shadows. Like yours." She nodded to where a shadow curled around his neck.

His eyes shifted as if he was considering. "I truly don't know anything about this new creature. But the dance is almost over. Come." He held out his hand to her.

She had a sudden, overpowering urge to put her hand in his, but a thought held her back. "If I disappear after what happened, my sisters will be beside themselves with worry."

The intensity in his stare called to something in her. "Thea. I need you there."

Steeling herself against the plea in his eyes, she said, "Not this time, Shadow Stranger. I'm not leaving my sisters alone when there are threats in these woods that I don't understand." She turned on her heel and walked way.

"Thea," he said in a low voice. "I can't give you answers if you don't join the dance."

She whirled around. "You rarely give straight answers anyway."

He shook his head, his face tight with anger. Then a doorway appeared, and he was gone.

17

Pixies are sometimes mistaken as delicate because of their small stature and gossamer wings. But in that tiny body dwells a giant's spirit. The most fragile and changeable thing in the world is not a pixie's wings, but a pixie's temper.

—Excharias, Sylvan poet

It was a long night, but no other threats appeared in the forest. Thea was relieved her father was not waiting as the patrol returned to Scarhamm. The leaders would report to Tordon at dawn, and Thea headed directly to her bedchamber, exhausted.

After a few hours' sleep, she put on her best brown trousers, green shirt, and a brown leathern vest that she wore on patrol, and left the fortress. She walked briskly, avoiding eye contact with the guards as she exited the gates. She didn't care to answer any questions, though at least this time she wasn't sneaking into a mysterious shadow realm.

The forest was alive with its midday bustle. Birds called to their mates while squirrels chattered in the treetops. The peaty scents of greenery held a hint of decay. Thea's boots trampled yellow and red leaves into mud on the path.

It was a long walk to her destination, which gave her plenty of time to think. There were too many things that didn't make sense, and no one in Scarhamm could help her put it all together.

First of all, Veleda's wards around Scarhamm were weakening. But that didn't explain why the Skrattis were able to come above the ground on any night, even when the moon wasn't full, and why Thirstwood's blood trees were not attacking them. Could Thea's father's powers be waning? It was the Sylvan king's connection with the trees that gave the Sylvans true protection.

She had to admit, her father hadn't been the same since his battle with Selkolla. When the Seer's lightning had struck him, he'd gone down and stayed there for too long. Thea remembered her blank-minded terror when she thought he was dead. She'd been so relieved when he'd recovered, but had he, completely? Even questioning his strength would be seen by her father as a betrayal. Still, the king had shown less attendance at training, and he'd barely gone to any revels. He didn't even go into the forest much anymore. *It would be so like him not to admit what he considered weakness.* Thea's steps grew heavy with anger, and she had to unclench her jaw.

Second, shadow creatures and silver trees like the ones in the Forgotten Realm were appearing in Thirstwood. Veleda had attributed this to the veils between realms breaking down. If nothing was done, would this world become part of that one? Or disappear altogether? Would the forest folk survive? And if they did, what kind of Sylvan lived in a forest of metal trees?

She shivered at the thought, lifting her face to reassure herself that the sun still shone. If that gloomy, hidden kingdom subsumed her world, it would be worse, even, than living in the Cryptlands. A realm with no sun? She half wished she'd visited sunny Welkincaster when Cassia had offered. She'd seen too many shadows lately.

Which brought her to her third point. She knew Damon was stringing her along the way he parceled out information in such small quantities. But she had to keep asking questions. *A lost Sylvan can be freed, but only if another is offered in her place.* Was the "lost Sylvan" her mother? And what could she do about those other poor folk trapped at Damon's dance?

The need for action made her want to unsheathe her sword and slash something. She needed to talk this out, but even if her cursèd throat didn't close up at the mere thought of mentioning the shadow realm, her father wasn't going to tell her anything, and Veleda's tongue was tied by her father's rules. Tordon and Tibald might know something, but they were loyal to her father, too. She could speak to her sisters, but she was certain they didn't know any more about this than she did.

To Thea's reckoning, that left a pixie Seer with a sharp tongue who would at least tell her the truth if she asked.

She reached the pixie settlement in late afternoon, only realizing she'd crossed a boundary when something whizzed past her ear. *An arrow?*

She put her hands up to show she meant no harm. No doubt there were about fifty more pixie bows trained on her. "It's me, Theodora, daughter of Silvanus. There's no need to shoot."

"Our pine needle arrows show the truth of things," a small voice said. "We had to make sure you weren't one of the shadows."

"Shadows?" Thea asked, her body tensing.

"They've thickened in the forest," one of the pixies replied. "Sometimes we see shapes like animals, but if you go near, they lose form and fade away."

Thea shuddered, remembering the beast that had grabbed Enora. Damon had also made his shadows into birds. Was he making them into other animals?

"Our arrows make them lose their form," another added. "It's hard to tell in twilight, so we couldn't be sure you were real." The pixie's tone became wary. "But what brings you to a pixie village, anyway, Sylvan?"

"I'm sorry to come here without an invitation," she said. "I seek audience with your wise young Seer, Autumn. I need her...esteemed guidance." Thea didn't know if that was flowery enough to soothe the pixies' pride, but it was the best she could do.

"Autumn is ill," said a voice from Thea's left. She made sure to turn slowly, keeping her hands up. "She's not taking visitors."

"Can I do anything to help?" Thea asked, not liking the idea of Autumn being sick, even if her words did bite sometimes.

Another voice piped up. "Come into the shrine. You may speak with our elder."

Thea's heart leaped with excitement. She'd never been invited into the pixies' shrine. She'd heard about it, of course. It was a special meeting place for the elders to dispense their prophecies, as well as a place of worship. The pixie religion was mysterious. They didn't share much with outsiders, so this would be a rare opportunity.

Suddenly, a familiar pixie with long white hair flew out from the trees. "Giantess, what are *you* doing here?"

"Winter?" Thea's lips parted in shock. "You're the elder?"

"Of course not." Winter's small eyes rolled upward. "Good blooming lilacs, these Sylvans are thick. Come this way, Giantess, and I will make sure you don't get lost. I know how confused you get in your own forest."

Pressing her lips together to stifle a scathing

reply, Thea followed Winter, who flew ahead, his wings beating almost as fast as a hummingbird's. He led her along paths that were so narrow, Thea had to turn her body sideways, branches scraping her stomach and back.

"Almost there," Winter assured her, dropping his voice to add, "if you can fit."

The path led to a round building that seemed to be carved from a hill, its open door barely large enough for Thea to crawl through. The interior was a circular space perhaps ten feet in diameter. Enormous by pixie standards. The plaster walls had been painted with a swirling design of interconnecting flowers, all their vines and stems leading to a sunflower motif on the ceiling. A round window in the center of the ceiling allowed the late afternoon light in.

"You may sit," Winter said, running a hand through his shiny hair before gesturing down. "Just don't squish anyone with your giant ar—"

"Oh, what now?" another high voice shouted. "Who are you and what brings you to my shrine?"

Her attention drawn to the voice, Thea saw a pixie woman with white hair done up in elaborate braids sitting on a toadstool in the center of the shrine. Her dress was bright yellow, and her mouth was puckered with irritation.

"My great-grandmother, Sunflower," Winter said in a whisper. "She's not as friendly as I am. Watch what you say."

Not as friendly…?

Thea, who was still on hands and knees, straightened as far as she could and bowed respectfully from the waist.

"You're a big one, even for a Sylvan," Sunflower said, looking up at her. "Trying to grow as tall as your father, I see. It hurts my neck to look up at you. I thought my great-grandson told you to sit. Don't you know how to take a kindly invitation? Sit, girl. Sit!"

With great care, Thea folded her—apparently huge—frame into a sitting position, crossing her legs so she took up as little space as possible.

"Well," the elder said. "That's marginally better. What's your name?"

"Theodora, but most call me Thea."

"I call her Giantess," Winter interjected.

"They're all giants to us," Sunflower said. "Not very innovative. Go back to your tutor and tell him to instruct you on how to have an imagination. The Ancients know you were born without one."

Winter grumbled something that sounded like "old witch." Thea coughed to cover his words.

"What's got you hauling yourself over to these parts?" Sunflower asked. "Not like you Huntsmen to take an interest in us."

"Of course we're interested," Thea assured her. "Our patrols regularly speak to your scouts. We protect all the forest folk."

"Do you? If that's so, why have your patrols ignored Autumn's warnings? She told you about the silver trees, didn't she? What have you done to stop them coming into our woods?"

"That's why I'm here," Thea said. "I have bits of information, but I can't put it all together on my own. I need her help."

Sunflower sighed. "My great-granddaughter has lately been incapacitated by her visions, but she has lucid moments. I suppose we could try. Calla!" she shouted. A nervous-looking pixie appeared in the doorway. "Bring Autumn. Tell her we've got a big one here."

A big one. Thea pressed her lips together,

recovering her patience with an effort. "Thank you for allowing me inside."

"Sacred place, this," Sunflower said, tapping the toadstool. "We worship our own deity. Not your Ancients. We thank the One who made the flowers and the mushrooms and the dew. You don't even know our deity's name, probably."

"No, I don't," Thea admitted, chagrined.

"Well, I'm not going to teach you," Sunflower snapped, as if Thea had insisted and needed to be put in her place. "You said you have some information. What is it?"

Thea paused, worried she might get thrown out if she said one wrong thing. "I...was going to wait until Autumn gets here."

"I'm here," Autumn said, her voice weak.

Thea turned her head toward the doorway, her heart contracting when she saw that Autumn was walking instead of flying. Autumn's hair was as bright auburn as ever, but her eyes were sunken, her skin pale. She came into the room and stopped at the toadstool, leaning on it for support. Surprisingly, Sunflower patted her shoulder in an affectionate way.

"I'm sorry you're not feeling well," Thea said. "Thank you for coming to see me."

"The visions won't stop," Autumn said, putting a hand to her temple. "I See the silver trees in Thirstwood, more each time. I think it's a warning of what's to come." Her eyes met Thea's, a bitter twist to her lips. "I suppose you don't believe me."

Thea leaned forward. "Of course I do!"

"Your other Huntsman didn't," she said, her eyes falling to stare at the floor. "I told that yellow-haired one last time he was at the Grotto." She furrowed her brow. "Durk."

"I call him Shirk," Winter said, "because he never listens to us."

"Burke?" Thea asked, annoyed to think how likely it sounded that Burke had dismissed Autumn's warnings. He didn't like magic. Well, neither did she, but she wasn't about to ignore a good source of information. "What did you tell him?"

"That I saw more trees, and this time...they were real. I could touch them."

Thea sucked in a breath. "Can you take me to them?"

Autumn frowned. "I wish I could. They'd disappeared by the time we returned to the same spot. That's why he didn't believe me. But it's a sign that what I saw in my vision is coming to pass."

"Do you know anything about it?" Sunflower asked, her brows forming a groove of worry as she gave Thea a harsh stare.

Thea opened her mouth, wondering what would come out. "I'm not sure how much I can say." Her shoulder muscles tensed with growing frustration. She had come here for answers, but she didn't even know if she could ask questions. Could she utter the words? She tried, swallowing against the thickness in her throat—it was restricting her breath. She tried to ask about the shadow king, but all that came out was a thin croak. Trying not to panic, she closed her eyes against the confusion in the elder pixie's stare. As the enchantment started to ease, she managed four words through gritted teeth: "A. Spell. Prevents me."

Sunflower's brow cleared as if she understood. "We can help with that," she said, snapping her fingers. "Winter? Some truth?"

Without hesitation, Winter flitted out, returning with a bow. He drew the string back, and Thea saw that a pine needle arrow was ready to fly at her.

"Wait, what will that—" The arrow hit her in the neck like a bee sting. Thea glared at Winter.

"A truth arrow," Sunflower explained. "Speak openly while you can."

Thea's eyes widened. Could she finally tell someone what had happened to her? "I think... Erebus, the king of shadows..." Relief coursed through her as the words poured out more freely. "...is behind the silver trees. And likely also the shadow creatures appearing in the forest." Her lips parted in shock that she was able to get the whole sentence out.

Sunflower's eyes darkened. "I know of him, of course. While other primordial beings had dominion over lightning, fire, wind, and weather, Erebus was the lord of dark places. His power was greatest in caves, deep crevasses, and the deeps of the ocean, all the spaces sunlight never touched."

Thea leaned forward. Finally, she was speaking to someone who knew the history of the Old Ones. "What can you tell me about him?"

Sunflower squinted. "Erebus fell in love with Solis, your Ancient sun goddess. She was much younger than him, but Solis fell in love with him, too."

"She fell victim to his charm magic, more likely," Autumn said.

Sunflower nodded in agreement. "The stories

say that although he had power over shadows, he fed off people filled with light. He had the ability to woo people into loving him. He might have taken Solis's life if not for the intervention of the other Old Ones. Charvelus, the primordial lord of stone and mountains, was protective of the young Ancients, and he forbade the union. Erebus threatened that if he couldn't have Solis, he would take her powers and plunge the world into darkness."

"What happened?" Thea asked, breathless at what Erebus had intended for the world.

"From what I remember," Sunflower said slowly, "Solis managed to run off with Erebus, but she started to lose her light when she was with him. Her peers, the other Ancients, along with Charvelus, came to her aid, punishing Erebus by removing most of his powers and depriving him of his followers. They placed him in darkness to rule over no more than shadows."

"So he was imprisoned?" Thea asked, already knowing that must be what the Forgotten Realm was—a prison whose walls were breaking down. "Alone?"

Winter interjected, sounding proud to be able

to add details. "Not alone! His followers were so loyal, their spirits came to him in death, even after Noctua created the Netherwhere as a haven for all ephemeral beings."

"Oh, so you do listen to your lessons sometimes," Sunflower said with feigned amazement.

Thea recalled Damon's shadows. Were those actually Erebus's loyal spirits?

Thea swallowed, realizing she had better say as much as she could while she was able. "I've been to a dark realm with shadows that seem to have minds of their own."

Sunflower's lips formed a perfect circle. At the same time, Autumn gasped, a hand going to her chest.

"What was it like?" Winter asked, sounding more curious than horrified.

"There's no sky, just a lot of silver trees," she said. "And a dark river that leads to a castle."

"Silver trees?" Autumn asked. "Like the ones appearing here?"

Thea nodded. "But they're not figments. They're cold to the touch, like metal."

"Did you meet anyone there?" Sunflower demanded, her eyes bright with urgency.

Thea hesitated, not sure how to sum up Damon. "About a dozen folk under some enchantment and a young man who controls the shadows."

"Erebus!" Sunflower said, her voice hoarse. "Though he is older than the Ancients, it is said he does not age. And you managed to escape? How?"

Thea opened her mouth to explain it wasn't Erebus but Damon... but did she know for sure? "He gave me a different name, but I suppose it could be him. As for escaping, I didn't. He let me leave."

"What does he look like?" Winter asked.

"He's very handsome." Her throat tightened. She put a hand to her neck, massaging. "I think I need another arrow."

Autumn looked to Sunflower, who sighed, her mouth turning down at the corners. "I'm afraid if we use too many at once, it could harm you. Come back in a few days and we can try again. In the meantime, we have a better understanding of the danger. It's worse than I thought. Much worse."

"Can we work together?" Thea asked, still laboring to speak, even though she was no longer trying to reveal anything about the shadow realm. The silencing spell had come back with a vengeance.

"Of course," Autumn said, rubbing her eyes. "We're grateful for the information you bring us. I'll tell you anything I See."

Sunflower nodded. "Your mother was the one Sylvan I felt I could speak freely to. Even your Court Seer tends to doubt our information. And your father has his own way of doing things." She gave Thea an assessing look, not hostile but not warm, either. "Trust is built over time, and you have taken the first steps."

Thea bowed in agreement. "Thank you. I'll do my best to help."

18

Take heed before stepping through a doorway to another realm. There is a danger when entering the land of spirits that one may become lost.

—Excharias, Sylvan poet

When Thea returned to her bedchamber, it was late evening, and another dress was waiting on her hearth.

A traitorous thrill went through her, as did her usual aversion to magic, as she moved to inspect it. She told herself this was merely another opportunity to find out more and to bring information back to the pixies.

The orange-and-black fabric was thicker than the previous gowns. She picked it up by the shoulders and saw that it wasn't a dress at all, but three pieces: a shirt, jacket, and trousers. The jacket had a long train, and wings had been sewn onto the back. They looked like butterfly wings, and the way they were sewn, it appeared they could move as she walked. The trousers were black and had pockets. Instead of the usual slippers, there was a pair of sturdy leather shoes with modest heels.

The choice of trousers, which would allow her ease of movement and a full stride, seemed almost...considerate. Was Damon that observant? Was this part of the charm he exerted over people, making them feel special and seen? Perhaps the same charm that Erebus had used on Solis—Thea should not underestimate it. Given what she'd learned from Sunflower, she needed to keep her guard up at all times. But she smoothed her hand over the cloth wings, helpless against appreciation for their beauty.

Should she accept this invitation? It happened to be her night off from patrol, so at least she wouldn't have to rush back. And she did need more information, especially now that she'd agreed to help the pixies.

Decision made, she threw off her patrol clothes and donned the outfit Damon had sent.

When she glanced at the looking glass, her eyes went wide. The clothes transformed her into a new creature, neither butterfly nor Sylvan, but a blend of both. She took a breath, noticing how the bodice tightened over her breasts. The neckline was... low. Heat ran through her veins at the idea of Damon seeing her in this.

She put on the shoes. Once again, she was taken through the forest to the walnut tree. The breath caught in her chest at a flash of silver in the darkness. It was there and gone in the blink of an eye, too quick to be sure she'd seen it.

Standing on the root brought her through the portal, and she emerged into the Forgotten Realm in the area of trees near the shore. As soon as her feet touched the finer gravel near the water, the boat arrived to take her across the river.

When she reached the castle, the couples were visible through the open doors, stepping slowly through their dances. Their eyes looked glassier than usual. By contrast, the lights in the ballroom looked brighter.

Damon was waiting in the doorway, his shadows like moving smudges against the backdrop of the ballroom lights. He was dressed all in black, a shirt with loose sleeves and a fitted vest. His hair was brushed off his forehead, his dark eyebrows as velvety as his vest.

He bowed from the waist as she approached,

his eyes never leaving hers. She watched a pulse jump in his throat, appreciating his reaction to her. As a flush swept into her cheeks, she came to a stop close enough that she could reach out and touch that dark hair if she wanted.

"I hardly know what to say," he said at last, his voice rough. He swallowed before continuing. "I congratulated myself on my design. I thought it would suit you. Now, I..." His nostrils flared as his eyes dipped to her shoulders, waist, and down to her feet. "I see I miscalculated."

Her shoulders were proudly straight as his eyes came back to hers. "It doesn't suit me?"

"It adores you," he said softly. "It shows you for what you should be. A queen."

She looked away, thrown off by a reminder of her mother. "I'll never be a queen. I don't want to be."

"A leader, then," he amended. His eyes conveyed something honeyed and thick. Her pulse responded. She could understand why others craved his attention. It was heady, and she enjoyed the thrill of risk.

He stayed still and silent, the moment stretching. Shadows wove around his neck and shoulders, like a moving collar to complement his black vest. His eyes moved up and met hers. "Do you like the clothes?"

She couldn't lie. "Yes. The outfit is surprisingly comfortable." *And I feel beautiful in it, especially with the way you're looking at me.*

"I—" He looked back at the ballroom for a moment, his shadows moving as slowly as the dancers. He seemed bothered, his face drawn into harsh lines. "Let's not go in there. Not tonight."

She looked at him in surprise. "You told me I have to come to the dance every night."

He swallowed. "Yes, that is the rule. But… you *are* here. I'm just changing the entertainment. We don't have to dance." He turned back to look at her, his eyes bright. "Why don't we go in the boat along the river? See where it takes us?"

She gave him a searching look. "Don't you know where it leads? Sometimes you talk as if you don't know this land well at all. This is your home."

"This has never been my home." His eyes shifted, and he sniffed the air. "Let's go somewhere else. This once."

Hearing the urgency in his tone, she put her hand in his without thinking. A spark of excitement skimmed through her at the texture of his skin, and she saw something happen in his eyes as their hands met. His lips parted, then softly closed. He looked as if he'd been struck speechless.

"The boat?" she asked, hearing the hoarseness in her own voice.

He nodded, his eyes never leaving hers.

She dropped her hand and turned away, her pulse pounding in her temples. She would have to be careful how much physical contact she allowed. *Allowed?* Inwardly, she laughed at herself. *She* had initiated contact. What about this invitation? Should she trust it? She had no idea where he meant to take her. And yet... somehow she did trust him, at least in this moment. In a way, she had no choice.

She embarked first, sitting on the bench seat while Damon stepped in and sat facing her. As the oars began turning, Damon spoke, his head turned to the side. "Take us anywhere. Stay on the water."

Thea wondered who he was talking to. Was there a spirit steering the boat? Shadows? She could ask, but he might count that as one of her allotted questions.

"What are you thinking, Sylvan?" he asked, the tone warm and inviting. "Something interesting is happening behind those entrancing brown eyes."

Thea couldn't help a pulse of pleasure at his compliment. No one had ever called her eyes *entrancing* before. "The dancers look worse off than last time."

After a pause, Damon appeared to decide something. "I have defenses around the castle so no one can spy on me. But most importantly, the dance feeds the magic. If even one dancer does not show up, my defenses are weakened."

Thea knew that revelry could feed magic. Sylvans believed that laughter and dance helped create the life force that kept the forest thriving. "So that's why you said I need to come here every night."

He inclined his head. "Your presence makes the castle stronger."

Does that mean I'm becoming weaker? Are you stealing my life force?

Instinctively, she felt he wouldn't answer such a direct question, even as more crowded her tongue.

What do you know about my mother? Do you even know anything, or is this all a lie? A game?

A way to worm the shadows of your realm into my world?

Are you Erebus?

Surely he wouldn't tell her, even if he was.

Damon leaned toward Thea, his hair falling over his eyes. Her fingers itched to sweep the strands back, to rake her fingers through his thick, luxurious dark hair. What would it be like to dishevel him properly? She bit the inside of her lip, the pain a reminder to stay alert.

He raised a brow. "You have a particularly bloodthirsty look about you. What's bothering you?"

"Your magic," she said flatly. "Stop using it on me."

Both brows rose. "What exactly do you think I'm doing?"

"Your... charm." She made a motion with her hand, indicating him. "The thing you use to lure folk into your realm. You don't have to cudgel me over the head with it."

He blinked twice, then a slow smile curved his lips. "Well."

She blew a piece of stray hair off her forehead, her eyes narrowing at the satisfaction in his eyes. "Well, what?"

His grin was so wide, it was almost insulting. "You think I'm using my charm on you."

She felt her jaw stiffen. "I want you to stop."

He laughed, low and rich, the sound bringing a frisson of awareness to the bare skin of her neck. She resisted the urge to rub her hands over her arms, glaring at him instead.

"Thea," he said, his lips twitching. "I'm not using my magic."

His denial only made her temper fray. "Don't lie."

His chin came up, his eyes losing some of that satisfied gleam. He looked around as if searching for some way to persuade her. "I used it in Thirstwood when I was trying to get you to wear the dresses. But not here." The smile in his eyes made him even more attractive. "However, you are charmed." He said it as if tasting, relishing the words.

She made a dismissive gesture, hating that she was probably blushing. "No one could fail to notice you're incredibly handsome. I'm sure it's part of the...lure. The trap." She turned her head to the side, trying to get control of herself. She'd intended to insult him, and he was clearly flattered.

"Come, Sylvan, you can look at me again," he

coaxed, laughter in his voice. "If it doesn't make you swoon."

"I do not," she spat, her hand going to a sword that wasn't there, "swoon." She turned back to glare at him. He was only inches away. If she leaned forward, she could take his cheek in her palm and... she shook her head to clear it. "Since I don't know what's true and what's not, I'd be foolish to find anything you say flattering. By that same logic, you shouldn't look so smug about what I said." She tried for an arch look, not sure she was pulling it off. "How do you know I was sincere?"

His lips twitched. "Ah, but Sylvans don't lie."

He had her there. He had her all muddled. The silent boat moved past more silver trees, reminding Thea of her mission tonight. Answers. She would start with something he might actually share. Perhaps he'd be inspired to boast if she phrased this skillfully. "You've been getting past our wards. No one has ever managed it. Scarhamm is the best protected place in Thirstwood, and somehow you've sent me dresses. Directly to my bedchamber, no less."

"Mm, yes, fire can create a convenient weak spot in the wards." He motioned to the dark shapes curling about his neck and wrists, like some sort of strange accessory. "And my shadows are very good at finding and exploiting weakness."

A flaw in the wards in her own bedchamber. She had to tell Veleda. "A rare direct answer, though not much of one. I suppose you won't tell me more."

He seemed to find her frustration amusing. "I shouldn't have told you that much. I shouldn't be tempted to answer these questions."

"But you *are* tempted," she pointed out, testing his resolve with a mischievous smile.

His smile softened, but the look in his eyes became more intense. "I reprimanded you for *your* directness when we first met, but I find I like it. No one in my life has ever been so forthright."

"You haven't known many Sylvans, then." As soon as she said it, she realized it couldn't be true. There was a Sylvan at his dance. It was too easy to let her guard down around him. "There are reports of silver trees in Thirstwood, and the only place I've seen them is here in your world. It seems to me that your realm is bleeding over into mine, and not just through my hearth. What does it mean?"

He seemed to sense her shift in mood, his face becoming more serious. "Your wards are, indeed, weakening. I believe your father's magic must be waning. My realm should not cross into yours, except in a few specific places where vestiges of old magic make the veil thin."

"Specific places," Thea repeated, her pulse picking up speed at the thought that he might finally tell her something important. "Like the walnut tree with the root that brings me here?"

He inclined his head. "That tree is one of the few that still belong to my father."

"Your father?" Thea asked, expecting him not to answer, to realize he'd said too much and shut down the conversation. But he surprised her.

"My father is Erebus," Damon said, a stillness about him as he waited for her reaction. "The king of shadows."

19

> Ancient magic still flows in the blood of those who walked the earth in ancient times, though some may never discover their own power.
> —Old Ones, Ancients, and the Folk

Damon was the shadow king's son.

The revelation was like a burning arrow dropped in Thea's lap. The oars continued to turn, the boat sliding through the smooth water in silence, but her thoughts were more like river rapids. She remembered suddenly that the pixie elder had assumed Damon was Erebus himself, but this made more sense. He had his father's powers over shadows. He had the ability to pull people to him, which Erebus used to lure people to this realm.

"Does that mean you're not the one behind all this?" She couldn't stop herself from hoping.

"Behind what?" Damon asked.

"The things from this realm coming into Thirstwood." She willed him to be honest with her. "Shadows and silver trees in my forest."

Damon's eyes never left hers. "Some shadows are mine, but only when I'm with them. The other ones belong to my father. He sends them above to spy, to test the boundaries, and to see how freely they can move about. And no, I'm not trying to take over Thirstwood. My father is the one who—" Damon looked around and shook his head, as if regretting how much he'd said.

Relief hit her, hearing that he wasn't trying to harm her world. "You're not attempting to take over, but he is."

Just then, the boat bumped up against something, jolting Thea off the seat. Damon's arms came around her, holding her for support. The contact sizzled through her. Even through the thick fabric of her bodice and his vest, she was excruciatingly aware of the sensation of her breasts pressing against his hard chest. It was enough to make her dizzy with longing. *Fight it*, she told herself.

"I'm all right," she said once she found her voice, noticing the tremble in her own limbs.

He took a second before letting her go. She

shifted back onto the seat and looked around, noting the castle was on her left. Had the boat merely taken them in a circle? "We're back here again."

"I guess I can't escape it," Damon said, his tone more bitter than she'd ever heard it. He stared at the castle, a flash of hatred contorting his face.

Thinking he needed a moment alone, Thea stepped from the boat. She heard Damon exhale and follow her, his feet crunching over the gravel. She went up the steps and entered through the open doors, blinking at the brightness. The couples were moving back and forth, lifting arms, turning, performing the same steps as before. But their faces were sheened with sweat, their eyes tired. They'd grown weaker.

Wait. There were only twenty-two dancers.

"What happened to the Sylvan?" she asked, turning to Damon, her stomach knotting.

Damon's face closed off, a mask of indifference settling over it. "His ninth night was last night. That's how long I can keep people here. After that, I owe them to my father."

She stared at him in shock. "Does that include me? Nine nights and then...?"

He swallowed and met her eyes. "Yes. After nine nights, every dancer must be presented to my father so he can give them a choice: stay or leave. I don't believe it's a true choice. My father would never allow anyone to go free. But they always stay. He makes most of them into silver trees. Occasionally, he will choose some to become shadows. My guess is that he picks the worst souls for that."

She stared at him, paralyzed by shock. Moments ago, she'd been relieved he wasn't behind the silver trees coming into Thirstwood. What a fool she'd been. Her pulse shot blood through her veins in readiness to fight. "What night is this for me?"

His lips tightened. "Your fourth."

Thea wanted to scream, but the formfitting jacket left her little room to breathe. "You've doomed me." When he said nothing, she had to curl her hands into fists to keep from striking him. "Why? Why do this to any of us?"

He turned his head to the side, a pulse beating in his cheek. "The dance gives power to Erebus, but some of it remains here. The castle, the boat. My little slice of the shadows. Without this, these shadows wouldn't stay with me."

"So you invite people here to power your

castle and keep your shadows loyal." Her heartbeat throbbed in her temples, her hands shaking. "And without them to shield you, I could kill you."

He turned back to stare at her, his eyes searching hers. "Which you no doubt long to do."

She wanted to take one of her blades and put it in his gut.

"They're more than shields," he said, tension in his voice revealing that he wasn't as calm as he appeared. "Protection, yes, but also power. Currency."

"Currency for what?" she asked. "I haven't seen anyone in this realm except dancers and your shadows."

"You haven't met my father." The word *father* held something ominous and dark.

"You're saying you have to be powerful or else he'll...what?" Her tone held a sneer, but she didn't care. She knew it felt horrible to disappoint one's father and king, but she wasn't feeling generous in the moment. "Do what you want and take the punishment later."

His eyebrows went up. "Is that what you do? Have you defied King Silvanus's express orders?"

"I would if the order was wrong." A few

months prior, her father had banished her sister Cassia from Scarhamm. Thankfully, the banishment hadn't stuck. But at the time, Thea had been ready to disobey her father if necessary. She would never hurt Cassia.

"What's the worst thing that ever happened to you when you displeased your father?" Damon asked. "The very worst thing?"

Thea paused, thinking. "I was thirteen. My father instructed me to be friendly to the son of an important Sylvan family visiting Scarhamm. Unfortunately, the son turned out to be a pig who took my friendliness as permission to stick his tongue down my throat." She could still feel the shock and rage of that experience all these years later. The feeling of being violated.

Damon's nostrils flared, fury blazing in his eyes. "Did you destroy him?"

Thea sometimes wished she had. "I pushed him into the river. Unfortunately for the pig, he couldn't swim. I fished him out, but my father didn't appreciate my generosity. After a blistering lecture, he ordered me beaten with a leather belt by one of the Huntsmen. My backside was sore for days." Her lips twisted in bitter satisfaction at the memory. "Worth it, though. I hope it made the pig think twice before doing that to anyone else. And he never came visiting again."

Damon didn't return her smile. "You didn't deserve that punishment."

"No. But my father wouldn't hear the reason. Later, he did and he...I think he regretted it." *Not that he ever apologized.* Thea watched the shadows moving over Damon's face, wondering if everyone had shadows. His were just visible. "What about you? What was the worst?"

He swallowed. "The worst isn't something I talk about. But I'll tell you the second worst. When I was seven, my father found me cowering." His lips pressed together, his expression blanking.

"Cowering in fear?" she asked, wanting to know this for some reason. "From what?"

He didn't meet her eyes, a bitter smile curving his lips. "His shadows tried to kill me, something they regularly attempted. My father thought it would make me strong to face their attacks alone. He always told me, 'They sense weakness, and that's when they devour. You can't show fear.'"

Thea noticed the stiffness in Damon's shoulders, as if he were trying to protect himself from the memory. "I still hadn't learned the lesson he was trying to teach me. I cried out for my father's help." He stopped speaking, and she saw that his breathing had quickened.

Thea couldn't stop herself from putting a hand on his arm, shivering when his shadows passed over her skin. "What did your father do?"

Damon raised a brow at her hand but smiled, the expression not reaching his eyes. "He put me into the cave, a prison for the shadows who are too wild to master, who swear no allegiance to anyone, even my father."

She swallowed the fury that welled up in her throat. "And he trapped you there? With them?"

Damon nodded. "For three days. When I came out, I was...different. I decided never to show weakness again. I faltered once out of pity...but was quickly reminded why that was a mistake."

"How did you falter?"

"I tried to help one of the folk my father was dooming to become a silver tree. I learned the lesson too late that no one can stand against him. I fared no better the second time I was imprisoned in the cave."

Thea let out an angry breath. "You were brave to stand up to him." She couldn't believe she had to explain that, but it was clear Damon needed to hear it. "And I don't believe your father's strength is as absolute as you think." There had to be a way to fight back.

His lips curved up, but he shook his head, as if she were naive. "I have shared enough memories for one night. I have told you far too much altogether."

"No one can swear off weakness," Thea argued, forcing herself to remove her hand from his arm. After all, she had no reason to comfort him. He had lured her here and planned to allow her to be trapped forever.

"Anything can be accomplished if you're willing to sacrifice." Damon's eyes grew thoughtful as they roved over her face. He looked down and away, then back at her. "Though I have never before had anything I was unwilling to let go."

The dancers' song ended, and there was a moment of silence before the strains of another, jauntier tune started up. Damon showed no reaction to the music.

"Do you actually like dancing?" she asked, still curious about him despite her disgust at what he'd done.

"No," he said sharply. "Wait. As you are so scrupulous about honesty, I will confess that I recently enjoyed dancing for two nights. Before that it had been a long time since I found it pleasant."

"You mean, before you started using the dance to harvest innocent spirits?"

His expression closed off. "Yes."

She took in the ballroom, the walls, the lights, the trappings of glamour that were no doubt as false as the prince's admiration.

It was a misleading, disguised battlefield. No blood, no swords, no stench of death. All you did was put on a dress, step into a dance, stare into a pair of beautiful dark eyes, and you found yourself defeated. Your life over. Your freedom forfeit.

"Will I die on the ninth night?" she asked bluntly, unable to look at Damon, dreading his answer.

His sharply indrawn breath was audible. "Enough, Thea."

"Because you don't like admitting how horrible you are?" She turned to look at him, too furious to care about the warning in his eyes. "Or because you're bored now that I'm not looking at you with doe eyes like the others?"

He didn't answer. She didn't think he would. His only words were "Root, take her home."

The portal opened, and Thea didn't spare Damon another look as she stepped through it, bracing herself for the topsy-turvy sensations of passing through. As she stepped into Thirstwood, her stomach felt sick.

What form would her spirit take on the ninth night? What would Erebus do with her spirit?

She didn't know. And she didn't intend to find out.

Learn your enemy's weakness, Tibald always said. *And exploit it.*

Thea had trained all her life with weapons, but that didn't mean she couldn't fight another way. She would figure out how to stop the king of this twisted, forgotten realm. Because if what Damon said was true, a clock was ticking, and sooner or later, she'd be drawn back here to pay with her life.

20

> A Sylvan never truly dies, because our spirits live on after death, first in our birth trees, and then, when that grows old or is cut down, in the Netherwhere with Noctua.
>
> —Excharias, Sylvan poet

Though it seemed like days had passed since she'd gone to the Forgotten Realm, it was morning when Thea returned home. Seeing everyone gathering for what appeared to be a larger patrol than usual, she rushed to her room to change, arriving at the yard along with another couple of stragglers. The patrols were assembled, groups of three and four standing in readiness to deploy. The Sylvan king stood in the center of the Huntsmen, which was unusual. Tordon usually organized the patrols ahead of time.

Enora moved through the crowd to Thea's

side, speaking quietly. "You used to be out here early every morning."

Thea sighed, giving a noncommittal shrug. She couldn't deal with her sister's concern right now.

Five more nights until she was trapped forever.

The Sylvan king turned his head, looking over his Huntsmen. The circles under his eyes were darker than Thea had ever seen. His antlers stretched as proud and wide as ever, but the head carrying them looked bent, as if the weight of responsibility was too much for him. Finally, he cleared his throat. Rain began falling as he spoke.

"Strange things are afoot in Thirstwood," the king said, his gravelly voice strong despite his appearance. "We have faced threats before, but the reports of a larger scucca has the Seers confounded. Right now, the wards on our walls are holding, but you are going into danger whenever you leave those gates. We were at war for many years, and you all fought faithfully. I trust that you will fight now for us, for me, as you have always done."

"Always!" Burke cried out, his voice strong and sure. "We'll never cower from our enemies, King Silvanus."

While Huntsmen agreed heartily, the word *cower* reminded Thea of Damon's story about being put into the cave simply for being afraid of the shadows. She had to steel herself against remembered sympathy. He didn't deserve it.

The Sylvan king nodded to his Second Huntsman in approval. "Do not fight an unknown enemy. If you see anything strange, report back to Scarhamm immediately."

"Why not kill first and report later?" Cedric asked, his grin infectious.

The weight of the Sylvan king's stare fell on him. "There are foes we cannot destroy with our swords. You would have been wise to learn that when we faced the scuccas."

Cedric bowed his head, his smile gone. "Yes, sire."

Tordon took over, his tone calm and assured as he gave specific instructions to each patrol.

"This is us," Enora said when it was their turn. "Coming?"

"In a minute," Thea said, meeting her sister's eyes. "I want to speak to Father."

Enora's eyes sharpened, clearly curious. When Thea said nothing more, she sighed in frustration and went off to meet Burke.

In minutes, the patrols had left the yard, and Tordon had returned to the fortress. Only Thea and her father remained. The rain picked up, falling faster. For a moment, Thea wondered if he had brought this bad weather. After all, the Sylvan king could summon storms at will.

"Where did you go tonight?" he asked, his voice full of suspicion.

Thea swallowed, not expecting him to interrogate her. She had meant to ask *him* questions. "What do you mean?" she prevaricated. "I'm here, ready for patrol."

He breathed in deeply, exhaling on a long breath. "You stink of magic. Tell me where you went."

The sound of pelting rain covered her gasp, but she knew her surprise showed on her face. She seemed less able to hide her emotions lately, and she didn't like it.

"You will tell me where you went," he commanded, the rumble of thunder on the edge of his words.

The Sylvan king had demanded an answer three times, and her tongue wanted to loosen, to tell him the truth. But when she opened her lips, her throat tightened. The shadow magic would not allow it. "I will not." She might have said she couldn't, but his growing temper was making hers rise to match.

Her father's eyes darkened with fury. "You dare speak to me in that tone."

"You have never spoken to me in *that* tone," she countered, her pulse throbbing in her temples. "I have a great deal more sympathy for Cassia now that I know how it feels to be lectured like this. What happened to your trust in me? Is it so easily broken?"

"You speak of trust? You stand on the edge of disaster, my daughter." Lightning flashed in the sky, illuminating Scarhamm's walls. "Remember who is ally and who is enemy. Some of you seem to be forgetting."

A reference to Cassia's Dracu? She couldn't believe she was standing up for him, but she wouldn't let that go unchallenged. "Zeru saved Enora's life when we were last on patrol."

He made a dismissive motion with one hand. "If you believe his motivations are pure, you are unfit to lead other Huntsmen."

She wanted to say more, so much more. To call his own leadership into question. But she wasn't ready to burn it all down. She had to ask her most important question before she said something she'd well and truly regret.

"What happened to my mother?" The question rolled out and sat there in a beat of breath-held silence. She put all her hope into her eyes.

Answer the question, Father. Care enough about me to tell me what I need to know.

A clap of thunder sounded overhead. Thea felt the hair on the back of her neck lift. Was he going to strike her with lightning? Would he go that far to silence her?

She stared into his eyes, refusing to look away. "Please."

"I forbid you to pursue this," he said, his voice harsher than ever. "You will find no satisfaction in the answer."

"What if I *need* that answer?" she cried, raising her voice to her father for the first time in her life. "What if it's about my own survival?" Her throat convulsed at the attempt to say more.

"Your survival?" The sky darkened as the king took a step toward her. "What have you done?"

Thea coughed, waiting for the magic to allow her to speak again. Her eyes held a clear plea. *Tell me.*

Thunderclouds curled overhead, lightning

strobing in their depths. "You will not go on patrol again until you have proven yourself trustworthy," the Sylvan king proclaimed. "Go to your bedchamber and stay there until I tell you otherwise."

In her fury, Thea found her voice. "You're putting me under house arrest for asking a question?"

"For your own protection." He lifted a hand to signal someone, and Thea turned to see Burke striding back toward them, Enora on his heels.

Enora came to a halt, looking between her father and her sister.

The king said coldly, "Thea is to stay in her bedchamber until further notice."

Enora's eyes rounded. "Why?"

Burke recovered more quickly. He nodded and put a hand on Thea's shoulder. "Come on, Huntsman."

Thea slapped his arm away. "I know the way to my own bedchamber! Touch me again and I'll break your fingers off."

Burke put his palms up and took a step back.

"Thea," Enora said, her voice confused and upset. But Thea was too angry to explain.

She stalked toward the fortress, knowing now

that it had been pointless to ask her father anything. He cared more about hiding the truth than he did about his own daughter.

Thea paced her bedchamber, her bare feet slapping the floorboards. She couldn't believe she was trapped in here.

She was still furious with Damon, and didn't even know if she could trust what he'd told her. What if he was lying and all she had to do was stay away from his world to be free? Somehow, she doubted that, but it was a possibility.

Exhaustion finally caught up to her, and she fell into a fitful sleep. She dreamed her mother was screaming at her, her mouth forming the words, "Run! Go!"

A knock made her sit up. She ran to her door and grabbed the handle, swearing when it didn't open. Someone must have locked it from the outside. Or maybe Veleda had been ordered to put a spell on it. Thea cursed them both, then called out, "Who is it?"

The knock came again, but it was coming from behind her. She spun around and ran to her window. A white-haired pixie was flying outside, rubbing his hands up and down his arms as he shivered.

"Winter," she said, shocked. Unlatching the window, she threw it open to a blast of cold air. The pixie flew inside, going straight to hover near her fireplace.

"Cold as a giant's fart out there," the pixie said, shuddering.

"For someone named Winter, you seem rather sensitive to the cold," she pointed out, grabbing a handkerchief from her wardrobe and holding it out to him. "Put it around you like a shawl," she suggested.

Winter wrinkled his nose. "Ew. No, thank you. I'd rather freeze."

"What are you doing here?" Thea asked, dropping the handkerchief on a table and sitting on the edge of her bed.

"Autumn had another vision, and she made me come here to tell you." He scowled into the flames in the hearth. "I hate that I owe her so many favors. Just because she told me which dice to bet on at the harvest festival so I could win a few petals. I didn't know I'd become her personal messenger." Suddenly, he looked at Thea, his eyes wide. "Don't tell anyone about the wagering.

Sunflower will cut my rations in half if she finds out."

Thea rolled her eyes. "I don't care that you cheated at dice. I'm on house arrest, and I can't leave my bedchamber. I hope you have some news that can help me."

Apparently warm enough now, Winter fluttered to Thea's chair and sat on the back, crossing one leg over the other, tossing his long hair over one shoulder. "I doubt it'll help you, but I'll tell you anyway. Autumn had a vision of shadows, like the ones in our forest. They were all around you, only you weren't afraid. She said it's like they were listening to you."

Thea's eyes widened. "And she thinks it was a vision of the future?"

"Possible future," Winter said, holding up his index finger. "Autumn says her visions are possible futures because they don't always come true." He grimaced. "I think that's her face-saving way of saying she's wrong sometimes. That's how I lost at dice in the end."

Thea waved a hand to indicate she was done with the dice talk. "Fine, so how do I do that? Control the shadows?"

Winter widened his eyes, a little sarcastically,

in Thea's opinion. "That's for you to figure out, isn't it?" He made a motion with his hand to indicate Thea. "All I know is, Autumn sees the silver trees in her visions all the time, and she thinks you're the only one who can help."

It wasn't much, but it was something. Thea bowed her head to him. "Thank you, Winter. I'll try to use the information you gave me."

With a brief nod, he flew into the air, heading for the window. "I'm sufficiently warmed to fly home."

"One problem, though," Thea said quickly, before he slipped away. "I can't leave this room. I'm locked in. Could you get word to my sister Cassia to come here? She's on patrol."

Winter's eyes shifted back and forth, a worried expression on his small face. "Would the Sylvan king be mad at me if he found out?"

"Yes," Thea said honestly. "You could be punished."

The pixie's sour expression gave her the answer before he spoke. "Sorry, Giantess, but I don't owe you any favors."

"I'm trying to save you and everyone else from becoming part of the Forgotten—!" Her mouth closed up violently, almost choking her.

"If you manage to save us from the silver trees, I'll owe you at least five favors," Winter promised unhelpfully. "Quick, Giantess. I have to go before anyone sees me."

Thea let out a frustrated breath, but she opened the window, sighing as Winter flew off into the distance. She'd never wished for wings more in her life.

The hours passed slowly, but they gave Thea time to make plans. She considered the message Autumn had sent and put that together with what she'd learned about the shadows so far. She knew there was a type of magic with an appetite for joy, sorrow, and suffering. Cassia's ring, the Solis Gemma, was powered by emotions pulled from the wearer. She remembered how Damon's shadows seemed to move faster or slower based on his mood. Sifting through it all, she came up with a theory that she thought was worth testing. Finally, the sun set, and darkness fell outside her window.

From one breath to the next, a pile of clothing appeared on her hearth. Thea rushed to grab it, barely glancing at the details before putting it on. Regarding herself in the mirror, she saw a long-sleeved tunic embroidered with an elaborate design of leaves, something clearly intended as a nod to her Sylvan heritage. It swept down over silky trousers, the legs so generous it was almost like a skirt. Beautiful and practical, but she had little time to appreciate that.

The shoes were soft leather half-boots that laced up the front. The most comfortable boots she'd ever worn. As soon as they were laced, they took her to the door. But something stopped them. She hovered, her feet tapping, but the door still wouldn't open.

The boots turned Thea toward her hearth. Her feet danced back and forth, and at first she thought the magic wasn't working. But soon a dot of light appeared among the flames. It grew and grew, and roots appeared, opening the edges of the portal wider until it was big enough to step through.

21

> To secure the goodwill of a shadow spirit, chaos must be embraced.
> —*The Little Book of Spells*

Thea's heartbeat fluttered in her neck as the boat slid across the water toward the castle, her senses on alert, her nerves stretched taut. She was going to do something very smart or extremely foolish, and she didn't know which it was yet. As the boat reached the shore, a soft, deep voice emerged from the darkness. "You came."

Thea spun to see Damon sitting on the ground a few feet away, as if he'd been waiting there.

"You didn't think I would?" she asked, her pulse throbbing faster at the sight of him. Even cast in shadows, he was a beautiful thing. The sparkling depth in his eyes, the velvet eyebrows, the sculpted face. His lips could inspire odes. For once, she didn't try to fight her reaction to him. She meant to *use* this attraction.

"I didn't know," he admitted. "You were angry. You had every right to be."

She was still furious. But she had an agenda, and that didn't include lambasting him all evening. Still, he'd think it odd if she was all sweetness after what he'd confessed.

"I can't forgive you for what you're doing," she told him, moving to stand closer. "But I don't know how else to get answers. Don't you think I deserve to at least understand why my life is forfeit?"

He put a hand to the ground and pushed lithely to his feet. The gracefulness of his movements made her shiver. "You deserve far better than that. I wish..." He held his hand out, then let it fall, as if he thought she wouldn't take it.

She reached down slowly, taking his hand in hers, warmth flooding her senses at the contact. "Dance with me?" Her voice was hoarse, her tone soft. She let her lips curve up. "Then answer my questions."

Though he seemed reluctant to enter the castle, his eyes warmed at her comment. "At least you've accepted how it works."

There were fewer couples than before. Eighteen folk left. Thea felt a lurch of pity to think what had happened to them, then fury at Damon all over again. She did her best to hide both, keeping her face impassive as she focused on the music and the steps. It was a Sylvan dance she well knew, and the same tune they had danced to at least five times. It struck her as oddly happy for this place of entrapment.

"You must like this music," she observed, careful not to phrase it as a question. "It plays almost every night."

Damon's eyebrows went up for a moment before he chuckled. "I suppose I do. I heard it at one of your revels." His glance fell away from hers for a moment, then he lifted his chin and met her eyes. "The first time I saw you. It was before your name day."

Thea sucked in a breath. "You were there before I ever saw you?"

"Not actually there. It's a projection of my image using my shadows. I can see and hear through them."

That made Thea shiver with unease. "What were you doing? Spying, I suppose."

He didn't look repentant. "First of all, testing if my shadows could get past your wards. You already know that fire thins the veil, and there's a large fireplace in your great hall. Your Seer should have known that and placed extra protection there."

Thea soaked in every word. She couldn't believe he was telling her so much. "That's why you were able to create a doorway in my bedchamber tonight."

His head tilted to the side. "Wait. The portal appears near my father's trees."

She'd assumed he was directly responsible. "I was locked in my bedchamber. The shoes danced in front of the hearth and a portal appeared."

His eyebrows went up, and he looked worried. "Creating a doorway is beyond my knowledge. Only my father could do something like that."

"Does he know about me?" she asked.

Damon paused for a few moments, the sound of the music covering what might have been a tense silence otherwise. "He knows you exist. He does not know you're here. But if he opened a portal, it makes me think he is planning to make contact with you." He put his hand on her shoulder, breaking time with the music. Her feet stopped moving, and she stared back at him.

He drew her away from the dance toward

the statue of Solis, where they'd spoken before. Thea's heart refused to calm. Part of her longed to allow herself to give in to what he made her feel. Another part knew that was foolish and deadly.

"What future do you want for yourself?" he asked, surprising her with the question. "If you had a choice?"

"I'd want to be what I am now," she told him. "A soldier in the Sylvan army. A defender of the forest folk. I want the freedom to protect the people I love."

"You must have ambitions," he said, his eyes urging her to tell him. "You are too impressive not to desire more."

"I do have one wish," she said, taking his hand, "but you'll have to pay to know that."

"What currency do you require?" he asked, his eyes lit with curiosity.

"Not much," she said, her heart beating double time. "Just a kiss."

Damon's eyes flared wide. "A kiss," he repeated, his shadows swirling rapidly around his neck and shoulders.

Why would they move faster now? Thea thought of Autumn's vision. How was Damon controlling the shadows? Or was he unable to control them in this moment? Thea could feel his pulse fluttering in his wrist, matching the manic rhythm of her own.

"Is that so much to ask?" She moved subtly closer, her head tilted up so that their lips were inches apart.

He took her other hand, sending a jolt of warm electricity through her. As he stared at her, unspeaking, she had a moment to second-guess her plan. She needed to test how loyal Damon's shadows were to him, but would a kiss make her more vulnerable?

If the shadows liked passion, well, she could supply them. If they liked strength, she was strong.

The warmth in Damon's eyes told her this attraction went both ways. If she could get him to lose a bit of that self-control, maybe the shadows would be drawn to her? It was a murky, vague plan, but it was a plan.

Some hesitation moved behind his eyes as he considered her request. "You were right, you know, not to touch me when we first met. Touch strengthens my magic."

"You can just say no, Shadow Stranger," she teased.

He took a step closer, bringing them an inch apart. Stars shone in his midnight eyes. "I only wanted to make sure you understood the risk."

"I live for risk." She tilted her head to the side, smiling up at him. "Didn't your shadow spies tell you that?"

He lifted a hand, his fingers threading into her loosely braided hair. When he grabbed the braid and tugged to get her chin to tilt up, she gasped. His fingers brushed her neck, sending warm shocks down her spine, her nipples hardening as he pressed against her. She met his eyes, knowing he could probably see the rapid pulse in her throat. She put a finger on his neck where his heart beat visibly, dragging it down to where his collar covered his skin. She watched his nostrils flare and his eyes dilate.

"What you do to me," he breathed, warm and spiced against her cheek. "You are surely hunting me, Sylvan. I have read about your father's history, you know. The Wild Hunt he undertook to cull the humans before your people moved into Thirstwood."

Thea blinked. She'd heard something about this from Cassia, and she now realized there was much she needed to question about her father and his history. But she didn't want to talk about that now.

Her fingers moved to his jaw, sliding toward the corner of his mouth. "Once, when I was on patrol, I was separated from the other Huntsmen and was cornered by a wolf."

He blinked at her topic change. "They say there are not many wolves left in Thirstwood. Did you kill it?"

She slid her finger along his bottom lip, watching as he sucked in a breath. "I couldn't. My father forbade any Huntsmen from killing the wolves in our forest. As you said, so few of them are left."

His hand slid to the back of her head, his touch pouring honey down her spine. "But surely it was a choice between your life and the wolf's?"

"Most people would say so." She traced the bow of his lip with her index finger, feeling him shudder against her. "I saw another choice. I sat against the trunk of a tree, knowing it would do its best to protect me. I told the tree to trap instead of kill the creature if it attacked. After that all I remember is my own white breath in the cold, and the wolf's yellow eyes staring at me."

Damon's fingers tensed as they cradled her nape. "Did it attack?"

Her eyes were fixed on his, which were rapt with attention. "It came right up to me. Snarled. I didn't react. It stared at me for a long time." Her eyes roved his perfect features, and she allowed herself to take pleasure in them, to allow his beauty to affect her so he could feel the joy running through her body. "I didn't challenge it, and it didn't challenge me. Two killers staring at each other in the dark." She snaked her arms around his back and rested her cheek against his shoulder, shivering at the feeling.

"Since you already had some practice defying your father, why didn't you kill it?" Damon asked, drawing away to meet her eyes again. His shadows moved closer to her, almost as if they were listening to her story. "It would have made your forest safer for every other creature."

"Who says I didn't?" She felt his indrawn breath, the warmth of his body at odds with the brush of shadows cooling her skin. They were all around her now, swirling into her hair, between her fingers, against her neck. She didn't find it as unpleasant as she'd expected. "How do you know I didn't have a cloak made from its pelt?"

His eyebrow lifted, his eyes deep as his hand slid to her upper back. "Then what would be the point of your story?"

She smiled, enjoying that he was paying attention. She lifted her left arm between them, showing the crisscross of white scars on her forearm. "I had to wrestle it to the ground and hold it there. Until it tired of snarling at me."

"That must have taken some strength," he observed, admiration in his expression.

"It was grueling," she agreed proudly. "But Sylvans are strong."

"That was a risk. You should have ended it." His hand tightened on her back. "Someone has to be prey."

"Sometimes," Thea said, "a predator is too beautiful to kill." She touched her lips to his chin, a heady feeling coming over her as he sucked in a sharp breath. She met his eyes before adding, "Besides, I've always liked wolves." And she lifted her face to his.

Her breath shivered out at the grazing of his lips against hers. Soft, inviting. *Oh, Ancients, the feel of him.* Better than she'd expected. Better than anything. She pressed closer, harder. Her hand caught in his hair, her fingers gripping him. He groaned, his hands moving over her back. His shadows swirled in rapid time to her pulse.

"Ancients save me," he whispered. "You taste sweet."

She pulled back for breath, knowing her own eyes must look as dazed, her own cheeks as flushed. She tried to think of the stable grooms she had thought handsome in Scarhamm. She couldn't even bring their faces to mind. "I can't remember what it felt like to be with anyone else. Your magic?" She couldn't help it. She wanted to know how much of this was real.

His eyebrows came together sharply. "No. I'm not using any magic on you, Thea. However, I don't care to hear about your previous lovers at the moment." Before she could argue, he added, "And don't talk about the future. Any future. There's only now."

That cooled her ardor. She might not have a future, and he was reminding her of it. But her plan was about finding the other option. Not killing the wolf, but not dying, either.

"Don't dismiss me so quickly," she said.

He gripped her shoulders and put a hairsbreadth of distance between them.

"Don't show me paths I can't travel." His

hands flexed on her shoulders, pulling her closer again as if he regretted that small distance. "Don't toy with the wolf, Thea."

She smiled up at him, a feline, predatory smile. "Without risk, where's the fun?" And pressed her lips once again to his.

The music faded to the back of her mind as she kissed the shadow prince. The only sound she cared about was his breath hitching and the rhythm of his heart pounding against hers.

When they finally drew apart, the shadows stayed with Thea. Just for a moment, before they returned to Damon. But it had been enough. Her heart raced, a heady triumph making her almost as dizzy as his kisses. He didn't seem to notice that his shadows had briefly clung to her. His lips were swollen, his eyes dazed on hers.

The song came to an end. Damon blinked, seeming to become aware of their surroundings. "I believe you owe me an answer," he said, straightening the collar of the shirt she'd put askew.

Thea raised her brows, fighting annoyance that he was coming back to reality faster than she could.

"Your secret ambition," he reminded her, his

hand moving into her hair as if he couldn't help himself.

"Oh, that." She nodded, planting a kiss on his wrist that made him inhale sharply. "Fair is fair." She flicked her eyes up to his. "What I want is to be First."

Damon nodded, approval in his warm gaze. "You're a natural leader. But you don't have to be promoted to First, Thea. You are already first."

Thea gave him a questioning look. "I'm only a lieutenant. What do you mean?"

He chuckled softly, as if her confusion amused him. "I think we have both answered enough questions for one night."

Thea was still holding Damon's hand. It felt warm and reassuring and solid, all the things he wasn't. She let go, but he held on a second longer. His eyes swept over her, hair to toes. Then he took a breath and said, "Take her home."

The white oval appeared. Thea took a step toward the root that emerged from the doorway. Had she met her goals tonight? He'd made her so muddled, she wasn't sure. She turned back and put her hand to his neck, feeling the shadows there, enjoying the look of longing in his eyes. He didn't seem to notice when the shadows clung to her fingers.

She took a breath, satisfied by that sign, and dropped her hand to her side. Yes, she was making progress. Though this growing need to be close to him made her wonder: At what cost?

"I'll see you tomorrow night," Damon said, his tone wistful. "Stay safe."

What an odd thing to say when he posed the greatest threat to her. Unspeaking, she turned her back and stepped through the portal.

22

> Although he was the king of shadows, Erebus longed for light. He sought the hand of Solis, whose brightness dazzled him.
>
> —Old Ones, Ancients, and the Folk

The following day was the longest of Thea's life. She passed a few hours with sleep, but after that, time crept by at a turtle's pace. Trapped in her bedchamber, she was cut off from everything that gave her purpose. She'd started to wonder if anyone was planning to feed her when she finally heard Rozie's voice, shrill with defiance. "I want to see her!"

"You can't." Cassia's softer tone. "She's not allowed to see anyone."

"And you're fine with that?" Rozie sounded furious. "After everything that happened, all the rules you've broken?"

"No," Cassia assured her calmly. "I have plans,

but I need time to carry them out so that no one else gets in trouble."

Rozie paused. "No one but you, you mean?"

"Correct. I'm used to being in trouble."

Thea put her hand against the door in sympathy. She now understood what it felt like for her sister to live under the storm cloud of their father's disapproval.

"What plans?" Rozie asked.

A note of mischief entered Cassia's tone. "Isn't it obvious? I'm going to take her out her window."

Thea cleared her throat, speaking through the door. "When are we planning this little heist? Because now would be good."

Rozie shrieked. "Thea! I tried your door but it's bolted and spelled. I demanded that Veleda remove the ward, but she wouldn't listen."

"Thank you for trying, Sproutling," Thea replied, grinning at Rozie's imperiousness. "Rude of her not to obey your orders, though."

"Worse than rude," Rozie grumbled. "I told her she'd be dismissed if she wasn't careful. She *laughed* at me."

"In answer to your question," Cassia said through the door, "I have to wait for nightfall.

Also, I really don't think I should be calling these plans through your door."

Thea frowned. Night wouldn't work. She had to go back to Iluna, to make more progress controlling Damon's shadows. The memory of Damon's lips filled her mind, though she told herself that had nothing to do with her mission, of course.

"Can't you create a distraction during the day?" Thea ventured.

Cassia sighed. "I don't want to involve many people, but... who do you think I should ask?"

"Enora isn't in on this?"

There was a short, heavy pause before Cassia answered. "Enora thinks this is for your own good. Father implied you're ill, and she believes him. She says you've been acting strange."

Thea put her back against the door, then straightened away from it as she felt the unpleasant tingle of Veleda's locking spell. Though it pained her to think of Enora losing faith in her, she couldn't altogether blame her. She *had* been acting strange. After all, she was looking forward to kissing a shadow prince who had lured her to a realm where her spirit was beholden to its banished ruler. If that wasn't proof of something wrong with her, what was?

"I'll get you out," Cassia said, her voice quiet and close to the door. "Hang on until after sunset. I have to wait until Veleda has come and gone. She said she'll be by tonight to bring you food."

Thea swallowed past a lump in her throat. Sylvans could go long periods without food as long as they had water and sunlight, but that didn't mean it was comfortable to do so. The petty cruelty of not bringing her food until nightfall did not escape her. Her father was truly furious. Well, let him be. She wasn't going to languish here waiting for his approval.

"Cassia, you're already doing so much," Thea said softly. "But can you do me another favor?"

The reply was quick and unhesitating. "Tell me and it's done."

"Can you fly to the pixie village and talk to Autumn or an elder named Sunflower? Or find Winter. He should pass the message on. I need Autumn to know that her theory seems to be correct. And ask if she's had any more visions. I can't explain any more than that." Her mouth was tightening even now.

"Of course, Thea," Cassia said. "I'll go now."

"Can I go with you, Cass?" Rozie asked in a pleading voice. "Please?"

"I can't fly *and* carry you," Cassia explained. "I'll be back as soon as I can to tell you what they said. All right?"

"Thank you," Thea said, a lump of gratitude in her throat. She wanted to apologize for not understanding what Cassia had gone through all these years, but she couldn't yet find the words. "I know it sounds unlikely, but if you come to my window and find me gone, don't worry."

Cassia sounded hesitant. "Thea, I don't see how you can get out of there without my help. What are you planning?"

"I... don't have all my plans figured out yet," Thea replied, which was overall true. Once she was free, she wasn't about to return to Scarhamm to be put back in her bedchamber until all this was settled. Either way, she'd get word to her sisters about her safety. Somehow. Still, it meant so much that Cassia was willing to try to help her escape. She realized how much she had always taken her gentlest sister for granted. "But Cass?" she added softly. "I love you."

Cassia sucked in a breath. "Thea, *are* you well?"

Thea laughed, her throat clogged with emotion. She didn't express her feelings enough if her sister thought she was dying simply because she'd said how she felt. "I'll be better when I'm out of here."

As she heard her sisters moving away, Rozie's voice carried faintly. "Could Zeru carry me to the pixies? I don't think he'll mind. Can you at least ask?"

Thea was bored out of her branches by the time a pale pink-and-mauve gown appeared on her hearth. She rushed forward and snatched it up. It was clear at once that it was quite different from the previous garments. The skirt was made from layer after layer of tulle. The satin bodice was covered in lacy frills. The dress was sleeveless, but long lace gloves were included, along with stockings. When Thea put the ensemble on, she felt constricted. There would be no ease of movement in this. The lace made her itchy. She turned to her looking glass, taking in the frilly confection. It fit well enough, but she didn't feel like herself in this.

Thea frowned. Damon had taken a step backward in his choice of dress. Did he think this was what she wanted?

She put on the satin slippers, though she preferred the soft leather boots he'd sent her the night before. Once they were snug, her feet immediately began dancing, the steps light and fast. In a few moments, a yellow dot of light appeared before her fireplace. The dot grew into a doorway, the roots reaching toward her like tentacles.

Dizziness took hold of her as she stepped through the portal, but she was less bothered than before. She felt a tremble of excitement in her limbs at the idea of seeing Damon again. She told herself that she was only eager to test his shadows, but she knew it was more than that. Rather than fighting it, she planned to use this feeling to lure his shadows. She only had two more nights before it would be too late to escape his father's curse.

The portal spit her out as it always did, but instead of stepping onto black gravel in the familiar silver forest, she found herself in a room with dark walls, its gold-edged tapestries barely visible in the dim light.

Disoriented, pulse racing, Thea took in her surroundings. As her eyes adjusted, she saw that she was standing in front of a black throne. Lounging on the throne was a man.

He could only be Erebus, king of shadows.

His hair was spun from dark satin. Bright gemstones and gold gleamed on his hands. Even as shadows moved over him, half-obscuring his features like clouds blocking the sun, he was nothing short of beautiful. At the edge of her mind, a haze of vague joy tried to gain entrance. Recognizing the tug of magic, she curled her hands into fists, forcing herself to move her eyes away from him. Once she'd averted her gaze, some of the effects ebbed, leaving her shakily aware of her vulnerability.

But she'd looked at him long enough to confirm something she'd already worked out. He was the one who had kissed her mother the night she'd disappeared. Here was the man who had taken her mother.

Another man stood on one side of the throne, a cowl covering his head and eyes. What she could see of his skin looked almost as gray as his robes. The whole of him, long face, long hair, and clothing, appeared to be fashioned from the pale dregs of hearth ash. On the other side of the throne was a single silver tree, its leaves chiming, though no wind blew. Its branches were bent away from Erebus, as if deprived of sunlight on one side, though no sunlight came from any direction in this place.

"At last, we meet," said the king. "The fair Theodora."

Heated rage pulsed in Thea's chest as she met his eyes. "Erebus, I presume?"

His lips curved in an amused smile that did not reach his eyes. "You accepted my dress."

Thea felt herself stiffen against a stinging sense of regret. She should have trusted her instinct that the dress was unlike the others Damon had sent. She'd been too desperate to escape her confinement to think clearly.

"Do you like it?" the king asked.

Even if she wanted to, she couldn't lie. "It's itchy and constricting."

A violent anger flashed in his eyes and disappeared so fast that Thea wondered if it was a trick of the dim light. "What would you like better?"

"Irrelevant," Thea said, "since I don't plan to put on another dress that you send."

The king's lips curved in a gentle smile, though his eyes were very cold. "Perhaps I can persuade you to change your mind."

Thea stared him down. "I wouldn't wager on it."

The king of shadows shifted on his throne. She had the sense she wasn't behaving as he'd expected. "Well, if you won't partake of my hospitality, I must insist that you provide me with conversation. Come closer." He patted the armrest. "I would like to see your features."

A branch on the silver tree shivered, and a leaf dropped onto the king's lap. He smiled as he picked it up, stroking it idly as he glanced at the tree. He said something under his breath that sounded like, "No need for dramatics."

As he directed his gaze back to Thea, she felt a pull of magic on her, a strangely soporific happiness. But while Damon's pull was more of a question, this was an order. To accept his invitation and to find it delightful.

She didn't move a hair. "I'm fine here."

His grin gained a hard edge. "I merely want to see you better." He snapped his fingers. "Prospect, some light."

The hooded figure raised his hands, tossing small objects into the air that lit with a green glow and cast an eerie aspect on the king's face.

"You are truly lovely," he pronounced after a lengthy inspection of Thea's features that made her want to draw a weapon. Why hadn't she brought one? No doubt his shadows were effective shields, as Damon's were, but she would like to test that theory. "I wonder what you would look like with flowers in your hair?" he mused.

"I wonder what you would look like with my knife in your neck." She restrained herself from saying it, but barely.

The king stroked his chin, looking puzzled. Likely most of his visitors did not wear expressions of fury as they stood before his throne. Perhaps Thea had some natural resistance to his ancient magic.

"We have a visitor, Father?" a familiar, melodious voice said.

Thea's heart stopped, then pulsed two quick beats together. She turned to face Damon, who was bowing to the king. He was as well-dressed and perfectly groomed as always. As he straightened, his midnight eyes met hers. They held no hint of recognition, as if they'd never met.

She couldn't help noticing the resemblance between father and son, wondering why she hadn't seen it before. But her memory of the shadow king had been hazy after so many years. Damon was carved as sharply, his features as beautiful. But there was something about him that she could reach out and touch, something real. It made no sense to feel relief at his presence, but she did.

"Hello," she said, wondering at his lack of greeting.

Before she could say more, Damon strode forward and bowed. "Welcome to our realm. I hope you will find it to your liking." He smiled as he straightened, but the blankness in his eyes chilled her.

He nodded once, tightly, the angles of his face sharper than she'd ever seen them. Then he took a breath and cleared his throat. "Would you mind if I continued bringing our guest to my dance?"

Erebus frowned heavily. "I intend to enjoy her company myself."

Damon looked down, then back up at his father in a placating way. "Just a few nights to bring joy to my little slice of our realm. Is that so much to ask?"

"Yes," the king said succinctly, his expression only softening when Thea looked at him. "But I am in a generous frame of mind. As this is such a festive night, I will allow it."

Festive? Thea wondered. There was no holiday

that she knew of. But she understood that she was on the knife edge of safety, and that she should listen rather than speak.

"Thank you, Father," Damon said, his face pale as he inclined his head. She saw the stiffness in his posture, the tension humming through him. "If it's not too much to ask, I'd like several nights at the dance."

"You ask much, my son," Erebus snapped. His fingers tapped an impatient beat on the armrest of his throne. "How many nights?"

"The full nine."

The king sat forward, his expression furious.

"Before you decide, my reasons are quite sound." Damon put his hands behind his back, his spine straight. The same posture Thea used when reporting to her own father. "First of all, there are fewer folk in the forest of late. Our silver trees appearing in Thirstwood has made everyone wary. But the dance must continue to bring cheer to our dark kingdom."

Thea understood that "cheer" really meant power for their kingdom.

"Secondly," Damon continued, "one strong soul is a greater boon to our dance than ten weaker ones. I have had weaker folk of late, regretfully. It is unfortunate that we have not devised a way to draw the strongest here."

The king launched an accusing look at the robed man called Prospect, who winced and bowed his head. His hands, which were laced together, tightened until the knuckles showed white.

"The silver trees are part of Prospect's efforts, but I expect him to be circumspect. As for the second point, we will make more progress on that venture once the snow falls and the folk above are in need of cheer. That is our time."

"Of course, sire," Prospect murmured. "The coming season is our best chance to gain an advantage, when nights are longest. The Sylvan wards are failing day by day."

Thea sucked in a breath. Though she already knew about the wards, it hit her hard to hear the Seer detailing the weaknesses of her people.

Erebus stared at Damon for a moment that stretched into uncomfortable territory. Finally, he nodded. "You must know this request inconveniences me. I have awaited the arrival of this fair Sylvan for a long time." He glanced at Thea, perhaps to gauge if she was flattered. She lifted her chin and stared back at him, unblinking.

"Remember that any guest who arrives here must be presented to me by the ninth night."

Thea swallowed. Somehow, though, the king didn't seem to know that she had been in this realm for six nights. And Damon was not telling him.

"And be careful what you say," the king went on, his shadows moving outward, almost like arms reaching for Damon. "I'll hear of it if you've been less than strict with your tongue. As has happened before."

"Put your faith in me, Father," Damon said. "I won't falter."

The chill in the king's eyes grew icy. "See that you don't. I expect you to do your duty by bringing more folk to your dance." His head tilted to the side as he swept Thea with a penetrating look. "Enjoy your time at the dance, fair Theodora. I look forward to seeing you again soon."

The scathing reply on Thea's tongue never found voice because Damon pulled her away by her arm. With a final, furious glance at the shadow-strewn throne, she lifted her chin and followed him. To her surprise, the throne room did not appear to be a room at all, but a massive space bounded by darkness. When they emerged from the obscuring magic that surrounded it, they stepped into a forest of silver trees. A gravel path took them toward a sheen of water in the distance.

Thea followed in silence. As they drew close, the boat floated up to meet them. She stepped in roughly, rocking the vessel in her angry haste so that Damon had to use his shadows to steady it as he joined her.

After a few minutes, the river bent and widened. The castle came into view, visible by its lit windows.

Thea couldn't hold her tongue any longer. She was not about to join his dance as if nothing had happened. "How did your father know so much about me?" She gestured down at herself and the dress she hated.

A muscle jumped in his cheek. "I'm assuming he used his shadows as spies."

"Which is what you did, too," she accused. Knowing the dress was from Erebus made her want to burn it immediately. "I can't believe I haven't demanded to know all this before! How have I let you convince me I can't ask questions, for the Ancients' sake? Enough. Either tell me what I need to know, or I start fighting back."

"Thea," Damon said.

His attempt to calm her fanned the flames of her anger. "Don't *Thea* me! You have been manipulating me, you've withheld vital information, and now he clearly has plans for me." The acquisitiveness in the king's eyes when he looked at her alarmed her on some deep level. Her hands were balled into fists in her lap, her nails scoring her palms. "Do you realize that it was your father who took my mother from me? And despite all your promises of answers, I still don't know where she is. What did he do to her, Damon? Answer me or I swear—"

"Thea." Damon swallowed, his skin paler than usual, his tone stiff. "You saw that silver tree next to my father's throne?"

"Of course," she answered, a sick feeling snaking into her gut at the look in his eyes.

"That," he said, slow and succinct, "is your mother."

23

> The spirits who become shadows in Erebus's realms are said to be the least fortunate because they have neither peace nor freedom. They are forced to do his bidding and are out of Noctua's reach. They will never be free.
>
> —*Old Ones, Ancients, and the Folk*

Shock burned through Thea's body, leaving her numb. Her throat tightened as she forced out a denial. "No. Her tree is in Thirstwood."

Damon shook his head, his eyes heavy with certainty. "This is not like a Sylvan going into her tree to rest. This is...a transmutation. Your mother *is* that silver tree."

Thea put a hand to her stomach and leaned over the side of the boat. She was going to be sick.

Damon muttered something, and the shadows moved closer to Thea. She reared back, but then she felt the cool sensation of them against her neck and realized Damon was doing this to ease her nausea. In a minute, her stomach settled.

After a few breaths, she managed to ask, "How?"

Damon spoke quickly. "Remember my father has sacred places in Thirstwood, remnants from bygone days when he had more power. Trees, fountains, rocks, small glades, groves. Some old pact, some ancient agreement, allows him to pull people from your realm into ours if they violate the boundaries of his spaces."

Thea had heard of such pacts, of course, and knew that the land folk were often custodians of sacred spaces. "My mother would have known where those places are. My father would have told her to stay away."

"The Sylvan king has put up barriers or hidden most of them," Damon explained. "Brambles or thick trees grow around them. However, there was a Sylvan girl who would not be put off by thorns. Perhaps she even viewed those barriers as challenges or sensed a great power half-concealed and was too curious for her own good.

Whatever the reason, she tore them away and climbed one of Erebus's trees."

Thea wished she could deny it. She almost didn't want to hear what happened next.

"The girl's mother came here and argued with the king," Damon went on. "But he would not be put off: He was owed the girl's spirit. The mother refuted his claim and went home. She tried to pretend it had never happened. But while she was in this realm, my father put a curse on her that made her sicken. When the queen grew so ill she could no longer survive, she returned."

Thea wished she didn't believe him. That this wasn't all her fault.

Damon was leaning forward, his elbows resting on his knees in a relaxed posture, but she felt the tension in him as he finished his story. "Finally, unable to deny the king's claim but unwilling to sacrifice her child, she offered her own spirit in her daughter's place."

"How do you know all this?" Thea asked, shivering. She had never noticed how cold it was here.

Damon met her eyes. "I was in the throne room when she was first brought here. And there again when she offered herself in your place."

Thea looked away to hide the tears that insisted on rolling down her cheeks. She put her hands over her face as a sob racked her chest. When was the last time she'd cried? She couldn't remember. But now she couldn't seem to stop. The pain she'd kept inside for so long insisted on being felt, and she was helpless against it. Damon's arm came around her back, and she allowed it, drawing comfort from his warmth. Finally, when her tears were spent, she wiped her face and straightened her back. Damon seemed to note her cue, and his arm fell away from her. She took a deep breath. Though her mind was still in shock over what she'd learned, something inside her eased, as if a tight knot had been untangled in her chest. She finally knew the truth and no longer needed to bear those secrets alone.

"Did you have anything to do with her imprisonment?" she asked, needing to know.

He looked away, his jaw hardening. "Prospect has crows in Thirstwood. Spies. He was the one who saw you climb the tree. He offered your mother the chance to give herself in your place. No doubt he felt the Sylvan queen was a bigger prize in my father's eyes than a mere girl." Damon looked at her. "But now..."

"I saw them kiss," Thea said unevenly. "I always thought she'd left us for him."

Damon made a sound of disgust. "He would have tried to charm her, and that could have been part of his attempt. I wouldn't assume your mother had a choice."

Thea's chest ached with regret, along with a renewed urge to murder King Erebus. All this time, she'd thought... The guilt threatened to crush her. "She sacrificed herself to save me."

"Yes."

Each breath was more painful than the last. All these years, she had blamed her mother for abandoning her. "She never deserved that," Thea said in a choking voice. "He shouldn't have made her stay in my place." Anger surged up, clearing her mind. "No one deserves to be trapped here."

"No, they don't," Damon agreed, surprising her. "But if there was a way to fight this, I'd have found it by now." He shook his head. "Even some of my shadows could still report to him. That's why I can say so little without risk. Though for now, it seems they have not told him about your presence here."

"Can I save her?" Thea asked, fixating on that point.

"Yes." His face lost expression, his eyes taking on a haunted look. "I tried to tell you on your second night here. You can take your mother's place. And she will be free."

Thea's mind reeled. That was too much to wrap her thoughts around. "Why the dresses?" she asked, needing a reprieve from the heavier questions.

He made a sound that seemed self-deprecating. "An invitation. A lure, I suppose, based on what my previous experience told me a young woman might like. The shoes were spelled to bring you to the tree."

"Did you know who I was when you sent me the first dress?"

Damon looked surprised that she'd ask. "Of course. I found the cracks in the wards of Scarhamm, but it took my shadows months before they could send it."

"If you can travel by root to Thirstwood, why not just talk to me when I was on patrol? Why send the dresses?"

A hint of humor lit Damon's eyes. "Do you think I'm foolish enough to risk accosting you in the woods without testing the waters first? You'd have skewered me."

Thea felt her lips twitch. "Most likely. But why me? What was your plan?"

Damon sighed, his eyes resting on the water for a few moments. "I thought it unfair that your mother was trapped here." He turned his head and met her eyes. "And her daughter, who had been the one who breached the boundary, was free. I wanted to give you the chance to make it right now that you're no longer a child."

Thea was struck by his sympathy, though it hurt to hear that he blamed her. "Why not tell me what was going on right from the beginning?"

He paused, his eyes shifting away from her for a moment. "I didn't trust you. I didn't know you."

Thea shivered at the memory of the way the king had looked at her, like she was something he could acquire. "And now that you do know me, will you tell me what your father wants from me?"

"He also wants you to take your mother's place. She's been here a long time, and a new presence will help power this realm and feed his shadows."

Take her place. As a silver tree.

The reality of it brought a fresh wave of nausea. This was where her mother had lived for seven years. Where she would remain unless Thea set her free. And if she did, this was where she herself would be for the rest of her life. Sylvans could live a very long time. She might live a thousand years trapped beside that awful king, miserable but sentient.

She looked at Damon with pure bitterness. Better to indulge her anger than to feel the guilt wrapped up with her mother's sacrifice. "Do the spirits trapped here eventually go to the Netherwhere? Is there freedom after death?"

Damon's eyes sharpened on hers. "I don't know."

She watched the boat's lantern reflected in his midnight eyes, the way shadows settled under his cheekbones, accentuating the angles of his face. A beauty used for something evil, to trap souls to feed this realm. "I want another way to free my mother that does not involve sacrificing my own freedom. I won't become one of your silver trees."

"The silver trees are not *mine*," he said, his tone furious. "Don't ever call them mine."

She scoffed. "They might as well be. What have you done to help those folk?"

"You don't know how unfair that is," Damon

whispered. "Every time I've tried to defy my father, I have barely survived the punishment."

She swallowed. She believed him. But could she trust him? After everything she now knew? That Damon had lured her here as some kind of fuel for his father's land of shadows, a prize he got to toy with for nine days before dooming her very spirit?

The problem was, she had no other options. "Well, you've never had an ally before."

Damon gave her a doubtful look. "You're offering to be my ally?"

"Yes. You don't seem to relish the idea of me taking my mother's place."

His lip curled. "I abhor it."

"Then tell me how to defy his claim. Is there any way I can free my mother without being trapped here myself?"

Damon's eyes stayed locked on hers. "Prospect can trade one spirit for another, but I've never seen that done, and no one who has been here nine nights has ever left."

So there's no hope. Thea had to put a hand to the edge of the boat to steady herself, as if she'd been dealt a blow.

Damon put a hand over hers, but she drew

it away. Thea saw they were nearing his castle. After a moment, he spoke again. A muscle jumped in his cheek, making it clear how dangerous he found it to tell her this. "I do think my father has a weakness. It's been many, many years since he went into Thirstwood. Until recently, the wards have kept his shadows from following him there. Other than the night he went to meet your mother, he remains in this realm. When I was a child, he started sending me in his place to hunt for folk."

"Hunt?" she asked.

"To bring folk here to become silver trees or shadows."

The boat reached the shore. Thea stood and stepped out. She was exhausted, but her mind was full of the vital information she'd received—answers she'd craved since her first meeting with Damon.

She couldn't let her mother languish here. That was not an option. Thea was a protector, her role and duty in life. She had always known it. And King Erebus was a power-hungry creature who enjoyed toying with those weaker than himself. She wanted to destroy him.

One of Damon's shadows touched her shoulder. Drawn to her fury? She had plenty of it. She wanted to kill someone. If she could pull Damon's shadows from him, could she use them to fight the king? Hold him at bay while she and her mother escaped? She stroked the shadow, willing it to stay longer. It lingered for another moment before returning to Damon.

"What calculations are going on behind those magnificent brown eyes?" Damon asked, an intense look of scrutiny filling his own. "It's like watching clouds move over the moon."

He was right that she was calculating her plans. When she returned to Thirstwood, she would head straight to the pixie village. Ask Autumn to commune with Thea's mother again. She might know if the king had a weakness. Though the idea of talking to her mother after all this time filled her with excitement, it also made her feel a depth of sadness she had shoved down for seven years.

As he watched her, his expression grew concerned. "You seem tired, Thea. Do you wish to return to Thirstwood? It's very late."

Thea blinked, realizing she hadn't spoken in

a couple of minutes. She had too much to consider. "Yes. I think I've learned enough for one night."

He looked as if he wanted to say more, but he kept glancing around as if he suspected they weren't alone. He inclined his head. "Tomorrow, then."

When the portal opened, Thea stepped through. But instead of stepping into the woods, she found herself back in her bedchamber. Trapped again.

She pounded a fist on her mantel, making the walls shake.

24

> Artifacts of the Ancients
> are much sought, but also
> misunderstood.
> —Old Ones, Ancients, and the Folk

The rest of the day threatened to crawl by almost as slowly as the previous one. Thea watched the Huntsmen practice in the training yard, wishing she was down there sparring with Cedric or Burke. Cassia's bright wings were easily visible, catching sunlight in a way that made them sparkle. Enora's pale hair was braided into her usual crown, and her movements were as graceful and economical as ever, something Thea had always admired about her elder sister. Rozie's bright shock of red hair was a moving spot of color as she wandered the edge of the yard, occasionally stopping by Tibald, making him bend his head to reply to whatever she had said.

Something made Rozie laugh, and Thea's heart contracted with love. She would die to protect any one of her sisters, but she had a soft spot in her heart for little Rozie, who she thought might be the best of them. A pained sort of longing hit Thea as she thought of the time with her sisters that could be stolen from her. She tried to memorize everything about the scene, not knowing when or if she might see it again. When training was over, her sisters turned and waved to her, Enora's face the most worried of the three. Thea waved back, trying to look like she didn't mind her confinement. But she was well aware that each of her sisters would know better.

After sleeping for a few hours, Thea sat at a small table for something she almost never did: She wrote a letter. She intended to produce a detailed account of what had happened to her in the shadow realm, but just as she began, her hand cramped painfully, and she could not form the letters. Disgusted by the restraint of the spell, she almost hurled the quill across the room, but that would only make more work for the lutin who cleaned the bedchambers. Instead, she composed a letter to Autumn: "If something happens to me, know that it went as I expected and tell my sisters everything you know."

There. Simple and direct and her hand had

only twinged once as she wrote the words "tell my sisters." She hoped Winter would return and find it, and deliver it to the other pixie.

The garments appeared on Thea's hearth in early evening.

Thea lifted the newest dress carefully. It was very heavy, and like nothing she'd ever seen. Gold scales ran over the tight-fitting bodice, down the skirt, ending halfway down the thighs. Under that, transparent black fabric flared out, showing glimpses of her legs. The shoulders were curved and came to a point. The sleeves were made of the same transparent black fabric as the skirt, flowing loose over her wrists and hiding her hands. There were no stockings or gloves this time.

Intrigued, she put on the dress, then stared at her reflection in the looking glass. It was unlike anything the Sylvans wore, in a style from a different place, born of a wild imagination. It said something about Damon that he had dreamed of this for her.

The gold scales felt cool against her skin, but soon warmed to her touch. Not gold, she realized, but another metal plated with gold. More like beautiful chain mail. She wondered at the significance of Damon sending her armor. A nod to their deal to be allies? If she was to wear armor, she needed a weapon. Remembering her wish for her dagger the previous night, she strapped the holster to her thigh.

She left her hair loose, trailing down her back. The shoes were black leather half boots with gold laces. She slid one on. As she was about to put on the second, she heard a murmuring outside her door, followed by the distinct sound of unlatching. She expected to see Cassia or maybe Rozie looking triumphant at her own cleverness...

Only to find herself facing the Court Seer. A zing of warning traveled up Thea's spine, though she kept her emotions hidden.

"Hello, Thea," Veleda said, coming into the room. "Did you know there's a major breach in our wards in your bedchamber?" Without waiting for a reply, the Seer moved to the fireplace. "Right here. And it stinks of magic." Veleda turned to face her, eyes burning with accusation as she looked her up and down. "You are wearing one of his dresses. How could you?"

"My mother—" It was all Thea could get out before her tongue froze.

Veleda's hands were curled into fists. "Yes, I

know. I confronted your father, and he told me the truth."

Thea's mouth dropped open. Her father told Veleda everything when he wouldn't tell her or her sisters?

"You are playing with forces far, far more powerful than you can handle. Your mother made an incredible sacrifice to keep you safe, and here you are, throwing it away."

Thea's hands curled into fists. "I'm trying to save her!"

The Seer suddenly looked tired. "Your father told me she's beyond saving."

Thea gasped at the coldness and finality of her father's view. "I don't believe that!"

"It doesn't matter what you believe," Veleda snapped. "You aren't going back there. I placed a spell on the breach so that you can't leave this way again." She swept her hand toward the hearth. "I'm afraid that dress is the last you'll receive from the shadow king."

"This is not from...him," Thea said, trying not to trigger the spell that would stop her tongue. "His son...helping. Allies." She had to choke the last part out before her throat closed altogether.

Veleda laughed. "If he has a son, he's cut from the same cloth as his father. I'd wager Erebus has him do all the nasty things he can no longer do himself. Do you realize they stole one of the artifacts of the Ancients? The silver cup of forgetfulness." She nodded at Thea's shocked expression. "That's what the king uses to confine spirits to his realm. He transforms them, and he makes them forget who they are so they won't break free."

Finally, the Seer was telling her something useful. "How do you counteract it?"

Veleda gave her an incredulous look. "Is that the folly you're pursuing? What has the son of the shadow king told you? You must stay away from him and that place."

"I won't abandon my mother."

"You have no choice." When Veleda came toward her, leaving the door unguarded, Thea did not hesitate. She dodged around her and rushed to leave. Or would have if she hadn't hit an invisible barrier that bounced her backward.

"It's warded," Veleda said calmly as Thea massaged her aching chest. "Only I can step through." She raised her eyebrows at Thea's expression. "You're looking at me like I'm your enemy. I'm only trying to protect you. It's easy for the shadow king and his son to manipulate innocent folk, and impossible to get free once you've realized you trusted the wrong person."

"You're trying to carry out my father's orders," Thea corrected. "Which are not going to protect any of us."

The Seer gave her a skeptical look. "What do you mean?"

"Thirstwood is in danger. If the veil falls..." Her tongue froze. Thea tried to curse but couldn't even get that out. She needed to warn everyone about the shadow king's plans to bring his creatures above and turn everyone into silver trees.

Veleda sighed in a pitying way. "I know you must think what you're doing is right—"

Thea cut her off. "You're not stopping me." Arguing was a waste of breath, especially if she couldn't speak openly. Thea wrapped her arms around Veleda, half carrying her to the doorway. A palpable resistance pressed hard against Thea in the threshold, but it didn't throw her backward this time—as she'd hoped. She'd guessed that the ward was designed to keep Thea in but to allow Veleda both entry and exit. Now, they were too closely entwined for the spell to work properly.

"No!" Veleda said, struggling against her as she started to speak a spell. Acting on instinct, Thea took her fist to Veleda's temple. It was a measured blow, just enough to knock the Seer unconscious. Veleda's eyes rolled back and her body went limp. Thea grabbed her as she fell, placing her gently in the doorway to keep the ward from working.

Quickly, she ran inside her bedchamber to grab the second boot. The moment she laced them up, the boots urged her forward. She stepped over Veleda's unconscious form, ran down the stairs and through the hallways, and past Huntsmen who clearly couldn't see her toward the main doors.

Only to find a massive figure was blocking the doorway that led out of the fortress.

Thea cursed roundly.

Her father.

It took a second to remember that she was invisible. If she was quiet, she could turn around and leave by another route.

The Sylvan king's antlered head lifted. He sniffed as if scenting prey, then raised his arm. He was holding a pair of slippers. Veleda must have snuck into Thea's bedchamber while she'd slept, found the discarded slippers, and taken them to her father. *I should have burned them!*

"Thea," he said, his voice a quiet rumble. "I know where you've been going."

Thea edged backward, step by step, relieved he could not see her. She longed to shout that if she didn't go, she'd be condemning her mother—his wife who'd once brought joy and laughter to the grim fortress—to eternal suffering.

"I know the magic that lures you," her father said, his head turning from left to right as his eyes moved over the entrance hall. "I smell it, as distinct as the night your mother returned from her first visit to the shadow realm." He paused, his gaze roving the entrance hall, fixing on a spot somewhere behind her. "You will not go there again."

In a quick, sharp movement, he reached out and grabbed her, his hand closing over her shoulder.

"Show yourself," the Sylvan king commanded, fire igniting in his eyes.

Thea winced as he found her other shoulder, both of his massive hands weighing her down. The time to be silent was over. "I'm going, Father."

"No." His hands flexed, tightening. Thea

sucked in a pained breath but didn't cry out. She'd endured far worse from past injuries.

"I have a chance to save my mother," she whispered.

His dark eyes reflected a torch on one wall, their flames indistinguishable from the flames that burned in his pupils. "She sacrificed herself to save you, and now you'll throw that in her face?"

"Why did you let her go?" she shouted back. "Why not fight him? That's your way with any other enemy. We fight! We don't give up!"

"There is no fighting him in his own realm," the king said. "Pacts and bargains were made long, long ago, and remain unbreakable."

"Why did you keep it all a secret?" She heard the emotion in her voice, accusation mixed with pleading but found herself unable to hide it. Suddenly, she felt like a child again, begging her father to go search for her mother, her hope painful, her future balanced on the edge of his decision. "Why didn't you reclaim his sacred spaces, rip his trees from the ground, fill his lakes and fountains, declare sovereignty over those parts of the forest? Why let him take anyone at all, least of all your own wife?"

Without seeming to realize it, her father had relaxed his grip on her shoulders, his head bowing so that his antlers loomed over her head. His eyes were flat and blank as he stared, not quite into hers, reminding her that she was still invisible. She could slip away now. She should. *Run!* But another part of her needed answers, longed to hear the truths he was finally telling her.

He spoke slowly, his eyes unfocused. "There is an old magic at work in the place where the shadow lord resides. An ancient magic. Not even I—" His lips slammed shut, and Thea realized he had been about to admit having limitations. Which he would never do. But she understood. Even he was not strong enough to fight the shadow king's magic.

"I have an ally," she told him. "I only need a few more nights." Her father's grip tightened again. "Trust me, Father. Have I ever failed you?"

"Not until recently," he said, his voice hardening to stone. "You have always held my highest trust. Until now."

Every word was a sharpened jab at her heart. "You can still trust me."

"Go back to your bedchamber where you're safe." He released one shoulder, holding the other as if he wanted to propel her there himself. "Throw whatever magic he sent you into the fire. Burn all memory of that place with it. Never speak of it, or your mother, again." He ignored her shocked gasp. "Then and only then will you regain my trust."

Her mouth opened and closed. He wanted her to pretend she hadn't found her mother, didn't know of her suffering?

"No!" she shouted, the word pulled from somewhere deep in her heart. "If I don't at least try to save her, I'll never be able to live with myself."

"If you fail, you won't live at all." His voice rose to a rough gale scouring over rocks. "If you go back there, you will be encased in silver, your spirit alive but helpless in a place with only cruelty and darkness."

So he knew what her mother was enduring. Thea's heart slammed, her stomach churning with horror.

"If you go, you will be lost, too," he said, his voice dropping to a thin wind after a rain. "I will not lose a wife and a daughter. I will not lose another." The flames in his pupils rose high as a terrible certainty came into his eyes. His hand shifted on her shoulder, and as he took a breath, his jaw firming, his intentions became as clear to Thea as if the decision had happened in her own mind. She knew the look he had before he pronounced punishment, before he sentenced someone to a week in a cell with only bread and water. He meant to subdue her by any means necessary. To haul her back bodily and lock her in her bedchamber until the threat had passed.

In a few nights, it would be too late to find another way out of all this.

Fast as thought, she knocked his hand from her shoulder and dodged as he swept toward her. His legs were apart, braced for steadiness, and in that moment, her smaller size was her advantage. Throwing herself forward feetfirst, she slid between his legs, using her hands to vault back to her feet. She took two steps, thinking she was free before her hair was grabbed, her head yanked backward.

She cried out, but knowing this was her father did not dull her warrior's instincts. She went into battle mode. Her hand went to her thigh under the skirt and drew her knife. But if she used a weapon on him, she might as well leave Scarhamm forever because she knew he would never forgive her. It was not so long ago that he had banished another daughter for a lesser betrayal. She threw her head back toward him, hitting his chest with her skull. He didn't let go, but she only needed that moment of surprise to slice off the hair he held, leaving him with a handful of dark brown strands, now visible.

He roared and came at her, blocking the door once more. "I forbid you to go, Theodora!" he said, his body as wide as he could make it, as if daring her to try to pass.

She feinted one way, knowing he must be listening for her movements, then feinted the other, knowing he would anticipate that, too. And when he was leaning left, she went right and skirted around him, making it all the way to the door.

Only to find it locked.

Her father's arms wrapped around her from behind. Cutting off any chance of escape. Ruining her chance of saving her mother. It was all there in her heart in that moment. That this was over. And she had lost for both her mother and herself.

Her father dragged her along the floor of the entrance hall, one arm tight about her torso, careless of the pressure that kept her from drawing a full breath, that made her ribs feel like they would crack. Sharp pain tore through her left side, making her gasp.

And then her boots started to move. They danced and danced, even as Thea's feet hardly touched the floor. The jerky movements somehow pulled her straight from her father's arms. She bolted for the door, which opened just as she reached it. *By what magic?* Shadows swirled around the lock, making it clear what had helped her.

She had no time to be terrified that shadows had appeared inside the fortress. She was outside before her father's footsteps pounded in pursuit. The Sylvan king called on his guard. "Close the gates!"

But the boots had the speed of magic, and soon the gates were behind her and she was in the forest.

25

> The Old Ones loved chaos and
> could not abide its cessation.
> In the end, they were willing
> to destroy their own children
> rather than be restrained.
> —OLD ONES, ANCIENTS, AND THE FOLK

ONCE IN THE SHADOW REALM, THEA fell to her knees, her breaths coming in shallow gasps, her heart quickening with pain. She put a hand to the right side of her chest, waiting for the worst of it to subside before she pushed to her feet, her steps uneven as she made her way toward the river. When the boat slid up silently beside her, she stepped in cautiously, mindful of her bruises, and perched on the seat.

As she reached shore, Damon was silhouetted in the doorway to the castle, cutting a sharp outline that highlighted his upright posture, his perfectly neat hair and clothing. She knew he was beautiful, dangerous, and deadly, but tonight, the shadow prince was more a friend to her than her own father.

Unable to execute her usual nimble jump, she stepped slowly from the boat, resisting the urge to hold her aching side as she made her way with ginger steps toward Damon. Something about her stance must have alerted him. He came down the steps in one jump, moving faster than she'd known he could, reaching for her before she could draw another breath. His warm hands held her upper arms, steadying her. She wanted to curl up against him and rest.

Dangerous, her mind warned. But she was too numb to listen.

"What's wrong?" he asked, the urgency of his tone weakening her defenses. A tingling behind her eyes worsened, Damon's concern activating something inside of her.

"My rib," she admitted, hating to admit vulnerability. She reminded herself she had already cried in front of him and had nothing to hide. "I think it might be broken."

He sucked in a breath, his hands tightening on hers. "Another battle with the Skrattis?"

Her lips curved in a bitter smile. "My father. He wasn't enthusiastic about me coming here."

Damon jerked in shock. She swallowed, watching his face transform in the scant light from the castle, darkening into a fury that could rival the Sylvan king's. The shadows clinging to his neck and shoulders writhed in agitation.

"What did he do?" Damon asked. It was more of an epithet than a question.

"Tried to stop me from leaving the fortress. I can't go home."

As she said it, she realized it was true, and the pain behind her eyes became intense. She turned her head to the side.

"Thea," Damon said, stepping close. His hand found the side of her neck, moving up to cup her chin so he could gently turn her back to face him. "What does he know about what's going on here?"

She met his eyes. "He knows my mother is trapped here. He knows I'll have to take her place to free her." She couldn't hide her bitterness. "He seems willing to let her rot rather than risk anything to save her."

"Don't say more right now," Damon said, his head moving from left to right. He sniffed once, and started to pull her toward the castle. "We have to go inside."

"What is it?" she asked, following him up the stairs.

He pulled the doors shut behind him, then wove a shadow between the handles, leaving it there as if to block it. He had never locked, or even closed, the doors before.

"What's going on?" she asked, her senses on alert. She moved her hand to her skirt, feeling for her knives. "Who are you trying to keep out?"

"Prospect," he said in a low voice. "He's been skulking. He's found some cracks in my protections. I don't think he believed the pretense that you and I had just met. He has a way of sniffing out lies. Come away from the windows." He pulled her to one of the corners where they often spoke, the darkness weaving around them. "The folk who dance here give my castle enough power to fend him off. But..." He gestured toward the ballroom, and Thea turned to follow his eyes. It was empty. Somehow, she hadn't even noticed. "Fewer sources of life force. Less magic. Less protection against enemies."

"Where are the dancers?" she asked, scanning the room to make sure she hadn't missed anyone. She knew it wasn't the ninth night for most of them. The black walls echoed the notes of one of the songs that often played here, but no feet moved in time to its melody.

Damon's nostrils flared, his eyes serious as he turned to face her. "I did something foolish."

Fear tightened her chest. What would the shadow prince consider foolish? "What did you do?"

He paused, sucking in a breath before continuing. "Last night, I..." His face went blank. "I couldn't do it. I couldn't bear to take another. Though I vowed I would never be weak again."

"What do you mean?" she asked, putting her hands to his cheeks to try to ground him in reality instead of the memory that was distressing him.

"I couldn't take their freedom." His eyes found hers and clung, like a man in a swift current who finds something solid to hold on to. "They should have been brought to my father and given the choice. Stay or leave." He paused, his eyes going unfocused as he again surveyed the empty ballroom. "Instead, I told them the truth. It seemed to wake them up. And I sent them home." He swallowed. "I have broken every rule."

"Will they be cursed, though?" Thea asked. "Will they sicken and die if they don't return?"

"I don't know. I think so. My only thought was at least they will be home among family for the time they have left."

He wrapped a shadow between his fingers, wearing it like a glove while smiling gently at it before he allowed it to curl around his arm. "Some of my shadows left me last night when I freed the dancers. They are probably telling my father of my great weakness." His face lost all expression, his eyes cold and hard as he stared at the black wall. "Something truly... unpleasant is in store for me. And despite my best efforts, I'm still not powerful enough to fight him."

"Then where can we go?" Thea asked, grabbing his wrist. "In Scarhamm, we have a war room that is warded on all sides from intrusions or eavesdroppers. Do you have anywhere like that?"

He was silent for a moment, thinking. "My own private quarters have always been beneath my father's notice, and I've made sure to evict all his shadows from there. We won't have long before he comes for me, though. Maybe one night."

She gripped his shoulder, trying to lend him some of her strength. "Then let's go back to your quarters, make plans, and leave before the night is through."

"Thea," he said, his eyes lacking the resolve she'd hoped to see. He looked more sad than determined. "I think your father was right that you shouldn't have come here."

She pulled her hands from him, taking a step back. "But you said my spirit is owed to your father and he'd find me in any case. And if I stayed away, I'd be abandoning my mother."

"What if I was wrong?" he said, his hands fisted by his sides as if to keep from reaching for her again. "My father claims a lot of things. Maybe I've been a fool to believe him. You should go above, hide within the walls of Scarhamm. I'll see what I can do to free your mother. I won't stop trying."

She pinned him with a sharp look. "That is not something I can leave in your hands. If it were your mother, would you entrust her safety to me?"

"Without hesitation," he said, honesty shining in his eyes. "But I would be by your side. I wouldn't leave you to face it alone." He gave her a look that said she'd made her point.

"Exactly." She relaxed a fraction.

"If you choose to stay in your mother's stead, you need to understand that I don't have the ability to free you. You will become like she is now. Trapped. Without speech. Without hope." His jaw clamped shut, his eyes looking haunted.

"I understand. It's my choice to make," Thea replied.

He looked angry, opened his mouth and closed it before replying. "I might never have the power to fight him. I can't become him." He looked as if he'd admitted something shameful.

She stepped forward to put her hands on his face, to tilt it gently so he would meet her eyes again. "I'm glad you will never be him. You have a strength of conscience that won't let you follow in his footsteps. You are so, so much better." And she touched her lips to his.

He closed his eyes, his arms coming around her. Their kiss was brief, harsh, and full of longing and promises neither of them could keep.

26

> The Ancients saw the shadow of
> their own deaths in the eyes
> of the Old Ones
> and began to make plans.
> —*Old Ones, Ancients, and the Folk*

The boat carried them along, steady and silent. A cloud of moon sprites moved ponderously over the water some distance away, creating a sparkling reflection on the smooth surface. A cool breeze ran its fingers through Thea's hair, ruffling the scales on her dress, the muted chime the only sound aside from her labored breathing. She sat across from Damon, her face as impassive as she could make it, though pain forced her to take shallow breaths.

"We need to make a stop first," Damon said, his eyes fixed on her face.

"Where?" Suspicion rose up at this change in plans.

He gave her a knowing look. "I can see you're in pain. I know someone who can help."

"Pain is irrelevant," she said firmly. "I have been injured more times than I can count. Bludgeoned, stabbed, bones broken—"

His expression darkened with each word. "Do you think I want to hear this?"

"—shot with an arrow, and nearly murdered while bathing in the river near my home. So, no, princeling, you do not need to worry about me. I'm as resilient as rocks and tough as boar hide."

"Rocks can split in half," he said, his eyes moving over her, his brows drawn slightly together, "and a boar's hide can be pierced with a lance. You are not invulnerable." When she would have spoken, he held up a hand to stop her. "Let me remind you, this is my realm. You can't find your way without my help. And right now, I am taking you to a healer."

His high-handedness annoyed her, but his concern warmed her at the same time. "Is this healer likely to tell your father our whereabouts?"

"No," he replied with steady conviction. "She won't tell anyone."

Thea couldn't decide if she was more insulted

or touched by his determination to take care of her. She decided to allow both feelings to exist simultaneously, focusing on the work of breathing, which was not easy.

In time, they reached an island, the boat scraping against a sandy shore. However, there was no carefully raked gravel. Instead, scrubby weeds grew on the sand. Thea wondered how plants grew here when she had seen no true growth anywhere else. There were no silver trees. A soft glow came from windows in a small house with a thatched roof, smoke swirling from its chimney.

Damon disembarked and held out a hand for her.

"Your healer's house?" Thea asked, her ribs aching fiercely as she allowed him to help her from the vessel.

"Healer, seamstress." He gave a slight shrug, his hand still holding hers, his other on her elbow. She felt tension humming through him and had the sense he was not as nonchalant as he pretended.

"Did she make my dresses?" She looked down at herself, realizing the metal scales must have given her some protection from her father's rough handling.

"Yes. You look incandescent in that, by the way." His eyes glowed with admiration, his hands flexing on her as if he wanted to draw her closer. "I'm sorry I didn't tell you before."

She had no defense against his compliment in her current condition, and let herself enjoy that one. "Thank you."

After a moment, he released her, turning and moving to the door. Thea saw that it was inlaid with seashells in a pretty, swirling pattern. Damon knocked once and went in.

Inside, a woman sat by the fireplace sewing. She had dark green hair with streaks of white, her features striking, her blue eyes large in a well-defined face. A naiad.

"Where have you been?" the woman asked, finally looking up. As she noticed Thea in the doorway, her face fell.

"Don't worry," Damon said, stepping in and motioning Thea to do the same. "This is Thea. She can be trusted."

"But to bring someone from the dance here?" the woman said, pushing to her feet. "Have you lost your senses?"

Thea's stomach knotted. She clearly wasn't welcome.

"No," Damon said, taking her waist in a firm grip. "I had merely hoped for help for my injured friend."

Thea submitted to Damon pulling her toward the woman.

"My name is Azra," the woman said, her eyes moving over Thea's face in a careful appraisal. "May I check your injury?"

Thea hesitated, then nodded. She said nothing as Azra felt her lower ribs. The healer's hands were warm and gentle.

"Are you having trouble breathing?" Azra asked, her voice kinder now as she looked into Thea's eyes. Probably seeing the signs of pain she couldn't hide.

Thea swallowed. "A little."

Azra tilted her head, pressing until Thea sucked in a breath. "It's cracked, but not broken. I'll bind it and then we'll see how it feels. Damon, go out and give us some privacy." When he hesitated, she added, "I need her to remove her gown." Azra gave him a raised-brow look of challenge. "You want to watch?"

He turned sharply on his heel and strode out.

Azra chuckled, her eyes crinkling at the corners. "I like to make him blush." She went to a cupboard that leaned against one wall and pulled out a basket, foraging in it until she found bandages and a little wrapped packet. "A poultice," she said, holding it up. "For the pain."

"I don't mind pain," Thea said, lifting her chin.

"But Damon minds it." Azra's eyes were shrewd as she looked Thea up and down. "He has always detested the suffering of others. He could never be a healer. Doesn't have the stomach for it."

Azra helped Thea remove her gown, her manner brisk but careful. When the dress was off, the woman held it up and looked at it, her eyes wistful. "Some of my best work. It looks like some of the scales fell off." Her gaze shifted to Thea. "I see now why Damon wanted me to make something special. You are unique."

Azra bound her ribs in an efficient manner, tying the cloth snugly at the end. She put the poultice against the wound, then clucked her tongue as she looked at Thea's arms. "You're all purple. Those bruises must hurt. I'll give the boy a tincture. Maybe he'll be able to convince you to put it on."

It occurred to Thea that the woman must

think her enchanted like the other dancers. "You overestimate his influence over me," she said, defensive at the idea. "I'm not one of those love-stricken guests who'll do anything to be with him."

"I can see you're not at all like the others," the woman said. "Or what I've heard about them, at any rate. Never met one, myself."

"You've never met any of the dancers?" Thea asked, wondering why she tensed to hear the answer.

Azra's eyes cooled. "You mean thralls. And no, he has never brought anyone to see me. He has told me about you, though."

Thea was surprised by that. "What did he say?"

"Good things," the woman said with a small smile. "Now, I've fixed you up as well as I can. But the dress won't fit over the bandages."

Thea looked longingly at the golden scales that felt like armor, but knew the garment wasn't practical. "Do you have anything you won't miss?"

"I've been working on something," Azra said, moving to a trunk set against the wall, reaching underneath a pile of fabric to pull something out. It was a filmy white dress, loose and almost transparent. It looked as if it were made from moonbeams and stars.

"It's too beautiful," Thea said. "I can't."

"You can and will," the woman said, putting it over her head as if she were a small child. Thea had no choice but to put her arms through the sleeves. Azra returned to the trunk and pulled out another garment, a sleeveless robe made from white feathers more beautiful than any Thea had ever seen. "This goes over the dress."

"Truly, I can't. It's obviously meant for someone special."

"I told you," Azra said, putting Thea's arms through the openings and smoothing it over her shoulders. "You are special. And now, you can invite Damon to come back inside."

Thea gave up on trying to understand this strange creature.

She went to the door and opened it. Damon's back was to her, his posture tense as he turned. As he caught sight of Thea, his lips parted on an indrawn breath. When he finally remembered to close his mouth, his eyes did not meet Thea's but went instead to Azra.

"Can you... give us a moment?" Damon said to Thea, his tone apologetic.

"Of course. I'll be in the boat."

Damon was only gone for a few minutes, but when he joined her, his face was tight with frustration.

"What did she say to you?" Thea asked, knowing it was none of her concern but curious.

He merely shook his head. As he waved a hand, the boat pushed off, traveling down the river once again. All was still and silent, the silver trees lining the riverbank on both sides.

"I forgot to thank her," Thea said, feeling a pang of guilt for her rudeness to someone who had eased her pain.

"You'll see her again, I expect," Damon said. "Or at least, she thinks you will. She has some of a Seer's gifts in addition to healing. In fact, she made that chain mail dress for you specifically because she thought you needed extra protection tonight."

Thea sucked in a surprised breath. She *had* needed it. "She used no spells to heal me, though." Veleda sometimes helped with the injured.

Damon watched the water, and Thea had the sense that he was dwelling on some sadness. "She doesn't have that kind of magic."

"I didn't know there were living folk in this

place," Thea said, hoping to draw out more information. "I thought it was the enchanted and their spirits, either shadows or silver trees."

Damon smiled, finally meeting her eyes. "Some have found themselves here through no fault of their own. Your mother is not the only one to have a curse put on her so that she would sicken if she left, who was forced to come back to this place. Most of them try to avoid attracting my father's attention. For obvious reasons."

Thea nodded, knowing there was more he wasn't telling her.

"Is your pain better?" he asked.

"Yes," she admitted. "I'm glad you took me there."

His eyes traveled over her feathery robe and the star-covered sleeves of her garment. "You look even more beautiful than you did in the gold."

She tried to ignore the helpless flush of pleasure at his compliment. Even now, she never knew how much was genuine. Her ribs ached, and she put a hand to them.

His hand reached out for hers, warm and reassuring. "We'll be there soon, and then you can rest."

27

> Noctua, Nerthus, and Solis knew that the Old Ones existed outside of death, so they could not be killed. Neither could they be bound or imprisoned. However, every hundred years or so, they needed sleep.
> —*Old Ones, Ancients, and the Folk*

The boat bumped the shore in an area thick with silver trees. At first glance, it appeared no different from other parts of Iluna: blanketed in darkness broken by the glow from the trees, black gravel underfoot, and an eerie silence. But as Damon helped her alight, she noticed the trees were brighter here, the air fresher. The gravel underfoot was finer, brushed neatly as if raked. He led her down a winding path to a door in what appeared to be a hill.

"This looks like a burial mound," Thea pointed out.

He chuckled. "Perhaps it's appropriate. I sleep like the dead."

He put his hand to the door, and the shadows darted forward and dealt with a lock, a loud click in the stillness. Damon motioned her in. A cramped entryway led to a hallway with doors inlaid with seashells and mother-of-pearl. An intimate hush filled the silence, making Thea's heartbeat loud in her ears. As they walked quietly side by side, Thea sensed that he was nervous.

"You don't bring people here much, do you?" she asked.

"Never," he said simply. He reached out and the shadows unlocked another door before he motioned her into a room.

It was so dark, Thea could see nothing as she crossed the threshold, but she heard Damon moving around. He must know the place so well, he didn't need light.

"A candle would be nice," she suggested.

"Sorry," he said, sounding contrite. "I don't often bother."

Candles flared to life, illuminating a bedchamber about twice the size of Thea's. A massive bed dominated the room, with black curtains enclosing it on three sides. Lacquer end tables held colorful rocks, shells, and worn pieces of sea glass that reflected the candlelight, casting dots of light on the walls. A shelf held books and scrolls, many of which looked very old. Some were even falling apart, as if they'd been read over and over.

"You like reading?" Thea asked, nodding her head toward one of the shelves.

"Yes," he said, and again she had the sense he was anxious. Was he so unused to sharing his personal space? Or maybe it was himself he was unused to sharing. "Though it's not easy to acquire books. I don't suppose you'd approve of how I've come by these."

"Not gifts from your dear father?" she asked dryly.

He didn't crack a smile. "No. He would call this a waste of time."

Her smile faded. Maybe she shouldn't make light of the shadow king. "Then I'm guessing you stole them on your trips to the land above."

"You would be correct. For the most part, anyway. One or two are from Azra. The ones on healing. She thought I might be interested. But I have no talent for that. My shadows are more interested in letting blood out of bodies than keeping it in."

Thea shivered, but she didn't know if it was the mention of his shadows' wish for violence or the chill in the air. Cold had permeated her bones on the boat ride, and the thin material did little to warm her.

Damon must have noticed because a blaze flared to life in a fireplace opposite the bed. Thea went to stand in front of it, putting her hands out to soak up heat. "Ah, that's better."

"You only have to tell me if you want something, and I'll do my best to get it for you," he said, coming to stand beside her. He reached out, then hesitated. She turned to smile at him, welcoming his touch with a tilt of her head. His fingertips brushed her neck as he moved a swath of her hair behind her shoulder, his hands running through it.

"Like the softest material ever woven," he said in an awed hush.

She shook her head. "Azra made some clothes that were softer. I feel bad for ruining so many things, now that I know who sewed them."

"She would understand," he said, swallowing. "But let's not talk about her. Or anyone else."

Thea turned to face him, watching the way the light and shadow played over his impossibly perfect features. His shadows moved slowly, as if tired.

He shook his head, blinking. "There is something so alive about you. An energy that fills a room. My shadows felt it from the moment you came to my realm." He paused, his lids growing heavy as he inhaled deeply. "It's like a breath of pure forest air, a wind from the mountains." He shook his head, his smile chagrined. "I should not try to be poetic. I'm not good at it."

"Is this the kind of thing you say to the folk above to lure them here?" she asked, unable to stop herself.

He pulled his hand from her shoulder, tension in his shoulders. "I don't usually have to go to the trouble."

"Your good looks are enough to befuddle them," she said.

His voice grew clipped, but she had the sense his anger was directed at himself. "My allure winds around their hearts, twisting them and tying them in knots, stealing their good sense, and dooming them."

She believed that he regretted his actions, but

she would not let him off so easily when he had trapped people's spirits the same way her mother's had been. She needed to know if his change of heart was permanent. "But you did it anyway."

He met her eyes. "I did, though I hated it. It's the only way to get power here. The only way to draw some of the shadows away from my father, which he allows for some reason. Maybe to test my strength. Maybe because he knows he is still stronger. I have never understood the game he plays with me." Thea watched his face darken, his hands fist at his sides. "But no matter how heartless I try to be, the shadows know my father is crueler. I can't gain their allegiance."

"What about these?" she asked, lifting a hand to point at the ones that wove around his neck like a scarf.

He put a hand to his neck as if stroking a cat. "These ones don't seem to care about cruelty, only emotion. I'm able to give them a surfeit of that. The hatred I feel for my father alone keeps them fed."

Thea wondered how all this could end. "Aren't you his heir? Won't you take the throne someday, anyway? Why not end the dance, leave this place, and come back to the throne when he dies? Last night you chose mercy. You can't go back to harvesting spirits. Surely, you see that."

"The word *heir* is meaningless in this case." Damon pulled a book from his shelf, opening its frail pages carefully. "Erebus is one of the Old Ones. He can't be killed. He will never die."

Thea's breath caught at this confirmation of what the pixies had told her. The Old Ones were primordial beings who came before the Ancients. What hope did she have of fighting Erebus?

"You know that my father's shadows are already finding cracks, coming into your forest, making new creatures out of whatever they find. What I don't know is whether or not my father or Prospect is encouraging them or if the shadows are innovating on their own."

"Does it matter?"

"It matters whether they are under my father's control. If his ambition has outstripped his power and the shadows get free…"

The idea of bloodthirsty shadows running rampant in Thirstwood was horrifying. "How did you plan to dethrone him?"

"The same way the Ancients took power from the Old Ones. They put them to sleep." Damon waved a hand toward a pile of scrolls. "Every three score years, my father has to go into a slumber for a full moon cycle. Without that sleep, he would start to age."

Thea understood that basic need for sleep. Sylvans had to go into their birth tree about once every twenty years or so to rest for a few weeks. They also retreated into their trees if they were ill or injured badly. The tree's energy repaired and rejuvenated them.

"There are signs he needs to sleep soon," Damon said. "And he's been pushing me to gather more folk for the dance. The more spirits guarding this realm, the more protected he will be in slumber."

"And you plan to keep him asleep?" she guessed.

"There's an artifact," he said, his eyes shining. "The lute of slumber. If I could only get my hands on that... You've heard of it?"

"If you'd asked me that six months ago, I would have said no. But now?" She thought of everything that had happened with the Solis Gemma, the artifact that her sister wore on her finger. "My sister, Cassia, told me stories of artifacts, everything she discovered in her research about her ring. I understand you have one here. The silver cup of forgetfulness?"

He watched her, his eyes piercing. "Yes. It's how my father makes the silver trees. But I don't believe it would work on him. After all, he's the one who stole it."

"Did he steal it himself?" Thea asked. "His shadows could have helped."

Damon regarded her thoughtfully. "I hadn't considered that. I suppose he might never have touched it."

"Which means he could be vulnerable to it," Thea added.

After a pause, Damon sighed. "Regardless, there'd be no way to get him to drink from it. His shadows protect him." He shook his head. "There are three artifacts that I know about: the cup, the lute, and the ring. Is it possible we can use the Solis Gemma to find the lute?"

Thea didn't see how. It wasn't as if the ring could answer questions. "I wouldn't pin my hopes on that. But if Cassia can help, she will." She hated to think that right now, Cassia must be worrying about her. Enora, too. Rozie would be beside herself. "I want to be able to tell my sisters everything, Damon. You said you had nothing to do with the magic that stops my tongue, but... is it true? Or can you tell your shadows to let me speak?"

Damon's expression tightened. "I don't know. I've never tried. But it's one thing to trust you. It's another to trust someone I have never met, even if she's your sister."

"I trust them with my life," Thea said. "Isn't that enough?"

"I trust no one like that," he said, still skeptical. "Except Azra."

That made Thea wonder. "It's easier to trust family," she said, hoping he would share how Azra was connected to him.

"Depending on the family," Damon said bitterly, reminding Thea who his father was. "As to that, here's the other reason I hoped I could win my father's throne." He picked up the book and turned the pages before handing it to her. "Read this."

The text appeared to be similar to Old Sylvan, but it was an older form mixed with Runic. Enora could read Runic, but neither Thea nor Cassia had ever bothered to learn.

"What does it mean?" she asked, admitting, "I can't read much of it."

"A Seer prophesied that Erebus could be brought down by someone who shares his unnatural power. That the corruption of thrall magic would come back to haunt him in the form of his own creation."

Thea tilted her head to the side. "You."

"He's sired many children over the years. He brought them all here, one by one, to test them. None of them survived. Only me. I believe he sees me as the one who could bring about that prophecy."

Thea's stomach roiled. "Why didn't he kill you, then?" she asked, ignoring the surge of rage that threatened to cloud her logic. "Eliminate the threat."

"He needs me to bring him new spirits. Since he either can't or won't go above anymore, and I have that ability." He paused, his eyes taking on that distant look she often saw when he talked about his father. "And I think he enjoys tormenting me too much to let me go easily. Despite my efforts to hide it, I think he knows I despise the work he makes me do. And that delights him."

"Did you ever think of just running away?" Thea asked.

He paused, his face closing off. "Of course I

have. In fact, I had it planned out once. But... even if I could go back to where I came from, my father would find me."

"Where you came from?" she asked, confused. Hadn't he always been in this realm?

"I wasn't born here," he said, his expression wistful. "I lived in an area with lakes and streams, near a waterfall. When I was five years old, I was ripped from my mother's arms and brought here alone, left in the dark with the shadows who tormented me to see if I could survive. I almost didn't."

"Damon," she said, stepping close to him. Though she wasn't the most practiced at offering sympathy, her heart ached, and she knew something needed to be said. "I'm sorry. What happened to your mother?"

"My father left her for dead after cursing her with a terrible illness." A murderous light came into his eyes, but he rubbed his forehead, hiding his face from her. "Anyway, he delights in letting me enjoy small victories only to punish me with them later. That was how the castle came to be. When I was about fifteen, I met some folk during my trips above. I actually enjoyed their revels and started to sneak out to them more and more. But my father found out and used one of his roots to bring many of them here. He took their spirits, in the end. I had to face the fact that people who had been kind to me were punished eternally for it." He pressed his lips together.

"It wasn't your fault," Thea said, stepping closer.

He shook his head, negating that. "There's something else in the prophecy. For Erebus to be defeated, a great sacrifice is needed."

"From the person who defeats him? What does that mean?"

"I think it means I have to give something up." He set the book down and looked at her. "Something I love."

"Hmm." She tugged at her lower lip, thinking. "Well, what do you value most?"

He braced his hand against the mantel as he stared into the flames. "There is someone I should have let go of long ago to protect her. The only person I know who ever managed to escape this realm, though she ended up coming back."

He turned his head and met her eyes, one half of his face burnished by firelight. "She found where my father had taken her son and followed in secret, at great risk to herself."

Damon paused, watching her reaction. Thea suspected she knew who he meant.

She merely nodded at him to go on.

"I gave her a safe haven—that small island hidden by my shadows—so I can visit. I have held on to the only good thing I ever had. The only person who ever cared about me."

Thea's heart clenched at the pain she saw in his eyes. "I wondered by the way she treated you and how you behaved toward her." She placed a hand on his shoulder. "Azra?"

Damon nodded. "My mother."

28

> The Ancients searched until they found artisans of great skill. First, they bade a lapidary find a perfect piece of amber, which was set into a gold ring. Second, they hired a silversmith to fashion an elaborately decorated cup. Finally, they commissioned the crafting of a lute made of the finest rosewood.
>
> —Old Ones, Ancients, and the Folk

"She loves you," Thea said, her throat thick with emotion at the thought of what Azra had sacrificed to be near her son. She lived in isolation in a dreary world where discovery would mean her death.

"Yes." Damon's lips twisted. "She didn't deserve any of what happened to her. The worst part is, because she once loved Erebus, she cannot leave this realm without his permission. He doesn't know she's here, but Prospect would be alerted. And either way, the curse is still upon her. She would sicken if she left. My mother found that out when she tried to escape once." He let out a long, slow breath.

"Some of your shadows guard her island?" Thea asked.

He nodded. "I leave the strongest and most loyal ones there. They even help to catch fish for her, and to gather firewood. I bring her fabric and she sews." He looked at Thea as if worried she'd accuse him of selfishness. "Not for my sake. That was her trade before my father… She's talented."

"Incredibly so. Both as a healer and tailor," Thea said, drawing a proud nod from Damon. "But because of that prophecy, you think you'll have to sacrifice her, your own mother, to defeat your father?"

Damon turned back to the fire. "I have never cared about anyone else. Well…" He turned to look her in the eye. "Until I met you."

Thea's breath caught in her chest, a lightness filling her as warmth spread to her hands. Could he truly feel so much for her in such a short time? They barely knew each other, after all. But she'd felt a connection to him from the moment they'd met. She reached out and placed her palm on his cheek, another burst of warmth coursing through her as his eyes fluttered closed.

"I wish we had more time," he said, his eyes opening to stare deeply into hers.

"So do I." Her mind turned over their situation quickly, trying to find a solution. If she couldn't tell people about the shadow realm, surely Damon could. And if not, well, they could at least enlist some allies in this fight.

"Come with me to Thirstwood. We'll get word to my sister and ask for access to the library in Welkincaster. I'll explain on the way."

"Prospect can tell whenever someone uses a root to enter or leave this realm," Damon said. "He'll know where we're going and he'll follow. At this point he'll have orders to bring me to my father for punishment. And he'll bring you back, too."

Thea cursed roundly. Another obstacle. Another problem she didn't know how to solve. She was drowning in a terrible sense that they were running out of time. She had never felt so much protective anger without any outlet. Normally, she'd love a good fight, but suddenly she felt exhausted.

"You need rest," Damon said, his eyes sharpening with concern as he noticed her expression. "Take my bed for a few hours."

Thea wanted to refuse, but she was falling asleep on her feet. "Maybe for an hour or two. But only if you rest, too."

He didn't argue, but smiled fondly at her frown. "I'll sleep by the fire."

Thea looked around. There was no other furniture but a wooden chair and an animal hide on the floor. She took his hand, enjoying the slightly rough texture of his skin, its warmth and strength. "Your bed is so large, I wouldn't even know you were in it. Share it with me, Damon."

He moved close, and the spice of his scent filled her mind. She wanted to taste him. His lips touched hers, moving lightly, tenderly. He put his hands on her shoulders and pulled her close. As she pressed against him, touching her tongue to his lips, his hands moved to her waist, then her back, clutching her closer.

Yes. This was what she wanted. His unbridled intensity. His need. His truth.

Their kiss was deep and long, tasting each other until Thea pulled away for air. As he pressed his hands tighter to her back, her ribs ached and she winced.

He immediately pulled away, shaking his head as if clearing it. "I'm sorry." Taking her hand firmly, he tugged her toward the bed. "Enough, Thea. You're in pain."

"There's more than one way to deal with pain," she said with a wicked grin. "Trust me, I've tried quite a few of them."

He lifted a brow at her, an uncertain look entering his eyes. "I suppose this is what jealousy feels like. I dislike it."

The prince of shades who has charmed so many, jealous? She placed her hands on his cheeks. "No need. My eyes are only for you right now."

"If I had my way..." he said, looking away from her, his expression one of longing.

She waited, nearly holding her breath out of curiosity. What did he want from her? What were his hopes?

He cleared his throat. "Best not to talk about the future."

Disappointment mixed with relief. She had

no idea what he might have said, but perhaps it was best if she didn't know.

"I agree." She put her arms around him, and his lips returned to hers. He took steps backward, pulling her with him. She broke the kiss as he sat on the bed. He pulled her into his lap.

"If you wanted me in bed, you only had to say so."

"*You* will be in the bed," he said firmly, his rapid pulse beating in his neck. "And *I* will be on the floor."

"Don't turn heroic now, Shadow Stranger. What good is that?" She met his overly serious gaze with a wider grin. "Is that really what you want?" She angled her head and hovered her lips near his neck, enjoying the satiny skin over corded strength. She pressed a kiss there, smiling as he sucked in a breath. When she pressed another kiss to the spot where his neck met his shoulder, he groaned. His shadows had started moving around her, like cats who wanted to be stroked. Thea wondered if Damon noticed.

His hands came to her upper arms, holding her away. "Thea. What if it's my magic making you feel this way?"

She pulled back, meeting his eyes. "I thought you said you weren't using it."

"I'm not," he agreed, his brows pulled together. "Firmly holding it in check as far as I know. But what if I'm not always aware of it? What if I want you so badly the magic is out of my control?"

She knew for certain that wasn't why she wanted him. She had learned to sense his magic. Meeting his father had made her even more aware of the charm and how it felt when it was being used on her.

No, it was *Damon* that was making her feel this way. "The magic isn't out of your control. Think, Damon. Does longing usually make you lose control of your powers?"

"No," he said, relaxing a fraction. "The only thing that makes me lose control of my power is..." His eyes shifted to hers, assessing.

She waited, wondering if he would trust her enough to tell her.

"Being trapped," he said in a low voice. "The fear that goes with being trapped, feeling as if I'm being buried alive. When I was in the cave, I lost control. I was a gibbering mess by the time Prospect came to pull me out."

Nausea turned her stomach at the thought of

what he must have endured, feeding the blaze of her anger toward his father. "What are the consequences of you losing control like that?"

He stared at the middle distance. "The trees outside the cave started to wither. For a week or so afterward, my charm seemed to come out in waves without me realizing it. I went above a few days later, and even the creatures of the forest were enchanted. A fox followed me for a while before I realized it was charmed, too." He frowned, one of his dark brows lifting. "You're laughing at me."

"You're comparing me to a lovesick fox. I can't help finding it funny. Don't you have a way to know when a woman has succumbed to your magic? Some way to test the hold you have over her before you ask her the crucial question about whether she wants to return home?"

His expression turned serious, his lip curling as if he found the idea distasteful. "I have never... tested to see if anyone was thoroughly enthralled."

"I mean, when they were willing to..." She nodded her chin to indicate the bed.

Damon pushed her away from him, only an inch or so but enough to make her pull in a breath as it jostled her aching ribs.

"I'm sorry," he said immediately, his eyes showing regret as he cradled her closer again. "I didn't mean to hurt you. But..." He cleared his throat. "You think I took them to bed."

She gave him a questioning look. "Well...it's logical to wonder."

"Never," he said, looking disappointed in her. "How could I? They were not acting of their own free will."

Relief coursed through her that he'd never crossed that line. Still, he couldn't be absolved of everything. "But after the ninth night, you presented them to your father, who turned them into silver trees."

"Yes." He took a deep breath, a faraway look in his eyes. "I know."

It reassured her that he didn't defend nor try to excuse his actions. His lips were drawn tight, his eyes downcast. Thea felt his tension and guilt. And though he needed to feel those things, she didn't like to see him lost in them. She put her hand inside the collar of his shirt, watching his eyes dilate. "There is something about you that draws me, even if I despise the things you've done."

He closed his eyes.

"I also have a father who is..." She hesitated. She still didn't feel right condemning her father to an outsider. "Harsh and unbending. I know what it's like to try to live up to someone with greater power than yourself. I've nearly killed myself more times than I can count doing things to impress my father." She blinked, surprised she had said that. A strange doubt had come over her lately, a suspicion that some of her beliefs were not as unshakable as she had thought. She wondered if some of her bedrocks were made of sand.

"You admire him," Damon observed.

"I used to want to be exactly like him." She shrugged. "Maybe I started questioning that need to please him when I first came here. I don't know. But I don't want to be as much like him as I once did. As you don't wish to be like yours."

"If I let that go, I let go of any hope of making this realm bearable. Any hope of saving people from falling into it. Any hope of saving myself." He wrapped his finger around a lock of her hair, tugging gently. "Any hope of happiness."

"Not necessarily." She put a hand to his cheek. "You have his shadow powers. I have strength, determination, and I can enlist my sisters. Not to mention my father's forest magic if we can convince him to face your father instead of running. He seems almost...scared."

"No one has ever challenged my father here. Not even Noctua, not even when he has broken vows. There is some pact that protects him. Maybe that's why he almost never leaves this realm."

"What if he hadn't come for my mother?" Thea asked. "Could she have avoided him?"

"She would have sickened and eventually died. If what my father says is true—though I am starting to question his claims—her spirit would have ended up here rather than going to the Netherwhere. But Thea, you have to rest. Please. Get some sleep."

Seeing his implacable determination, she sighed and moved from his lap, crawling on hands and knees to the head of the bed where fluffy pillows beckoned. A groan from Damon made her smile. He must have turned his head to watch her, seeing her body through the filmy fabric.

"I will sleep on one condition." She turned the covers back, a black quilt edged with fur. She patted the space next to her. "You have to sleep in the bed with me. Not on the floor. You're no good to me if you're exhausted tomorrow."

He rubbed his face. "You are determined to torment me." Sighing, he dropped his hands to his lap and looked at her with his starry night eyes. "Fine. I will sleep in the bed. *Sleep*, Thea. I do not take advantage of young women in my realm. Not even the one I want above all others."

She smiled to herself as she closed her eyes. Her Sylvan senses told her he was indeed being truthful with her about wanting her above all others. And the rest of it, too. He wanted her. Badly. That was good. Because she didn't know how long she could go without having him.

29

Solis drew light from the sun, placing it into the amber gemstone. Nerthus dug deep into the ground to where the earth slumbered, and fed this somnolence into the cup. Noctua wove a lullaby into the rosewood lute, calling on the magic she used to soothe spirits into peace.

—*Old Ones, Ancients, and the Folk*

THE SHADOW CREATURE REACHED out with distorted hands, its long fingers stretching toward Thea's face. She scrambled backward in a crab walk of terror. Her back hit the trunk of a tree. Its branches wrapped around her, as if she were an intruder in the forest. She struggled against its hold, but it clutched her tighter, whispering: "You'll never leave here…"

Thea sat up, panting, her eyes wide, searching

the shadows. But then she turned her head and saw Damon, his eyes worried as they stared into hers. Shadows rested around him like fallen scarves. It seemed they slept, too. She reached out to him, needing to touch something solid and real.

"You were having a bad dream." His voice was scratchy from sleep, and he had a soft, tousled look that made Thea's heart contract. "What was it?"

Her stomach churned at the sensation of being trapped. She didn't want to talk about it. "I'm cold. Warm me."

"Thea." Her name was tinged with warning. "This is not a good idea." But he sighed and lifted the blanket to reveal the empty space between them. Eagerly, she filled it, wriggling close to him, her whole body relaxing as she pressed against him breast to hip, her legs tangling with his. A part of her wondered why she perceived him as safe and comforting when he could be the most dangerous person she'd ever known. But she didn't want to think, only to feel.

For a few minutes, they didn't speak. Damon reached up and put a hand to her head, tentatively at first, moving his palm over her temple then tangling his fingers in her hair as he pulled them through toward her nape. Thea closed her eyes, letting herself bask in the pleasure of his touch.

"So soft," he whispered. Amusement crept into his voice as he added, "The deadliest daughter of the Sylvan king winding around me like a house cat is not something I could have imagined."

"Enora might take offense at you calling me the deadliest." She opened her eyes, grinning mischievously. "But you would be right."

Damon's lips twitched. "Humblest, too."

Thea swept a hand over his arm, enjoying how his muscles tensed and relaxed under her hand. "I've never actually spent the night with anyone." At least, she had never gone to sleep and woken up with anyone else.

"Elaborate?" He lifted an eyebrow.

She shrugged. "Sylvans aren't shy about coupling, but there are different rules for the king's daughters. We're supposed to behave with more decorum. I don't invite anyone into my bedchamber. And it wouldn't look good if I spent the night in anyone else's."

"You talk so openly about these things." The

expression in his eyes was curious to the point of awe.

"I don't suppose you have anyone to talk to," she guessed. "Prospect doesn't seem like the type to dispense useful advice."

His lip curled. "I've never been fool enough to ask him. And he's not a topic I'm eager to talk about at the moment, either, if I'm honest."

"Which I think you are sometimes. Honest, that is." She turned her head to breathe in his scent, which she found intoxicating.

He lifted the edge of her collar to trace a fingertip over her collarbone. "You are tempting beyond words."

"This dress is barely there. Almost as if your mother was trying to push us together." She tilted her head to check his expression. "Some people might think your decision to bring me to meet your mother was a meaningful gesture." She treated him to a wide grin. "Didn't you worry you'd give me ideas?"

He barked a laugh. "What? That I was eligible for marriage? Thea, please. Who would ever marry me? Who would want to live here?"

She bit her lip, thinking of the lack of sun, the emptiness, the shadows watching and listening everywhere. The only people who stayed were enchanted.

"I used to dream of escaping," he said, his body curving around her subtly, as if he wasn't aware he was doing it. "But I have become too much a part of this realm. Even if I were to leave here, my shadows would follow. I would enchant every creature I see. This is the only place I can fully control my magic. I'm as trapped here as the silver trees."

Underlying his light tone was a vein of deep sadness. It made Thea's chest ache—the thought of him being so alone forever. She had an urge to give him hope. She wanted him. And now she knew his magic had nothing to do with it. Finding out more about him, about his attempts to defy his father, his efforts to save his mother, made her see him in a new light. He wanted to get out of this realm, this life. It was up to him how to do that, but she might be able to help.

"Have you considered you might be controlling it the wrong way? Your shadows like it when we kiss." She cupped his cheek in her palm, enjoying its planes, and rubbed her lips across his, absorbing his groan with a flutter of pleasure. "How do you know they wouldn't be as enticed by passion as they are by cruelty? Have you ever tried it?"

"I'm intrigued," he said, his eyes as dark as midnight, his pulse jumping visibly in his neck. "Are you offering to help me perform a test?"

She kissed her way up to that pulse point. "I think I've made it clear that I am."

His breathing grew heavy, his rapid pulse swelling under her lips. He shifted, his muscles taut against her wherever they touched.

"I want you," he breathed, "like I have never wanted anyone or anything in my entire life."

She felt the same. Her hand found where his shirt met his waistband. She straddled him, letting the covers fall off to pool on her legs. Her breasts were near his face, his eyes on her with such intensity, it made her heart stutter. She slid her fingers through his hair, knowing he liked that.

His eyes closed. "I can't fight this."

A rush of heady power washed over her. The hard muscles of his stomach contracted under her touch. "I only want to do what gives you pleasure."

"Anything you do to me will give me pleasure," he said hoarsely. "Unless you gut me with one of those knives you wear on your thigh. Or if you leave."

"Then we agree," she whispered, flutters of desire pulling low in her belly. She'd forgotten about the knives, though. Those would have to go. She reached down and unbuckled the thigh strap that held them.

Damon's eyes followed the movement. "It would be a great disappointment if you killed me now, Thea. In case you were considering it."

She laughed, adoring the way he looked at her as if she were something divine. A few days ago, she might have contemplated using the daggers on him. Might have planned it. But not now.

After dropping the knives on the floor, she came back to him, sliding her body along his, and watched his pupils dilate, his lips parting for air. "Please," he said simply, as if she would know what he needed.

She did.

As he drew the filmy material from her body, Thea looked down at him, all burnished in firelight that hugged the muscular curves and lean hollows of his body, and thought, *He is the shadow prince.* Then immediately after, *It doesn't matter. I want him.*

When he lifted himself up, bracing on one elbow as his lips moved to her chest, his tongue as soft as a butterfly's wing, she lost all ability to think.

30

> The magic of the Old Ones is chaotic by nature. It is hard to control, and harder still to bear for any mortal.
> —*A Seer's Guide*

Pleasure drowned out her pain, and by the time Thea slept, she'd all but forgotten her cracked rib. When she woke, she opened her eyes to brighter light but no fire in the fireplace. Her hand came out to search for Damon, but the sheets were cold and empty.

She sat up, letting the blanket fall from her, then as quickly snatched it back over herself. A gray cowled figure sat in the chair by the fire.

"Prospect," she spat, the word a curse on her tongue. "Get out."

The Seer's chin lifted. "Don't think I care anything for your state of undress. I am here by orders of my king. I am to bring you to him."

"I haven't been here nine nights, you toad," she told him, hurling a pillow. His shadows snaked out and deflected it. Thea contemplated more projectiles, but no doubt he'd block them, too.

Prospect's hood cast shadows that blended with the darkness swirling around him. "The number of nights has no bearing. The king demands to see you. Now."

She looked around the room, starting to feel the tendrils of fear. "Where is Damon?"

Prospect pushed to his feet. "He reported to his father hours ago. Come. Don't keep him waiting."

Thea clutched at hope that this was a bluff. "Damon wouldn't leave without telling me."

"He wasn't given a choice." Prospect took a step toward the bed. "You don't seem to understand how things work here. The king commands. We obey. If someone resists, he sends his shadows to enforce his word. There is no method by which to fight him. Not here. And soon, not above, either. Soon, your world will be a part of his."

Her heart slammed her aching ribs at the reminder that there was so much more at stake than herself and her mother.

Prospect opened the door, allowing in a blast of cold air. "Hurry. Meet your fate bravely like the Huntsman you are so proud to be."

Thea's back stiffened, her pride responding to his challenge. She threw off the blanket and got to her feet, snarling when the Seer didn't look away, "You seem to care a little for my state of undress. Avert your eyes, Seer, or I'll take them out."

He turned his head away. "Your bravado won't help you."

"Then what will?" It was a gamble to ask, knowing he wasn't likely to tell her anything useful, much less the truth.

"Only the Ancients can save you now." The Seer's eyes were mostly hidden by shadow, but she caught his expression in profile, which was stiff and serious. "And this realm is untouched even by them."

She yanked the filmy gown over her head, grabbing the feather robe. "What are you, anyway?" she asked as she put her arms through the openings. "Sylvan, Azpian, human, what?"

"Old," he said, his voice acerbic. "Now hurry. The king doesn't like to be kept waiting."

Thea felt as if she were still naked as she stood in front of King Erebus's dark throne, his shadows whirling like smoke. Cold seeped from the gravel stones beneath the thin soles of her slippers, making her shiver. She wished she were wearing armor instead of the thin gown and robe.

"The Sylvan queen's daughter," Prospect said, bowing.

Thea's stomach lurched as she noticed her mother's silver tree leaning toward the throne instead of away. As she watched, one of the branches touched the king's shoulder, a quiet scrape of bark against cloth. Erebus's eyes narrowed. Casually, he reached up and plucked a leaf from it, smiling as he brought it to his lips. "Ah, my lovely Coventina, how sad I will be to see you go. You have given me such comfort, staying by my side in the eternal night of my realm. I have peeled your bark in my anger, stripped you of your leaves, and yet you still stay, your spirit as strong as ever, feeding my power."

As Thea imagined the cruelties her mother had endured, she couldn't control her fury. "You're weak!" she shouted, taking a step toward him. "Stealing power from those who have no choice, abusing folk with no defense against you. Taking their freedom. You're a monster."

The king's shadows moved toward Thea, and she braced herself for their attack, but instead, they swirled around her for a moment before Erebus made a gesture, calling them back. He looked puzzled, as if he hadn't expected that. His eyes swept over her in a thorough appraisal. "My willow," he said, as if that were an endearment. "So strong, so confident. Perhaps with all that passion, your leaves will be sweeter than your mother's. I still find hers to be somewhat bitter." He bit into the leaf he held, the rip of his teeth making Thea wince at the implication: that he was devouring a part of her mother, taking from her spirit, taking what was not given freely.

She wanted him dead. No, not just dead… *obliterated*, as if he'd never been.

"You don't seem surprised to learn that it is your mother here, beside me." He tilted his head toward the tree. "No doubt my son told you."

"Where's Damon?" Thea demanded, still desperately scanning the corners for signs of him.

"He is taking some time away to think," Erebus replied, his light tone at odds with the menace in his eyes. "You see, he has been disobedient and must feel the consequences."

Thea hated him more and more with each

word. "I want to see him." When he tugged at another silver leaf, she took two steps toward him, halting when his shadows snaked out to block her. "If you touch my mother one more time, I will dismember you."

His laugh rose and faded into the void all around them. "Your bravado is entertaining. But pointless."

A shiver ran through her at the cold certainty in his eyes. Thea crossed her arms, trying to hold herself together. "You had no right to demand my presence here. I don't have to appear before you until my ninth night."

"Ah," he said, tapping his chin. "You have heard the rules, and you believe I must abide by them. How charmingly innocent. Those were merely privileges I offered to Damon so he could gain some magic for his small domain. And I grew impatient to see you."

Impatient to see if she was stronger than her mother? Thea's stomach churned at the terrible choice she would be offered, though she knew in her heart how she would decide. She could not leave her mother here when she could send her home to Enora, Cassia, and especially Rozie—who needed a mother more than ever at her age.

And... maybe someday Damon would find a way to free her. The thought gave her a little comfort. "I know my choice," she said. "Offer it to me and be done."

"There is," the king said slowly, "another possibility."

Thea raised her chin, knowing he must be playing with her. "What is it?"

He rested his head against the back of the throne, staring down at her through half-lowered lids. "Your first option is to trade places with your mother. You will never be able to speak nor move, aside from a slight shake of branches now and then when you are in a mood, as your mother is frequently of late." He glanced at the tree beside him, smiling slightly. "But you will be my most prized of silver trees, getting my attention daily for the rest of your blessed existence." He turned his head to the Seer. "Not a bad choice, wouldn't you say, Prospect?"

"No, sire," the Seer agreed eagerly. "A generous offer, indeed."

Thea glared at Prospect. She wished she could stab the insufferable sycophant in the throat so he could never simper again.

"But I feel so generous," the king went on,

"that I am offering a second option." His expression changed to one of woe. Thea was reminded of a poor playactor who'd once performed in Scarhamm's great hall. "You are healthy. Strong. Young. All the qualities I've needed by my side and lacked until fate delivered you to me."

Thea's tiny spark of hope was dying. She had the feeling he was about to offer her something worse than being bound in silver.

"My shadows are drawn to desire, revelry, wildness, and chaos," he went on. "They sense all these things in you. Damon, on the other hand, has always had to fight to gain their allegiance. I thought perhaps he had potential, but in the end, I was disappointed. My son has shown himself to be weak."

"He's twice the man you are," Thea said, sick to think this was the abuse Damon had to endure.

Erebus moved his index finger in a small gesture, and the shadows converged on her, slamming into her back and shoulders and taking her to her knees. The sharp gravel cut through the thin cloth and into her skin, drawing blood. She met the king's eyes, refusing to bow her head.

"As I said, strong." His tone was triumphant.

"Unbending. Unwavering. Because of these qualities, I am offering you another choice. You may free your mother and also keep your own freedom, Theodora. All you need do is swear allegiance to me... with a Sylvan vow."

Thea's lips parted, her breath coming in short bursts. That was his offer? That was not freedom. Pledging to follow Erebus would be worse than being a mere witness to his cruelty. He would expect her to perpetrate atrocities along with him.

"I understand my choices," Thea said. "Let me be clear, Erebus. I have no intention of swearing allegiance to someone as petty and cruel as you."

A shadow came forward and wrapped around her face over her mouth, silencing her. Another shadow took a hunk of hair at the back of her head and forced her to look at the king. She put all her hatred into her stare.

Erebus stared back, his lips curving as he noticed the branches waving near his face. "Coventina, my love." He reached up and stroked a finger over one silver bough. "Your daughter is so much prettier when she's quiet, don't you think?" The branches shook violently, one of the leaves falling onto the king's shoulder. He brushed it off, with an air of lazy amusement. "So emotional. You really must calm yourself."

Thea's throat ached as she grappled with the shadows over her mouth, trying to fling them off so she could tell him what she thought of his suggestions.

"Another small detail before you decide," King Erebus added, pausing for an agonizingly long moment before continuing. "Damon is in the cave. I assume he's told you of it?"

Thea tried to suck in a breath and choked on shadows.

"He is trapped there with no way out." The king pretended to sound sad, but his eyes were bright with pleasure. "He is cold, scared, sick with worry for you. And dying."

Her body jerked as she registered that last word.

"I'm afraid I was rather displeased with him when I reminded him of his duty and...well, he did not apologize. We had a disagreement. He ended up in rather poorer condition than when you last saw him." He added a head shake, false regret oozing from him like stale sweat.

Thea managed to grasp one of the shades. She yanked it away from her mouth, sucking in air. "You're saying I can save him?"

The king's lips parted, and Thea wondered if the fact that she'd moved a shadow of her own volition shocked him. But he soon hid his consternation behind a mask of calm. "If you choose the offer to swear allegiance to me, I will order him taken from the cave and allow Prospect to heal him."

"Can he truly do that?" she shot back, glaring at the Seer.

Erebus nodded. "He is a surprisingly effective healer when he is allowed to be. Prospect? A demonstration."

The Seer came forward, stopping out of Thea's reach. "My shadows sense you are injured." The dark shapes swirled about her torso, causing a tingling in her ribs that made her gasp. When she took another full breath, her pain was gone. She glanced up at Prospect, surprised.

"You see I am telling the truth," the king said. "Prospect will heal Damon. If you make the right choice."

The idea of letting Damon die coiled through Thea like a poisonous snake, leaving her cold. "I want Damon healed immediately, here where I can see him."

Triumph flashed in Erebus's eyes. He clapped his hands as he stood. "I am delighted you have chosen to vow allegiance to me. Damon will be relieved as well."

Thea looked at him in disbelief, disgusted that he could speak so lightly of his son's pain. "You'd really let your son die?"

"Many of my children have died," he replied, one brow raised as if confused by her outburst. "Only one is meant to survive, and perhaps Damon is not the one."

"You filthy pile of wolf dung—" she spat before the shadows silenced her.

Erebus shook his head. "A slow learner. But you *will* learn."

Thea wondered what torments were in store for her because of this one choice.

And whether even she, as strong as she was, could bear it.

31

> While Solis tested the power of her amber ring, and Nerthus worked on her silver cup, Noctua took the rosewood lute to a village where the folk were gathered and began to play.
>
> —*Old Ones, Ancients, and the Folk*

"Step close to your mother's tree," Prospect instructed.

Thea shivered as she placed her hands against the cold trunk, trying to connect with her mother's spirit. There was a sense of rage and fear, but it was distant, like an echo.

"Tell her you have chosen to take her place," Prospect said. "Tell her she is free from her confinement."

Thea pressed her forehead against the cold metal, willing her mother to hear. "Mother, please listen." She felt a sob rising in her throat.

"I made a bargain for your freedom. Break your bonds. Come back to us."

Prospect produced a silver goblet from a fold in his robes. Thea turned her head to get a better look, knowing this was an artifact of the Ancients. Its silver was embossed with an image of sleeping animals. She saw an owl, a deer, and a fox. Prospect poured liquid from the cup onto the roots of the tree, muttering in the language of the Ancients as he did so. Shadows swirled, creating an inky column that darkened to midnight. Specks of silver danced like stars. The Seer's voice grew louder. A frigid breeze lifted the hairs on the back of Thea's neck, and a tugging sensation in the center of her chest signaled the spell was taking hold of her, too. There was a crack and an explosion of silver shards. Thea covered her head with her arms, turning away. When it was over, she blinked and rubbed her eyes, noticing that some of the silver had embedded itself in her skin. It reminded her of Cassia's gold freckles.

As the column of shadows ebbed away, Thea saw that the king held her mother in his arms. Fury at that made her stride forward. But her mother's body was limp. Thea's heart clenched tight. "Is she...?"

She reached out unsteadily to touch her mother's wrist. A pulse beat there, and her skin was warm. A sob escaped Thea's throat before she stifled it. "I'll take her."

Erebus's eyebrows rose, but Thea didn't wait for him to agree. She gently put her arm behind her mother's back, shivering in revulsion as she touched the king's chest. Scooping her other arm under her mother's knees, she pulled her into her lap, taking a seat on the floor. She put her hand to the beloved warm cheek and felt tears covering her own. "Mother, please. Wake up."

Queen Coventina blinked, her eyes bleary as she stared up into Thea's. Her eyebrows came together, and for a moment she said nothing. Thea tried to smile but wasn't sure she managed it.

"Thea?" the queen asked, her breath coming in gasps. "Is it you?"

Thea started to tremble. "It's me." Her voice was hoarse. "I came to find you."

The queen's hazel eyes were bright with love, but a second later, they filled with horror. "I don't want you here, Thea!" Her name caught on a sob.

Thea's eyes were damp, the tears unstoppable.

"You've been here long enough. Go home to Enora and Cassia and Rozie. They need you."

The king stepped closer, staring down at the queen with a wide smile. "Your daughter has agreed to take your place at my side."

"Step away, Theodora," her mother said, her tone as cold as a winter morning.

"Why?" Thea asked, a knot of worry tightening in her stomach.

"I must pay a debt that has grown far too great over many years," her mother said firmly. "Step back. Now."

"You can't fight him, Mother, especially not here, in his own realm." Her mother, like her father, had some connection with the trees that went beyond most Sylvans. But surely it wouldn't be enough to win against an Old One.

Her mother wasn't listening. Wind swirled around her, fluttering her green robes and lifting her greenish-gold hair, picking up dust and bits of silver bark and leaves that had fallen from her. The whirling column of green light was threaded with knifelike silver shards.

Erebus frowned. Thea hoped her mother would be able to do some damage to him.

The gale exploded. The silver leaves became

knives that flew at the king's face and chest. His shadows trembled as the shards sunk into them, shielding him.

A momentary hush was broken by laughter. "Oh, Coventina," Erebus gasped, mirth making his voice crack. "Nothing can kill me. Don't you know that by now?"

"This isn't the end," she rasped in furious loathing. "I have listened silently all these years, heard your every secret. I know your weaknesses."

"Prospect," Erebus said, all hints of laughter gone, "I fear we will not be able to enjoy the queen's presence any longer. I have lost a taste for her bitter leaves. Return her to the forest where she belongs."

"Not without Thea." The queen stepped back, grabbing Thea's arm and wrenching her to her side. "I won't leave without her." When the king's expression darkened, she turned to Prospect. "Seer, let us go. Send us by root. Leave us be forever. I have paid enough penance. Surely, those years of suffering were enough!"

The Seer was as silent as the king.

Finally, the queen turned to Thea. "Tell them. Tell them you choose to leave. Come with me."

Thea trembled with the urge to do just that. If only she could.

But she'd agreed to swear allegiance to Erebus. If she didn't, Damon would die. Even putting her own feelings aside, he was the best hope of defeating his father. The silver trees in Thirstwood, the weakness in the wards—they were signs Erebus was breaking out of his prison. She and Damon together would have to stop it.

"I can't, Mother," she said, softly but firmly. She wished she could explain. "I can't go."

Her mother's eyes grew desperate, her grip tightening. "I made your father vow not to let you come here to save me. I knew you would try to find me someday."

Was that why her father had tried so hard to stop her? "Mother." She felt tears rise to her eyes once more. "*I* have made a vow. To stay."

"Curse your vow!" Queen Coventina cried, though Thea knew she couldn't mean that. "You're my daughter. I'm taking you home."

Thea felt the desperate tug on her arm, as if she were a child who could be guided in the right direction. For a second, she wished she could go back to the time when she had been, when everything could be solved with the wiping of tears and soft words and a mother's embrace. A sharp pain made her breastbone ache, as if her heart were tearing in half.

She swallowed against the thickness in her throat. "I have one chance to save us," she whispered. "To save everyone. You must know what he's planning. Please, Mother."

Queen Coventina's expression twisted with pain and denial. Thea waited, meeting her mother's eyes until she saw the anger turn to sadness, and from there, resignation. Her face sagged, making her look old for the first time in Thea's memory. At least she could warn everyone in Scarhamm when she returned. Maybe they would come up with a way to fight the incursion of shadows.

The queen kissed her daughter's cheek. "You can beat him," she whispered. "Strength wins the shades. My power was too constricted by my form as a silver tree, but you are strong and determined. I'm convinced you can find a way."

"I'm sorry you can't witness your daughter swear allegiance to me," the king said, sounding impatient at being ignored.

The queen's hands clenched on Thea's, her

head turning with swift fury toward the king. "I would rather witness your disemboweled carcass being gnawed by my husband's hounds."

Erebus stared hard into her eyes as he said, "Root, take the queen home."

A root furled out of the darkness, landing at her mother's feet. As Thea helped her mother step onto it, a portal grew, too bright in the gloom. The tears in Queen Coventina's eyes shone like diamonds.

"I'll see you again," Thea choked, knowing that could be the closest she'd ever come to lying. Squeezing her mother's hand, she saw a flash of love and worry before she let go. Another step, and her mother was gone.

32

> When Noctua played a joyful tune, the folk laughed and danced. Even the shadows seemed to revel, taking on minds of their own.
> —Old Ones, Ancients, and the Folk

THEA WIPED HER TEARS BEFORE TURNing to face Erebus. It was time for him to keep the next part of his bargain. She spoke with cold clarity. "Heal Damon."

The king stared back at her, unspeaking, his magic battering her mind. Like a current rushing along a dam, it tested her, trying to find a crack in her mental walls. Thea marveled at his sudden mood changes. He could be furious and emotional one moment, cold and calculating the next. He seemed to vacillate between trying to inspire fear or devotion, perhaps the two mixed together to confuse and unbalance. Or maybe he had little experience with anyone able to defy him. His charm rushed through her mind, as wild and insistent as a river bursting with snow melt from the mountains. It swept her up, turning her mind over, twirling her sense of self into eddies.

Somehow, though, she was not lost in it. She allowed the wildness to pass and found herself at the center, still Thea. The king's brows drew together in confusion as he watched her face, his scrutiny as fierce as the power that flowed from him. She held on to herself and stared back, taking a relieved breath when she realized she'd been practicing resisting since she'd met Damon.

The shadows moved toward her, but no longer with menace. *Drawn*, she thought. *Drawn to strength*, as her mother had said.

Erebus broke into her thoughts with a sharp command. "Prospect! Retrieve my son."

The Seer rushed off, disappearing into the gloom. After what felt like an age, his gray robes came into view. Damon leaned heavily against his left side, his steps labored. His pale face was striped with blood. His shadows were gone. Thea wanted to rush to him, but she held still as he and the Seer drew closer.

Prospect lowered Damon to the stone flags

before the king. Damon's eyes fluttered open. When they met Thea's, his look was feverish, his eyes dilated, as if he wasn't quite lucid.

Erebus spoke with a detached sort of pride. "My son is difficult to kill."

Thea turned her back on him, the hatred she felt making her long to slay him right now.

Prospect went to his knees. Shadows swirled over Damon's body, converging like fish weaving between rocks. When they cleared, Damon's eyes were closed. He looked so vulnerable.

"He's asleep," Prospect said, looking at Thea, then the king. "He needs rest. But the worst of his wounds are healed."

Thea watched Damon's chest rise and fall in a slow rhythm. His skin was a healthier hue. She took a breath, some of the tension leaving her body.

"Well, my willow?" King Erebus said with a mocking tone that made her back straighten against it. "I have met my end of the bargain."

He was right. This was what she had agreed to do, but now that the moment was upon her, she fought a surge of unfamiliar panic.

Erebus offered his arm to Thea, his eyes on her as he instructed his Seer. "Prospect, let us make this vow official. The altar."

Thea pretended she didn't notice his proffered arm, turning away to follow Prospect, who led them to a stone slab in the center of a circle of trees.

From the silver branches hung lanterns containing moon sprites, their tiny bodies pressed against the glass. Everything in this place was either trapped or subjugated. The thought of spending the rest of her life here made Thea's heart thud in thick, painful beats. She wanted to run as she'd never wanted to run before.

"Stand here," Prospect told her.

Thea noticed rusty streaks on the stone. From sacrifices? How appropriate. She felt like one.

She stepped onto the slab. What had appeared to be scratches in the stone on closer inspection seemed to be Runic characters. She wished she knew what they meant. Perhaps Erebus wanted to ensure this vow was as binding as possible. If what Prospect had said about the Ancients having no power here was true, that meant Noctua could not enforce vows in this place. But maybe some other power did. Perhaps the shadows or Erebus himself.

Erebus stepped onto the altar next to her. She moved to put more distance between them, but he merely smiled and took her arm, drawing her to the center. She battled an overpowering urge to plant her fist in his belly. The shadows would only stop her, and the attempt would amuse him.

It occurred to Thea that it was almost like a wedding ceremony. But instead of candles, there were trapped moon sprites. Instead of family and friends to witness the event, there were shadows writhing toward her, their cold tendrils stroking her neck and chin. Instead of a priestess of the Ancients officiating the ceremony, a Seer in filthy robes stood awkwardly in front of herself and the king.

"Prospect," Erebus said, staring deep into Thea's eyes, "you may begin."

"Repeat after me," the Seer intoned. "I, Theodora, daughter of Silvanus…" He paused and waited.

Thea repeated his words, unable to keep the anger out of her voice. "I, Theodora, daughter of Coventina and Silvanus…" Adding her mother's name seemed like an act of defiance, but the king only raised a brow, his eyes intensely triumphant.

Prospect went on. "…do swear a Sylvan oath to be obedient to King Erebus."

Thea paused. "Do swear…" She couldn't say

it. She couldn't. Her throat was tight, her chest aching as if she were about to tell a lie. She stared at Erebus mutely, unable to continue.

"Say it." It was low and sharp, a nasty command that gave her a good idea how he would treat her in the future.

She almost choked. "It feels... like a lie."

Erebus raised his arm to backhand her. But she was faster, blocking with her own arm. Erebus grabbed her wrist, squeezing it painfully while she contemplated whether to knee him or punch him. The shadows did nothing, which Thea found interesting.

Prospect cleared his throat. "Perhaps there is some variant of the vow that you will find acceptable, my liege."

"This is not up to *her*," Erebus spat. But after a moment, he let Thea go.

She took a step back, her mind racing. Could she get out of this? Damon was healed, or so the Seer claimed, and her mother was free. What prevented her from refusing to adhere to this ridiculous deal?

The king must have realized that possibility, or he read her thoughts in her eyes. "I will kill Damon in front of you," he promised. "Slowly."

She believed him. Closing her eyes, she considered what she could say that might satisfy the bargain. She had to force the words out. "What if I promise to stay in your realm unless you allow me to leave?"

"Not enough," Erebus said. "Vow not to defy me."

Thea felt again the mental pressure—less of a current, more of a heavy, insistent pull like the undertow of river rapids. His magic was trying to sway her, to bind her to him. Disgust turned her stomach, forcing her to swallow and take a deep breath.

"I vow not to defy you." She hated him.

He smiled, his magic softening. Perhaps he thought it was working. "Vow to follow my every instruction."

"I've made my promise!" Thea shouted, reaching some internal limit. "Let that be enough. Or kill Damon and then kill me. And be done."

They stared at each other for a few moments. Thea's stomach roiled, wondering which way the king would go.

"Fine," the king said in a bored voice, though she heard the undercurrent of rage clearly enough. "Prospect, take her to the guest cottage to dress. I have sent out invitations. We should expect visitors tonight."

Desperate to escape his presence, Thea didn't ask what he meant. She wasted no time following the Seer down a path of purple stone between silver trees. It led to a cottage, the walls inlaid with moldings of silver and hung with rich tapestries.

"Who stays here?" Thea asked, not liking this place at all.

Prospect ran his finger along a lacquer table, his lip curling at the dust. "No one recently. In the past, his wives."

Thea put a hand to her stomach. "I'm going to be sick."

"Do not," the Seer said, "throw up on the tapestries. The king will be displeased."

Thea made a mental note to throw up on the tapestries.

"The shadows will dress you," Prospect said, turning to leave.

"Wait," Thea said. "I don't need any help!"

No sooner had the Seer shut the door than the shadows converged, pulling a dark shape from a trunk in the corner. The garment was made of black silk with black seed pearls stitched into its bodice, and a collar of cobwebs. Thea longed to disappear, to shrink away, but she remained still as the shadows slid pins into her hair and placed a silver tiara on her brow. The metal was so cold, it made her forehead ache, but after a minute, it warmed to her skin.

Why the crown? Was she to play the role of queen? For a moment, she truly thought she might throw up. But she took a deep breath and stepped from the cottage.

Prospect looked her up and down, nodding once before he turned away. "Follow me."

A short, silent boat ride ended at Damon's castle. Thea's breath locked in her throat. Surely the king couldn't be planning to receive guests here? But the vessel scraped onto the familiar shore, and Prospect got out, halting to wait for her in the doorway. Reluctantly, Thea followed, taking slow steps inside.

The ballroom was full of Azpians and…others. There were Skrattis, pit sprites, and imps, but there were also things she had never seen before, possibly from lower realms very few would brave. There were creatures with too many teeth to fit in their mouths, insect-like beings that crawled with multiple legs, things with antennae that waved slowly as if tasting the air, and bulbous eyes that stared at her as if she were something good to eat.

Erebus was seated on a dark throne on a dais at the far end of the ballroom. As Thea moved toward the king, hands and tentacles reached out to touch her, the creatures making strange, guttural noises. She tried not to shiver.

Conscious of the many watching eyes, she inclined her head. She felt the intensity of the king's regard as she lifted her chin and inspected the room. "Your subjects?"

The king turned a satisfied eye on the hideous assembly. "Some of these creatures swear fealty to no one, not even the Dracu queen. They've come to celebrate our alliance."

"You invited such wild creatures into your realm?"

Erebus had the air of a conqueror about him. "They have felt the swelling of power and come to pay tribute. Fealty will be the next step. It was a boon to have the Sylvan queen's spirit in my realm, but far greater to have the blood of Silvanus himself in the form of his daughter. The fact that I was able to win the allegiance of my old enemy speaks to my power."

Before Thea could ask what he meant that her father was an old enemy, or argue his claim that he'd "won" anything, he took her hand and planted a kiss on her knuckles. A murmuring of approval from the guests made Erebus smile against her skin.

"I did not agree to be manhandled," Thea said, tugging her hand away. She glared at him, wondering if she could make any threats that she could truthfully carry out. How much would her vow prevent her from defying him?

"This crowd enjoys theatrics," he said, his smile cold.

Noticing heads turning, Thea looked toward the doorway. The newcomer was hidden by two tall Skrattis, to whom he was speaking low words of greeting, but a thrill of recognition ran through Thea at the sound of his voice. She knew him even before the crowd parted. If she heard his voice a thousand years from now, she would know it.

Damon looked as healthy as if nothing had befallen him, as if the past hours had been a bad dream. His skin was smooth and unmarred, his hair clean, its dark strands swept back from his forehead in a carefree way. He wore a velvet coat of midnight with a white cravat, a diamond brooch shining under the lights, which were brighter than ever. As he came within touching distance, he bowed low, his hair shining like the black seed pearls on Thea's dress.

"My father and king," he said in a deep, respectful tone. Then his eyes flicked up to meet Thea's. He bowed to her. "First of Shadows."

Thea frowned, disliking the sound of that but unsure she'd heard him correctly among all the din of the creatures. "What did you call me?"

"My son told me you wanted to be First Huntsman," Erebus explained. "I hope you approve of your new title."

Thea gripped the side of his throne, needing something to steady her. Why would Damon tell him that? It was shared in confidence after their first kiss. Maybe he had spoken under duress when the shadows had attacked him or when he'd been in the cave. She tried not to blame him. But the last thing she wanted was to have a title from the shadow king, especially a perversion of the one she had tried so hard to earn in the Sylvan army.

"You are well, my son?" Erebus asked, his tone warm.

Damon's eyes moved from his father to Thea. "All is as it should be. As it was meant to be."

A sick feeling twisted Thea's stomach, making her throat twitch with the urge to gag. "That's going a bit far, don't you think?"

The crowd had gone silent but for soft shuffling and buzzing, the creatures listening to this exchange.

"Not at all," Damon said, his smile fixed in place. "Our realm needed someone strong to increase our power forever. Your allegiance will bring the Sylvans to our side."

"It will not," Thea said, wondering if he was repeating nonsense he'd heard from Erebus. "How can you say that?"

Prospect entered the ballroom, his stained fingers coming up to remove his hood. He was not as old as she'd thought, though his skin was an unhealthy gray. "First of Shadows, I had no doubt you would someday come here to free your mother."

"In time," Damon said, "your people will come to love my father. As everyone does in the end." Thea's hand ached from gripping the side of the throne. Damon couldn't mean any of this.

He was acting like he was in league with Prospect, whom he didn't trust at all.

Damon took a step forward, a new seriousness entering his eyes. "I thank you for saving my life with your bargain, Thea. Though"—he looked at his father—"my father wouldn't have let me die. You'll come to understand that sometimes he does things that are painful, but ultimately for the best."

Thea stifled a bitter laugh. If this was a performance for the king's benefit, perhaps she should go along with it. But part of her was starting to doubt. Her eyes roved over his face for some sign of truth. This had to be a ruse, a trick to put his father off-balance, or to protect her.

King Erebus leaned on his elbow, bending toward Thea as if delivering an aside. "Though I was wroth to hear that my son did not tell me when you first came to my realm, I believe his claim that he wanted to assess your strength before presenting you to me on your ninth night. And now, knowing your stubborn nature, I must allow if it weren't for his persistence, it's possible you would have never come."

Thea couldn't believe this. If she'd known her

mother was trapped here, she would have come sooner. But Damon had clearly sold his father a story to appease his temper.

Erebus turned back to Damon, speaking louder. "My son, ask for a boon, and it's yours."

Thea's heart did a double beat, and her breath caught in her chest. Would he ask for her freedom?

"Anything?" Damon asked, his posture straightening, the relaxed air leaving him suddenly. The tension in his body and the look in his eyes spoke of terror and hope.

Erebus waved a hand impatiently.

Thea waited, her breath shallow, unable to hide her hope as her eyes met Damon's. He took a deep, audible breath, and his eyes shifted away from hers. "Father, I have a confession. My mother did not die as you once thought. I have kept Azra here, hidden and safe until the day when you would reward me by granting my greatest wish. And that is to lift the curse that binds my mother to this realm. I want the spell that keeps her in this place to be lifted."

Shock hit Thea like a blow. He hadn't been thinking of her at all. The reality hollowed out her stomach. Numbness came to her rescue, and suddenly it seemed as if she were observing a scene entirely separate from herself. She watched Damon's hands shake, knowing he was risking everything. Despite her tumultuous emotions, her stomach clenched, imagining what Erebus would do.

Tension built in the silence. Erebus's frown acted on the shadows like an oncoming storm, making them spread out like dark clouds over the ballroom. "You've done *what*?"

Damon straightened. "Strike me down if you wish. But if you want to reward me, let my mother leave this realm, and me along with her. You don't need me now that you have your First of Shadows. Then all will be even between us."

Thea's heart jerked painfully. *And me along with her!* He meant to leave, too? As the pieces fit together in Thea's mind, she tried not to scream her disbelief. Damon was framing it like a trade: her freedom for his mother's. Had he planned this all along?

Erebus seemed to ponder his son's request. A profound hush had fallen over the guests. One small creature tittered, the laugh perversely loud in the stillness. Erebus turned his head to look at Thea. She had the sense he was measuring her value to him and weighing it against the urge to kill his son for his betrayal. At that moment, she almost wished for the latter.

"What do you think, my First? Should we allow it?" His eyes were sharp on her, as if he actually cared how she answered.

He was giving *her* the choice?

She could say no. She could crush Damon's hopes the way he'd crushed hers, cause him unbearable pain in revenge for what she'd have to face in her future. But all she could think was that she knew what it was like to have a mother trapped in the shadow realm.

"Set his mother free," she said, hating that her voice shook with the pain of betrayal.

Damon gave her a look so warm with gratitude, it almost broke her down. She had to turn her head away to protect herself. He might have wounded her, but she didn't need to let him see where she bled.

Erebus stared at Damon so long, Thea wondered if he might ignore her advice and kill his son. But his rage seemed to evaporate, and his tone dripped contempt. "I don't need you anymore, Damon. I never did. Take your mother and go."

Damon bowed his head. "Father. Thank you."

Thea heard the relief in his voice. Stark *relief* when he had traded her freedom for his mother's. When he had lied to her and made her care for him, more than she'd even realized until this moment. As the heat of shame crept up her throat, he raised his head and boldly met her eyes. "Goodbye, my First."

"I am not your anything," Thea spat, taking a shuddering breath before launching another attack. "I hope your mother enjoys her freedom, knowing it was bought at my expense."

"I won't tell her," he said, his eyes somber. "She has always been unable to bear the suffering of others."

Thea's heart felt as if it were being clutched in a gauntleted fist. Damon didn't seem to spare a thought for *her* suffering. It took a moment to speak past that tightness. "Unlike her son."

Damon's eyelids fluttered, and she wondered if she'd hit a vulnerable spot even his shadows couldn't protect. "It seems I am my father's son, after all."

"That's a choice," she shot back. "You're choosing that path, Damon."

The blankness in his expression chilled her. "It's the path my feet know best."

As he turned away, she closed her eyes. She would not watch him leave. There was a shuffling sound as creatures moved aside for his departure. At the last moment, she opened her eyes, helpless against the promise of a final glimpse.

He was already lost in shadows.

33

> When Noctua played a tune
> of mourning, the folk wept.
> The shadows called for more
> music and grief to feed them.
> —*Old Ones, Ancients, and the Folk*

Thea tried to save them.

Night after night, new folk came to Iluna. In the ballroom of Damon's castle—now the king's—they danced and cavorted in front of the throne. On the first night, they were merry. The second night, their cheeks were too red, their eyes glassy. By the third night, they didn't know their own names.

"Who is bringing them here?" Thea asked one morning after the folk had left by root. She had given up trying to persuade Erebus toward mercy. Her fury and disgust only amused him. And her vow gave her no recourse to defy him.

"They are drawn to the power *you* have

brought me," Erebus said. "You, my First of Shadows."

Thea fought the urge to gag at his implication that it was her fault. She didn't believe him, anyway. She knew someone had to be luring people here.

Every night, she approached the creatures who had come to join the dance, one by one. "Leave," she told them bluntly. "Save yourselves! If you don't leave now, you never will." Erebus didn't stop her, only laughed at her folly. Time after time, they looked at her, smiled, and kept dancing.

One night, there was a Sylvan girl, perhaps from one of the villages, who looked like Rozie, though a few years older—ginger hair, freckles, curious eyes. It made Thea sick, the thought of her being trapped here.

"Why did you come?" Thea asked, gripping the girl's slim shoulders harder than she intended.

The Sylvan drew a breath and turned startled eyes up to Thea's. "He asked."

Thea forced herself to loosen her grip, though she wanted to shake answers out of the girl. "Who asked?" Had Prospect been rounding up folk to bring here?

She blinked, as if struggling to remember. "The prince."

Thea paused, her pulse jumping. "The king, you mean?"

The girl shook her head, her eyes wide. "The young prince in the woods. He invites us here to dance. My mother warned me not to go, but the prince seemed so agreeable. So handsome."

Thea's head reared back as if she'd been struck. *No!* Damon could not still be using his powers to lure new spirits to his father's realm. Not when he had won his mother's freedom, and his own as well. It was sick. Twisted. Unforgivable. Could she have been that wrong about him?

"Go!" Thea shook her. She was ready to slap the girl if that might wake her up. "If you don't leave now, you'll be trapped here forever. Save yourself!"

The girl frowned in confusion. "Maybe. I..."

A deep voice crooned from behind Thea, making her tense in revulsion.

"Calm, my dear," said King Erebus, putting on his best charm. "Is it not a fine night? Dance with me." And he put out a hand to the girl, inviting her.

"No!" Thea turned on him, despising him

more than ever. "I won't let you." She reached for him, her nails talons that would rake the skin from his face. But the shadows held her wrists and forearms in a fierce, painful grip, lacerating her arms until blood poured down. She managed to break free, but more shadows snaked out and held her fast.

"Get off me," she seethed, spitting at the shadows in her fury. They twitched, as if her outrage excited them.

Through all this, the girl's eyes stayed on the king as if she could not pull them away. "But I love to dance!" And she took his hand.

In nine days, the Sylvan girl was a delicate silver tree.

Thea's free hours were spent devising ways to kill her sworn liege. None of them were viable, but it was the only thing that gave her satisfaction.

When she slept, she dreamed of a pair of lying midnight eyes.

As days wore into weeks, the sky of Thea's mind grew darker. No one who came to the dance seemed able to resist the king's spell. She stood beside the throne as the same scenes passed before her. Dances. Endless dances. And more silver trees, trees, trees.

Thea could almost feel her inner fire dimming, her confidence in herself ebbing away like a tide that never rolls in again. She could hardly remember how it felt to stand in the sun.

Had she ever? Maybe everything was an illusion. Perhaps, in the end, nothing was real.

Over time, her enemy became hope. It was by far more painful than despair.

As she left her cottage one night to make her way to the dance, something rustled in the silver trees.

"You look terrible." It was a voice she knew.

A pixie voice.

Thea gasped and turned but saw no one. "Winter?" she whispered, searching the silver trees.

A tiny head popped out from behind a trunk, a small hand waving at her. "I hardly recognized you, Giantess."

Thea half worried she was imagining him. "How are you here?"

"That's a long story filled with my bravery. No time for that now." He flew toward her, and she saw that he was dressed all in silver, his hair and clothing blending in with the trees. "Scarhamm has been in an uproar since your mother returned. Everyone is determined to find a way to help you. The Sylvan queen insists you will rise up against him."

"I'd love nothing more than to murder him," Thea assured Winter. "But his shadows are too strong."

Winter gave her a critical look. "Your mother tried to tell you: Take them, Giantess. Take them for your own."

"I've tried," she said, suddenly furious. "Don't you think I've tried? I've tried nothing else since the moment I made that cursèd vow of allegiance."

"Yes, yes, I'm sure you've tried to bully them to your side with your signature bluntness. But have you tried wooing them?" He gave her a coquettish look.

She crossed her arms. "With what? Blood and pain and suffering? I can't outdo Erebus in that way."

Winter's lips twisted. "Surely they like something besides cruelty."

She had already tried that with Damon and hadn't even won his shadows to her side. But she recited the options in a deadpan voice. "Desire. Revelry if it's out of control. Wildness. Chaos."

His eyes widened, a smile curving his lips. "Then be desire. Be wild. Be chaos."

For so many years, she'd had to keep a secret so great that she could not allow herself to speak unguardedly, even for a moment. She'd spent years learning how to be efficient, controlled, precise. And she'd already tried to win the shadows through every method imaginable. It hadn't worked. "I've tried using desire. As for the rest, I don't know how."

"Well, you have to find a way," he said, one hand coming to his hip, though he was still afloat, wings flapping. "Where is the vaunted tactician when we need her?"

Thea felt as if Winter had hit her with a pine needle arrow in the center of her chest. He was right. She had all but given up. That wasn't like her. And she realized she hadn't even asked about her sisters.

"My sisters are well?" she asked anxiously.

"As well as can be. They said to tell you they'll never rest until you're free. I'm told your youngest sister, Rozenna, has snuck out to try to find you no less than four times."

Thea had to blink against a sudden moisture in her eyes.

"Did..." She swallowed, remembering the last time she'd left Scarhamm. "Did my father have a message for me?"

Winter's face froze. "He is concerned, too, of course."

Something about the look on his face screamed *lie*. "What are you not telling me, Winter?"

The pixie looked away for a quick second, then back at her, his face serious. "I haven't seen your father myself, but there are reports he is ill. And more and more silver trees are appearing in the forest. Your mother has explained how the shadow king is trying to take over Thirstwood. He is weakening the forest, and that is weakening King Silvanus. Your father has not risen from his bed in days."

A new fear rose up in her heart. "I can't believe I'm trapped here when they need me most. I hate this." But despite that, Thea felt a surge of pride that she'd freed her mother, who was now home, safe. She put her finger out in something of a handshake. "Thank you, Winter. You've given me hope."

"Everyone wants to help you," Winter said.

"Not only the Sylvans but all your forest allies. Most importantly, the pixies."

A lump of emotion lodged in Thea's throat. They were all fighting for her. Of course they were. Why had she ever thought otherwise? She was angry with herself for considering giving in to despair. Her sisters would never stop searching for her, even if she never saw them again. And if her father had lost faith in her, well, she had faith in herself.

"Someone is coming." The pixie backed away, floating into the branches of a tree where he blended in. "Find a way, Giantess."

A moment later, footsteps sounded nearby. Thea turned and straightened, her stomach dropping when she saw that it was Erebus. He was as impeccably dressed as ever, his white cravat only a few shades lighter than his pale face. The perfection of his features struck her as that of a poisoned moth, the beauty of its colors a warning not to touch.

"My First of Shadows," he said, and his magic swirled around her, searching for cracks in her mental armor.

"Am I First of Shadows?" Thea challenged. "Because if so, why do I not have any of my own?"

His lips tightened at her demand, his eyes sharpening on hers. Perhaps he sensed the change in her. "You are needed at the revel. It isn't the same there without you." The cloying, false gentleness set her off as much as his dismissal.

"No." She crossed her arms. "You only want to torment me because you know I despise it. I'm not going to attend that sick dance ever again."

Storm clouds moved through his eyes. "You swore not to defy me."

She stood firm, bracing her feet on the ground, reminding herself she was strong. "You yourself said Noctua can't enforce vows in this realm."

"You are going the revel," he snarled, grabbing her upper arm in a biting grip and shoving her against a tree. After a moment of shock, her years of battle experience rushed forward. She had his throat in her hand before his shadows could react. A heartbeat later, they swooped in, prying her fingers off one by one, but she held on as long as she could. She met Erebus's stare even as he choked and gasped. Finally, when he was free, he stared at her with undisguised hatred. "You'll pay for that."

"What's worse than what I'm already enduring?" she asked. "I watch night after night as you turn those poor souls into trees, and I can't do anything to stop it. You don't think that's bad enough?"

"Clearly not. You need to learn respect." He waved a hand, and suddenly Prospect was there, stepping from the shadows. "Take her to the cave," Erebus said, his hand massaging his throat.

Prospect moved forward immediately, his hand reaching out toward her.

"Don't touch me," Thea warned, weighing whether Prospect's shadows would be strong enough to hold her. Her blood was up, the need to fight pounding through her veins. But she remembered that Winter was nearby, and if she was in real danger, he might be rash enough to come to her aid. She could not bear the thought of him dying for her.

Prospect merely put his hands up, palms out. "I am certain there is no need. I'll show you the way."

"I hope," said the king, "by the time you return, you will be in a more reasonable frame of mind."

34

> When Noctua played the sweet strains of a lullaby, the folk yawned, rubbed their eyes, and fell into a deep sleep. As the music ended, the shadows crept away to find more of what they had been fed and now craved: revelry, music, and grief.
>
> —OLD ONES, ANCIENTS, AND THE FOLK

PROSPECT HALTED AT THE BASE OF A black cliff, holding up a bog sprite lantern. "I'll go no closer."

Thea could make out the deeper darkness of the cave's entrance. She sniffed the air, turning her head slowly, as she would if she were on patrol in the forest, her hunter's instincts on alert. "There are shadows in there?"

Prospect made a rough sound of amusement, as if he'd forgotten how to laugh. "They are so wild, even the king could not win their allegiance."

Thea might have thought he was trying to scare her, but that description matched what Damon had told her about the cave. She imagined him thrown into that darkness as a child. Though she was still furious with Damon for lying, and disgusted with herself for believing him, she had sympathy for his younger self. Every child deserved a protector, and he'd had none.

"So this was Damon's punishment," she said, a lump in her throat as she imagined how terrified he must have been. "To be trapped with the most vicious spirits of all."

"Yes." There was no regret in the Seer's voice.

Thea turned on him, her hands fisted. "And you didn't stop it. You didn't defend a child in need."

He held her eyes. "To defend him would have meant my own death."

From what she understood, he hadn't even tried. She turned away, despising him and everyone in this cursèd realm. She did not want to go into the cave or stay in this horrible place one moment longer. But she lifted her chin and took a step forward. She would not cower.

Prospect gave her one last warning. "Do not trust anything you see or hear. The spirits deceive."

She paused before stepping over the threshold, wondering why he was trying to help her. "How long am I to be left in here?"

The Seer spread his hands. "It depends on the king's whim. Sometimes Damon was in here for several days."

Though the idea made her stomach crawl, if Damon as a child could bear it, so could she. An invisible veil of magic pressed against her body as she entered, as if a hundred horsehair brushes slid over her. Once inside, she tested the ward and found it to be as solid as the rocky cliff. She was trapped.

She took a single shallow breath before turning to face the interior, the scant light from the doorway reaching inches inside the cave. Stepping into darkness, she felt her way around the perimeter with outstretched hands. The space was not large, perhaps twenty paces deep before the wall started to curve back toward the entrance.

It wasn't long before she heard rustling, a *scritch scritch* of small animal feet. Rats? How had they survived in this barren environment? The noise grew until it sounded like a dozen or so. When the sounds drew close, Thea darted forward with her hand outstretched to grab one. It felt solid under her palm for one moment before it dissipated like mist.

Shadows.

The figment rats scratched the floor around her for several minutes. She thought of Damon being trapped here when he was young. Rodents would be horribly frightening to a child in the dark alone. But she had faced much worse.

Snarls came next. Something larger approached, padding over the cave floor. A wolf? Teeth grazed her arm, cutting her skin. She snarled back as she reached for it, but the wolf turned to smoke, and her hand passed through cold air.

An unfair fight! There was nothing worse.

She listened to the wolf's movements as it padded around her. It snapped at her, rushing forward and retreating. She pushed the animal's mouth away before it could clamp onto her arm. The next time, it was too fast, leaving a bloody gash. Thea gasped in pain, but after a while, her senses attuning to it, she was able to judge the shadow wolf's location by sound, and used her forearms to smash its maw from her before it could bite her again.

Next came spiders. The tiny insect figments crawled all over the cave walls, jumping onto her hair and shoulders, skittering down her back. She shouted and pressed her body against the wall, squishing them into mist. She forced herself to focus, to steady her breathing so she didn't panic.

In a moment, the spiders changed. Snakes coiled around her ankles, hissing. She thought again of how scared Damon must have been as a boy trapped in here with these things, and anger rose inside her, hot and fierce, sharpening her senses. She grabbed the snakes before they could turn to mist, hurling them away from her.

"Enough of these games," she said aloud. "Challenge me."

A moment later, something large approached, its loud panting filling the small space. A paw swiped out and raked long claws down Thea's face, drawing blood and knocking her to the floor.

Paralyzed with pain and fear, she couldn't move for agonizing seconds. The feel of hot breath on her face made her push to her feet and stumble back.

"A bear?" she asked, keeping her distance while using one hand on the wall as a guide. She and the shadow bear did a sort of dance, the animal lunging for her while she leaped right or left, always out of reach, until it hissed at her in frustration. The panting ceased.

Silence followed. *What next?*

Face the greatest enemy of the Sylvans, said several hissing voices speaking together.

"A Dracu?" Thea guessed, motioning an invitation in the dark. Dracu were fast, and so were the shadows. She listened, dodging as best she could, but soon, a blade sliced Thea's shoulder, missing her cheek by inches.

"Unfair to use a blade," she snapped, moving by sound alone, guessing where the shadow Dracu might be. "I have no weapon."

Fair? the shadows spat. *There is no such thing.*

Suddenly, there were at least two Dracu. Three? More? Thea used her forearms to block, but their attacks struck home. Soon, she was covered in blood and sweat, the air stinging her wounds.

Cry mercy, the shadows hissed.

"You first." Thea blocked, then finally managed to grab one of the false Dracu by the hair, which turned to cold mist under her fingers. A knife cut her back. Her arm. Her leg. There were too many. She would go down fighting. All she could do.

The shadows made a sound like laughter. *Cry mercy!*

"Is this what you did to Damon?" she asked, blocking and dodging while more and more shadow knives cut her skin. "To a helpless child?"

No answer. Thea hated the shadows in that moment. Despised them as she'd never hated anything.

He hates us, too, they whispered. *The shadow prince.*

Suddenly, the attacks stopped. Thea stared at the darkness, anticipating another attack, her entire body throbbing in pain. "What's wrong?" she asked finally. "Is it more amusing to watch me bleed to death slowly?"

Thea wondered: Did they actually *want* to kill her? It would be easy. But a dead body would provide no entertainment.

The thick quiet was broken as voices cried out in the dark. "*Thea! Thea, help us!*"

She gasped, not expecting this new kind of attack. Her sisters? Rozie's voice rose to a shriek. *"Thea! I need you!"*

Don't trust anything you see or hear, Prospect had said. It wasn't real. But it tore at Thea's heart, touching on her worst fear—that she wouldn't be able to protect the people she loved. She covered her ears, but the sounds seemed to pierce her skull. This was so much worse than the cut of a dagger. *"Thea! Help me! Help!"*

Her stomach heaved. As the voices went on and on, she shivered violently, wishing death on the shadow king, his son, and Prospect for putting her here. Finally, she snapped. "Shut up, you foul things. Be silent!"

The voices grew louder.

Real or not, they were breaking her down, making her sick, making her question her sanity. She closed her eyes and leaned her head back against the wall, her stomach roiling as they continued their cries.

The sounds of battle came next. Clangs and shouts and the cries of her sisters shrieking in pain, gasping their last breaths. It sounded so real. After a few minutes, tears made cold tracks down her cheeks.

You should have killed Erebus while you could, they sang. *Your weakness will mean your sisters' deaths.*

"So you claim," she replied, her lip trembling. "But the future isn't fixed."

Wind came from nowhere, a gale so strong it pinned her to the wall. The shadows grew louder, spitting terror in every way imaginable and in forms she had never imagined. The cries of children. Animals in pain. Images appeared in the darkness, terrible images. War. Death. Destruction. Lightning crashing and fire consuming the forest. A chasm rending the ground and lava pouring from it. The oceans covering the earth. Stars falling from the heavens like sparks. The sun going dark.

Images from the future, the spirits said. *Your future.*

"Then I will live a long life," Thea said, though her body shook uncontrollably, "if I am to see the end of all things."

You will never leave here. We vow it.

Days seemed to pass. Weeks? Thea experienced no hunger or thirst, nothing that would help her gauge the passage of time. Her cuts burned, but the bleeding seemed to have stopped. The shadows tormented her until she was half-mad. It seemed she was to be left here forever.

"What do you want?" she cried aloud, unable to bear it.

We remain here. Trapped by Erebus the Betrayer.

That made her sit up. "Who were you before you came to the cave?"

They paused. *The souls of the folk, like the others. But we are those who would not obey him.* Another pause, then: *We will kill you. Kill you and devour your spirit.*

"I would not obey Erebus, either!" Thea shouted. "So kill me if you can, but know that you are doing his work for him!" She pushed to her feet, readying for their next attack. But how long could she hold them off? She was used to relying on her combat skills to save her, but the shadows weren't like any other foe. She couldn't defeat them, couldn't even make them bleed. Was there another way? Sylvans were known for making deals. Why not offer the shadows a bargain, something they were desperate to have? She had little time to consider the details, so she trusted her instincts. "Or you can bind yourselves to me, and I will give you freedom from this place—"

We serve no one! If we wouldn't obey him, we shall not obey you.

"Because he is empty of everything you crave," she said. "His shadows want cruelty, but you want something else." She listened, trying to gauge their reaction, hoping they were so bored by their eons of tormenting others that they would be tempted by her offer.

She waited, but the shadows went quiet.

It gave her time to think. Even if she knew how to set these shadows free, she couldn't risk it. They were too dangerous to be left loose. Instead, she was offering them a Sylvan bargain, which would commit her to tending these shadows for the rest of her life—the worst shadows, the most violent of spirits, so evil that Erebus himself, with all his cruelty, could not win their allegiance. What would they want from her? What would they expect? What would happen if they grew bored and turned on her? Still, she would do anything to help save Thirstwood from Erebus.

Erebus must have wanted her allegiance for a reason. He had hinted at her bloodline, her powerful parents, born long ago in a time of greater magic. Perhaps she had something inside her that drew the shades. Something even she didn't understand.

We could kill you, the spirits said.

"Then do it." Thea lifted her chin, daring them. She let them sense her fearlessness. "Erebus is weak. His cruelty is born of fear. Test me. Fight me again. I will never beg for mercy. Never yield. I'm not like him." She paused, sensing interest in their silence. "If it's freedom from the cave you want, I'll try to release you, but you have to remain with me. You will have more chaos and revelry than you can drink in if you stay at my side." She believed what she said was true. There was no end to the threats her people faced, and perhaps she was her father's daughter because she didn't mind the challenge. She wanted to fight.

You are a curious thing, they said, voices softer now. *A thing that loves death as much as we do.*

"Death never frightened me."

She felt the shadows approach like animals scenting food. They growled, some of them shrieking words in an ancient tongue. Cursing her, even as they moved toward her.

There is one thing. It pulls us. We sense a hunger for death in you. A wish to kill.

Thea wanted to deny it. She opened her

mouth to refute it. But the shadows were right. She was her father's daughter, as Damon was his father's son. And a part of her loved war.

There. She could admit it to the shadows.

If you promise us chaos and death, destruction and tears, we will join with you.

Thea closed her eyes. "I promise you battles until there are no more to be fought. I won't stop until Erebus is defeated."

But would she be able to stop at all?

As the shades wove around her, circling her wrists like bracelets and settling around her neck like a fur collar, she found her mind floating to a state of euphoria. It was a new kind of power that gloried in wildness instead of perfection, freedom over precision. She let herself savor it, trying to let go of the need to exert control. She *would* be mistress of the shadows. No matter how she had to change to do it.

Over time, her cuts healed, and she experimented with the shadows. It was strange at first to consider them allies, but soon she became fascinated by them. They were unpredictable, fickle, and imaginative, taking shapes of animals she had never seen—some things she wasn't sure existed. At first, she didn't trust them not to hurt her, but it seemed they had committed to the bargain, and she began to let her guard down. With practice and attention, she could hear their thoughts without them speaking.

It felt as if they were learning her, too. She found she could influence their shapes, and they chose the one she liked best. They became butterflies. Deadly ones. Her weapons against the betrayer.

Weapons against anyone who would hurt you, they whispered.

When light appeared at the cave entrance, Thea rose to her feet and smiled.

35

> Nerthus feared that the power of the ring, lute, and cup might not be enough to subdue the Old Ones. Even if they slept, they could one day wake, and their vengeance would be terrible. It was safer to also make them forget. She crept into Noctua's realm and drew water from a river that made spirits forget their past lives, adding it to the cup of silver.
>
> —Old Ones, Ancients, and the Folk

Prospect's voice came through the cave's entrance. "Your penitence is complete. King Erebus releases you!"

Thea could see the ward trapping her inside, like a layer of rippling water between her and the outside. Prospect must have some spell that would allow her to step through but keep the shadows contained.

Or so he thought.

The shadows rested on her back in the form of butterflies, their wings inky and delicate. It was like wearing the winged jacket Damon had given her. The memory stabbed her heart, so she pushed it aside, focusing on the ward she must step through. The invisible barrier pressed at her, squeezing her lungs.

She held her breath, willing this to work. She'd used Veleda to pass through the ward in the doorway of her bedchamber. She hoped the shadows could pass through the cave's wards if they were part of her. But this containment spell was much more powerful than Veleda's. She could feel the weight of it, the way it bent the air.

She took one step, her face encountering the strange feeling of the ward. Another. The magic pressed against her, making her skin feel as if it were being pulled tight. A third step made the ward snap together behind her, releasing her to the other side. She put a hand to her shoulder, feeling the wing of a butterfly. Her shadows had stayed with her, tasting freedom for the first time in an age.

It gave her a sense of protectiveness knowing

they were inseparable. She took another step away from the cave. The glow from the silver trees seemed painfully bright. Her eyes had learned to love the dark.

Prospect stood a few feet away. He was smaller than she remembered, his eyes wide as he looked her over. "You are well, First of Shadows?" His hands twitched with nerves, his shadows swirling.

She smiled at the title, which now felt earned. Her body hummed with the power that her shadows—her butterflies—were giving her. Is this what the king felt when he amassed new spirits? It was exquisite.

Thea beckoned to Prospect's shadows. "Come to me," she commanded.

The Seer's face was a mask of horror as the darkness around him moved toward Thea, sinuous and graceful, curving around her waist and into her hair.

"What are you doing?" Prospect cried, his hands opening and closing as if he could pull them back. "Please. To be without them here could mean my death. The king is mercurial. If he sets his shadows on me in a fit of rage, I'll have no protection!"

The Seer fell to his knees, his hands clasped together so tight she could see the curve of his knuckle bones. Begging her for mercy after he'd just put her in the cave for days? She lifted her skirts and stepped around him.

As she swept along paths through the silver forest, the Seer trotted after her, his robes swishing nervously. "The shadows from the cave follow no one. They were imprisoned for the safety of everyone, most especially you and the king."

Thea turned on her heel, whipping around so fast the Seer took a step back, his eyes wide. "Never again put me in the same category as Erebus," she told him. "It will be the last thing you say."

The Seer drew a sharp breath through his nose. "I understand."

"Where is he?" she demanded.

"In the castle, entertaining guests."

Strength wins the shades, her mother had said. She had never felt stronger. "Take me to him."

The lights of Damon's castle were dim.

It seemed the king had run through the folk she'd seen last time, perhaps turning them into more silver trees. The strange creatures from the lower realms were back. But instead of glassy, vacant stares, their eyes were wild. They shrieked and ran across the filthy tiles and up the walls, talons extended as they shredded paint, fabric, and one another. Blood streaked the floor. Here and there were bits of some opalescent liquid as if insects had been squashed.

Thea toed a drunken imp who was nursing the dregs of a bottle of fruit wine out of her way. She strolled from the door to the throne, where the king sat with his chin on his hand. He was pretending to be bored, to not care about her arrival, but she could feel his anticipation. No doubt he expected her to beg forgiveness.

When she drew close, she did not bow. She stared at him, wondering how someone so small could have almost broken her.

"Had enough of the cave, my willow?" he asked, his smile as slick as the bug grime on the walls.

"On the contrary," she said calmly despite the screeches and shouts coming from all around them. "It was an interesting experience."

His brows twitched up. "But not one you would soon repeat. My son always despised it.

Perhaps that is why he ran like a frightened child from my realm. A pity he turned out to be so weak." Though Erebus's mouth still twisted in a bitter smile, his fingers drummed on his armrest, and his eyes held a brooding look. She surmised he was far more upset about Damon's defection than he let on.

Thea would neither defend nor condemn Damon to a man who had never deserved to be a father. Instead of responding, she took her time surveying her surroundings. There were creatures killing each other on the ballroom floor. Two insect-like things were tearing each other apart. Fractured chaos. Pointless violence. The predictable lowness of it all. It showed Erebus for what he was. She sensed his shadows in a way she hadn't before, and noted they were not as thick or as fast-moving or as deep. It was time to show Erebus that she had not been humbled as he'd intended.

She waited for him to meet her eyes before she spoke. "Your shadows are bored."

Erebus's head went back as if he'd been slapped. "What's that? Are you begging me for more punishment?"

She raised her voice so the assembled mob

could hear. "Your chaos is becoming as unvaried and tedious as any mundane task. Even the shadows you took from Damon were happier with him." Saying Damon's name hurt, but the point was to catch the king off guard, and she could think of no better way than a hit to his pride. It must gall him that the son he'd so enjoyed tormenting had finally left.

"Prospect," the king said silkily, his movements slow and calculated. "Take my First back to the cave. Strike that, she is no longer First. I name her Last." He grinned, satisfied with his new name for her.

"Belay that," Thea ordered before he could continue, using the voice of command that she used with her Huntsmen. "Take Erebus instead."

A quiet fell over the ballroom, inch by inch, spreading like a ripple in a pond, leaving only a whisper of a cold breeze.

"I can't do that," Prospect said, his voice a fearful rasp.

Thea snapped her fingers as if remembering something. "No, you can't. I have your shadows." She made a twisting gesture, calling one of the butterflies to her hand. As it alighted, she allowed the others to flutter free from where they'd hidden behind her back, making a beautiful black cloud of moving wings around her. "It seems I will have to do it myself."

The seconds slowed as if time itself were shocked by her brazenness. As Thea had hoped, the creatures from the depths began leaving, no doubt unwilling to risk themselves in the coming confrontation.

A flush of rage suffused Erebus's features. His lips drew back from his teeth, and for a moment, he looked as ugly as his soul. He flexed his shoulders and opened his arms, and his shadows spread out like feathers, forming dark wings at his back. A breath later, the feathers turned to blades, which arched and curved as if aiming for Thea. The rush to the door intensified, the guests' talons and claws making a racket on the smooth tile floors. In a minute, only Thea, Erebus, and Prospect were left.

"I honored you by naming you First of Shadows," the king said, his voice hardly more than a whisper of rage. "And you disgrace me like this. Your power could have burned bright beside me. Now you will eat the ashes of your failure."

Thea pulled her own shades closer, making them into the shield she would need. "But

I became what you wanted me to be. *First of Shadows.* So I don't burn bright. Not anymore."

He panted heavily, his shadow-blades trembling as if they couldn't wait to sink into her vulnerable flesh. "No, you don't," he snarled. "You are thoroughly disappointing."

"I burn *darkly*," Thea finished.

And unleashed her shadows.

36

The Ancients agreed that each item must be tested before they were used on the Old Ones. As Solis used her ring to create dreams, and Noctua played her lute, Nerthus filled the silver cup with nectar and gave it to a brave, strong human warrior. But to her dismay, the second the liquid touched his lips, he fell to the ground. So great was the magic that his heart forgot to beat. His death disturbed Nerthus so much, she hid the cup so it could harm no one else. But the cup's shadow spoke to Erebus, as all dark spirits can, and told him where to find it.

—*Old Ones, Ancients, and the Folk*

Erebus's knives homed in on Thea, curving like arrows loosed from some impossible bow that locked onto a single target. As she watched them come for her heart, she tensed, trusting her own shadows.

Her shield held, but the jarring impact sent her airborne. She landed hard, the breath knocked out of her. Erebus's shadows followed, trying to find a way past her shield. She struggled to breathe, her chest aching as the king's footsteps neared.

Erebus seemed to grow in height, his own shadow a long, misshapen thing on the wall behind him. The ground quaked with each of his steps as he neared. Thea felt her insides being shaken and wondered wildly if he meant to step on her and if her bones would grind together into dust. Each footfall left a crack in the floor, releasing steam from the fissures, bringing the scents of magma and other unnamed things. Finally, he halted, and the world stilled, allowing Thea to catch her breath.

"Hubris," he said, staring down at her with triumph. His eyes burned with real fire, his face taking on an animal shape as his mouth stretched in a grimace of hatred. His body seemed to grow, becoming larger than a bear's, larger than any creature Thea had seen—a monster that would steal the sleep from those who saw it. This was a form she had never imagined, something wild and primal that made her chest tighten with rising panic. Erebus made a wide-armed gesture, retrieving his shadows as if he were gathering a dark harvest into his arms. He moved his fingers, and the shadows turned into knives, then he made a downward motion with his palms. The blades rained upon her, cutting her cheeks and scalp before she covered her head. They sliced into her arms and back, the cuts burning as if they were filled with poison. At that moment, Thea felt in her bones that Erebus was one of the Old Ones. Cold. Monstrous. Merciless. A creature who'd existed long before things like morality and conscience. She had defied him with all the confidence that she was stronger.

But I didn't win his shadows. The failure seared into her mind.

His voice had the intonation of a furious deity. "You spit on my generosity. You dreamed you had power in my realm. Now you bleed at my feet."

Thea drew a painful breath. "I don't regret

anything." Though her voice was thin, she hoped he heard the perfect truth in her words.

He spat a guttural word in a tongue she didn't know. "Then you will become one of my silver trees. Not a commander but a thrall. *You* have decided that, Theodora. I offer everyone a choice, and you have made yours."

She stared into his fiery eyes and spoke the truth despite her fear. "You *take*. You manipulate and violate. You are surely the worst of the Old Ones. You create nothing. Your power is stolen."

He sucked in a breath and a wind raged around the ballroom, his shadows obscuring him for a moment so that only his red eyes glowed through. "Then I will steal one last thing from you. Your spirit will serve me quietly when you would not."

The room darkened. Thea lifted her head in time to see a host of shadows moving in through the open doorway. They kept coming and coming, an endless dark tide of night, filling every corner of the ballroom, blocking out light from the lanterns. The air pressure increased until her chest hurt as if it were being crushed. Her beleaguered heart ached. She was going to die painfully, and no one would know what had happened to her. A gasp escaped her throat. "Prospect's shadows gave you a false sense of confidence." Erebus sounded as if he were smiling at her obvious pain. "You thought it was proof you are powerful. But it only means he is weak."

A light flared, illuminating Prospect. Erebus turned to face the Seer, whose pale hands trembled as he bowed to the king. "My king, you cannot blame me. I put her in the cave as you ordered, but instead of emerging subdued as she should, she was...changed in some way that drew my shadows to her." He shook his head, his gray eyes settling on Thea with loathing. "It was not my fault."

Erebus stepped toward the Seer, his footfalls reverberating through the room. "You disgust me. When you came into my realm, you promised to bring me the best and strongest folk from above. Instead, my son far surpassed your abilities."

"*I* brought you the Sylvan queen!" Prospect cried, his thin face twisted in some mixture of rage and plea. "It was my crow who saw her daughter violate your boundary!"

Erebus's voice lowered to its usual volume but was filled with contempt. "And for that, I will spare your life. But your last act as my Seer will be to use the silver cup on the Sylvan king's daughter."

"You can't mean that," the Seer argued, his eyes pleading. "I have served you faithfully for ages. You can't mean to send me away."

Erebus's shadows moved menacingly over the Seer. "Make her drink, then take your shadows back. Perhaps, if you grovel for a hundred years, I'll consider forgiving you."

Prospect nodded, but his face was still twisted in resentment. Thea had taken his shadows, and he had no reason to help her, but if she could play on his bitterness, poke at his pride… "Prospect isn't one of your thralls to be ordered around. He's strong enough to defy you if he wishes," she said hoarsely. It might be a waste of the breath that was rapidly leaving her body, but she had to try.

Prospect stared at her for a moment, something measuring in his eyes. But then he lifted his chin, his face set in lines of determination as he moved toward her. She tried to get up, but her legs were weak, so she pushed herself backward on the floor, her hands slipping on her own blood. The Seer reached toward her and plucked a cup of pure silver from the shadows around Thea, grimacing as he touched it.

"Don't!" Thea cried, managing to push to her feet. But before she could run, Erebus's shadows swept to her, grabbing her arms and holding them to her sides so she couldn't fight. More shadows held her still, preventing her from turning her face away.

She watched with a sense of violent outrage mixed with helplessness, her heart slamming as Prospect brought the cup closer, his fingers stretched around the base of the goblet. All she could think of was the image of her mother as a silver tree, her branches straining away from the throne, unable to escape. Her eyes pricked with tears, but she pressed her lips together, determined to fight him to the last. The cup touched her cheek. It burned colder than ice, a painful chill that ran into her skull and down her back, making her shake. She tried to turn her head away, but the shadows held her fast.

Prospect bent to whisper in her ear, and what he said shocked her into stillness.

"Pretend to drink." It was no louder than the beat of butterfly wings.

Pretend? Thea made an involuntary sound

in her throat, more surprise than anything, but when King Erebus laughed, she realized he must be enjoying what he perceived as her pain at the burn of the cup. She made a pantomime of drinking as the cup was pressed to the edge of her lips, but no liquid touched her skin.

Prospect returned the cup to the shadows, mouthing something to them as he did so.

The shades moved downward, and Thea watched as her feet turned silver, then transformed into roots that spread out over the ballroom floor. She gasped in horror as the silver moved upward in a pattern like the whorls of tree bark, covering her body from ankles to waist and rising, molding to her curves. In moments, she was encased in a sheath of silver, her arms become branches, among others reaching toward the sky.

But she felt her heart beating and the warmth of her own blood rushing through her veins. She took a shuddering breath, almost certain her mother had not been able to breathe when she had been a silver tree.

The shadows had created a shining illusion.

The king walked up, reaching out to touch her. Thea held her breath. His finger ran along her arm. She bit her lip to keep from spitting in his face. Finally, he stepped back, shaking his head. "So strong. So misguided. Such a disappointment. She will serve me better in this form."

As he turned away, Thea let her breath out slowly. The shadows had succeeded in fooling the king. And Prospect had told them to do it. She didn't know which was more surprising.

Erebus spoke once more, his voice drawing farther away. "The Sylvan king's daughter has shown me that it is past time to pay a visit to Thirstwood, to remind the folk who I am. Prospect, if you want forgiveness for your failures, retrieve your errant shadows and meet me by the walnut tree."

Thea waited for the Seer to do just that, but Prospect did not come to take the shadows disguising her. She heard his voice one more time, soft and bitter. "You are on your own, girl. Your people will pay the price for your folly."

A second later, the door closed with a clang.

Thea's legs shook. Lightheaded with blood loss, injured, exhausted, she crumpled to the floor, and her mind fell into darkness.

37

When Noctua played her lute to put the Old Ones to sleep, Erebus alone was left awake. The cup's shadow had warned him of the danger, covering his ears to block the music. Solis fought him, but even her ring of light was no match for all his shadows. Unable to subdue him, the Ancients combined their powers and banished him to a realm where he could harm no one.

—Old Ones, Ancients, and the Folk

"Giantess! Wake up!"

Thea opened her eyes. She was lying on the floor in the ballroom. A glimmer of light came from a single sconce on the wall. Her tree glamour was gone. Butterflies hovered around her. A silver pixie flew among them, his long hair tangled, his eyes wide in his small face.

Thea sat up abruptly. "Winter! Get out of here!" Her voice was shredded, barely audible.

Winter made a placating gesture. "It's all right, Giantess. King Erebus is not here. What happened?"

Thea massaged her aching chest where her shadow shield had pressed into her, and assessed her wounds. The bleeding had stopped. "I set my shadows against his. He won."

Winter clucked. "You're not a silver tree and you're not dead. I'd call that a draw against the shadow king."

Thea pondered Erebus's final words, how he had plans in Thirstwood. Her heart clenched at the thought. The shadows seemed to sense her distress, fluttering closer. "We have to get home," Thea said.

"Yes," Winter said. "Except we can't. Our way out of here lies across the water, and that lumpy gray Seer took the boat. I can fly but..." He gestured to her, grimacing.

So Prospect had saved her life but taken the boat, leaving her trapped. *Fickle Seer.*

Thea bit her lip against a groan of pain and

pushed to her feet. The only light outside came from a handful of moon sprites that wheeled slowly overhead, far fewer than before. It seemed they'd all but abandoned Damon's castle. Perhaps without his dance, there was no longer the right kind of magic to draw them.

Thea moved to the edge of the water, its soft lapping the only sound. "Is it safe to swim?"

Winter shuddered. "I wouldn't. I've seen things in there. Things I can't name. I suspect they'd find you a hearty meal."

Thea exhaled a puff of breath. "That's what I was afraid of." She spoke to the shadows hovering around her shoulders. "Can you help?"

After a pause, the butterflies surrounded her, attaching to her arms, back, and legs. They formed something like a harness around her chest and waist, cinching tight as they lifted her feet an inch off the ground.

"Is this a good idea?" Winter asked, his face openly doubtful.

"It's my *only* idea," Thea replied, kicking experimentally to see what happened. The butterflies lifted her higher, making her gasp before she added, "Which makes it good enough."

"Daft Sylvan logic," the pixie muttered.

The butterflies flapped in unison, lifting her higher. She sucked in a terrified breath, her heart beating hard against her ribs as they took her over the water.

"If they drop you," Winter said, flying beside her, "I'll try to distract the ravenous predators while you swim to the other side."

Thea couldn't manage a reply. She closed her eyes so she wouldn't see the shapes moving below the dark, glassy surface.

In minutes that seemed far longer, she reached the opposite shore. When the shadows set her down, she took gulping breaths, relieved to be on solid ground. Her butterflies rested on her shoulders and in her hair. "Thank you," she said softly.

"I'm glad they didn't drop you," Winter said, shuddering dramatically. "I wasn't really going to risk my life to distract the predators. I only said that to make you feel better."

Thea smiled wryly. "Very comforting."

As Winter flew along gravel paths through the silver forest, Thea followed, her injuries slowing her steps so that Winter had to keep stopping and waiting for her. Finally, he pointed at a larger silver tree. "I remember this spot. This should be close enough. Root! Take us home!"

"You can command the root?" Thea was shocked. "Is that how you got into the shadow realm?"

Winter ignored her, his focus completely on his task. "By the power of the Sylvan queen," he shouted, a hint of panic in his voice, "take us home!"

After a brief pause, a root snaked out of the darkness. Thea stepped on it, and the familiar portal of light grew and grew until it was large enough to walk through. Winter didn't hesitate before flying forward. Thea followed, desperate to find herself back in Thirstwood.

Suddenly, the scents of the forest were all around her, the needle-strewn path under her feet. Relief flooded her, making her lightheaded. Night had fallen, but the area was familiar. It thrilled her to be once again among real trees, poplars and firs and oaks, the smells so vivid and alive. It brought an immediate sense of security. She would never again take the forest for granted.

"How long have I been gone?" she asked, feeling comforted that her butterflies were still with her, though fewer than before. She didn't know if some had been lost in the clash with Erebus's shadows or if some had left her, but she was glad for the ones that had stayed.

Winter looked up at the moon as if for guidance. "I've lost track, but it's been over a month."

Thea's chest ached at the thought of how long she'd been gone, but it had seemed like far more time had passed in the cave. She counted herself lucky to have escaped at all. "How did you manage to enter Iluna?"

"Veleda used the remnants of magic from a pair of slippers in your bedchamber to call the root of the walnut tree."

Thea was glad she hadn't thrown all the clothing into the fire.

She gave him a grateful look. "The pixies are indeed the greatest of the forest folk." She lifted her head and sniffed the air. "Scarhamm is this way."

Winter flew beside Thea, who walked as fast as she was able through impenetrably dark paths. Sometimes, she had to feel her way along. A few times, she stopped to rest, though she didn't allow herself to stop for long. Finally, Scarhamm's towers came into view. The lanterns on the walls had never been such a welcome sight. But strangely, she saw no Huntsmen on the watchtower.

When she saw a guard on the wall, she lifted her arm and called out. "It's me, Thea! And our good pixie friend, Winter."

She expected an uproar of relieved greetings, but the guards were quiet. She supposed the recent threats had everyone unnerved. She hadn't let herself think about what it would feel like to come home, but when the gates opened and a tall woman with greenish-gold hair swept from them in great haste, a sob rose in Thea's throat.

"Mother?" Her heart felt as if it would burst.

"My daughter," the Sylvan queen said, beckoning to her.

Thea ran to her mother, reaching out to pull her close. But she didn't feel the embrace of warm, soft arms. Her mother's arms remained at her sides.

Thea looked into her mother's hazel eyes, trying to figure out what was wrong.

"Thank you for freeing me," Queen Coventina said. "With your help, we will bring the rest of the silver trees into Thirstwood. And together, we will serve Erebus faithfully."

38

Erebus knew that regaining his lost freedom required shadows and spirits to do his bidding. He needed to draw them to his prison, and keep them there. Killing was of no use to Erebus. If the folk died, their spirits merely went to Noctua's realm. He wanted to keep the spirits for himself, to give power to his realm. He hired a Seer to discover the cup's secrets, to test various brews on the folk who came to his master's dark realm.

—*Old Ones, Ancients, and the Folk*

Thea stepped back, her pulse slamming, suspicion sharpening her senses. "Who are you?"

The queen tilted her head. "Did you think I would spend seven years in Iluna and remain unchanged? What a sad homecoming my return has been. My husband's power is waning. He is ill, his magic weakening day by day. A strong ruler is ready to step into his place. No one is more powerful than the Old Ones, and Erebus is the most cunning among them. Only he escaped the long slumber enforced by the Ancients."

"Is that true or was he already imprisoned?" Thea asked, taking another step back. After all, they didn't know the full story. "Maybe they ignored him because he was of no consequence."

Rage flashed in her mother's eyes. "He has bided his time like a seed in the ground, awaiting the right conditions to sprout. The cracks in the veil between realms have given him a chance. Selkolla's magic damaged the Sylvan wards, and now they are breaking down. It's only a matter of time before the Forgotten Realm comes through."

This was all wrong. Her mother's rage, the way she was talking about Erebus, this obsession with power… "You're not the Sylvan queen." Thea backed away, her eyes searching for allies. Where were the archers on the wall? The guards at the gate? Even the patrols should be returning soon. It must be close to morning. Where was her father? Then she remembered that Winter had said he was bedridden. Scarhamm was more vulnerable than it had ever been.

"Please, Theodora," the fake queen said, holding out her hand. "King Erebus is willing to forgive you."

"Forgive me?" Thea laughed harshly. "He tried to turn me into one of his trees. As far as he knows, I'm trapped in silver."

"Prospect's ruse didn't fool him for long." The queen, or whoever she was, took a step forward. "He could have gone back to kill you, but he wanted to see what you would do next. As he hoped, you have come home."

Thea did not believe a word. She took another step backward.

"My First of Shadows," a deep, silky voice crooned from behind her.

Thea spun to see Erebus moving toward her with a warm smile of welcome. "Your mother is right. I was rash before, when I deemed your usefulness to be at an end. You've shown yourself to be cunning and strong. Worthy."

"I don't believe any of this," Thea said, still

scanning the walls for help as she stepped toward the trees, careful to put distance between herself and Erebus and the thing that called itself her mother. "Am I still in the cave? Dreaming?"

Another voice spoke from the edge of the forest. "It's not a dream, Thea."

Damon!

Thea spun to see Damon emerge from the trees to the north, his clothing as tidy as if about to step into the ballroom for the first dance of the night. She knew he'd betrayed her, but to this extent? Was he truly so evil?

Damon gave her a crooked smile. "For so long, all my plans were to free my mother. I invited you to my realm intending to trade you for her, and it worked. But now that we're free, I've realized there's nowhere for us to go. Nowhere safe from the breakdown of veils. It's time to make amends with my father. It's time to reunite the realms." He lifted his hand, and a silver tree appeared next to him. "Accept it, Thea."

If what he was saying was true, why did she have to accept it? Why were they trying so hard to get her to believe them? "Where are my sisters?" she asked.

"Enora isn't well," the queen said, her face falling. "I'm afraid she was struck with an illness. Cassia, too. Even poor little Rozie."

Thea's hands fisted. Erebus had cursed her sisters? "No!" Her scream echoed against Scarhamm's walls. The blood trees shook their branches, sensing violence to come.

Erebus nodded. "I had to find some way to make you understand. If you don't join with us, your sisters will wither and die the way your mother almost did."

"Let me see them!" Thea repeated, her voice rising. "I won't believe you until I see for myself."

Erebus motioned with one hand. Moments later, three solemn figures shuffled from the gates of Scarhamm—Enora's silver hair glowed in the lantern light as she supported Cassia on one side and Rozie on the other.

"No, please," Thea whispered. "Please may it not be true."

Thea moved as quickly as she could, her hand trembling as she reached out toward Enora. Touching her shoulder made her sister wince in pain.

"One of the guards let the shadow king inside

the gates," Enora whispered, her eyes forlorn. "All he had to do was speak to them, and they let him in."

Thea wanted to vomit. Erebus had charmed the Huntsmen guards into letting him through the walls. And once inside, Veleda's wards no longer protected against his magic.

"He cursed you?" Thea asked, her eyes taking in Enora's wan cheeks, the dark circles under Cassia's eyes, and Rozie's feverish flush.

"He said we would sicken until you returned," Cassia said.

Rozie coughed. "I ache all over. I can't sleep. Thea, please, make it stop."

Thea closed her eyes, her heart hurting, her temples aching. But was this too pat? Too perfectly aimed at her heart?

She didn't know. She swallowed and turned to face Erebus, who was watching their exchange with an amused expression.

"Will you finally accept the truth, Theodora?" he asked.

"I'd rather know an ugly truth over a pretty lie," she said. "That's why your magic doesn't work on me." As soon as she said it, she felt that it was right. "But I don't trust you. Any of you." She turned to her sisters. "I'm sorry."

Enora's face registered hurt. "We're sick, Thea. Can't you see that? All the secrets you've kept have led to this. If you'd only told me, I could have helped you. We all could have."

"I couldn't!" Thea cried, that accusation hitting her like a blow to the chest. "I tried!"

"Or did your obsession with a shadow prince stop your tongue?" Cassia asked, her eyes sad. "You were always suspicious of Zeru, and now look who you've trusted. What you've brought on us."

It wasn't like Cassia to be so harsh. And although their illness reminded her of her mother's, it wasn't this bad until after a couple of years of decline. Somehow, they'd weakened in only hours. "Where's Veleda?" she asked.

No one spoke. Erebus's eyes shifted. Damon stilled.

"I want to see Veleda." Thea crossed her arms, refusing to give in.

"The time for demands is over," Erebus said, striding forward, his hand reaching for her. "Come with us, Theodora. We will talk terms, as you Sylvans did with the Azpians when you made a pact of peace. Remember your vow of allegiance to me. That is the only way to save your sisters."

Thea stepped back and back, keeping out of Erebus's reach, though she knew it was taking her closer to Damon, who was now only about twenty feet behind her. Everyone was closing in.

A whizzing noise broke the silence. Thea turned toward the sound. Out of the trees, a small, pale shape flew. *Winter!* She had all but forgotten he was here. He was holding a bow, his expression determined.

"Our pine needle arrows show the truth of things," Winter reminded her. "Watch."

As he shot an arrow at Damon, the figure exploded into shadows. Thea gasped at the illusion.

Winter nocked another arrow and shot it at the Sylvan queen, who dissolved into darkness.

Neither of them were real.

Winter nocked a third needle, loosing it at Enora. She cried out and put a hand to her neck, looking startled. She did not turn into shadows, but blinked as if she was coming out of a dream. "What's going on?"

"Kill him!" Erebus made a motion with both

hands. The shadows turned into hunting birds, the entire flock diving toward Winter.

The pixie's wide eyes took up most of his face as he hovered, frozen by fear.

Thea's heart stuttered. "You can outfly the shadows. Go!"

Winter whirled and darted away, a silver blur that disappeared into the trees with shadow birds on his tail.

Erebus strode toward Thea and her sisters, determination and vengeance clear on his features.

"Run!" Thea breathed, taking Rozie by the shoulders and turning her toward the gates. "The war room." Of all the places that might be safe, that was the best option.

"We can't," Enora said, her eyes still dazed as if she'd woken from a dream. "We *are* sick, Thea. Go. I'll try to get Cass and Rozie away."

No. She wouldn't run. She turned toward Erebus. She would stand and fight. She opened her hands, calling her butterflies to her.

Erebus laughed. "Have you forgotten you tried to fight me mere hours ago? I left you bloody on the floor. What makes you think now will be any different?"

"Because I'm not alone here," she said, digging her heels into the ground of Thirstwood, feeling the strength of its trees, and calling to her shadows, asking them, willing them to fight for her. *My hatred for Erebus knows no bounds*, she told them. *And my love for my sisters is even stronger.*

We are here. We will rise against him.

"There's nowhere safe for you if you defy me," Erebus said. "Nowhere. Haven't you figured that out, Theodora?"

Something shook the ground, a quake that knocked Thea to her knees. She heard Cassia gasp and Rozie groan, but she had no time to turn her head to check on them.

Silver trees began appearing, popping up out of nowhere, splitting the trunks of some of the trees, supplanting the trees of Thirstwood. And with them came... things. Some were familiar, Azpians like Skrattis, pit sprites, and drakes. Others, Thea had only ever seen in the Forgotten Realm—like the insects with bulbous eyes.

"Why stop at merging *two* realms?" Erebus asked, his smile wide, his teeth bright in the light of the lanterns on the walls. "There are so many more pockets of the world that were sealed off by the Ancients because they were too dangerous to mortals. But I am not so small-minded."

More unfathomable creatures dug their way out of the ground, Thea looked desperately at her sisters, willing them to get inside the fortress gates before it was too late.

"I invited all the realms here. And look, some have accepted my invitation," Erebus went on. "So tell me, Theodora: Do you care to dance?"

39

> Finally, the Seer perfected a brew that would be of use to Erebus. The drinkers lost the memory of their mortal forms. In this way, the king of shadows could keep their spirits bound, transforming them into creatures of his own design, each silver like the cup.
>
> —Old Ones, Ancients, and the Folk

So many enemies were rushing toward Scarhamm. Scaly lizards breathed fire onto the walls, blackening them with scorch marks. Other creatures piled kindling from the forest into heaps, lighting them ablaze and dancing around as if in celebration. Scores of them moved closer to Thea and her sisters, their eyes aglow with death.

Chaos.

Screams filled the air as the creatures came tearing at her. There were hairy wild boars with serpentine tails. Doglike animals with long snouts that bared sharp teeth shining with spittle, their leathery ears flat as they ran faster than the Sylvan king's hounds. Things that looked like overgrown flies covered in fish scales flew ahead of the rest.

"Enna?" Thea called out, not wanting to turn her head for even a second.

"At your back, as always," Enora said, her voice inches behind.

"We're here," said Cass, her voice breathless but determined.

"Can you fly?" Thea asked. "Take Rozie to safety?"

"I can try," Cassia said, but in seconds the creatures were too close. They'd take her right back down.

Protective energy swirled inside Thea. Her shadows responded, creating a dome around herself and her sisters. A moment later, a shattering blow hit her shield. She saw Rozie stumble, but Cassia helped her up. Thea drew strength from the support of her sisters at her back.

Creatures shrieked and clawed at the barrier,

their eyes just visible through the darkness. Thea could feel their claws on her shadows as if they raked her own skin. She gasped for breath, desperately tired, agonized by how much strength it took to hold the shield.

Erebus's voice floated to her. "Your vow of allegiance gives me power, Thea. You thought to break it in my realm where Noctua can't reach, but here, you will die if you do. Obey me or die."

"Death," Thea whispered, "over allegiance to you."

A pressure filled the air inside her shield. He might not be able to break it…yet…but he was stealing the air. Thea drew breath with difficulty.

"You can kill me," she said, "but you'll remember every word I've said: Your grand plan is nothing. You want folk to worship you again? Why would they? Look at the world you're creating. You have nothing. And you are nothing." She gasped, her lungs starving. "That's why you tormented Damon. You knew he was…more than you'll ever be."

She fell to her knees, her head light. She turned to speak to her sisters. "I can't hold it much longer." She hated admitting that failure.

"Drop the shield, Thea," Cassia gasped. "I can get in one... blast with my ring!"

It seemed like a huge risk, but Cassia was right. Thea nodded. "One, two..."

"Three!" Rozie cried.

The creatures had piled on top of one another in their desperate bid to break the shield. The dozens leaning on the barrier came crashing in like a wave of claws and teeth. At that moment, Cassia sent a searing blast from her ring, so bright that Thea was blinded. She heard bodies hitting the ground. Screams and shrieks echoed, Erebus's shout of rage rising over it all.

Thea gulped air, filling her starving lungs, and rubbed her eyes. The creatures were writhing on the ground.

More shouts... but these were Sylvan voices! Thea turned to see armed Huntsmen pouring from the gates of Scarhamm. Had the blast broken Erebus's enchantment over them? But then she saw a host of pixies with bows flying along with the Huntsmen. Winter must have flown like mad for reinforcements! Maybe the magic of their pine arrows had brought the Huntsmen out of Erebus's charm.

Finally, a great antlered figure stepped from the gates. "Erebus," said the Sylvan king. "At last." His skin was paler than she'd ever seen, his steps slow, but he was here. A thrill of triumph ran up Thea's spine to see the death and revenge etched clear in her father's eyes. He was a creature of war, and right now she was glad of it.

But there was no time to celebrate. Shadows grabbed her, and Thea was lifted and thrown as if she weighed nothing, her body landing hard on the cold earth, away from the fray. Above her, Erebus looked down, his eyes completely black. Darkness covered the sky. He'd cut her off from everyone else, the two of them locked in a void.

Thea pushed to her feet. The Huntsmen would deal with the incapacitated creatures. Her father would protect her sisters. She could focus solely on the task at hand.

It was time to test her shadows against Erebus.

"You are nothing," he spat, his eyes pure hatred.

"Then why bother with me?" she asked. Thea lifted her arms. Her shadows grew until they became giant moths as large as vultures, their wings inscribed with what looked like pale eyes.

Erebus's darkness changed, becoming wolves

with rough fur, their maws snapping, white fangs bright against the dark.

Some of her shadows became black hunting cats with yellow eyes and long pale teeth.

As the two sides met, growls, roars, snarls, and cries erupted as darkness descended. Thea was caught between them, the sharp claws slicing her. The outcome of this fight would determine whether her sisters, her people, everyone in Thirstwood was safe. She imagined what would happen if she lost and let out a battle cry, letting the protective emotions wash over her and feed her shadows, urging them to fight, devour, destroy. Embracing the chaos around her after so many years of precision and perfection.

She looked up to see Erebus holding a shadow shaped like a curved blade in one hand. He lifted his arm, ready to bring it down on her.

"And to think my son loves you still," Erebus whispered. "Fool."

"Oh, Father," a smooth voice said from behind the king. "I thought petty name-calling was behind us."

40

At first, Erebus didn't know that the spirits lived inside these new bodies, awake and aware, trapped and in agony. When the Seer told him of their suffering, Erebus laughed. Their pain fed his shadows, making the realm stronger.

—Old Ones, Ancients, and the Folk

Erebus whirled. A figure was illuminated by a lantern held in one hand. But Thea already knew who it was before she saw him—his voice, his scent, the feeling of his presence in the air.

Damon.

As Erebus's shadows whirled in confusion, Thea's butterflies returned to her, their wings shrinking as they settled on her shoulders and in her hair. She sensed their curiosity, as if they wanted to watch this confrontation, to gauge who would be the winner.

"My son," Erebus said, hiding the blade behind his back. "This Sylvan girl is a threat to both of us and must be dealt with if we are to rule together."

"Thea is most definitely a threat," Damon agreed.

As he approached, the darkness of the bubble that surrounded them thinned. Thea could see the clash of Huntsmen and creatures fighting by Scarhamm's walls. The Sylvan king's sword was a scythe, harvesting death rattles and blood.

Light from the bonfires filtered in, catching the planes and angles of Damon's face, delineating every beautiful line and curve. Thea was ashamed to realize how much pleasure she found in looking at him, even now.

"I am glad you see her for what she is," Erebus said, bringing the shadow blade from behind his back. "Shall I give you the honor, my son?"

Damon put his hand out for the blade, his face a mask of cruelty. In that moment, Thea could not remember ever seeing softness in him. All memory of their time together was wiped away in the intensity of this. He was death personified, a walking embodiment of a last breath. If they'd been on the same side in this conflict, she might have admired him.

But he was going to kill her. He had traded her freedom for his mother's, and now he would trade her life for his father's forgiveness.

His eyes shifted to hers, but she could not name the look in them. Her heart pounded, her blood warming to panic in her veins. No shield could hold forever.

She hoped her sisters had made it inside the war room. She wished she could embrace them one last time. There was so much more she wanted to do if only she had more days ahead. She would spend less time training. More time laughing. Less time worrying the truce wouldn't hold. More time finding common ground.

Damon took a step closer, one hand holding the blade. With his other hand, he reached out toward her as if inviting her to dance with him. She gave him a hate-filled look, furious that he was using this moment to mock her. She had never done anything to deserve this.

He blinked, the expression on his face changing to one of inquiry. She saw the thickness of his lashes, the way the shadows fell on the curves of his face. Shadows had always loved him.

"I'll haunt you as a spirit," she swore, hating that her voice shook. "I'll make your life a misery. I'll never leave you alone."

"Promise?" He bent his head, and for a moment, she thought he would touch his lips to hers. But they merely brushed her cheek in a warm caress of two words. "The cup."

"What?" Thea jerked her head up, her eyes snapping to his. He was asking her for the silver cup? Prospect had hidden it in shadows, but... wait, *she* had his shadows!

Damon made a motion with his hand. A butterfly lifted from her shoulder and alighted in his palm. It unfurled to reveal the silver goblet, its polished surface catching orange firelight.

In a blur of movement, Damon turned to his father, seizing his shoulder and pressing the cup against Erebus's cheek.

Erebus froze as if turned to stone, letting out a groan of pain. His lips moved slowly as he spoke in a fierce whisper. "What... are you doing?"

"Feel his terror," Damon said to the shadows. "My father's power is waning. You've grown bored with his petty cruelty. Go to the First of Shadows. She is stronger. Braver. More enticing in every possible way. Cleave to her, and she will never betray you."

Shadow by shadow, they swirled together in a dark cloud. Thea felt their ambivalence, some of them reluctant, even hateful—but they came to her. Maybe they were persuaded by Damon's words, or by the new power they sensed in him. She sensed it, too. Her head was reeling, her breath coming in shallow bursts. She trembled at the feeling of so many shadows around her.

"You'll be my butterflies," she told them, emanating the strength they craved.

Damon gave her a lopsided smile. "My First," he said softly. "I knew you were meant for this."

"Think very carefully about what you do next," Erebus snarled. "There will be no forgiveness for you this time, Damon, unless you take this foul cup from my skin and kill the girl. Then we will discuss your future."

"It burns, doesn't it?" Damon asked, shoving it closer. "An item made by the Ancients to weaken and overcome the Old Ones, who had outgrown their time in this world. This is the cup of forgetfulness, once used to help put them to sleep. You, Father, have lost the right of wakefulness. Sleep now, and be at peace for the first time in your miserable existence."

"No!" Erebus screamed, the word ending on a gasp of pain as Damon pressed the silver tighter against his cheek. "I will cover the earth with my shadows, and all will bow to me."

"You have no shadows," Thea pointed out, becoming accustomed to their presence. "They're mine now."

Erebus's eyes shifted to her, and she had never seen so much loathing. "You deserve what is coming. You and all your people. I've been weakening the walls of my prison for millennia, and the walls that hold the Old Ones have been thinned, too. Without me holding my realm strong, the rest of them will be released. They will destroy everything you hold dear. Freeing me now is the only way to save yourselves."

"We'll find another way," Thea said, coming to stand toe to toe with him.

He bared his teeth. "When my brethren wake, we will have a revel of destruction unlike anything—"

"I could force you to drink," Damon interrupted, his voice calm, low, and as silky as ever.

"But I will offer you a choice: The cup? Or eternal torment?"

"You think you're strong enough to trap me? To torture me endlessly?" Erebus said, his voice almost hysterical.

The barrier of darkness around them dissolved.

A heavy footfall came before a large, antlered figure approached, his animal shadow falling over the shadow king, his sword dripping the ichor blood of creatures with no place in this world.

"Erebus the Betrayer," said the Sylvan king, his hair matted, his face drawn in lines of fatigue. "This has long been coming. It will take many, many years to repay you for what you have done to me."

Erebus's chest was rising and falling quickly. "Unfair. This is your home, Silvanus. Fight me in territory where we're evenly matched."

"Was it fair that you took my wife? That you took my daughter?" Thunder rumbled overhead and lightning flashed, illuminating the Sylvan king and the Huntsmen.

Thea had never seen her father look so dangerous. So wild.

And behind him, the sky was orange. Dawn was breaking over Thirstwood.

Wind shook trees, shaking leaves from branches. Rain poured, lashing the Huntsmen and their enemies as they fought. Lightning flashed in an endless strobe. The bonfires hissed, their flames dying.

"I did nothing wrong," Erebus screamed. "It was *your* carelessness that led to Coventina's capture. You should have warned your people. It wasn't my fault you are so frightened of weakness that you could not admit my power still thrived in your forest!" Though his words held fury, Erebus's body trembled as he twisted the rings on his fingers.

Thea thought how small he looked without his shadows.

"Let us test my 'weakness' here in *my* home, Erebus," said Silvanus, king of the forest, as he walked closer, his steps shaking the ground. "I will be as merciful to you as you have been to all the folk who were lured into your realm."

"I choose the cup," Erebus whispered, his eyes wide with terror. "My son. The cup!"

His shout was drowned by a clap of thunder. Between one flash of lightning and the next, Damon tipped the cup to his father's lips, administering the brew. Silver flowed over the ground, roots spreading. Each flash of lightning showed more, from Erebus's ankles to his waist, and finally, his arms lifted as branches that touched the sunrise.

Some of the branches glinted gold, red, blue, and green—his rings, strung like decorations for a revel.

Thea realized they were all that was left of Erebus the Betrayer.

41

> Erebus refused to free the spirits, declaring that anyone foolish enough to be bound should be bound forever.
> —*Old Ones, Ancients, and the Folk*

THREE WEEKS LATER, QUEEN COVENtina sat at a table with her daughters in the great hall, the glass doors behind them framing the garden. The evergreen shrubs had been trimmed into topiaries of forest creatures by Cassia and her mother, who'd spent hours together on sunny days reconnecting after their long separation. Thea wasn't much help at gardening, and her shadows didn't like the sun, but she often sat on a bench while they worked, comforted by her mother's presence. If you looked at a certain angle, you could see the top of Erebus's tree, its silver bark reflecting sunlight.

The shadows had started accompanying Thea to training on overcast days, though she instructed them forcefully *not* to interfere on her behalf. And they enjoyed the dim interior of Scarhamm, seeming to find it dark enough for their comfort as they explored their new home. The Huntsmen were clearly wary, but she hoped they'd grow used to the shadows in time.

Currently, Thea and her mother and sisters sat in the great hall with some important guests. Enora sipped mint tea from a porcelain cup in the shape of a tulip while Cassia held a slim pewter mug filled with nectar. Rozie was trying to eat a honey cake as messily as possible, or so Thea assumed based on the amount of crumbs on her dress. Thea herself held a tankard of spiced cider, grateful for its warmth. Her butterflies explored the space, sitting on rafters or alighting on the hearth, some resting on her shoulders.

Three pixie guests sat on the table, each with a thimble of blueberry juice. There had been no revels since the queen's return, but she had invited small groups of folk to the fortress in order to reintroduce herself to society slowly. Her health had been fully restored, and she said she had years to make up for as host of Scarhamm.

"I have so much to thank you for," Queen Coventina said to the pixies. "I hardly know where to begin. Without you, the Huntsmen—even myself and the king—would have remained spellbound by Erebus's charm, unable to fight back. We owe everything to you."

Sunflower inclined her head, her white hair braided like a crown. "We were glad to put our skills to use. When the forest is under threat, all of us are under threat. There is no division between pixies and Sylvans in times of need."

Thea was impressed and surprised at how gracious that answer had been. The pixies were treating her mother with great kindness, rather than with the barbs to which Thea was accustomed. Perhaps everyone had sympathy for the queen after she'd lost so many years trapped in Iluna.

Winter was dressed in brown furs that contrasted nicely with his pale hair. As hero of the fight against Erebus—or so he claimed—there was already a lutin ballad written about him. "Autumn thought I was wasting my time making so many pine needle arrows, but *I* said—"

"I never said that," Autumn snapped from next to him. "And why are you the hero of the story when it was my visions that directed everything you did?"

Thea was glad to see how clear Autumn's eyes looked now that her visions of silver trees had stopped. Thea noted that her hair was almost as bright as Rozie's, who sat across from her. Maybe they would become friends.

"Well, you kept sending me on errands," Winter sniped back, setting down his thimble with a thump. "Several of which nearly got me killed."

"You were extremely brave," Thea interjected. "Thank you for coming to get me in Iluna. If not for you, I'd still be trapped there."

"Or devoured by ravenous fish creatures," Winter said with a shudder. "Did I mention some of them had two mouths?"

"No," Thea said, grimacing. "I'm glad you didn't tell me that when I was flying over the water."

"Well, I deserve some recognition, too," Autumn interjected. "I was sicker than a squashed tree vole for weeks. Your Court Seer didn't even believe me."

"I feel terrible about that," Veleda said.

Thea turned in surprise to see the Court Seer approaching the table. Thea had barely seen her of late. As the Sylvan king had been renewing his protections over Thirstwood's roots, Veleda had been working on reinforcing the wards in and around Scarhamm. She bowed to the queen, then to Sunflower, before turning back to Autumn. "I came to make my apologies and ask if you'll still be my apprentice."

"I'll think about it," Autumn said, not meeting Veleda's eyes. After a slow sip from her thimble, she added, "If you give me lessons in a room more suited to pixie sensibilities. I can't think in that dungeon of yours."

Veleda's face set in annoyed lines, but after a speaking look from the queen, Veleda nodded and said, "There's a room on the second floor we can try."

How things were changing in Scarhamm now that the queen was home.

"I want to thank you again," Queen Coventina said, placing her hand near Autumn, "for listening when I spoke to you in my spirit form. You were a lifeline for me when I overheard Erebus's plans and could do nothing to stop him. You helped me warn my daughter." She looked over at Thea, who smiled. She still couldn't believe her mother was actually here.

After a while, the conversation wound down, and the pixies took their leave. Enora kissed the queen's cheek and gave her a warm embrace before saying, "I have to meet with Tordon. We're organizing tonight's patrol. Though there haven't been any Skratti attacks recently, we can't rule it out. And there are still scuccas here and there."

The queen nodded. "Be safe."

Rozie hopped up next. "I'm going to see if Mr. Himmy is back from hunting. He brings me dead mice."

"Of course," the queen said, almost successfully hiding her distaste for the idea. "Dead mice are meant as tributes."

"He yowls until I tell him he's a good boy." Rozie grimaced. "I don't mind, but Cassia doesn't like his noises."

"He sounds so sad," Cassia said, pushing to her feet and stretching her wings. "I always think maybe I'm supposed to feed him. But then I look at his dimensions and think I'd better not." She put her arm around her mother, squeezing as she said, "I'm going to meet Zeru for a quick trip to the clouds. You should come visit."

"Soon," the queen said, smiling, though Thea had the sense she wasn't ready to leave Scarhamm yet.

When everyone else had gone, Thea scooted

over on the bench and rested her head on her mother's shoulder. It was such a privilege to be able to do that.

"Thank you, Theodora," Queen Coventina said. "For all you've done."

"You've thanked me a dozen times," Thea reminded her. "Two dozen."

Her mother's voice was choked with emotion. "I never thought I'd escape. I didn't intend to leave. I thought that was the only way to protect you."

Thea swallowed a thick lump of feeling in her throat. She was starting to get used to having those. *Emotions.* "I know."

"I made your father swear never to tell you what happened to me."

"I know that, too," Thea said. "But he shouldn't have let you go."

The queen sighed. "Thea, believe it or not, I am formidable when I make up my mind, and I have a great deal of power over your father. I insisted. Because if you had gone to that place, I would have died. I wouldn't have *wanted* to live. Do you hear me?"

"I think I understand a little," Thea admitted. "When I knew you were trapped, there was no chance I would have left you. I suppose if you love someone enough, their suffering is worse than your own."

"Exactly." Her mother's hand smoothed her hair, and Thea sighed, knowing she'd never take that caress for granted again.

A few minutes later, Thea felt a shift in the air and turned to see her father entering the room.

The queen didn't turn, but her back posture changed, stiffening slightly. Thea stood, knowing they would want to be left alone. On her way out, she faced her father for a moment, waiting to see what he'd say to her. He hadn't apologized for anything, and since her return, she'd sensed tension between Tordon, Tibald, and the king. She'd also heard muttering among the Huntsmen. They now knew the Sylvan king had lied to them about the whereabouts of his queen, and though some understood the reasons, no one would trust him in the same way again. *He isn't truly Sylvan*, Thea had realized. He was their king, and yet he was something older, something wilder that they didn't quite understand.

Thea continued to wait, refusing to make things easier on her father. She still craved an admission that he'd been wrong. She wanted him to at least admit he should have helped her rather than hindered her.

His dark eyes stayed locked on hers, his head tilting in acknowledgment. "My daughter."

Thea felt a pinprick of tears at his warm tone. Was that supposed to be an apology? Why couldn't he say what he meant? Even now, when she could hear the rasp in his voice, see the dark circles under his eyes—the signs that his health was still recovering from Erebus's incursion into the forest—he could not admit vulnerability in any way. She sighed and moved past him, knowing that was all he would give.

As she walked out, she heard her parents talking and hovered in the doorway. It was obvious the Sylvan king was incredibly relieved to have his wife home again. Anyone could see that he loved her.

As Thea turned for one last look at them, silhouetted by the afternoon light, she saw her mother reach out and place a hand on her father's arm. He bent and kissed the top of her head. Silvanus murmured something, and with his low tone and the deep baritone rumble, it was hard to make out. But it sounded like, "My love."

Thea's throat was thick as she made her way

to her bedchamber, her chest aching in ways she wished she could deny. Her own arms hurt for the person she'd held, who had felt so right to her not long ago. She knew full well that she shouldn't want him, and hated that he had disappeared without even a parting word. She had to accept she might never see him again.

When she reached her room, her eyes went immediately to her hearth. She despised how her heart sank when she saw that all it contained was ashes.

42

> Some say Erebus's trapped spirits need only remember who they are to be freed.
> —*Old Ones, Ancients, and the Folk*

As the days grew shorter and colder, the trees shook off their leaves to make a fiery carpet on the forest floor. One night in early winter, long after dark, Thea caught herself staring at her hearth. The fire had died down, but the embers still glowed orange. When she realized her chest was tight with longing, she kicked off her bedding and sat up, stirring up the shadows that had been at rest around her. Nothing was going to appear in her bedchamber. Scarhamm's wards had been restored, as they should be.

She despised that she could not forget the shadow prince. She had always been good at shoving unimportant things out of her mind, but she couldn't seem to do that with him. It was humiliating considering he clearly wasn't thinking about her. He hadn't even tried to contact her.

As time went on, she'd realized the worst part was that she would never get a chance to say what she needed to say to him. She couldn't vent her hurt, or accuse him of misleading her, or tell him why she'd never trust him again. At times, it felt as if she'd imagined him, along with all her experiences in the Forgotten Realm. And yet, sometimes on patrol she caught the barest scent of magic, the specific combination of silver and water and darkness unique to Iluna.

Unable to bear her own restlessness, she strode to her wardrobe and yanked out her patrol gear. She wasn't scheduled for duty, but she might as well do something useful and check on the pixies. As her shadows swirled around her, she grabbed a lantern and her canvas bag and headed out of the fortress. She waved to the guards on the wall, making sure to spit on the large silver tree outside the gates.

Once in the forest, she sniffed the air, detecting the promise of snow. She hoped the change of season would release her from this unpleasant mood. Her long legs ate up the distance, and within a couple of hours, she was approaching the trees lit with clusters of moon sprites, tiny archers waiting in the branches.

"It's me," Thea said, raising one hand palm-out, the other holding the lantern. "The Sylvan king's daughter."

One of the pixies smiled, her teeth shining in the sprites' glow. "There's no need to check if you're real. Haven't seen a shadow thing in a while. No scuccas, either."

"Do you know what happened to them?" Thea asked. The Sylvan patrols had also noticed the absence of scuccas, but no one knew where they'd gone.

"I figured those evil shrubs just wandered off a cliff," one pixie replied.

"Nonsense," another said. "Sunflower says their spirits were freed. She sensed them leaving the forest."

Thea pondered that as she followed the path to the small cottage tucked into tree branches where Autumn and Winter lived. Knocking softly with one knuckle, she waited to see if anyone was awake.

Autumn's face appeared in the window, grinning widely. She turned and spoke to someone behind her. The door opened and Winter emerged, his wings brushing Thea's hair as he flew near her face. Autumn also flitted out, perching on a tiny porch that jutted from the front of the cottage.

"Sunflower is asleep," Autumn whispered with a finger to her lips, nodding to the cottage next door. "What are you doing here?"

Thea opened the bag, reaching in. "I brought you something."

"Let me guess." Autumn rolled her eyes toward her cousin. "More pine needles."

Thea's hand stilled. She'd been gathering pine needles to keep busy, bringing them to the pixies by the bagful every couple of weeks or so. Maybe she had overdone it.

Autumn seemed to notice her hesitation. "We can always use more."

"Just used some today, in fact," Winter said, flying into the cottage and returning with a handful of arrows. "These are for you. In case you need to find out the truth of things. They don't just shatter illusions, you know. They can also make anyone speak the truth. Not much use on you honest Sylvans, but useful on *other* folk. Autumn had a vision that—"

Autumn reached out and pinched his arm,

ignoring Winter's outraged gasp. "Your future holds a smack if you keep talking."

Winter rubbed his arm and glared back at her. "I hope your next vision is of something disgusting."

"Like a blizzard?" Autumn asked, twisting her lips. "I've already Seen it. Tomorrow." She shuddered.

"I adore snow." Winter sighed, his chest expanding as he took in a lungful of chilly air.

Autumn flicked her hair over her shoulder. "Oddling."

Thea smiled at their antics. "Do you know anything about the scuccas leaving Thirstwood?" she asked, looking between them. "Your guards mentioned they hadn't seen any in some time."

Winter snorted, tilting his head toward his cousin. "She has a theory on who released their spirits."

Autumn glared hard at him. "What I *know* is that a certain snowflake is going to get melted if he isn't careful."

That led to more barbs and threats, and Thea could get no straight answers out of the pixies. After a few more useless prompts, and having satisfied herself that they were perfectly fine, she said goodbye and left, walking more slowly on her way back. She considered going to the Grotto, but didn't feel like being in random company. She was halfway home when a twig snapped on the path behind her. Unsheathing her blade, she lifted her lantern high. "Identify yourself."

The silence made her uneasy. She was about to start throwing knives in the direction of the sound when a voice darker than a winter's night replied. "I'm a stranger in need of help."

The air froze in her chest. She had not heard his voice in so long.

Thea swallowed and put away her blade. "What kind of help?" Her voice was breathless, so she tried to steady it.

"I...find myself lost in a place I have never been before," he replied, the rasp of his voice both familiar and different than she remembered. He sounded...tired.

"Thirstwood isn't kind to strangers," she said. When her father had reinforced the wards, he'd also strengthened the blood trees. "You'll want to watch yourself."

"I was hoping a Sylvan would accompany me. To assure my safety."

A pleasant weightlessness came over Thea, spreading to her limbs. She could not help the elation that coursed through her at his presence, even now. But her mind raced, questioning this. As usual, she chose directness over games. "What do you want, Damon?"

She heard his indrawn breath, as if he were giving himself a moment to prepare. "I know I'm not welcome here. But I had to see you."

"Why?" Her pulse leaped at those words, but she knew better than to trust him.

After a pause, Damon said, "I grow bored in my realm. No visitors to pass the time. As a Sylvan, you understand the need for revelry."

Disappointment washed through her. Was that all? Still, she was curious enough to want answers. "I thought you'd left Iluna."

"As it turned out, I couldn't leave," he said. "And my mother decided the Forgotten Realm is her home as long as I'm there."

"What do you mean you *couldn't* leave?" Thea took a step closer, needing a glimpse of his face. Maybe she could read something in his expression.

"I've discovered my father was telling the truth about the realm being a buffer," he said.

"The real reason he harvested all those spirits was to thin the walls of his prison. But his spells also thinned the barriers between your world and the one that holds the sleeping primordials. The veils need to be restored or else the Old Ones *could* wake."

Thea digested that as best she could in the moment. "But...you hate it there."

"I did hate it there," he agreed. "But someone has to keep it strong, and I don't see who else will do this work."

Thea couldn't believe he'd chosen to do something so selfless, sacrificing his dreams of escape to protect...well, everyone. Her people and her family would be safer with him guarding that realm. She realized it was exactly what she would do in his shoes. "So you went back," she said, admiration clear in her voice.

"I never left." He paused, his voice lowering.

"What do you mean, you never left?" Had he been there, hiding, when she'd thought he'd escaped with Azra? That made no sense, and if it was true, only made her angry. He had never tried to help her after she made her bargain with Erebus. After she'd been put into the cave.

Thea took another step toward him, the lantern light picking up his outline. Another step and she could see his face, though shadows hid the nuances of his expression. Her heart slammed faster, as if it knew him better than she did.

"I freed my mother, but then I tried to come back to you," Damon said. "I should have known my father wouldn't allow me to return. He trapped me on an island in the river for a while, until my shadows found a way out, and that's when I followed you into Thirstwood. In the end, there was one sacrifice I wasn't willing to make."

"What sacrifice?"

"You."

Thea halted, her lantern raised, her heart jerking painfully while her eyes took a slow inventory of the man before her. He hadn't changed and yet he had. The planes of his face were sharper, the corners of his lips held tighter than she remembered, his eyes more sunken.

Now was her chance to tell him what she needed to say. "You still left me, Damon. You used me to free your mother and threw me to your father's mercy. After I saved you from death in the cave."

His swallow was audible. "Thank you for saving me. Why did you do it?"

Thea wished she could be as casual and dishonest as he was. To hurt him with a lie. But she was a Sylvan. "I couldn't let you die."

His eyes closed for a few seconds that stretched while Thea's chest ached with remembered pain. "I'm sorry," he said finally. "I can only imagine how you must hate me."

He *couldn't* imagine her hurt. But she forced herself to speak truth. "I'm angry. I'm furious. I feel betrayed. But... I don't hate you."

He paused, a thread of hope in his curiosity. "Why not?"

She shrugged one shoulder, an angry gesture as if she were throwing off his probing questions. "I haven't managed it yet." Her honest nature made her add, "And you did return to help me bind Erebus. I don't think I could have done that without you. I also understand the need to save your mother. I'd have done anything to free mine."

Damon sighed, his shadows moving slowly between himself and the lantern, reminding Thea that there were some loyal ones that had never left him. One strayed closer to Thea, and she allowed it. One of her own shadows twined together with it as if they liked each other.

"I should have done that to him long ago," Damon admitted finally. "Bound him in silver."

"He might have been too strong for that in Iluna," Thea pointed out. "He had far less power here in Thirstwood."

"You are generous," Damon said, "to defend me after what I've done."

"Yes, I am." Thea drew herself up, lifting her chin as she heard his warm chuckle. "Did you expect me to be modest?"

He put his palms up, his eyes moving over her face. "I think I know you better than that."

"Do you?" She gave him a skeptical look, noting the hungry way he stared at her. "We've known each other such a short time."

He took a step closer, and his eyes sparkled with the reflected torchlight. "Sometimes it's not about the hours spent but what's shared in those hours. If you see a person for who they truly are, what does it matter how long it took?"

She put out her hand. Damon looked surprised, staring at it blankly for a few seconds before he took it, sending a tingle of awareness through her palm. Thea set the lantern on the ground before reaching into her pocket. Her fingers grasped a pine needle arrow, drew it out, and jammed it into the fleshy part of his palm.

He sucked in a breath. "What is that?"

"Pine arrow." She pushed the needle deeper, recalling Winter saying that it had to draw blood to work. "Pixie made. Enchanted."

Damon swallowed. "I feel its effects."

"Tell me why you came here tonight." Her own skin warmed at the heat of him, the rapid drumbeat of his heart under her fingertips.

"I..." He pressed his lips together until they turned white, his eyes accusing. "Underhanded to force this out of me, Sylvan. I didn't think you were cruel."

She held his hand tightly, not blinking. "Then you don't know me well, after all."

He looked away, then back at her sharply, his voice breathless as the words poured out. "I don't want to live my life without you. I curse myself for the decisions that led me to lose you. I worry I'll never be content again. I want to shut you out of my thoughts but there you are, every minute." With his free hand, he massaged his temple, as if it ached. "I know you would never want to live in Iluna with me, and yet I would do almost anything to earn your forgiveness. I am weary of being without you." His lips pressed together again, his brows furrowing as a frustrated sound came from his throat. Finally, he said through gritted teeth, his eyes accusing, "Pixie spells are wicked."

Thea's senses reeled from his confessions. She sifted through what he'd said—putting most of it aside for the moment. "What would you do to earn my forgiveness?"

"I freed the scuccas," he said, his eyes steady on hers. "I've come into Thirstwood every night until it was done. The witch's thrall magic still lingers, and most of them fought me, but I was able to release their spirits with the help of my shadows." He moved his hand, and she let go. He rolled up both sleeves, showing angry scratches that could have come from branches. "I had hoped that my efforts would mean something to you."

Thea's lips parted as she looked at the red gashes on his arms. *He* had freed the scuccas. For her sake. She took a steadying breath. "Go on."

He tugged his sleeves down and stood straighter, meeting her eyes. "I am working on freeing the silver trees in Iluna... the ones I'm able to save.

Those that have been in the realm too long... well, the best we can do is to send their spirits to Noctua, according to Prospect."

Thea's chest expanded in a relieved sigh at that news. She'd worried their spirits would be trapped in Iluna forever. But her lip curled at the mention of Prospect. "I thought the Seer had fled."

Damon nodded. "After we dealt with Erebus, I kept thinking about what he'd said about the veils between realms. I needed to know if it was true. So I searched until I found Prospect in the Cryptlands. He'd been captured by the Skrattis, the fool, so I had to use my shadows to... *negotiate* his release. I have bruises from that, too, but they are in rather less obvious places, and I can't show you here." He lifted a brow at her.

She folded her arms, resisting the urge to smile. "I can't believe you rescued Prospect."

Damon's look told her he couldn't believe it, either. "Unfortunately, I need his help to strengthen the barriers. But some nights, when he is prattling on about spells, I'm tempted to jump into that monster-infested river so I won't have to listen anymore."

Thea couldn't repress a laugh. "That feckless Seer helped save me by deceiving your father, then stole the boat and trapped me there."

Damon shook his head, anger darkening his eyes. "Typical. He is useful about a fifth of the time. I haven't decided whether to kill him when I'm done with him."

"You won't."

Damon tilted his head. "No?"

"You won't reward his help with murder, even if he is odious. You'll be fair and show him more mercy than he deserves."

He looked away. "We'll see."

"You are not your father," Thea said softly. She saw the moment the compliment hit home, and warmth softened his eyes as they met hers again. But the pixie spell wouldn't last, and she wanted to know all his truth. "What will you do if you finally earn my forgiveness?"

He shook his head, blinking. "Whatever you want. I thought...I could invite you and your sisters to the dance. Iluna could be a place of revelry. With free folk who remain free," he added quickly.

"Merriment is fine," she said, liking that idea,

"but if you think Iluna is a barrier to the Old Ones waking, we need to find out more about that."

"We?" His eyes widened.

Thea lifted her hand and brushed it against the shadow that circled his throat, not touching him directly. He shivered, his nostrils flaring. Seeming to recover himself, he gave a single, slow nod. "It might take some time. Research. Experimentation. Dedication to the task. I might need you there often."

"However," she added, "it's doubtful I'll be allowed to return to Iluna at all. My father and mother won't like it."

"Ah." He looked down, clearing his throat.

"So your first task would be to win *their* forgiveness," she clarified.

"Mmm." He sounded skeptical. "I would have better luck fighting a hundred more scuccas."

Thea decided he'd earned a morsel of hope. "My mother says you argued for her freedom when she was first trapped."

He looked up sharply. "She remembers that?"

Thea nodded. "She thinks you have goodness in you, but you didn't have much chance to practice it. My father, however, will be harder to persuade."

He let out a slow breath. "My father and your father were old enemies. I would have to do something exceedingly impressive to make King Silvanus change his mind about me."

"Agreed." Thea reached out and touched his cheek, enjoying his quick inhale. "And even if you do gain their trust," she said, hearing the betraying emotion in her own voice, "you'll still need to prove yourself to me. That's more important."

Damon's chest rose and fell as he pressed his face into her hand. "Yes. That is *most* important."

Thea felt as if she were on the edge of something, poised to leap over a deep crevasse that might be too wide to clear. Then again, maybe it was more like jumping off a rock into the Scar, knowing the water would break her fall. The thrill of risk blended with the promise of reward, enticing her. She liked both too much to back away from this.

"You are never to lie to me again," she said, her fingers sliding into his hair. As soft and thick as she remembered.

Damon reached up and gripped her hand,

speaking in a firm voice. "I vow never to lie to you again, Theodora. In Noctua's name."

Thea gasped, shocked. "A vow to Noctua is sacred. It's not like being in Iluna, cut off from the Ancients. If you break this one, she'll take your life."

He stared at her, his eyes telling her he understood. She stared back, absorbing what he'd just done for her. An owl hooted in the distance, and it seemed to Thea that Noctua herself had replied to his promise. The other night birds hushed in the silence.

"The effects of the pine needle will be wearing off," she said finally, lifting his hand to remove the tiny arrow, then brushing at the spot of blood that welled up in its place. "But now that you made that foolish promise, I suppose it doesn't matter." She bent her head and pressed her lips to the wound, tasting the copper of his blood. It felt as if she had made a pact, too. That she would fight for him for as long as he fought for her.

Damon's hand was gentle as he took her face and tilted it so he could look into her eyes. "Please tell me I have some hope of earning your trust again, Thea."

Warmth at his look, his tone, and everything

he'd said spread through her body, leaving a lightness in its wake. And the feel of him against her, solid and real and there for her, now and in her future...it meant something. And she was herself with him in ways she was not with anyone else. She wanted him, and couldn't imagine a time when she wouldn't.

"I am devising tasks," she said, sliding her hands to his back, spreading her fingers to savor the muscles that rippled under her palms, pulling him toward her until their chests touched. She absorbed his shudder of pleasure as if it were her own. "Tasks you'll have to perform to gain my approval." She touched her tongue to the corner of his lips, very lightly.

"Without question," he breathed.

He made promises to her without speaking, and she decided to believe every single one.

Epilogue

> Revel, Sylvans, though danger
> lurks under our roots!
> Remind yourselves of joy,
> though our enemies rise with
> the full moon.
>
> —Excharias, Sylvan poet

Two months later, Thea stared at the dress on her hearth. Her heartbeat doubled, but not from fear. She moved forward, her fingers tingling with anticipation even before she lifted the soft fabric. The dress was black, fitted, and completely plain. No frills. No ribbons or ruffles. No adornment whatsoever.

She smiled as she realized the adornment would be her shadows. Currently, her butterflies filled her bedchamber, covering the walls, wardrobe, curtains, and window.

She took her time getting ready. First, a bath. Then, she brushed out her hair. When her skin had dried, she slid on the filmy undergarments. Next, the silky gown. Then a pair of black lace gloves.

Before putting on the boots, Thea took a moment to check the looking glass. Her cheeks were rosy with excitement, her hair a few shades lighter than the dress but dark in contrast to her skin, which had lost some of its summer tan. She didn't know what she was anymore—Huntsman, Sylvan king's daughter, or patroness of shadows—but she felt more herself than she had in a long time.

The tension coiled inside her as she realized she would be returning to Iluna for the first time since she'd escaped. Would her memories come rushing back? Would she hate it there?

What she did know was that Damon had managed to persuade the Sylvan king and queen that he was trustworthy. He had made several trips to Scarhamm over the past two months, and discussed his efforts to reinforce the walls of Iluna. At first, the meetings had been tense, full of suspicion and questioning. But the Sylvan queen clearly had a soft spot for him and smoothed over the worst moments.

The most frustrating part was that Thea had not been alone with Damon once.

However, the fact that this dress had appeared on Thea's hearth meant that the Sylvan king had instructed Veleda to make an exception to her wards. For tonight only? Thea shook her head. She didn't know. Of course, he hadn't bothered to tell her about his change of heart. She supposed that was typical of her father, and she couldn't expect any different.

As she sat on her bed to put on the black leather knee-high boots with heels, her door burst open. "Thea, I got a dress on my fireplace!" Rozie hopped inside, waving a yellow gown in the air like a prize. "Did you get one? Enora and Cassia—"

Cassia peeked her head in. "Did you ask if she got a dress? Never mind, I can see she did." She grinned.

The door opened wider, and Enora traipsed in, spinning so the skirt of her teal dress widened out in a bell shape. "I want to know how this thing was tailored to my exact size. It's slightly eerie. Who made this? I mean, it's lovely. Honestly, the most beautiful thing I've ever worn."

"Thea got one, too!" Rozie cried. "It looks magnificent!"

Thea had to catch her breath at this sudden tumult. "Enora, really? You received a magical item out of nowhere and just put it on?"

"We knew who it must be from," Enora said haughtily. "It's an invitation to dance. You explained that to us. Remember?"

"Yes." She swallowed, uncertain how her sisters felt about Damon and the shadow realm, even though he had spoken to them all several times over the past months, and the interactions had been polite. "Do you want to go?"

"Obviously!" Rozie cried. "Give me a minute to put it on. Be right back." And she left in a yellow blur.

Once they were all clothed, Thea gathered her butterflies, inviting them to alight on her dress.

"That looks stunning," Enora said, and Cassia nodded. Rozie blinked in awe.

Thea instructed her sisters to put their slippers on at the same time. "As soon as they're on, they'll lead us to the root that will take us to Iluna," she said, wondering if this was a good idea.

They each put their slippers on. Nothing happened.

Had Damon left enchantment out of these new clothes, perhaps to give them a choice over whether they accepted his invitation? "I suppose they don't need to be enchanted now that I know the way."

The four daughters of the Sylvan king walked in silence from the gates of Scarhamm.

When they reached the walnut tree, Thea stepped onto the root without hesitation. The portal formed, grew, and she entered, holding Rozie's hand and drawing her along.

The boat ride was quiet, her sisters taking in their surroundings. "If I'd come here alone, I would have been terrified," Rozie whispered. "But I guess it's kind of pretty."

"Yes," Thea said. It was quite beautiful in its way. The river reflected the lanterns in the distance. The moon sprites wheeled freely over the black castle. For the first time, Thea realized that Damon had never put the sprites in cages the way his father had. Another sign that he had never been meant to follow in his father's footsteps.

When they reached the gravel shore, Thea stepped out first, helping each of her sisters alight. Music filtered from the castle, a lilting Sylvan melody.

"Next time," she said quietly to Cassia, "you can bring Zeru. Does he like to dance?"

"I'm teaching him," Cassia said shyly, her smile full of gratitude. "Will there be a next time?"

Before Thea could answer, a golden-brown shape materialized in the air behind Cassia. Rozie shouted and pointed. Thea gasped, her hand going to the knife she had brought just in case she needed it. What was it? She'd never seen anything like that here or...anywhere. It looked like a flying...fox? Thea drew her blade.

"Don't!" Cassia cried out, her lips stretching into a wide grin. "It's Voz! Remember I told you about the Vozarra from the welkins? She can only appear in spirit realms like Welkincaster. And I guess, like Iluna." She laughed, looking delighted as the creature came close, alighting next to Cassia. "How did you find me?"

The fox didn't speak, but Cassia behaved as if it had. "Oh, that's clever. I'm so glad you're here. You can come with us to the dance."

Thea shook her head, marveling at this strange turn of events. But if her sister was happy, so was she. "Welcome, Voz," she said, realizing how beautiful the creature was with its golden eyes and the copper in its brown fur. Its wings were lovely, almost like Cassia's.

When they reached the castle, Thea was the first to enter. Her breath stopped as she saw that Damon stood alone in the center of the ballroom. He was wearing an ebony jacket in the same fabric as her dress, his shirt and trousers also black. His face looked pale, his expression formal. He made a low, elegant bow and swept his hand to the side. "Welcome, daughters of the Sylvan king. Would you care to dance?"

There were no other dancers, and the ballroom echoed with the emptiness. It was quite different from a Sylvan revel.

Enora composed herself first. "Thank you for the beautiful dress! Your seamstress is incredibly talented."

Damon inclined his head. "My mother. She is nearby if you want to meet her. I asked her to wait until I'd welcomed you."

"Of course we want to meet her!" Cassia said, moving forward to clasp Damon's hands in greeting. Damon raised his brows at the flying fox who was making herself at home exploring the ballroom, but he said nothing. "I love my gown, too." Hers was emerald, the same shade as Zeru's eyes, which had to be a thoughtful touch on Damon's part based on what he'd heard about Cassia's Dracu.

Rozie was uncharacteristically quiet. Thea wondered if she was finding herself a little dazzled by all this. The ballroom was brighter than ever, its silver and black furnishings rich and stately.

Finally, Thea could no longer stall. She stepped up to Damon, inclining her head to him. Her shadows swirled around her, a few of them flitting over to Damon to rest on his shoulders. "Thank you for inviting us."

He bowed again at the waist, his face set in formal lines. "Thank you for accepting. You look stunning, as I knew you would."

Thea tried to smile. This was more awkward than she'd thought it would be. It felt strange to be back in this place under such different circumstances. She couldn't shake off the past so quickly.

Enora and Cassia took Rozie around the room, talking and laughing, probably to give her time alone with Damon.

But a pulse jumping in Damon's throat showed that he was not as unruffled as he appeared. Thea thought of everything he had done to make amends, freeing the scuccas as well as many of the silver trees, and finally winning her parents' approval. She decided she was ready to offer him another morsel of hope.

"I have a problem you might be able to help me with," she said casually, or as calmly as she could manage.

"Oh?" He took a step closer, his eyes keen on hers. "What is it?"

"My butterflies need more excitement than they're getting in Scarhamm. I'm afraid there's not much going on in my bedchamber of late."

Damon's lips curved up in a slow grin. "Can I admit I'm relieved to hear that?"

Thea couldn't help but fight a smile. "I'm wondering if I can bring them here from time to time. If you invite anyone here, that is. For revels."

He nodded, the intensity in his eyes warm and fixed on her. "I wanted you to see that it's not like it was before. I believe this realm still needs folk to come here to lend power to it, but no one will ever be forced to stay. I promise you that."

"I had already figured as much." She reached out and took his hand, noting his indrawn breath as their skin touched.

His eyes shone with admiration. "I'm in awe of you, Thea."

The way he looked at her... nothing made her feel more powerful. Not even her shadows. "I have to warn you, I'm not the type who changes my mind. Once I commit to something, I stick it out. And if I want something, I go after it."

Damon nodded, his eyes clinging to hers. "And what is it that you want, Thea?"

She stepped into his arms, pressing herself to him chest to thigh, and felt his heart slamming against hers. "I'd like to come back here tomorrow night." She put her lips to his ear. "Alone."

Damon's unsteady chuckle stirred the hair at her temple, sending a pleasant tickle down her spine. "I would like that, too." His raspy voice made her shiver. "I already have your dress in mind."

"Oh?"

"It will be"—his lips slid along her cheek, his head bending to press a kiss to the side of her neck—"minimal."

Thea turned her head and caught his lips with hers, taking his face in her hands and running her fingers through his hair. For the next few minutes, she had no thought for anyone but Damon.

Rozie's titter made them split apart. "You call that dancing?"

Thea turned her head to see Enora was teaching Rozie steps in the dance, and Cassia was talking with Azra, who was grinning at them. Thea nodded a greeting, her cheeks heating to think they'd had an audience.

As Damon took Thea's hand, she suddenly remembered why he had to stay here.

Sensing her change of mood, he leaned in and asked, "What's wrong?"

Thea hated to bring up something serious when her sisters were enjoying themselves, but it was better to face the darkness. "What do we do if we can't stop the thinning of the walls between my world and the primordials? What if the Old Ones do wake?"

"If they do," Damon said, "can you imagine a better group of folk to deal with them?" He tilted his head to indicate her sisters, chuckling as his gaze fell on Rozie. "Your youngest sister alone could probably take them on. She'd order the Old Ones back to sleep, and they'd be terrified enough to obey."

Thea laughed, relaxing into Damon's arms

and letting the problems of tomorrow fade to the back of her mind.

As they danced, Thea's butterflies flew in a cloud over the ballroom, wheeling to the music like blackbirds on a clear morning. Cassia's winged fox cavorted with them, chasing them in a game they all seemed to enjoy.

And the silver candles flared like shooting stars, their brightness making the darkness more beautiful.

Acknowledgments

I'm forever grateful to the team at New Leaf Literary, especially my agent Suzie Townsend, always my steadfast support and sounding board. Keifer Ludwig, I appreciate your perceptive notes! Thanks also to Tracy Williams and Olivia Coleman for all you do.

Huge thanks to the team at Little, Brown Books for Young Readers, especially my editor extraordinaire, Deirdre Jones, for your perceptive notes, excellent ideas, and attention to detail at every stage! Thank you, Jessica Levine, for taking care of so much. To the marketing, publicity, and sales teams—Savannah Kennelly, Cheryl Lew, Christie Michel, Emilie Polster, Mary McCue, Victoria Stapleton, Danielle Cantarella, and Allie Stewart—thank you for doing everything you can to get my books into readers' hands! Shout-out to editor-in-chief Alvina Ling, publisher Megan Tingley, and deputy publisher Jackie Engel. My sincerest gratitude to manufacturing coordinator Kimberly Stella, production editor Annie McDonnell, and copyeditor Starr Baer. I honestly don't know how you put up with my gazillion logic and continuity errors! Much admiration to Sasha Illingworth, Patrick Hulse, and Tuesday Hadden for your beautiful cover concepts and interior design.

Micaela Alcaino, thank you for making my cover dreams come true! I still can't believe my luck.

Thanks to Molly Powell and the whole team at Hodder & Stoughton for all your hard work.

Jen Hawkins, Mary Ann Marlowe, Summer Spence, Ron Walters, and Kristin Wright, thank you for being my most steadfast friends, critique partners, and shenanigators. Nicki Pau Preto, Morgan Rhodes, and Maureen McGowan, thank you for the vital Zoom chats and check-ins. Grateful hugs to Anabel, Brooke, Crystal, Guida, and Sarah of the Lady Seals, without whom I would probably have given up on writing early on. Robin and Skye, thanks for being my first and forever reading buddies. And to the Writing Wrecking Crew—Brittni Brinn, C. M. Forest, Vanessa Shields, and Ben Van Dongen—thank you for the coffee shop chats, the online check-ins, and local events!

Mom and Dad, love you forever. Erik and Mark, thanks for being the best brothers! Biggest hugs to Fred, Donna, Heather, Jill, Todd, Zoe, and Quinton for your incredible support. All my love to Darren, Nicklas, Aleksander, and Lukas for making my life so happy, and for being the voices of reason when I need it.

A special thank-you to librarians and booksellers for your passion and dedication in getting books into readers' hands.

My sincerest and warmest thanks to readers for giving my words a chance!

CELEBRATING 100 YEARS OF PUBLISHING

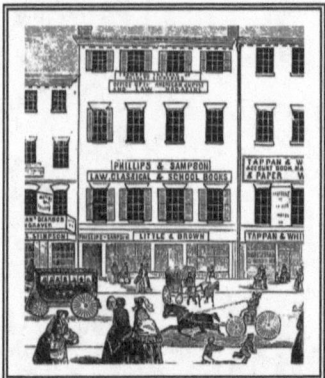

Dear Reader,

You may have noticed the words "Little, Brown and Company" on the title page of this book and wondered what they mean. Well, Charles C. Little and James Brown were the founders of this publishing house, and the "and Company" is all the editors, designers, marketers, publicists, salespeople, and more who help produce each book and bring it to readers like you. Little, Brown was founded in Boston, Massachusetts, in 1837, and some of its early publications included *The Writings of George Washington* and *The Works of Benjamin Franklin*. The catalog grew to feature works by Emily Dickinson and Louisa May Alcott, among many other notable authors. In 1926, recognizing that the literature we read when we are young has a deep and lasting influence and requires expert curation, the company appointed an editor to lead a dedicated children's department.

In 2026, Little, Brown Books for Young Readers celebrates one hundred years of excellence in publishing. Today, we are a division of Hachette Livre, the third-largest publisher in the world, and we are based in New York City. Our staff has grown from a team of two to more than one hundred people. And with the changes in technology, our books are read by more readers, in more ways, and in more countries than ever before. However, one thing has not changed: our commitment to providing a supportive home for all creators and superb stories for all readers. Thank you for being one of them.

Megan Tingley
Megan Tingley
President and Publisher

LITTLE, BROWN AND COMPANY
BOOKS FOR YOUNG READERS

To learn more about Little, Brown's history, authors, and books, please visit LBYR.com.